COLD BLOWS THE WIND

COLD BLOWS THE WIND

Catherine Meyrick

Courante Publishing

Published by Courante Publishing, Melbourne, Australia.
courantepublishing@gmail.com

Cover Design by Jenny Quinlan, Historical Fiction Book Covers.
Cover image: Hobart from the Bay by J. W. Beattie, courtesy of the State Library of Victoria.

A catalogue record for this book is available from the National Library of Australia.

ISBN: 0648250852
ISBN-13: 978-06482508-5-2

This book is written in Australian English, both formal and vernacular, and uses Australian grammar, spelling and publishing conventions.

For
Sarah and Francis

Between 1803 and 1853, approximately 75,000 convicts were transported to Van Diemen's Land; of these, 13,500 were women. Sentences served, many went on to lives of comparative comfort and respectability, far better than they would have had in the British Isles, from where most of them had come. Others did not—their lives and those of their children were marked by poverty and hardship similar to that found throughout Britain at this time. Yet, despite their struggles, in the fresh air and clear light of Tasmania, as Van Diemen's Land was called from 1856, many retained and passed on to their children a zest for life and a healthy disrespect for the pretensions of their so-called betters that helped see them through the worst of times.

1

March 1878

Ellen looked down at her open hand and pressed her lips tightly together. Her palm was reddened by scrubbing that had failed to remove the blacking from the creases. She was supposed to do washing, ironing and, if there wasn't enough of that, dusting and odd jobs, not cleaning and painting stoves and fire grates. If she didn't get the black paste off, there would be stains on everything she touched, including Mrs Bryce's fancy white tablecloths.

Ellen continued to stare down as Mrs Bryce carefully counted coins into her hand. She had given her two shillings extra. Ellen paused—should she say something? Was the old bat testing her?

She slowly raised her eyes. 'That's too much, Mrs Bryce.'

'I am paying you what you are worth, Ellen.'

Ellen couldn't keep her eyebrows from shooting up.

Mrs Bryce smiled sweetly, as if she meant what she was saying. 'When Mrs Turner visited last week, she complimented me on the table napkins, not only their whiteness but the way they were ironed and folded. It seems her girl is nowhere near as competent as you are.' Her pale eyelashes fluttered as she spoke. 'And when I heard what she was paying her, I thought I should give you a little more.'

Ellen fought against a bubble of laughter. Mrs Bryce was afraid Mrs Turner, or one of her other friends, would lure her away. Mrs Turner was likely paying her girl three shillings more.

As if she could read Ellen's mind, Mrs Bryce said, 'Now don't be getting ideas about leaving here. Most would not be as understanding as I have been. Not everyone agrees with me, but if we don't give honest work to girls like you, we know what you will end up doing to make ends meet.'

The smug old bitch, she wouldn't let it go. One day Ellen would

1

tell her exactly where she could shove her job.

She forced a polite smile. 'Thank you, Mrs Bryce. I'll be back on Monday. My hands should be properly clean by then.'

Mrs Bryce nodded. 'Yes, they should.' She paused, her eyelashes fluttering faster than before, as if she was thinking hard. 'Rather than employing a new girl to do the fireplaces, you could do them. I want them done thoroughly. You could come in on Fridays.'

Ellen frowned. 'For the same pay?'

'No, my dear, I will give you one shilling and sixpence extra, on top of what I have paid you today.'

Mrs Bryce winced as Ellen whistled.

Ellen smiled, genuinely this time. 'Thank you, Mrs Bryce.' What she could do with three shillings and sixpence extra! Start getting winter clothes for Billy and perhaps have enough left over for herself.

~

Ellen hummed as she walked along Liverpool Street, stopping to stare into the large windows of Mather's store and Perkins and Nephew's with their displays of pretty hats—straw and felt, decorated with ribbons and brightly dyed feathers. She sighed—even with her extra shillings she could never buy one of these. Still, she could buy some ribbon or flowers at one of the cheaper drapers and tidy her old hat. She hugged her shawl tighter, a sharp breeze tugging at her skirts despite the bright sunshine.

She stopped and waited on the footpath as a horse was led out from the blacksmith's, still dreaming of what she would buy if she could save her extra shillings for a few weeks. Perhaps she could get a new pair of gloves, dark ones that wouldn't show the stains. She strolled across Barrack Street and moved to the edge of the footpath, thinking to cross to the other side of Liverpool Street.

'Hey, Ellen!' A voice cut through her daydreams. 'Come and have a drink with us.'

Damn! She should have crossed the road earlier.

A group of young men stood outside the Rob Roy Inn, jostling each other and laughing. Work was finished for the day or, more probably, they had slept in and fronted up late so they hadn't been taken on. They clearly had nothing better to do than drink and annoy passing women.

Ellen kept walking. 'You are joking, Dan Rogers.'

'Don't be like that, sweetheart.' A gangly youth of Ellen's age slid his arm around her waist.

'Go to buggery. I'm not your sweetheart.' She elbowed him sharply and watched for a break in the stream of carts and buggies heading up and down the street.

'Don't give yourself airs, *sweetheart*,' he sneered. 'We all know what you're like.'

Ellen turned, her eyes blazing. 'You bastard!'

'You'd know all about bastards,' he said, a smirk on his narrow ratty face.

Ellen stalked towards him, thumping her hands against his shoulders.

Rogers stumbled back against the wall of the pub.

'You watch what you say, you little turd. My brothers will be back any day.'

He swallowed, his Adam's apple wobbling. 'I'm not scared of them.'

It was Ellen's turn to smirk. 'I heard, last time, Will only had to look at you and you pissed your pants.'

She marched away from him, across the street, dodging a pile of horse manure.

'You showed her, mate.' The laughter rumbled behind her but, this time at least, it wasn't directed at her.

~

Ellen slammed through the door into the kitchen, pulling the pins from her hat, her light brown hair tumbling down.

'Why are there so many bloody useless loafers in this town?' She stabbed the hatpins back into her hat and placed it on the battered sideboard alongside her mother's hat, the pile of her father's old newspapers and an assortment of other bits and pieces no one could work out where to put.

Mam turned from the stove, a gleam of amusement in her dark eyes. 'What's happened, my love?'

'Dan Rogers and his mates, outside the Rob Roy, giving me lip.' Ellen ran her fingers through her thick hair and twisted it back into a neatish knot.

'And you gave them a piece of your mind,' her father said from behind his week-old newspaper.

Her two youngest sisters, Alice and Jane, sitting at the end of the table, paused their game of cat's cradle and watched, trying not to grin.

'I did.' Ellen raised her chin. 'No one messes with a Thompson.'

'No.' Her father looked over his paper, his hazel eyes fierce. 'They do not.'

'And Mrs Bryce,' Ellen said, pushing the last of her hairpins into place, 'had me blacking the fireplaces. She said there wasn't enough ironing today, so it was either do the fireplaces or not get paid at all. Said it like she was doing me a favour.'

'Money's money, Ellen.' Dad lowered his newspaper.

'But, Dad, look at my hands.' She held them out. 'Her and her blasted fireplaces. Next thing she'll have me emptying her piss pot.'

Her father raised his voice. 'Language, girl.'

'You can talk.'

'I'm an old man—I can say and do as I like.' He lifted his paper again. 'You're little more than a young wench.'

Knowing he couldn't see her, Ellen poked her tongue out.

Jane and Alice stared at each other, stifling their giggles.

Bessie, two years younger than Ellen, sat by the window, her attention on the seam of the underbodice she was mending.

Her back to the room, Mam stirred the large pot simmering on the stove. 'You haven't given her a piece of your mind and lost the job?'

'No, but it's beyond me why these old women can't do their own housework like the rest of us.'

'You wouldn't have a job if they did.' Mary Ann, her elder sister, walked in and dumped her hat beside Ellen's.

Mary Ann was so damned practical.

'You haven't spent the day cleaning fireplaces. Do you know how many fireplaces that house has?'

'There are days where I think I'd prefer cleaning fireplaces to dusting china dogs and vases.' Mary Ann pulled a face and said in a plummy voice, 'That plate is Wedgwood, my dear. It is worth more than you are ever likely to earn in a year.'

'What's the point of that?' Alice asked.

Mary Ann shrugged. 'It's pretty, but not much use if you can't eat off it.' She raised an eyebrow, grinning. 'So what are her un-mentionables like?'

'Drawers big enough to make a sail for a clipper.'

'Show some respect,' Dad laughed.

'The table needs to be set,' Mam called over her shoulder.

Mary Ann looked across at the younger girls. 'Come on, you two, get on with it.'

Jane spread the cloth on the table, and Alice set the cutlery. Bessie was still sewing, off in a world of her own.

'Bessie, wake up.' Mary Ann raised her voice. 'I'm surprised you haven't had an accident at Peacock's the way you wander about in a dream.'

Colour spread up Bessie's cheeks. 'I don't work in the tin shop or make the jam. I pack the tins into crates.' She walked over and put her sewing on the sideboard. She took out the plates and carried them to her mother. 'And I concentrate on what I do,' she added, scowling.

Ellen watched her sister, back at the table now cutting slices from a loaf of bread, her head down, her chin puckered as if she were about to cry. Although she had her mother's dark eyes, Bessie seemed to lack the fight Mam and the rest of the Thompsons had and, of all the girls, was the one most likely to be bossed about by Mary Ann. There was nothing Ellen could do to help her.

She glanced around the room. 'How's my darling boy been today?'

'A perfect angel,' Mam said. 'He's still asleep in the front room.'

'I hope that doesn't mean he will be awake half the night.'

She walked out of the kitchen and into the front room that was both sitting room and bedroom for her brothers when they were at home. Bending over the cot in the corner of the room, she gently crooned to the sleeping child. 'Time to wake up, Billy boy. Time to have tea.'

Ellen scooped him up, covering his cheeks with kisses as he squirmed and grizzled.

'Who's got a wet bottom?' She bounced him gently. 'We'd better fix that.'

His napkin changed, she carried him back to the kitchen.

Alice, at eight already a sure hand with her nephew, held out her arms. Ellen placed him on her lap and pressed her nose to Billy's head, drinking in the blissful scent that was her baby boy.

Alice grinned into Billy's face as he reached for her nose. She poked his with her finger. Billy blew little bubbles back at her.

Over at the stove, Ellen spooned a small portion of the stew — more potato than meat — into a dish, mashed it with a fork and set it on the table to cool. An apron covering her dark work dress, she slid onto the bench beside Alice and took the child back, jigging him on her knee as he started to grizzle again.

'You're hungry, aren't you, my little darling? Let's see if this is cool enough.' She stirred the stew around, tested a spoonful against her lip, and offered it to the baby.

Billy opened his mouth and willingly swallowed it down.

Mam began to ladle the stew onto plates, and Bessie and Jane placed them on the table. Dad put his paper aside as the rest seated themselves on the benches and assorted chairs either side of the table.

Ellen ate a mouthful of her stew, then continued to feed Billy.

'I wonder where Will is now,' Mary Ann said.

Dad finished chewing. 'Out in the middle of the ocean. They can go months without making land. He said this would be a long tour.'

Mam's eyes shone but she said brightly, 'George should be home soon.'

They all turned as the front door slammed.

'Speak of the devil,' Dad laughed.

'George,' the young women all squealed together, jumping up from their seats and crowding around their brother.

'My, you do smell sweet.' Ellen stood on tiptoes to kiss his cheek, Billy on her hip.

'Of course I do.' He dumped his kitbag against the wall. 'I've been to the Turkish baths and had a shave. A new set of clothes too.' He spun in front of her. 'What do you think of the jacket?'

Ellen ran her eyes over the single-breasted jacket in blue checked wool. 'Very smart.' She screwed up her nose. 'I can still smell whale oil.'

'Smell or no smell, it pays well.' He looked around the room. 'Will not here?'

'He's been and gone in the time you've been away,' Dad said. 'Off on the *Emily Downing* at the start of the month.'

'Sit down, son.' Mam was back at the stove, ladling stew onto a plate. 'Bessie, cut your brother some bread.'

'Shove up, Ellen.' George sat on the bench beside Ellen. 'I could eat a horse.'

'No horse in the pot here,' Mam snorted.

George turned to Ellen, his eyes on the child on her lap. 'And

7

who do we have here?'

'Your nephew.'

'Who's the father?'

There was silence in the room.

'You are blunt, aren't you?' Ellen said, a twist to her mouth.

'Well,' George grinned, 'I've learnt babies don't just appear on the doorstep.'

'That mongrel John Collins.'

'And he didn't marry you.' It was a statement not a question.

'No, and I wouldn't have him if he was served up on a platter with an apple in his mouth.'

'Do you want me to have a *word* with him?'

'He cleared out soon as I told him. Didn't give Will or Dad a chance to have a *serious word* with him.'

'What's the lad called?' He grinned at the boy and took his chubby fingers in his, shaking them gently.

Billy eyed his uncle warily and buried his face against Ellen's shoulder.

'William John Thompson.'

'Not George—I am disappointed.'

'I'll call the next one George.'

'Next one?' George arched an eyebrow.

'Oh, I'll have a ring on my finger before then. A big one I can wave under old Mrs Bryce's nose.'

2

Harry leant against the railing as the sky gradually lightened to a pink-tinged grey. He could barely tear his eyes away from the mountain rising behind the town, the fluted columns of the cliff face near the summit kissed by the rising sun.

The *Southern Cross* hooted loud and long as it steamed towards the wharf. He pulled his bedroll closer as two seamen thudded past. Cabin passengers had begun to emerge to watch as the steamer pulled slowly alongside the pier. Their servants were busy hauling their luggage out ready for the gangway to be lowered. Harry heard, through the door behind him, a sailor calling below for the steerage passengers to come on deck. He had escaped the sour fug of sweat and vomit as soon as he woke. The heavy seas and wind overnight had not made the journey easy. It had been bad enough with only five of them. It would be unbearable when it was full and in winter when they couldn't come on deck.

The steerage passengers had been told to wait until the cabin class had alighted but Harry saw a gap and slipped behind the first group down the gangway. Money didn't make them any better than he was.

He made his way through the crowd on the pier toward the town, scanning faces as he went. His father had said he came into town every couple of days. Would he recognise him after all this time? He'd said he rode a white horse—Harry could see a piebald and a grey, but no white anywhere in sight. A surprising longing for Eliza swept over him. She would have everything organised, know what to do and where to go. He took a deep breath. The past was the past.

He walked away from the docks with its tangle of masts, hooting steamers and the general thud and hubbub of a working port busy with cargoes loading and unloading. In the distance, the mountain rose above the town giving him an idea of the direction he should go, but he needed to work out the streets that would take him there.

Hobart Town's streets looked to be laid out in straight lines. Settled on hilly ground, the town sloped upwards towards the mountain. Most of the larger buildings were of stone, many two or three-storeyed, the public buildings with grand pillars and porticos, the shops sporting awnings or verandahs, some trimmed in fine iron lace.

Harry buttoned his coat against a sharp gust of wind. Although the sky was clear and the sun shining, the wind was cold. Good thing the old man had warned him to bring a coat and thick socks.

Carts and drays, buggies and traps rolled down the street, women with baskets over their arms were out and busy, men in smart suits and shabbier workingmen moved with purpose along the footpaths and across the roads, here and there a loafer was already at work holding a street lamp up. The smell of baking bread wafted through an open door. Harry's stomach grumbled—he could do with tea and a bun at least. He hadn't eaten much on the crossing, fearful it would not stay down. He wondered how the old man had survived it, four months he had said, halfway across the world in the hold of a ship. They made them tough back then.

Harry whistled as he came out of the small refreshment room— scalding tea and a meat pie straight from the oven and he was fit to face anything this new town threw at him. He dodged his way across the street to where a carter was loading crates and tight packed sacks onto a wagon. Two blinkered horses stood munching at the feed in the bags hanging from their heads.

'Excuse me, mate.'

The carter straightened up. He was a half head taller than Harry, broad across the shoulders and around ten years younger.

'Could you point me in the direction of the Huon Road?'

'Going that way myself—as far as Fern Tree. Where are you off to?'

'The Springs on Mount Wellington.'

'I'll drop you at the start of the Fingerpost Track. Got business up there with the Old Man of the Mountain?'

Harry frowned, not understanding.

'Old Woods—he's lived on the mountain since God knows when.'

'How much for the ride?'

'Give me a hand loading this lot and we'll be square.' He held out a broad calloused hand. 'Bob Flanagan's the name.'

Harry offered an equally calloused hand. 'Harry Woods.'

Bob's clear blue eyes lit with interest. 'Related?'

'His son.'

'Didn't know the old man had children.'

Harry threw his swag into the wagon and hefted a sack.

Bob seemed to take the hint. 'S'pose, we had better get on with the job.'

The wagon lumbered its way through the streets, Bob pointing out the sights of Hobart Town and offering free advice—the best place for a feed, the cleanest lodgings at a decent rate, where to avoid if you didn't want watered beer or a fight every night.

As the road rose, the town fell behind them. Harry turned and looked back. On the outskirts, houses were set well apart, neat behind their orderly fences. Farther off, the town seemed to be a mass of buildings huddled beside the river sparkling in the morning sunlight. Beyond the river, hills rolled along the horizon.

Bob clearly liked to talk and as long as he got an answer, he seemed satisfied. Harry's terse replies did not stem his flow.

'First trip to Tasmania?'

'Yes.'

'Must have been a while since you've seen your father.'

'Thirty-odd years.' Harry kept his eyes on the road ahead, aware that Bob was staring at him.

'You would have been a nipper when you saw him last.'

Harry nodded. 'I was.'

Bob whistled between his teeth. 'Where are you from, Harry?'

'Western Australia. Born in Fremantle.'

'Warm place, from what I've heard.'

'Warm enough.' He gazed at the cloudless sky. The earlier cool breeze had disappeared. 'It's pleasant here.'

'Today it is.' He glanced at Harry's nearly new coat. 'Come winter, you'll need that coat.'

They drew aside as another cart passed in the opposite direction. In places the land beside the road was fenced but the farther they travelled, towering trees pressed close at the sides of the road, and banks of tree ferns stood more than three times taller than a man. Above it all, the mountain loomed, the pattern of the rock near the summit clear.

Bob pulled back on the reins and called to the horses. They halted opposite a clearly marked track through the trees.

'If you follow that track through there, it will take you right up to the Springs. Bit of a hike, and steep too, but you can't miss it.'

Harry jumped down, pulled his swag out from the tray of the wagon and slung it across his back. 'Thanks for the lift, Bob. Much obliged.'

'No trouble at all. Might call in one day for a drop of the old man's *poitín*—it's a fine brew considering he's an Englishman.' He tipped his hat and with a flick of the reins he called to the horses and the wagon rumbled off.

Harry crossed the road, past a tall stump with initials carved into it—the work of visiting climbers, he supposed—to a tree with signs nailed on, the fingerpost. One sign pointed to 'The Fern Tree', whatever or wherever that was, the other to the Springs.

Harry tramped along the path. It was well made in parts, rough in others, stones and leaf litter underfoot. Fallen branches had been pushed to the side in a few places. Gum trees soared towards the blue sky, here and there logs lay on the ground, furred with moss. The silence was broken by intermittent birdcalls. Light fell in shafts through the canopy. He stopped when the track flattened out, sweating with the effort of the steep climb, and took off his coat. Taking a deep breath, he drank in the clean scent of the bush, and looked back through a break in the trees. He could see for miles. Hobart Town and the river glimmered in crystal light. He slung his jacket over one shoulder and plodded on as the track climbed higher.

3

Nearly an hour on from the fingerpost, Harry walked into a clearing. Several buildings were set among the bushes—a couple of huts, a barn with a horse grazing beside it, and a cottage built of wooden slabs with a shingle roof, a stone chimney at one end. Trees soared behind, the mountain top dominating the sky-line to the right.

Two young women sat together on a bench beside the door to the cottage, well-dressed and assured, chatting amiably to a tiny woman wearing a large apron and an old-fashioned frilled bonnet. Two men stood talking with a tall elderly man who was pointing towards the mountain top.

Harry had not imagined there would be strangers present. He stood, hesitant, on the path leading up the slope to the cottage. The old man was as lean and wiry as Harry remembered him but his hair was white now and sparse; his beard followed the line of his jaw, the rest of his face clean-shaven. Despite the years, his stance was the same. His distinctive laugh carried on the still air.

The old man looked up. 'Come over, sir.' He walked towards Harry. 'Have you come to climb the mountain? If you have food that needs cooking, my wife will see to it for you, have it ready when we return ...' His voice died away. 'Harry?'

'Dad?'

The old man was beside him, his arms around him. 'You've got your mother's eyes,' he croaked, barely above a whisper.

Harry swallowed. He clung to the old man, tight—as tightly as a boy clinging to a father about to be transported to an island hanging off the other end of the continent.

The others paused in their conversation, watching the pair.

The old man turned back to them, his arm across Harry's

14

shoulder. 'This is my son, young Harry—all the way from Swan River.'

'Perth? Western Australia?' one of the young women said.

The old man nodded.

The young woman wore a narrow-brimmed hat with a vivid green ribbon bunched around the crown and tied beneath her chin.

Eliza would have liked the hat. Harry frowned, pushing the thought away.

'You're a long way from home,' said an older man, fully kitted out in what looked to be walking gear bought specially for this outing.

'That, I am.' It felt like an entirely new world.

The old man drew Harry away to a bench at the other side of the door to the cottage where the old woman now stood, a mug in her hand.

'Harry, this is Jane, my wife.'

Harry raised his hat. 'Pleased to meet you.'

He took off his swag and set it against the bench.

Jane handed him the mug of dark tea. 'You'll be hungry after your tramp up from Hobart Town.' She placed a dish with a scone and a handful of raspberries on the seat beside him.

He sipped the tea, heavily sweetened with sugar. 'Aaah, just the way I like it.' He smiled at her.

Her stern face broke into a wide grin. 'It's welcome you are, young Harry.' Her voice had a distinct Scottish lilt.

The young women had returned to their conversation about a party to be held the following night, but as Harry ate, the older of the two men questioned him about his journey and life in Western Australia; the progress of the railways; the difference the East-West Telegraph line, completed the previous year, had made. Harry knew little about the railways but could tell him of his time working on the telegraph line between Perth and Adelaide.

His son—Harry assumed it was his son as the resemblance between the two was clear—gazed around, clearly bored. 'Do you think we could get going soon?' he said to no one in particular.

Harry stood up, his tea and scone finished.

The old man grabbed a tall wooden staff from beside the door. 'Come along, Harry, I'll show you to the top.'

He led the way at a leisurely pace, Harry beside him, answering the visitors' stream of questions as they walked around the side of the cottage. They had come from Victoria and were enjoying every sight Tasmania had to offer.

The second young woman, fresh-faced and wearing a hat trimmed in more modest pink, asked, 'How high would you say we are, Mr Woods?'

'The mountain is four and a half thousand feet.' The old man chuckled. 'Not that I've measured her myself.'

'It's a wonder a hotel hasn't been built up here,' the younger climber said. 'What you need is a proper road to bring people by carriage right to the Springs. You would have visitors in the hundreds all through the year.'

'Ever been here in winter?' The old man's bushy eyebrows joined together as he frowned.

'No, but with a decent road that wouldn't be a problem.'

'Snow two foot deep, cloud covering the mountain. Not much for these hundreds of visitors to see,' the old man muttered.

The narrow path rose steeply, a thickly wooded gully on one side, a clear running stream on the other. Boulders and occasional logs lay across the path which, despite their skirts, the young women managed to clamber over. They passed a turf-roofed hut of stone some way above the Springs.

'That's the icehouse.' The old man nodded towards the hut. 'Ice is stored there in winter, packed tight so the swells in Hobart Town can have it in their drinks in summer.'

The young woman in the green beribboned hat caught up with

the old man. 'Can we see the Rocking Stone?'

'It's not far out of our way,' he said.

'I doubt there's enough time,' said the older climber.

'We've come to see Hobart Town at its most beauteous,' the younger man drawled.

Harry stared at him, judging him a man who had never done a day's honest labour.

He felt the tug of effort on the muscles at the back of his thighs as the track narrowed and became rockier, the upright gum trees giving way to stunted eucalypts and windswept scrub. An ancient fall of rocks lay across the track, opening out the breathtaking view toward Hobart Town and the river. There was no sound of bird-life, only the rushing of the wind.

The track went higher, the climb harder going. Harry glanced back at the young women—they seemed to be taking it in their stride. Despite their pretty hats, both wore sturdy walking boots.

The old man halted, leaning on his staff. Harry saw the strain in his face, the laboured breathing. In the letter he had sent to Harry last December, he had said he was failing. It was clear it had not been a ploy to get him here. The visitors seemed not to notice the effort it took him.

'The Ploughed Field,' the old man announced as if the plain that stretched out before him was all his own work.

A plain of huge rocks heaped one on the other spread out. In places snow was still trapped in the deep crevices between the rocks, in others tufts of stunted grass struggled against the wind. The old man led the way as they skirted the rock field. Up high now and in the open, the chill wind was constant, whistling past them. Harry turned as the young woman in the plainer hat shrieked. She struggled to keep her skirts down as the wind ballooned them around her, giving him a pleasing view of the lace trimming on her drawers. He glanced towards his father who winked back at him.

The final ascent was steep, steeper even than the Fingerpost

Track. Boulders of all sizes, grey, rust-coloured, speckled with lichen, covered the summit. Some stood tall, grouped together like sentinels, others were spread out across the plain. Stunted scrub grew between them, prostrate tea-trees, broom-like shrubs in orange and yellow, reds and whites, cushions of low-growing yellow and green shrubs. As if the height was not enough, there was a massive cairn of stones close packed at the top of the mountain, a flag post at its centre. Even the ladies climbed up and sat, staring out at the view. The sky was a clear blue out to the horizon. The light glittered on the river and its white beaches as it opened out to the south where it merged with the sea. To the north, the river wound like a broad silvery thread through rolling hills. And below lay Hobart Town—a delicate model set in the folds at the mountain's foot.

Harry felt like an eagle in its eyrie—it was no wonder the old man had stayed on here. The troubles of the town, of the whole world, seemed so far away.

The old man stood below Harry, near his legs. 'A couple of trips up here, son, and you could take them by yourself.'

'I wouldn't have your stories, though.'

'A few nights by the fire with a warming drop and you'll know all I know.'

Harry grinned.

Miss Green Ribbon, her hand firmly clamped on her hat as the wind gusted, called across to them, oblivious of their conversation. 'Mr Woods, will you settle a question for us? How did you arrive in Hobart Town?'

The old man winked at Harry and turned his attention to the young women seated demurely side by side on the large rocks beside the cairn. 'Well ladies, it was a long time ago but I was a sailor on a man o'war. After a shore leave where I had met the woman of my dreams ...'

The fresh-faced girl giggled.

'... I couldn't bear to be without my love,' the old man continued, 'so I leapt from the ship and swam for shore. I hid on the mountain until the hue and cry died down and have never left the place.'

Harry listened, amused. A whole world opened up. Here, the past could be whatever he wished it to be.

'And where would we be without Mr Woods to guide us?' the older climber said. 'I hear he has rescued many a climber lost on the mountain.'

'There have been a few,' the old man nodded, 'quite a few.'

Their return was taken carefully, making sure no one fell or turned an ankle on the steep journey back down the track. By the time they arrived back at the Springs, Jane Woods had the group's picnic ready for them—their pies warmed, their sandwiches and cakes set out on plates. She lugged a kettle-sized teapot around, filling their cups as they discussed their plans for tomorrow. The meal over, they thanked her for her hospitality. Grannie Woods they called her and pressed coins into her palm which she slid into her apron pocket. The old man accompanied them to the finger-post where a carriage was now waiting to take them back into Hobart Town. Harry went along, carrying their empty hamper. It did nothing to improve his opinion of the younger of the two men that he needed a man nearly twice his age to carry his wicker basket.

The day drew in, the trees casting long shadows over the clearing, a heavy chill on the air. *This is summer*, Harry thought. Bob was right, he would need his thick coat come winter. Thick gloves too. He almost laughed. He had never worn gloves in winter before.

4

A fire burned steadily in the large fireplace that extended across the end wall of the cottage, the air thick with the smell of cooking. His mouth watering, Harry slid along the bench behind the table at the centre of the room. The old man sat at one end as Jane served a stew of vegetables seasoned with lumps of bacon; thick slices of bread lay on a plate on the table.

There was no conversation as they devoured the meal. Harry had never enjoyed a meal more. Eliza's Sunday roasts were nothing on this. He cleaned his plate, sopping up the gravy with the bread.

'That was a fine meal,' he said to Jane as she took the plates away.

Her face lit up. 'You're quite welcome, young Harry.'

He sat back, waiting for the usual cup of tea that had followed a meal in Perth.

The old man went to the sideboard where a small flagon stood and filled a jug. He called Harry over to the chairs by the hearth and handed him an earthenware mug, pouring a generous measure of spirit into it. 'My own brew,' he said proudly. 'I keep the still out in the bottom hut.' He jerked his head towards the door.

Harry swallowed a mouthful and spluttered, gasping. It was as if he had drunk liquid fire.

'Give the lad some water with it,' Jane chuckled as she sat down beside them, nursing her own mug. ''Tis the best *mountain dew* you'll ever taste, young Harry.'

The old man splashed a small measure of water into Harry's mug. 'It was my brew that decided Jane here to set her cap at me.' He winked at the old woman.

She grinned. 'Aye, that and his gift of the gab.'

The playfulness surprised Harry. Once the early days were over, marriage seemed to be an uneasy truce between most of the couples he knew.

When he had his breath back, he asked, 'How many parties do you take up the mountain each day?'

The old man stared into the fire. 'Ten, fifteen years ago, in the height of summer we would have hundreds trooping up here. I'd often go to the top twice a day. I've even taken a party up to watch the sunrise and then in the afternoon taken another to Wellington Falls and back. These days I can barely manage one.' He sighed as if exhausted at the thought of it. 'I'm not as young as I was, nearing a hundred now.'

Harry raised an eyebrow. Nearing eighty was closer the mark but, as he had realised, here on the mountain, you could spin whatever tale you wanted.

'We had a couple of girls here, great guides they were.'

Jane snorted. 'We treated them like daughters, yet they took themselves off with a couple of *gentlemen* last year.'

The old man peered into his mug. 'No goodbyes, not a backward look.'

'I couldn't get here any sooner,' Harry said into the silence. 'I left Perth as soon as I got your letter, but I had to stop off in Adelaide and Melbourne to earn enough for the fare.' He sipped at his drink, careful this time. 'Thought I could work my way over on a steamer—they laughed when I asked, said I was too old to be starting out. They were probably right. It was rough in the Bight— I heaved the whole way from Albany to Adelaide.'

The old man gave a great bark of laughter.

Jane lifted her mug and downed the contents in one long swallow. She smacked her lips, and took a pipe from her apron pocket. After teasing out the contents of the bowl and adding more tobacco from a pouch she kept in her apron pocket, she lit it. With a couple of puffs to get it drawing, she sat back in her chair, utterly content with the world.

'Your mother said, when she came from England with her parents, she spewed from Portsmouth to the Cape, but was right after that. No problem at all when we came here from Swan River.'

Harry took a swig, swallowed with a shudder, and forced out the question that had eaten at him for years. 'What happened to her?'

The old man shrugged. 'It was a mess and all my fault. I thought we could get me assigned to her and we could live together like a normal family—I'd seen it done in New South Wales. And once we were settled here, we would send for you and Sarah.' A twist to his mouth, he said, 'But they added three years to my sentence because I had done time in New South Wales, and sent me to Port Arthur as I was a *hardened criminal*. I was there two and a half years. She was gone when I got my Probation Pass and came back to Hobart Town.'

Harry stared into his mug. They had all sailed out of his life, his mother and his two little sisters, never seen again. His sisters were a blur, vague memories of laughter, squeals and running feet.

'It was bitterly cold when we got here.' The old man shook his head slowly. 'Heard she couldn't find work—she had your two little sisters with her, she said they were too young to leave behind.'

'If you had brought Sarah and me, we would have found work.' He couldn't keep the bitterness from his voice.

'She fell ill,' the old man said, ignoring Harry's comment, 'and was in the Colonial Hospital for a while. Got jack of waiting, I s'pose. Hope she found herself another man to take good care of her. She deserved better than me.'

Whatever she deserved, she shouldn't have deserted her older children. Harry scowled at the logs glowing in the fireplace. 'She could have come back to Fremantle—we were all there. Not just Sarah and me but Gran and Grandad—they would have helped her.' His voice creaked. 'She didn't have to go in the first place.'

The old man spoke as if he were discussing something of no

great concern. 'She married me but she was always respectable. I doubt she could have stood the shame if she'd stayed in Fremantle.' He picked up the jug from beside the hearth and refilled his mug. 'And old Joe and your grandmother are gone now?'

Harry stood and took the jug. 'Yes,' he said, pouring most of what remained into Jane's mug. He tipped the rest into his own and set the jug down. 'All gone—Gran and Grandad Broughton dead and Mum cleared off God knows where.'

'But not Sarah, not your sister.' The old man's eyes glistened as he said her name. Sarah, his firstborn, his favourite. He had her name tattooed across his right forearm, the rest of his children mere initials on his left.

'No, not Sarah,' Harry said. She had not left Perth but she had as good as deserted him—married the year after their parents had left, her attention on her almost annual child, some now well into adulthood. Harry stared, silent, into the hissing flames.

'Don't make the lad miserable,' Jane said. She broke into song.

> *There lived a man in yonder glen,*
> *And John Blunt was his name, O*

She looked at Harry and his father. 'Come on you two—join in.'

> *Rise up, rise up, auld Luckie, he says,*
> *Rise up, and bar the door.*

Harry had no doubt, had she been a few years younger she would have had him up dancing.

~

Harry woke, his head throbbing, his mouth parched. He couldn't remember getting himself to bed. He lay on the bed in the second room of the cottage, a rough blanket over him. He could hear the old woman in the next room, singing softly to herself as she moved around.

He struggled to sit up, wincing with the pain gripping his head. Swinging his legs off the bed, he braced himself as he bent down to pull on the boots set neatly on the floor. He had slept in his clothes! He could imagine what Eliza would have made of that.

Jane turned from the fireplace where she was stirring the pot hanging over the flames as he came out into the larger room.

'Good morning, young Harry.' Her eyes twinkled. 'Sleep well?'

'A bit too well.' Bright daylight poured through the doorway almost blinding him. 'Can I get some water to wash?'

'Aye, but first break your fast.'

Harry sat at the table, and she set in front of him a bowl of porridge and a cup of strong black tea.

'There's no milk,' she said, pushing a dish of sugar towards him.

He dug out a spoonful and sprinkled his porridge generously, heaping a couple more into his tea—exactly what his grumbling stomach needed.

He gazed around the room in the daylight. The walls had been whitewashed once but were now heavily smoke-stained. The old couple's bed stood in the far corner, a tall cupboard and a sideboard against the other walls. Faded blue curtains were pulled back from the window, the morning light spilling onto the floor.

'You've not a strong head for the drink.' The old woman sat opposite him, sipping her own cup of tea.

'No.' Eliza had tended towards Temperance but hadn't minded him having an occasional drink with the rest of the family. He had only seen her truly angry the few times he had rolled home, singing at the top of his lungs, with Frank, one of Sarah's sons-in-law.

'We'll learn you to drink up here. Himself brews a fine drop. Many a visitor comes mainly for a sup.'

Jane looked to be in her sixties, nowhere near as old as his father. In repose her face was stony, the effects of life's unkindness plain in her eyes. Yet, as he had discovered last night, she could talk the leg off a table once she got going and was full of an impish humour.

When he had drunk the last of his tea, he stood up. 'Thank you, that was just what I needed.' He paused a moment. 'What should

I call you—Mrs Woods?' He wouldn't be calling her mother but it didn't seem right to call her by her first name.

'We're no swells here.' She screwed up her face, thoughtful. 'These days most people call me Grannie. That'll do.'

'Grannie it is.' Not that she was anything like his own grandmother had been.

He went back to the other room. He picked up his swag from the floor, unrolled it on the bed and took out a clean shirt and a comb.

Grannie came in and placed a bucket, half-filled with steaming water, on the floor beside the ancient washstand set next to the window.

Harry watched as Grannie rifled through a cupboard in the corner of the room. 'Where's Dad?' he asked.

'Gone off to town early, he does every couple of days.' She handed him a towel. 'He should be back by dinner time.' She pulled the door closed behind her as she left.

This smaller room was clearly the bedroom. Harry wondered why the old couple didn't sleep in here. He supposed the other room was warmer in winter. Perhaps they used it for overnight guests, but he doubted anyone had stayed in years. There were chairs stacked in one corner, boxes piled beside the cupboard—it had the air of a storeroom. Not exactly the sort of place a paying guest would want.

He walked out into the clearing ten minutes later, face washed, hair and beard combed, a clean shirt, feeling much more himself. The air was clear, a hint of warmth in the breeze. He stood listening to the silence that had struck him on his climb yesterday. It was a silence alive with movement—the stirring of the breeze through foliage, the rustle of the undergrowth, the call of unfamiliar birds —not silence at all but the absence of human noise.

The old man led a bony white horse up from the track, a half-filled sack slung over the saddle. He untied the sack and held it out to Harry. 'Take this in to Jane, son, while I see to the horse.' He led the horse towards the barn, but turned, beaming. 'I still can't believe my eyes.'

After handing over the sack, Harry walked from the cottage to where the old man stood staring at a fair-sized garden behind the barn—cabbages, carrots, swedes and parsnips were laid out in neat rows, as well as staked canes of blackcurrants, gooseberries and raspberries. All around watercress and mint ran riot.

'The raspberry canes are looking ragged,' he said to the old man. 'They'll need a hard prune soon.'

'That they will.' The old man nodded. 'The apple tree needs pruning. The last of the potatoes need to be dug up. The roof needs patching. There are a couple of chairs need mending.' He crossed his arms. 'I'm not up to much these days.'

'I'll get on to it,' Harry said. 'Time to earn my keep.'

'You're staying?' There was longing in the old man's voice.

'I am.' For now. It was as good a place as any at the moment.

The old man showed him around—the huts, the barn with its store of wood, a shelter attached to one side for the horse. The whole place had a tired air, yet Harry could see the idyll it must have been when his father was younger and stronger and could keep the place in good repair. They climbed to the track above the cottage and followed the path towards the south, the old man showing him the troughing, wood and masonry, and the pipes carrying the water from the mountain to the reservoir holding Hobart Town's water supply.

'How often does it snow?'

'When doesn't it snow?' the old man chuckled. 'Even in summer there can be snow at the top. In a few weeks we'll start to feel the cold and by mid-winter we will be snowed in.'

'Never seen snow.'

'Wait a couple of months and you'll have seen more than you could ever want.'

5

April 1878

Ellen hummed as she walked along Liverpool Street, more than happy with the contents of the parcel she held tight against her. She had saved the extra shillings for the past few weeks and not given in to the temptation to buy ribbon, feathers or flowers to decorate her hat. Today she had bought not only an almost new woollen coat for herself but one for Billy that would last through winter the next two years. It was far too big for him now but it was a bargain too good to let go. They both looked clean and smelt of nothing other than camphor but she would hang them in the yard for a day. And she might sneak them into Mrs Bryce's next washing day and go over them with the potions in the laundry for cleaning gowns, jackets and coats.

She glanced ahead to check whether she needed to cross the street before she got to the Rob Roy, slowing her step at the sight of George and Alice standing with that skinny rat, Dan Rogers. George held a bundle in his arms too, a squirming bundle.

Ellen hurried up to them, scowling as she looked from George to Dan. 'What's going on here?'

George grinned at her. 'We thought we'd give young Billy some air.' There was a glitter in his eyes. 'And then we ran into my mate, Dan, here.' He nodded toward Dan. 'That's right, isn't it, Dan?'

Dan nodded his head furiously.

'And Dan was saying what a fine lad Billy is.'

Ellen raised her eyebrows. 'Was he?' She passed her parcel to Alice and took Billy, settling him on her hip and pressed her nose against his hair, breathing in deeply. She looked up to see Dan Roger's forced smile.

'Tell her yourself, Dan.' George grinned.

The Adam's apple in Dan's scrawny neck bobbed up and down

as he swallowed. 'He's a grand lad, he certainly is.' There was strain around his eyes.

Ellen wondered what George had threatened him with.

'I know,' she said, still unsmiling. 'He takes after his mother's family.'

'And Dan was saying he wants to give you something for the lad.'

Ellen pressed her lips tight shut against the laughter bubbling up. She almost felt sorry for the skinny gutter rat.

Dan's eyes had bulged with surprise but he obediently put his hand in his pocket and pulled out a shilling. 'Sorry, Ellen, I'm a bit short at the moment.'

'Not so short you can't buy a mate a drink for old time's sake.' George threw his arm over Dan's shoulder and steered him into the bar.

Ellen held tight to the coin. She'd buy Billy a toy, that brightly coloured spinning top she had seen in the window of the pawn-shop. She could already hear his burbling laugh.

Alice beside her, Ellen walked smartly across the street ahead of a couple of carts trundling down the hill. 'How did George manage that?'

'He asked him how his mate Hawkes was and Dan's knees went wobbly.'

'I'll remember that if there's a next time.' She had forgotten Dan Rogers was related to Hawkes. Will and George had done a month in gaol three years ago for the hiding they had given him. Rogers should remember that Thompsons never forgot a wrong.

'George said he'd get him to make up for being rude to you.'

'I wish the mongrel wasn't rude to me in the first place.'

'Perhaps he's sweet on you,' Alice said.

'What? No. He's just a nasty little rat picking on someone he thinks is weaker.' She stopped and stared at her sister. She was only eight years old. 'Where did you get the idea boys behave like that?

You're too young ...'

'From you and Mary Ann. I listen.' Alice skipped along beside Ellen.

They turned into Watchhouse Lane, past the mercifully quiet Sunday School on the corner. The children bellowing out their raucous hymns on Sunday mornings made sleeping late almost impossible.

'Anyway.' Alice spun around and skipped backwards as she spoke. 'George said, with Easter coming, we should go up to the Springs and see Grannie and Mr Woods.'

'Oooh, that would be good. We can all go and make a real party of it.'

'Mr Woods has his son staying with him.'

'I didn't know he had a son.'

'He's come from wherever Mr Woods was from, but he's old.'

Halfway along the lane, Ellen pushed open the gate with her foot. 'I suppose he would be. Mr Woods is ancient. How do you know all this?'

Alice skipped in and stood holding the door for Ellen. 'I listen.' She grinned.

'As long as you learn from what you hear,' Ellen said, hoping her sister would learn enough not to get involved with feckless men.

6

To begin with, Harry followed as the old man led parties of climbers along the tracks through the bush and scrub and across the rocky expanses up to the pinnacle. On days when there were no visitors, he explored the mountain. He visited the Rocking Stone, a large ovalish rock balancing on a base nearly as big that rocked when touched. He walked along the Watercourse Track above the Springs, following the stone and, later, wooden channel carrying water from the mountain springs to feed into Fork Creek and Browns River and be transported along wooden troughing to Hobart Town's reservoir. He detoured from the track to the monument to John Smith, a ship's surgeon who had become lost and died on the mountain not long before the old man had come to live at the Springs. Farther on, he struggled down gullies and over fallen trees and rocks covered with mosses of varying colours, through damp forest with tree-ferns, tea trees and wildflowers, the sound of running water a constant presence. He came to the Fern Tree Bower, a man-made retreat planted with three rows of tree ferns and with tables and seats of planks set about for picnickers to use. He had gone from there to see the Silver Falls, overhung with creepers and spreading fronds of ferns and sassafras, its water cascading like a flow of silver in the light.

He took his father's directions and walked to the end of the Watercourse Track, then followed a winding and rocky track around the south of the mountainside, passing through the Potato Fields, a slope of lichen-covered boulders and scree. Nearly two hours on, he arrived at the Wellington Falls and stood awestruck as he watched the rush of water cascading over the rocks and down the sheer cliff face.

As his knowledge of the mountain grew, he cautiously made his way through the bush towards the Organ Pipes, the wall of rock he had noticed when he first arrived in Hobart Town. He pushed past snow gums with their dark spirals of peeling bark but could find no clear trail. He stopped at a fall of rocks and boulders, spread down the mountain like a stream. Doubt crept in. He had no idea how stable the rocks were, whether, if he tried to cross, he would stumble and fall headlong down the mountainside. He turned away from the towering columns of rock and gazed out across the south of the island to the sea, exhilarated. The mountain was a world in itself, beautiful and dangerous, well-travelled yet still holding secrets. And although he had only been here a few weeks, Harry felt he knew her well enough to take visitors where they wanted to go. And he was free to come and go as he pleased, no one to answer to but himself.

Within a fortnight of Harry arriving, the old man had caught a heavy cold, complete with a hacking cough that left him breathless. Harry had taken over without too many doubts. Young men often wanted nothing more than a few directions. Parties of mountain climbers, especially those including ladies, wanted all the help they could get. They were the ones most eager for tales, not only of the mountain but of the old man's life—and Harry's too. He had developed a patter almost as good as his father's. When the mood took him, he embellished his own story of 'roo hunting with his father and laying the telegraph with tales he had heard of others' lives in the West: exploring the interior and pearl fishing up north. Many who wouldn't have given him the time of day in town hung on his words. He was young Mr Woods or, with the more hearty, Harry the younger.

~

Harry struck the axe into the chopping block and, fists at his hips, stretched his shoulders back as a couple of fresh-faced young men bounded up the path from the Fingerpost Track to the cottage.

They glanced from Harry, standing at the barn door, to the old man sitting in front of the cottage.

'We were told in Hobart Town we could get a drink here,' said the taller of the two.

'Tea, for certain, and a drop of something more if you want,' the old man said. 'My wife will cook any food you have brought with you and have it ready when you come down again.'

'We won't need that. We've brought sandwiches and plan to eat them when we reach the top.'

'Tea would be excellent,' the shorter said.

The old man nodded. 'Take a seat, sirs, and my wife will bring you tea.'

Grannie came out with her teapot and cups.

The taller man pulled a flask from his coat pocket and poured a generous splash into each cup.

Grannie eyed the flask as she passed around scones, but neither seemed to notice her.

She took her pot inside and brought out a steaming mug, which she carried over to the barn. She handed it to Harry and glanced towards the pair, shaking her head.

Harry stood outside the barn and drank the heavily sweetened tea, watching.

The old man, seated beside the cottage door, puffed on his pipe and, after a bout of coughing, said, 'You'll be wanting a guide, then.'

'Not at all, we know the way.'

'Been up here before?'

They shook their heads.

'I'm from Risdon,' the taller said, 'and James here is from Melbourne, but we've been given directions.'

'I've hiked in the Grampians,' added James.

'The mountain here has a mind of her own,' the old man said. 'The weather is changeable this time of year. A clear morning can have pelting rain or even snow by the afternoon. And if cloud comes down, chance is you won't find the way back.'

'Don't worry,' the taller said as if he were talking to a nervous old woman. 'We know what we're doing.'

Scowling, the old man glared at their backs as they headed off towards the track.

Shadow spread across the clearing mid-afternoon as the sun slipped behind darkening clouds. The old man called to Harry, who was on the roof, hammering rough wooden shingles onto the places where leaks had appeared during the last downpour.

'Any sight of those young fools?'

Harry straightened up and gazed through the trees towards the Ice House Track. 'Can't see anything.'

The old man muttered and went back into the cottage.

By nightfall, fog had drifted around the Springs. The old man stood peering through the window. 'They should be back by now.' He turned to Harry. 'Will you light the lamp, son? When the fog lifts, it will give them something to guide them home.'

The large lamp was fixed to the wall of the cottage outside the door. The old man had told Harry he had put it up near twenty years earlier as a beacon to those lost on the mountain. He liked to think the light was a sign that the Old Man of the Mountain, as they called him, was watching over them all.

The rain started as they finished their evening meal, driving sheets of it. Harry glanced at the roof to the places he had spent the afternoon patching. They seemed to be watertight. He took a seat beside his father at the hearth, both of them nursing a mug of the old man's *mountain dew*. Grannie was crooning an old lullaby to herself.

'Should we go out and look for them?' Harry asked. Not that he wanted to. It was wet and dark outside. He was likely to get lost himself.

'Too hard in this weather.' The old man sighed. 'We could do it in clear moonlight and if we had more men.'

'Perhaps they took another track.'

'They said they were coming back this way but might have changed their minds and gone back along the track to New Town.' He glared into the fire. 'Nothing we can do tonight but pray they have found shelter somewhere. The mountain can be cruel when she puts her mind to it.'

Harry went outside to relieve himself. He stood in the doorway of the cottage and cooeed into the night.

There was no answer.

As he closed the door, his father said, 'I have that old blunderbuss. I used to have a horn attached to it, and when I set it off, you could hear it all over the mountain. He scratched his head. 'Don't know what happened to the horn. If you fired it, the sound would still carry.'

Harry looked towards the ancient weapon leaning against the wall at the far corner of the room.

'I've never used one.' He walked over and picked up the firearm, peering down the flared barrel. 'What do you put in it? Shot?'

'Or stones and rocks. And gunpowder and a bit of wadding. You'd have to go out and collect the stones.'

'Don't know that wet stones and gunpowder would work well.' He returned the blunderbuss to its place and went to the fire.

'Miserable weather to be out in.' The old man groaned as he stood and moved, stiff jointed, to the door. He stared out into the rain.

'Close the door,' Grannie called over her shoulder, 'you'll catch yourself another cold. There's naught you can do.'

The banked fire took the chill off the room overnight. Harry's bed had been dragged from the bedroom to the corner along from the old couple's bed. Wrapped tight in his blankets, Harry slept soundly. In the dim morning light, he woke to Grannie's groan as she struggled out of bed and padded over to the fire to stir it to life.

He forced himself out of bed, and pulled on his trousers.

The old man was up, dressed in his coat, a scarf tight across the lower part of his face. 'I'm going to the police office on the Huon Road.'

'I'll go if you want.'

'No.' He shook his head. 'I'll do it.'

Harry watched him, leaning heavily on his staff as he walked down the path to the track. He supposed it was pride—the Old Man of the Mountain felt those who clambered over it were his responsibility.

A search party of a dozen men passed on their way to the pinnacle in the afternoon. Harry toyed with the idea of joining them, but he was no bushman—once off the main tracks, and without his father's directions, he'd likely get lost himself. He was certain, though, in the old days, the old man would have been out at dawn leading them.

The day drew on, and the party did not return. The old man was uneasy, talking of those who had been lost in the past, those he had searched for. He paced the room, making frequent trips outside.

'Have you sprung a leak?' Grannie called to him.

He glared at her. She muttered under her breath that they weren't living in a barn.

Harry woke at first light, the old couple still asleep. He dressed quietly and took himself down to the police office further along the Huon Road, near Fern Tree.

He was halfway back along the Fingerpost Track when he met his father.

'Any news?'

'They've been found on the New Norfolk side of Sorell Creek.' Harry had only the roughest idea of where that was other than some distance away.

'Lucky this time, young fools—they should have taken a guide.

Harry nodded. The mountain's stunning views came with the

35

price of steep precipices.

'Another month and there'll be snow.' The old man gazed around him. 'They'd not last a night in the open then.'

Harry stood outside the cottage, staring towards the track down to the fingerpost. The weather had cleared yesterday morning, Easter Sunday, to a bright but brisk day and today, despite overnight showers, looked to be even better. Climbers had begun arriving early, just as they had yesterday. Unfortunately, most stopped only for a cup of tea, often with a fortifying splash of the old man's *mountain dew*. Some strode on up the track accompanied by a guide from the town.

The old man came out and sat beside the doorway, his unlit pipe in his mouth. He was taking his rest today, breathless after prolonged bouts of coughing overnight.

Harry turned to him. 'I thought there would be more than this.'

They needed the money the climbers brought in. There were so many things that could only be bought—flour, tea, sugar at very least. Today was a holiday and the old man had said that visitors swarmed up the mountain on holidays. Winter would be here soon and no one would venture as far as the Springs.

Harry watched as his father drew on his now lit pipe and near coughed his lungs up.

'It's still early,' he gasped, 'still early.'

Voices carried up the track. A party of three young men burst into the clearing, full of high spirits and laughter. They spoke over each other. 'Can we get a guide? 'They said in Hobart Town ...' 'We need a guide to the top of the mountain.'

Harry stepped forward. 'I can guide you to the pinnacle or anywhere else.'

The deal was quickly done, money changed hands and they were off. Harry felt that he was herding puppies. The young men bounded ahead, darted back full of questions, and were off again.

Harry did his best to answer anything they asked—what he didn't know, he made up. They didn't stay long at the pinnacle. Each climbed to the top of the cairn with no more than a glance out across the view of Hobart Town and the hills, the inlets and the sea beyond and then they were off, back down the mountain.

'We're in a hurry, want to be at New Norfolk by nightfall.' 'Haven't much time, need to fit in as much as we can.' 'We've only got a week.'

When they reached the end of the track, just above the Springs, Harry stopped to take in the view. The young men did not wait— the mountain was a challenge to be conquered, not an experience to enjoy.

Harry stood gazing out. The day had warmed, the sky was bright and clear. There was nothing in Perth to compare to this view. He wondered what Eliza would think of it. He shook his head, angry at himself. Despite his best efforts, he still thought of her—not every day, but often enough she came to mind. If he were honest, he missed her bright chatter, missed her warm body beside him at night, missed having someone care for his comfort. With Perth behind him, he had been certain he would not miss her at all. She was the past. He must do what he had always done— concentrate on the here and now.

Voices carried from the Springs below, women as well as men. It sounded like a party.

Harry walked along the side of the cottage and out into the clearing. There seemed to be women everywhere, their skirts spread around them, bursts of muted colour among the greenery, blues and a rusty red, two-toned checks. An older woman with faded sandy hair sat on the bench beside the door, her hat lying on the seat beside her. The rest, ranging in age from about eight years old to two young women of twenty or so, sat on logs or on chairs dragged out from the cottage. Grannie moved among them with her teapot, refilling cups. Instead of the stony face she usually showed to strangers, she wore a bright grin.

Harry's father stood talking with two men. The elder was a tall spare fellow, not unlike the old man to look at, the same shaved face and beard along the jawline, grey rather than white as he was about twenty years younger. Beside him was a much younger man, heavily freckled, a sailor by the mass of tattoos below his rolled-up sleeves. These were not the initials of family members like the old man had on his arms but elaborate pictures, a horse's head, crossed flags, an anchor, stars on his hands.

'Harry, meet Bill and George Thompson.' His father turned back to the two men. 'My son, Harry Woods the younger.'

The elder man held out his hand. 'Pleased to meet you, Harry the younger.' He waved his hand towards the group of women. 'And these are my lady and my daughters.'

Harry raised his hat to Mrs Thompson, a tiny woman shorter even than Grannie, who had joined the men. The three younger girls gave Harry a passing glance, more interested in the antics of the baby they had with them, a sturdy child of around six months, who was trying to stand on the youngest and pull her fringe. The baby fell back in her lap and began to cry. The woman Harry supposed was the child's mother held out her arms and the youngest girl passed the baby to her. She seemed to be aware of Harry's gaze and glanced across at him. She was pleasant looking, her face made for smiling. His stomach gave an unexpected lurch. He shook his head to clear it—she must be George Thompson's wife.

Bill Thompson passed a flask around, Mrs Thompson and Grannie both making sure they got their share. Harry took a swig. He was hungry and would have preferred a cup of tea.

The young woman smiled at him. 'Should you be having that on an empty stomach, Mr Woods?' She stood, the child on her hip, and picked up a tin. 'Here, have a sandwich.' The scent of roses washed over him. He closed his eyes a moment. The memory of Eliza's gentle violet perfume faded.

'Thank you.' He took a sandwich and sat on the bench by the door. At a loss for words, he bit into the sandwich: cheese and pickle. It disappeared in three bites—it had been a long time since breakfast.

'Go on, have another.' Mischief in her grey-blue eyes, she grinned as if she were flirting with him.

He glanced across at George who winked back. Harry's eyes widened, unsure what was happening.

The baby started to wail. 'Poor Billy is teething.' The woman stuck her finger in the child's mouth, rubbing his gums.

'Don't know much about babies,' Harry said.

'You have none yourself, Mr Woods?'

There had been no such blessing. 'No, Mrs Thompson.'

'No need to be formal. I'm Sarah Ellen but family call me Ellen, you can too.'

He wasn't being drawn into this game. 'Your husband might have something to say about that.' He glanced at George again.

'My husband? Oh, you mean George?' Her laughter pealed around the clearing. 'He's my brother. No Billy's father ran a mile when he heard Billy was on the way. Afraid Will, my other brother, would give him a right thumping. Bastard!' She said the word under her breath.

Harry blinked. He had never heard a decent woman speak like that before. His pulse bounced surprisingly.

'So where are you from, Mr Woods?'

Even when she wasn't smiling, there was amusement in her eyes. Her skin was clear and unblemished, her lips perfect.

He realised he was sitting dumb, staring at her. Her chin had the slightest dimple.

'I'm from Perth but born in Fremantle on the other side of the Swan River.' He stopped. Why was he giving her his life story? 'If I'm to call you Ellen, you should call me Harry.' He smiled—he couldn't stop himself.

'Oh, I will.' Her eyelashes fluttered lightly. 'Are Mr and Mrs Woods from Perth too?'

'My father was there from the start of settlement. Mrs Woods is his second wife, he met her here.'

The baby began grizzling again. Ellen looked down, rocking him in her arms. 'My little darling needs a sleep.'

He watched her walk away towards her sisters—the straightness of her back, the tilt of her head, the sway of her hips.

Harry got up and helped himself to a cup of Grannie's stewed tea and one of the scones set out on a plate. He had finished when a small party arrived wanting to be taken to the pinnacle.

As he moved off with them, Ellen gave Harry a dazzling smile. He grinned back, aware of his own ridiculousness—he suspected he was near old enough to be her father.

8

May 1878

The wind howled, great lashing gusts pelting rain, but there were no drips through the roof. The chinks in the walls and windows had been stuffed with rags and daubed over with mud, now dried hard. The wind was kept out but the heat from the fire didn't extend far from the hearth.

Harry sat alongside the old couple, a blanket over his shoulders, his boots practically in the fire. 'What do you do most of the winter?'

'This and that—it's all I can do to make sure the path is clear down to the road and keep an eye on the waterways, see they are free of branches and rubbish.' The old man groaned. 'Even that is getting too much for me now.'

'The money from summer tides us over,' Grannie said, answering Harry's unspoken question.

'No visitors?'

'One or two in June, but from July to the start of October there are none most years. Too much snow and not much to see when there is cloud covering the top.' The old man drew on his pipe and started coughing.

Harry hunched tighter into his blanket. He had his coat, his gloves and two pairs of socks on and still his ears and the tip of his nose were icy. It was May, not even winter and already he'd had his fill of snow. He didn't know how he would survive cooped indoors for months on end with little to do.

'Perhaps I could get a job in the town. It would bring in a bit extra.' He paused, thinking out how it could work. 'Don't know that I could do it living up here.' It came to him like a visitation. 'I'd need a room in town, but I could come here on Sundays and help with the paths and anything else that needs doing.'

The old man spoke slowly. 'It's been a treat having you here, but that's a grand idea.'

Harry's only thought was that it would be warmer in the town.

~

The windows shook and the door slammed shut behind Ellen as the wind almost blew her into the kitchen.

'I'm not going out again, not for anything.' She pulled off her hat and gloves and sniffed. 'It's smoky in here.'

Mary Ann sat close by the fire. 'It's the wind whistling down the chimney, when the fancy takes it, blowing smoke everywhere.'

Ellen laughed. 'Mrs Bryce had to pay me more than she expected today. She asked me to come in to make the house perfect for when Mr Bryce comes back from Melbourne on Monday. I was supposed to leave at twelve but the silly old bat hasn't had her chimney swept since last year. The gale shook the soot loose and blew it all over her front parlour. She was so near to tears, I actually felt sorry for her.'

Dad poked his feet closer to the fire. 'Feels like snow.'

'It's white halfway down the mountain,' Ellen said, dragging a chair next to Alice who was holding Billy. 'Come here, Billy, my darling.' She hauled him onto her lap and smothered him with kisses. The child squirmed but she held him tight, rocking him.

The rain slashed against the window.

'Where's Mam?'

Mary Ann nodded towards their father. 'Ask him.'

'Dad?' Ellen said.

Her father sat puffing on his pipe, staring at the stove.

She raised her voice. 'Dad!'

'At Campbell Street, I suppose.'

Ellen gaped. 'In the House of Correction?' She handed Billy back to Alice and moved over in front of her father.

'She met a mate from the old days. She was a barmaid in the Labour in Vain too. I left them sitting in the Rob Roy last night, arms around each other, singing like long-lost sisters.

'You left her there! Anything could have happened to her.'

'It's only across the road and your mother knows how to look after herself. I called in at the police office on the way to work and she was waiting to go to court. Drunk and incapable.' He chuckled. 'It's a wonder it wasn't obscene language as well.'

Ellen stood, hands on her hips. 'You didn't go and pay her fine?'

'She hadn't been to court and I had to get to work.'

'But after work?'

Her father shrugged and didn't meet Ellen's eyes. 'I forgot.'

'Forgot your wife!' She clamped her mouth shut on the words she wanted to scream at him. How could he forget the woman he had been married to for over twenty-five years, had eight children with, and buried one? It wasn't as if they were always rowing—they seemed to enjoy each other's company still. And, after all that, how could a man forget his wife and leave her to be locked up in the House of Correction? If someone like her father didn't care enough, what hope did Ellen and her sisters have of finding a man to stick with them through life's ups and downs?

She glared at him, breathing through her nose. 'Well, you had better go and get her now.'

'S'pose I should. But they probably won't let her out until the morning.'

'You can at least try,' Ellen said.

Dad got up off his chair and stuck his hand in his pocket. 'Here Bessie.' He tipped a few coins into her hand. 'Go over to the Rob Roy and get us a couple of bottles. Your mum will be wanting a hair of the dog when she comes home.'

Ellen looked at her sisters. 'We need to get this fire burning properly and some tea on. Did anyone think to buy bread?'

As the front door slammed shut behind their father, a burst of cold air blasted into the room.

'Jane, can you find that old blanket to hang over the door? It might stop some of the draft.' Ellen rattled in the pantry cupboard. 'It will be potatoes and bacon for tea tonight. Plenty to go around though.'

She straightened up and folded her arms tight across her bosom for warmth. 'It must be freezing at the Springs at the moment.'

'I bet young Mr Woods hasn't seen snow before,' Alice said.

'He'll see plenty now.' Mary Ann stood and moved away from the stove as Ellen put wood into the firebox. 'There wouldn't be much work for him either. It must be hard in winter up there.'

Ellen thought of the way Harry Woods had smiled as he'd moved off with his party of climbers, the light in his eyes as if he couldn't help smiling at her. He was a bit older than she was but nowhere near as old as Mam and Dad. He seemed more courteous than the men she knew. Was he the sort to leave his wife in the lock-up overnight? Was he even the sort who would have anything to do with a woman who could end up there?

9

Harry began his walk down the mountain in the grey early light. The air was eerily still, the bird chatter and the rustle of the bush absent. He tramped steadily, the snow seeping through his boots, careful on the steep track from the Springs. The old man had fashioned him a staff to help with walking on uneven and slippery ground. He hid it among the tree fern when he got to the Huon Road.

Once he was on the road, it was easier going. He had expected there would be a stream of carts and drays on a Monday morning, but the road was empty. All still sensibly tucked up in bed perhaps. He had been walking for near an hour as the road slowly flattened, in places the mountain fell steeply away beside the road. The sun had risen into a clear blue sky. The journey towards Hobart Town was pleasant in its way—Harry had no need to rush, enjoying the quiet and the brisk clean air. He caught glimpses of the town and the water through the thinning trees.

Saturday's storm had left its mark on the town—branches and other rubbish piled against buildings and along lanes, water pooled in the gutters and the ruts and potholes in middle of the streets. The wind was still blowing cold down the mountain.

Harry pulled his coat tight as he walked down Davey Street towards the docks. The sight of the water and the masts and rigging of the ships thrilled him. He need not stay. He could catch the steamer to Melbourne, try his luck there, leave his burdens behind. The longer he stayed, the greater they would be. He had come to Hobart Town, free of care for anyone but himself and had felt, those first few days, that he could almost be, almost do, anything he wanted. But responsibility for the old ones had fallen on him and he hadn't fought it.

He didn't know how easy it would be to find a job. But he was willing to do nearly anything and would ask at every place that looked like it used labourers. If it wasn't so early, he could call into one of the many pubs—there seemed to be one on every corner. They were always a useful place for information of any sort and someone there was sure to know where there was work to be had.

He tried a couple of woodyards. All had taken on labourers for the day, but he was told to turn up early tomorrow and see what was offering. Before he went to find somewhere to stay, he decided to try one last sawmill at the lower end of Elizabeth Street. Thudding and hammering could be heard over the whine of the saw as a small army of men worked on buildings in various stages of construction. Piles of charred wood and rubbish were dumped at one side of the yard—there must have been a fire of some sort. Perhaps they had need of one more man.

Harry stepped into the yard and approached a burly man of about his own age standing, hands on hips, watching a lad stepping like a tightrope walker along the angle of the roof of a half-finished building.

'Bloody young fool,' the man muttered under his breath. He turned, scowling. 'What do you want?'

'I'm looking for work. Name's Harry Woods.'

His scowl deepened, his attention back on the youth on the roof. 'Got nothing today.' He turned his head, peering hard at Harry. 'Woods did you say? Related to the old man at the Springs?'

'His son.'

His face relaxed. 'He's a grand old fellow—found my brother when he lost himself up there a few years back. They say he's been here almost as long as Hobart Town itself.' The man gave Harry his full attention. 'What can you do?'

'Shingle splitting, carting and carrying. I'm willing to turn my hand to anything.'

'Plenty of carting and carrying here at the moment. Ever

operated a circular saw?'

This was no time for exaggerating his experience. 'No, but I've seen one used. The best I can say is I've used a two-man saw felling trees.'

'We get the trees already felled. At the moment it's mainly lugging timber and sawing firewood. I'll give you a try.' He glanced back at the building where the lad was now working his way down a ladder. 'If you're satisfactory, I'll take you on regular but no playing the fool on the roof or around the saws.'

'Far too old for that,' Harry laughed.

'I'm Jack Davis.' He held out his hand and shook Harry's firmly. 'Be at the gate at seven tomorrow, rain or shine.'

Davis moved away from Harry and bellowed, 'Bowen! Get yourself down here. Now!'

The young fool does need a good roaring at, Harry thought. Put a foot wrong and he could end up on the ground with a broken back.

He walked out into Elizabeth Street, whistling—the world was almost as full of possibilities as it had been when he arrived.

'Harry. Harry Woods.' Bob Flanagan pulled back on the reins and drew his wagon alongside Harry.

Harry moved to the edge of the footpath, out of the way of those hurrying up and down the street. 'G'day Bob.'

'Off home already?' He nodded towards the swag slung across Harry's back.

'No, I've just found myself a job.' He jerked his head in the direction of the woodyard. 'Start tomorrow.'

'Plenty of work there—they had a big fire in March, just before you arrived. As soon as the fire was out, they started rebuilding. Where are you off to now?'

'Looking for lodgings.'

'Hop up, I'll take you around to Mrs Hennessy's. Her place is clean, and the rate is reasonable. The tucker's not bad, not all gravy and gristle like they serve up at some places.'

Harry threw his swag into the back of the wagon and clambered up. He'd barely spent any time in the town since he had arrived. From high on Bob's wagon, he had a good view of the streets—the variety of the shops, women in all sorts of hats from the pretty to the serviceable, businessmen and working men, people from all walks of life and, as they were near the docks, from nearly everywhere on earth.

Bob drew up outside a neat weatherboard house at the top of Bathurst Street. He got out the feedbags, hung them from the horses' heads, and climbed the steps onto the verandah. He rapped the doorknocker and looked back at Harry. 'Make sure you wipe your feet. She doesn't like mud on the floors.'

A substantial woman wearing a startlingly white apron, opened the door, her steely grey hair pulled back into a tight bun. At the sight of Bob, the sternness in her face melted into a broad smile. 'Bob, my boy, 'tis wonderful to see you.'

Bob stepped forward and kissed her on the cheek. 'It's grand to see you again, Aunty. Sorry, it's been too long.'

'That it has. You must bring Mary and the little ones round to see me one Sunday.' She looked Harry up and down. 'And who is this you have with you?'

'This is my mate Harry Woods. He's the son of the Old Man of the Mountain.'

'Indeed.' She smiled at Harry, but not as brightly as she had at Bob. 'It is a pleasure to meet you, Mr Woods.'

Harry took off his hat. 'The pleasure is mine, Mrs Hennessy.'

'Aunty,' Bob said quickly, 'I wondered if you had a room to spare. Harry has come down to work in town for the winter and needs somewhere to stay.'

'And you can vouch for him?'

'That I can.'

Harry kept the surprise from his face—Bob barely knew him—

but he was grateful that Bob saw in him the decency Bob himself clearly possessed.

Mrs Hennessy paused, her eyebrows raised as if she did not altogether believe Bob. 'I do have an unoccupied room at present. And as it's you recommending Mr Woods, I'll take him without written references.' The unspoken words *If it doesn't work out, I'll hold you personally responsible*, hung in the air. She turned to Harry. 'This is an extremely respectable house, Mr Woods. I know I need not say this, as you are Bob's friend but I'll say it all the same. No drinking in your room. No coming in at night roaring drunk. And no sneaking women in—you'll be out the door if you do, no matter what the hour.'

Harry blinked at her bluntness. 'I wouldn't dream of it, Mrs Hennessy.'

She stared straight at him as if she could read his hiddenmost thoughts. 'I'm not concerned with what you dream of, Mr Woods, it is what you do that is my business. And I want my board on the dot at half past six on Friday night, before the evening meal.'

'That's so you don't spend your pay at the pub.' Bob grinned.

'Dinner will be at seven o'clock. You can have a glass of porter with it if you wish. And you may sit in the parlour as long as you are not in your work clothes. We often sit there after dinner and sing a few songs. Do you play an instrument, Mr Woods?'

'No, Mrs Hennessy, but I like a song or two.'

'Do join us.' She smiled at him, a picture of sweetness. 'Now I will show you to your room.'

Bob followed them up.

It was a small room, but all Harry needed was a place to sleep and to keep his few belongings.

Mrs Hennessy left them after Harry had paid his week's board from the money he had kept aside for his fare away from Hobart Town, should he need it. He dumped his swag on the floor and squeezed past the end of the bed to the window. He could see a corner of the mountain beyond the roof of the house next door.

'Is it to your liking?' Bob asked.

'It's better than I'd hoped. Thanks, Bob. I doubt she would have taken me off the street without you.'

'She is fussy but then you need to be in this town.'

'She's your aunt?'

'A cousin of some sort, of my father's—both from the same village in Kilkenny.'

Harry grinned at him. 'You are a handy man to know.'

'I am indeed. Now I think it's time for lunch, and you can buy me a glass of beer in one of Hobart Town's *evil* public houses.'

'That sounds like a very good idea.'

10

Harry whistled as he headed up Macquarie Street late on Saturday afternoon. It had been a good week. His board was paid, a couple of shillings put by in his room for the next week, and there was still the weighty jingle of coins in his pocket.

The work was heavy, lifting and carting mostly, but he enjoyed being among men who knew what they were doing. There were overseers, but as long as he did his work, he was left to get on with it. Davis seemed a decent sort. He had let Harry go an hour early so he could make it up to the Springs before nightfall. For the rest, all that mattered was a man's ability to do his job, to answer joke with joke and not to put on airs. Harry hated those who thought they were a cut above the rest, and he was not alone in that.

It was a pity that he would be missing tea at Mrs Hennessy's. Her cooking was more than satisfactory—nothing fancy, the same plain, filling meals his grandmother had made. In the evening, her lodgers gathered in the parlour, eight in all. For the most, they were clerks and counterhands; only one other was a labourer like Harry. Most were churchgoing types, sober and hardworking.

The snow-capped mountain was ahead of him. The road appeared to lead straight to it. Perhaps rather than following the Huon Road, which twisted and turned, it would be quicker to follow Macquarie Street. There must be a track that led from the street straight up the mountain. But so late in the day, he was sure to get lost if he tried to find it.

He crossed the street. Time to get onto Davey Street where there was a chance of being offered a ride.

'Harry Woods.' George Thompson detached himself from the fence he had been leaning against. 'Saw you coming, mate, and decided to wait. Where are you off to?'

'Up to the Springs. Need to give the old man a hand.'

'Don't you do that most days?'

'I'm working in town for the winter.'

'Got time for a drink?'

Harry grinned. 'Why not?' One drink wouldn't hurt.

George threw his arm over Harry's shoulder and steered him towards a pub further along the street. 'Now Harry, tell me about Western Australia, I've a mind to go somewhere warmer.'

~

Harry stared at the closing door as a gust of icy mist blew in. Outside the fog was thick, too thick for stumbling his way up the mountain. He wondered how late it was but didn't care.

George had bought the first drink, and Harry had been obliged to buy the second. It had gone on from there. He was introduced to everyone who came through the door. George Thompson was well-known and the life of any party.

George sang 'Where have you been all the day, my boy Willie?' with a couple of verses of his own invention, others joining in the refrain, Harry with them. As soon as he finished, Harry began.

O where are you going to, my pretty little dear,
With your red rosy cheeks, and your coal black hair?

A woman sat beside him and answered his verses.

I'm going a-milking, kind sir, she answered me,
And it's dabbling in the dew makes the milkmaids fair.

By the end of the song, she had slid her arm through his, her head resting against his shoulder.

As the last notes faded, an old fellow in the corner stood and started singing, his voice shaky.

They chain us two by two, and whip and lash along.

The whole bar erupted as one.

They cut off our provisions if we do the least thing wrong,
They march us in the burning sun until our feet are sore,
So hard's our lot now we are got upon Van Diemen's shore.

Some stood, their singing fierce, others sat crooning, but all stared back into a living past.

The anger and the sorrow of the song vanished almost as soon as the song ended—a fiddle was brought out and tables and stools were pushed back against the wall. The landlord stood behind the bar, arms crossed, frowning. There were rules about singing and dancing in public houses, but there was little he could do with this lot set on dancing.

George danced a hornpipe first, then two women joined him. The woman beside Harry—Moll, he thought she was called—grabbed him by the hands and dragged him to his feet. She was past thirty and must have been pretty when younger, but her face showed the wear of hard living. Still, he felt his pulse leap when she smiled at him and brushed close as they passed each other in the reel. It was good to have a woman in his arms again.

When the fiddler took a break, Harry and Moll fell onto the bench against the wall. The room continued spinning about. Harry sat still, pinpricks of sweat across his forehead, around his mouth. He lurched up from his seat and staggered out the door, barely making it to the side of the inn before he brought up the evening's beer—it crossed his mind that all he had eaten since breakfast was a lump of bread and cheese.

The cold air sobered him. His hand went to his pocket and the coins left there, less than half of what he had started out with. He could not possibly have spent so much, but he knew he had.

The night was pitch black, an icy wind swirling around corners. It was too dark to try to get up to the Springs. If he tried, he'd likely fall and break a leg and die of exposure.

Harry felt his way along the wall to the stables at the rear of the inn and eased himself into an empty stall. It was dry and warmer by far than outside. He heard the slam of the door and a burst of song carrying on the air. Darkness closed over him.

~

Harry's head throbbed as he clambered up the track towards the Springs. He had woken in the gloom, certain it was later than it seemed, the mountain top hidden by ragged cloud. It was Sunday morning so the road had been empty. He jingled the coins in his pocket. At least he wasn't coming home empty-handed. Home. He almost laughed out loud at the word. The cottage at the Springs was unlike any home he had ever had. Home had always involved a woman's care—his mother, his grandmother, Eliza. Old Jane Woods didn't come into it. He couldn't imagine her mending his socks, or making him brandy and hot milk when he was ill. She would more than likely drink the brandy herself.

There was nothing to see but the trail ahead, nothing to keep him from maudlin memories—his father as he had been when he'd last seen him in Fremantle. He had been wiry and full of life, his hair and shaggy eyebrows dark. His sense of humour seemed to be the one thing that had survived through the years.

He had taught Harry how to fell a tree, to split shingles straight and clean. He was skilled with wood, taught him the perfection of a good join. Yet he had always said he was a shoemaker, from a long line of shoemakers. Harry supposed it was true, he had seen him mend boots, but it was not how he had supported his family. He had willingly worked at anything that had offered—boatman, shingle splitter, duck and kangaroo hunter.

By the time he was ten, Harry was working most days with his father. He had felt almost a man when they took a break from the wood splitting, sitting on a log, eating bread and cheese, drinking brewed tea loaded with sugar—often with a splash of something stronger added to his father's but never to the boy's.

'You're not old enough. Best not to get the taste too early—it can lead to ruin, my lad.'

He'd told Harry stories of where he had come from, another world with houses of stone, rolling hills and gentle skies. It was no wonder he had stayed on here in Tasmania—it could almost be the place of his tales.

Then there was the day they had come for his father. The police had surrounded the house. The old man had set loaded muskets at each window and had shouldered his double-barrelled shotgun. But when they had threatened Harry's mother, he had gone like a lamb.

Harry hadn't believed the story of the stolen silver thimble. He was certain it was as his mother had said, she had been given it long before the night the old man was supposed to have broken into John Wicksteed's store. Once his father had gone, Wicksteed had crossed the street every time he saw Harry coming. He hated Wicksteed—the guilty lying bastard.

The day before his father had sailed, he had held Harry tight, eyes shining. 'Look after your sister, son.' He had stood back and tousled Harry's hair. 'Seven years—it's not forever.' He had raised an eyebrow. 'Might be less if I behave.'

Seven years transportation to Van Diemen's Land. To a boy, seven years was a lifetime and Van Diemen's Land as far away as the moon. And his mother had gone too, on the same boat as his father, taking his little sisters with her. He had liked the look of schooners with their triangular sails, their elegance in the water, but there was no pleasure in the sight of this one. He had felt small and lost staring out at the horizon as the *Champion* disappeared into the glittering sea.

He had kicked a stone hard. It had skittered along the wharf and bounced off towards a lumper lining barrels up for loading onto a ketch.

'Hey! Boy! Watch what you're doing,' he had yelled.

Harry had slouched back to his grandfather's cart and sat in silence as they had driven back to the farm near Rockingham. He had run off as soon as they'd arrived and hidden in the scrub, not coming home until after dark. Granny Broughton had been waiting for him, his meal in the oven. She'd repeated what his mother had said, that they would send for him and Sarah when they were settled—only a year, two at most. He hadn't believed it. Granny had folded him against her ample bosom. He'd clung to her, convulsed with sobs. He had not cried since.

~

Harry's mouth was parched and his clothes damp by the time he reached the Springs.

The old man broke into a broad grin. 'Harry, you look as if you have climbed out of the grave.'

'Feel like it too.' He walked over and stood on the hearth.

'Night on the town?'

'It was meant to be a single drink with George Thompson.'

'No such thing as a single drink with the Thompsons.' The old man sloshed a fair measure of his brew into a mug. 'Here—hair of the dog.'

Harry shook his head, his stomach lurching.

The old man pressed the mug into his hands. There was nothing for it. He gulped it down, his stomach balking at the fiery liquid. But it stayed put, and he was soon well enough to face a bowl of Grannie's porridge.

He handed over most of the coins. 'Sorry. There isn't that much—the *night on the town* was expensive.'

'Better than nothing at all,' the old man said.

His bowl of porridge finished, he went into the barn, picked up the axe. The old man had clearly done no chopping since Harry had left—the blade was as keen as he had left it. He turned to the wood pile and began, chopping the logs, splitting kindling, carting it into the cottage. He made a sizeable stack along from the fireplace so his father wouldn't have to go out in the rain or snow to get it.

Harry left in the middle of the afternoon and was back at Mrs Hennessy's well before time for the evening meal. As soon as the meal was over, he took himself off to bed. He smiled into the dark—it was a good thing he had been heading for the Springs on Saturday—she would not have been pleased to have him roll in on Saturday night singing his lungs out. He didn't regret his evening spent with George Thompson, but he had to be careful he didn't make a habit of it. He was too old to be carousing into the night and working like a dog by day.

11

September 1878

If there had been no one around to see her, Ellen would have skipped along the street. The sun was shining and the days were finally stretching out, although it was still chilly. Snow dusted the upper slopes of Mount Wellington, as it had all through winter.

George was home, and he had promised to take her and Mary Ann to the dancing room on Campbell Street tonight. She could have some fun, and he would be nearby if anyone got ideas she didn't like. Maybe she'd meet someone nice. Someone who was as sweet on her as she would be on him. She knew it didn't pay to dream too much but, in the sunshine, a neat house with a garden and a man who would love Billy as much as his own children seemed possible. Ellen knew very well that even in the better sort of houses where the women had nice clothes and new furniture, there were nasty secrets that in the workers' cottages were common knowledge. Well, she wasn't having a husband who would lay into her—Will and George would see to that.

She caught sight of Harry Woods coming towards her. She'd thought of him, now and again, over the past few months. George had said he was working in the town but their paths hadn't crossed until now. The moment she'd set eyes on him at the Springs, she'd known there was something about him. She liked the way he looked—the weathered skin and the nose that was a bit too big to be handsome somehow made him more attractive. His hair and beard were dark, and there were crinkles of laughter at the corners of his eyes, hinting that he didn't take life too seriously. And those brown eyes asked to be gazed deeply into. He was older than she was, but not that old. He seemed to be alive to the world around him, though at the moment his mind was miles away.

She drew level with him, and he still hadn't noticed her. She wondered what he was thinking about.

'Forgotten who I am Mr Woods?' Her cheeks dimpled.

He stopped. 'Miss Thompson.' His smile spread into his eyes. He seemed to mean it when he raised his hat and said, 'A pleasure to see you again.'

'I'm pleased to see you too.' She ignored the flush spreading up her neck.

He drew her to the side of the footpath, out of the way of others hurrying home. She could feel the weight of his hand on her arm through the layers of cloth. She went to place her own hand on his but caught herself in time.

'It's late to be heading up the mountain.'

'I'm boarding here in town, but I should be back at the Springs in a few weeks.'

'Where are you staying?'

'At Mrs Hennessy's.'

She screwed up her nose. 'That must be fun. She's a right old battleaxe.'

'She has her rules but she's a fair cook.' He looked around. 'Where's the lad?'

'At home with the family.' Ellen took a quick breath. 'Mam said if I ran into you, I should invite you to tea.'

'That is kind of her.' He hadn't taken his eyes from her face.

Ellen rushed on. 'She wants to make up for George leading you astray a few months back.'

'I wasn't exactly unwilling,' he said dryly.

'I'm sure you weren't.' She couldn't stop herself from smiling at him. 'All the same, Mam wants you for tea. Come on Sunday evening.'

'Thank you, I will.' He was grinning as if Ellen had made his day. 'I'd better be off, can't keep Mrs Hennessy waiting.' He tipped his hat again. 'I look forward to Sunday.'

Ellen walked a few steps past him and turned back, watching as

he crossed Liverpool Street, neatly sidestepping the muddy potholes. She was sure there was a spring in his step that hadn't been
there before. She smiled to herself and walked soberly home,
although she still felt like skipping.

~

The light of the gas lamps gave the dancing room a golden glow,
hiding away the shabby corners and bringing a rich red sheen to the
heavy curtains hanging over the windows. At one end, the band
played. It was exaggerating to call a man on the piano and another
with a fiddle a band, but they knew all the tunes people enjoyed
dancing to and that was all that mattered.

Ellen turned beneath her dancing partner's raised arm and
moved on to the next man. She groaned quietly. It was William
Cook, a smooth-faced nob in a flash suit who, along with his mate
Thomas Armstrong, appeared at these places annoyingly often,
slumming it because they assumed the women here were easy. As
they swirled around, Cook's right hand resting lightly at Ellen's
waist, she could see Mary Ann dancing with George's mate Tom
Budd and George dancing with a girl who had taken his fleeting
fancy. It was a comfort to know they were nearby.

Ellen loved the progressive dances that made up the early part
of the evening. You didn't stay long with any one partner, and it
gave you a chance to judge who was a good dancer and who wasn't,
who had made an effort and was not still covered with dust or
stinking from his day's work, who had roaming hands and thought
the women here were his for the taking, like Cook and Armstrong.

She skipped back and forth with Cook, his arm now around her
waist, her fingers touching his shoulder. As she turned to move on,
he slid his hand down her hip towards her backside.

'You watch yourself,' she called over her shoulder as she moved
on to the next dancer. Damn! It was Thomas Armstrong.

'I haven't seen you here before, Miss.' He had the sort of face
most would call handsome, but his grey eyes were cold and hard.

Ellen knew that when she told him he had, several times, he would say that it wasn't possible because he would never forget a girl as beautiful as her. Then she was supposed to swoon into his arms so he could drag her off to the nearest dark corner. Did any woman ever fall for that sort of rubbish?

'Oh, you have,' Ellen said, unsmiling. 'I've had the so-called pleasure of dancing with you several times.'

That seemed to put him off; he said nothing more. Nowhere near soon enough, Ellen took the hand of the next dancer, Jack Williams, who lived around the corner in Molle Street, a decent bloke without any airs.

The music changed, and they formed a circle dance. These dances were fun, but a bit slow. After the band's break, what Ellen thought of as the real dancing would begin.

She glanced about. George was nowhere to be seen. He would have gone out and through the fence to the pub next door as all that was on offer at the stall at the back of the room was fruit punch and lemonade. Dancing halls were not permitted to serve alcohol or have any association with pubs, and pubs were not meant to have singing or dancing, but many found ways to get around the rules.

When the music stopped, Ellen went over to Mary Ann, who was sitting against the wall, sipping a glass of fruit punch.

'I suppose George has gone off for a real drink.'

'Yes, and Tom too.'

She sat beside Mary Ann. 'Can I have a sip?'

Mary Ann passed her the glass.

'You must have got in early—the drink stall is crowded at the moment.'

'Tom bought it for me before he left.'

Ellen handed the glass back and grinned. 'You two seem to be getting on well. Is he nice?'

Mary Ann shrugged, not giving much away. 'Nice enough.

He's done a couple of trips with Will as well as George.'

George and Tom wandered back in as the band started playing again, a polka this time.

Ellen grabbed George's hand. 'Come on, you promised me one dance tonight.'

She loved the polka. It was an exuberant dance, especially the way it was danced here. It didn't matter how good or bad your partner was, they could clomp along and it still was fun—as long as they didn't trample on your feet. George had barely let go of her hand when she was swept away by someone else. She never had any difficulty finding someone to dance with. Many of the men here she knew. Hobart was not so large a town, and most of those who came here knew not to mess with Will and George Thompson's sisters.

As she spun around the room, she wondered if Harry Woods was a good dancer, wondered whether he liked a drink with his dancing or if he would prefer one of the legal rooms, where there was no drink and the men were generally better behaved. One thing was certain, the legal rooms were not places where the likes of Cook and Armstrong went to have their fun.

Mary Ann was dancing with Tom Budd—she hadn't danced with anyone else all night. They did seem suited. Tom was not as tall as George but was a couple of inches taller than Mary Ann, dark-haired with a scar on his forehead, probably from a fight like most of George's.

George was clearly enjoying his dance with yet another girl. He was laughing as she spoke, the girl gazing up at him, lovestruck, poor thing. Ellen's brothers rarely settled their attention on anyone for long. But they were still young—George was only twenty-two and Will two years older.

Ellen noticed Armstrong and Cook leaning against the far wall. They had been missing for a while, off in the pub no doubt. As their gaze followed the dancers, they looked to be passing sly comments to each other and sniggering. Perhaps she was imagining it, but they seemed to be watching her in particular.

She was dancing with Jack Williams again when the music slowed to a waltz. He was polite and had a reputation as a steady worker and not much of a drinker. Unfortunately, his dragon of a mother would be more than unimpressed if he tried bringing Ellen home.

Armstrong stepped in their way. 'My turn now, I believe.'

Jack looked at Ellen, a slight frown on his face. 'Do you want to?'

She shrugged. 'It won't hurt, Jack, but I will dance with you again later.'

He nodded to her and disappeared between the other dancers.

Armstrong smiled at Ellen. 'I know you wanted me to come over. I've seen the way you've been eyeing me all night.'

She glared at him. He was making it up. She had glanced their way a couple of times and only to check where they were. The pair made her uneasy.

They had made no more than a couple of turns when Armstrong's hand slid down her hip. She grabbed it and placed it back at her waist.

'Try that again and you'll be dancing on your own.'

He smirked, amused.

The music slowed further. She wished they'd play a polka again so they could dance with a decent distance between them.

Armstrong moved closer, pressing himself against her as they slowly moved in perfect step together. He stank of whisky, and his cologne was overpowering—he must have drenched himself in it.

Although he danced well, there was nothing about him Ellen liked.

'I've had enough.' She let his hand go and tried to move away.

'And I haven't had near enough.' He clamped his hand on her buttock.

The small pad tied beneath her skirt to make a bustle and the cloth of her overskirt caught up and pinned on one hip offered no protection.

Ellen stood still. 'Let me go.'

Another couple almost collided with them. Others stopped and watched.

'I suppose you want to be paid first,' he sneered. 'How much?'

Ellen slammed her fists into his shoulders, but he held her tighter.

'Let the lady go, mate.' Jack Williams was beside her.

'Lady!' Armstrong scoffed. He looked Jack up and down. 'And you mind your own business, *mate.*'

'You heard the man. Let her go.' George stepped in front of Jack.

'Make me.' Armstrong pushed Ellen away and swung a fist at George's head.

George ducked. He brought his head up, smashing his forehead against Armstrong's nose. Blood flooded over his chin, soaking into his expensive white shirt.

Ellen scrambled backwards. Armstrong was as likely to turn on her.

Cook, now at Armstrong's side, took a swing at Jack. Tom lunged towards him and brought his elbow up across his throat. The room erupted with an almighty roar. Men were everywhere— grappling, punching, kicking, gouging. There was no sense in who was belting into whom.

Mary Ann grabbed Ellen's arm and dragged her towards the door. 'We have to get out of here.'

The music had stopped, the musicians gone. Women were screaming. Glass smashed down near the drink stall.

They pushed their way through those already streaming out through the door, mostly women and a handful of men, and ran through the yard of the adjoining pub, out into the street.

'Slow down now,' Mary Ann said. 'We need to act as if we know nothing about any dancing room.'

She handed Ellen her shawl.

Ellen, her heart still pounding, wrapped it tight around her shoulders. 'You thought to grab this?' Her sister was truly the most sensible of them all.

'I saw the look on George's face and knew exactly what would happen.' She exhaled heavily through her nose. 'Once the coppers arrive, they'll assume any poor woman in there is on the town.'

'They always assume the worst of us, like that pig Armstrong.'

They turned at the sound of pounding feet behind them.

George and Tom ran up to them, barely out of breath. Tom had a red patch on his cheek that would be a lovely bruise tomorrow. George, despite a split lip, was grinning widely.

He wiped away the trickle of blood on his chin with the back of his hand. 'Now that was a fine end to the night.' As they turned into Liverpool Street, he slid his arm through Ellen's. 'What I would describe as almost a perfect evening—a couple of drinks, a few dances with a pretty girl and a fight. All that's missing's not fit for discussion with my sisters.'

Behind them, Tom, walking with his arm around Mary Ann, laughed.

Ellen rolled her eyes. That might be George's perfect evening, but it wasn't hers. She wanted to dance with a man who was good-looking, polite and a decent dancer, someone who would treat her like a lady, not a whore.

Now Harry Woods was polite and seemed to think no less of her even though she had a child. In fact, she was nearly certain he actually liked her. She hoped he was every bit as nice as he seemed. And that he liked dancing.

12

Ellen sprang up from her chair and was halfway across the room before the rap on the door had finished.

'Someone's keen,' Dad laughed.

Ignoring him, Ellen hurried to the door. She paused and took a deep breath. She knew she had said the invitation was from her mother, but she felt as if Harry was coming to see her. She pulled the door open and there he was, his hat in his hand, two bottles of beer tightly cradled in his other arm.

'Miss Thompson.' He grinned, his eyes on hers.

Ellen's pulse gave a leap. He did look pleased to see her. She felt as if a dozen brightly coloured butterflies were flitting around her stomach.

'Ellen, please. I've told you that before.'

'And I'm Harry,' he said, his eyes still smiling.

'I know.' She raised her eyebrows. 'Now come in before they start yelling at me for letting the cold in.' Ellen stood back against the wall to let him pass.

'Harry, mate, come on in.' George threw an arm over Harry's shoulder as soon as he was through the kitchen door.

The younger girls politely said hello, but Ellen could see Mary Ann was sizing him up. Bessie, kneeling in the corner beside Billy, was building a rickety tower of blocks that he knocked down, gurgling with laughter.

He stopped when he caught sight of Harry and eyed him warily.

Ellen went over and lifted him onto her hip.

'Come on, Billy, meet Mr Woods.' The boy scowled and turned his face away, burying it against Ellen's neck.

Ellen sat at the table with the boy, her lips against his silky hair. She had hoped he would take to Harry straightaway—it would have been a sign.

'He's shy,' Harry said gently. 'It's better if children are a bit wary of strangers.'

Ellen looked up at him. 'That's right.'

Harry offered Dad his gift.

'That will go down a treat.' He slapped Harry on the back. 'You certainly know the way to get on a father's good side.'

Harry's colour darkened—was he blushing?

Ellen lowered her eyes and tried to hide her smile, wondering if it was good manners on Harry's part, or if he really was buttering up her father.

The meal was served almost immediately, a hearty stew with bread and butter. The whole family sat close around the table on an assortment of stools, benches and chairs, Billy on Ellen's knee. He fought to get the spoon from her as she tried to feed him. When she thought he had eaten enough, she surrendered the spoon. As much went into his hair and across his cheeks as into his mouth. He happily burbled away as he played with the spoon.

Harry was hoeing into the meal with as much relish as George and polished off the gravy with the bread. He swallowed the last of his bread and said, 'That was delicious, Mrs Thompson, just like my grandmother used to make.'

Mary Ann stood and went to the stove, pouring water from the kettle into the teapot standing on the hob. Jane collected the empty plates and placed them beside the washing tub on the bench beneath the kitchen window.

Ellen lifted Billy off her lap and handed him to Alice. 'There's cake as well.'

'Take a big slice, Harry,' Dad said. 'Ellen baked the cake special-ly for you.'

She brought the pound cake out of the pantry cupboard. It had turned out perfectly, a lovely golden brown on top, sprinkled with sugar.

'Don't be silly, Dad.' Ellen concentrated on cutting the slices evenly, trying to ignore the heat rising up her neck. 'I often make a cake on Sundays.'

Mary Ann, busy pouring the tea, snorted and tried to cover it with a cough.

Alice, holding Billy and attempting to wipe the remains of his meal from his hands and face, opened her mouth, 'But ...' A jab in the ribs from Jane silenced her.

Mam sat back, warming her hands around her teacup. 'So you're staying with old Mrs Hennessy.'

'Yes, on weekdays. I go up the mountain on Saturday afternoon, back by Sunday night.'

'No time for play,' Dad said.

'No, unfortunately. I need to keep an eye on the old folk.'

'I've seen you striding along towards the Huon Road on a Saturday.' George stretched back in his chair. 'Too fast for me to catch up. I'd started to wonder if you were avoiding me.'

Harry shook his head. 'I need to be quick, don't want to be climbing up the track in the dark.'

'Summer is on its way, longer days.' George put his empty teacup down. 'Time for a beer, I think.' He went to the sideboard and opened one of Harry's bottles of beer. Glasses were passed to all but the younger girls, and, drinks in hand, the questioning began.

'Where was your father from?' Dad asked.

'England.'

'But where? It's a big place.'

Harry shrugged. 'Cheltenham I think it's called, wherever that is.'

Dad nodded. 'About eighty or so miles south of Stoke on Trent, where I was. Pretty place, from what I've heard.'

'And, Mrs Thompson, are you from there too?'

Before Mam could answer, Dad said, 'Beth here is English or

Scottish depending on her fancy on the day.'

Mam rolled her eyes. 'We moved around the border. My parents were Scottish, but I were sent here from Carlisle.'

His hazel eyes intent on Harry, Dad asked, 'Now, young feller, what did you do in Perth?'

'This and that. I'll turn my hand to whatever makes a penny.'

Ellen frowned. Why was he being vague? Was he hiding something? Perhaps he had been in gaol. It might not be a problem, depending on his crime.

George clearly thought the same. 'Ever been in gaol, Harry?'

Harry sat up in his chair, his mouth open, as if he was shocked by the suggestion. 'No.' He paused, frowning, perhaps trying to work out why he had been asked. 'My grandfather had a farm. I worked on that for a few years,' he finally said. 'Then did a bit of wandering, joined a party exploring the interior, tried my hand at fishing.'

Ellen listened as he talked of the country he had travelled through—the scenery, the sheer rock walls, the great boulders in all manner of reds and browns, the floods, the wildflowers bursting into bloom as the waters receded. The way Harry described it all, it was as good as the stories Dad read out from the paper.

'Later I worked on the East-West Telegraph line.'

Harry spoke of the heat and the sand, the scarcity of fresh water, the transport of logs by sea, hauling them ashore and through the coastal scrub to the route of the telegraph line, the raising of the poles and the stringing of the wires overhead, the cheering as the two lines, from Perth and from Adelaide, were finally joined at Eucla. Although his descriptions were not as vivid as before, Ellen thought they seemed more real.

'You didn't think to come and visit your father when you were younger?' Mam said.

'It never crossed my mind. There was plenty to do in Western Australia.'

'Your father said he was a shoemaker in England,' Dad said.

'Just like you.' Ellen smiled at her father.

'He didn't do much of it in Western Australia. It was mostly fencing, shingle splitting, a bit of carpentry and hunting ducks and kangaroos.'

'You must have been young when Mr Woods came here.' Mam stared straight at him, a line between her brows.

Ellen wondered if she was concerned at the thought of a little boy left without his father or puzzling out his age.

Harry nodded. 'I was.' He added nothing more.

'And your mother?'

'Dead.' His terse response brought an end to the interrogation.

'This is getting morbid,' George said. 'Time for a song, I think.' He grinned across at his nephew.

Where have you been all the day,
Billy boy, Billy boy?

As George sang, the others joined in with him.

When he had finished, Mam and Mary Ann sang 'The elphin knight' together. Ellen crooned along with them, Billy in her arms. She was aware of Harry watching as she rocked Billy, his head resting against her breast.

When Harry's turn came, he sang 'The dark-eyed gypsy'.

Harry sang it at a faster pace than Ellen had heard it before and she thought it sounded so much better. But the song had a line, sung by the lady, that Ellen hated—*What do I care for my children O?* She stared down at her beautiful boy, his head nodding towards sleep. As if a mother would think like that. But whatever the words, Harry had a rich voice and she could listen to it all evening.

Ellen sang a soft lullaby. Billy was sound asleep by the end. She rose quietly and whispered, 'Goodnight, Harry,' as she stepped past him.

As she carried the boy from the room, she heard Harry say, 'It's been a grand evening but I must go, need to be up early for work.'

A cork squeaked and popped. The whisky bottle, no doubt.

'A parting glass,' George said.

Poor Harry. Ellen wondered if he had the will to limit it to one drink in face of George's insistence.

Leaving Billy asleep in bed beside Alice, she went down to go out to the privy. As she stepped into the yard, she almost collided with Harry.

She moved aside to let him pass. 'Now tell me you would have had a better Sunday evening with Mrs Hennessy?'

'I'd be lying if I did,' Harry said.

'Good thing I invited you.'

She could see his smile in the moonlight. She wanted to reach out, feel the prickle of his beard against her fingertips.

'Wasn't it your mother's invitation?'

'It was, once I told her you were coming.' Ellen stood, her eyes lingering on his face. 'I suppose you'll be off back to Mrs Hennessy soon.'

He nodded. 'Yes, after I've said my goodbyes.'

'Well, goodbye, Harry.' She moved towards him and stretched up, touching her lips to his cheek. Harry turned his head, moving into her kiss. He slid an arm around her waist and pulled her close, kissing her as if he would swallow her. Her lips parted under the pressure of his mouth and she kissed him back hungrily for an endless moment.

She moved her hands up to his chest and stepped back from him, shaken. No kiss had ever made her feel this way.

He caught her hand and held it. 'Now that felt more like hello than goodbye.'

Ellen didn't trust herself to speak. Smiling, she slowly withdrew her fingers and walked away towards the privy in the far corner of the yard, shared with the other house on their side of the lane. She stood in the shadows, trying to gather her thoughts. The kiss had made her weak-kneed. Every part of her had seemed to melt.

From over by the back door, she heard her brother say, 'What are you doing out here, Harry? I hope you haven't brought up the day's takings? Mam will be disappointed—that was a good stew.'

'No. Just a bit unsteady. The cold hit me when I came outside.' Harry's voice brought back that melting feeling.

'Looks like I'll have to teach you to drink, mate.' She could imagine George now slapping Harry on the back.

'I'll be on my way, George. Got to be up early tomorrow.'

'If you need to be up bright and early, rum's the thing,' George said. 'My brother Will says ...' Their voices faded as they went back into the house.

Ellen came out into the middle of the yard, staring at the millions of bright pinpricks in the inky sky. Her arms spread wide, she twirled around, her skirts spinning out. She wanted to laugh for pure joy.

13

On Saturday, Harry woke to the sound of an empty cart rattling along Bathurst Street. He knew he should get up but slowly drifted back towards sleep and the dream he had reluctantly woken from all week—Ellen Thompson, warm and willing, in his arms. He forced his eyes open and lay staring at the ceiling. How many times had he relived his memory of last Sunday? Ellen pressed against him, her eager kisses. And he had started it—her intention had been simply to kiss him on the cheek. But wasn't that encouragement? He lay there, his eyes wide. Eliza. He pushed thought of her away. It was over seven months now. She was the past.

Harry groaned and stretched his arms above his head. He must get up. He hadn't taken the day off work to spend it in bed. On Wednesday, Harry had gone to Davis, the foreman, and said he needed to spend more time up the Springs. The gradually lengthening days with the arrival of spring meant there was plenty to be done. It wouldn't be long until he would have to spend all of his time up there.

He forced himself out of bed and pulled on his trousers, went over to the washstand, yawned and stretched again. After splashing cold water on his face, he raked a comb through his hair and beard.

He paused at the sound of a light tapping. Was that his door? It wasn't Mrs Hennessy's sharp rap. Harry struggled into his shirt and quickly buttoned it. He buckled his belt as he opened the door.

Ellen stood in the doorway.

Harry's heart thumped as he forced his morning fantasies away. 'Ellen.'

Her eyes glided from the unmade bed and fixed firmly on his face.

'I hoped I'd catch you before you left. Mam said to bring you this.' She held out a parcel wrapped in a checked tea towel and a stoppered bottle. 'Just a bit of bread and cheese and some tea. It's a hungry walk up there.' She was rushing on, gabbling almost. 'I'm sure this won't spoil whatever Grannie Woods has ready for you.' She smiled, a dimple in one cheek. 'Bring the bottle and tea towel back next time you visit.'

'Thank you, Ellen.' He took the warm bottle and the parcel, his eyes lingering on her lips, her neck disappearing into her high buttoned jacket. 'I'd invite you in, but Mrs Hennessy would have something to say about that.'

'I'm sure she would. I saw her heading off to the shops as I arrived.'

'I did wonder why she wasn't chaperoning you.'

Ellen rolled her eyes. 'She wouldn't have let me past the front door.'

'Thank you again. Thank your mother.' He didn't know what else to say. Perhaps he should kiss her on the cheek. No, that was not a good idea. 'I'll think of you when I eat them.'

She smiled, a sparkle of mischief in her eyes. 'You do that.' She glanced along the passageway towards the stairs. 'I must be off.' She leant towards him and pecked him on the cheek, her hand resting on his arm.

Harry stood in the doorway watching the sway of her hips, the flick of the hem of her skirt as she sped towards the stairs.

~

Ellen nearly collided with Mrs Hennessy at the foot of the staircase.

'I thought it was you lurking across the road,' Mrs Hennessy said, her lips pursed. 'What are you doing in my house?'

'I had something to give to Har... Mr Woods.'

'I'm sure you did.'

Ellen pressed her lips together, heat rising up her face as she glared at the older woman.

'You keep your claws out of Mr Woods. He's a decent hard-working man. Too good for the likes of you and too old by far.'

Ellen's mouth twisted. 'More to your taste, is he?'

'You insolent little piece of work. Your whole family is no better than it should be. The stories I could tell.'

'No doubt you could, grandma, but that has more to do with your own filthy mind. There are enough tales about you, how you came here and what you did to get by.' Ellen was making it up as she went but, true or not, if she wasn't careful, the old woman would burst a blood vessel.

Mrs Hennessy spluttered, 'You, you ... I'll warn him to stay away from you and your family.' She jerked away and hauled herself up the stairs. 'Now get out of my house.'

Ellen slammed the door behind her.

Bloody Mrs Hennessy would spoil everything. Harry wouldn't come near her after that old beast got in his ear. And, of course, he would believe it—there was Billy to show she was no good. She marched on, tears pricking at the corners of her eyes. She hadn't had much say in that. John Collins had been good-looking and fun—as long as he got what he wanted. There was no point saying no to him—he'd turn nasty if you did but, she supposed, he wasn't unusual in that. And once Billy was on the way, he had refused to have anything to do with her, said if she had gone with him, who was to say she hadn't gone with half a dozen others. The pig! And he'd cleared out before Will or Dad had had the chance to give him a damn good thumping. Anyway, Billy was a Thompson. Better off without his good-for-nothing father.

'Ellen! Ellen!'

She turned, hoping it was Harry come to tell her to ignore the old besom's nasty tongue.

George dodged between the carts as he ran across the road. 'Where are you off to?'

'Oh, George,' she wailed, looking away from him, her chin

quivering. 'I don't know. I wanted a walk.'

He caught her by the hand. 'What's wrong?'

'That old bitch Hennessy tore into me a few minutes ago.'

'What?' He scowled. 'In the street?'

'No,' she sniffed. 'I was in her house.'

He raised an eyebrow and grinned. 'Calling on Harry Woods, eh?'

'I was doing a message for Mam. She asked me to drop some food off for him, a sandwich to eat on his way up the mountain. He said last Sunday he would be going to the Springs early today.'

'I think Mam might want to adopt him—needs another boy to care for with Will away.'

Ellen's face crumpled. 'It's not fair. Nothing's fair.'

'Cheer up, sis.' He linked his arm through hers. 'I'll buy you some ribbons or a spray of those cloth flowers you like to pin to your dresses.'

'Just paid, are you?'

'I am. Flush with money.'

'All right, let's go to Kerr and Young's. I'll try on every hat there and you can make sure that old woman in trousers behind the counter treats me like a lady.'

'That's my girl.' He stopped in the middle of the footpath. 'And, if Harry Woods doesn't behave himself, you know he will have your brothers to answer to.'

She leant her head against his shoulder. 'Dad's right, it's only family you can count on.'

~

Ellen sat by the stove, her eyes straying to the clock every few minutes.

'Are you expecting a caller?' Mary Ann asked.

'No.' Ellen crossed her arms and stared at the kettle sitting at the back of the stove. 'I was wondering if it's time for bed.'

'If you're tired, go now, lass,' Mam said.

'If I go too early, I won't sleep.'

Mary Ann shook her head and smirked.

Ellen decided to ignore her.

Harry Woods should call in and thank her mother for the sandwich, but it was dark outside. He was probably in bed already. He did seem reliable and hardworking, so he would want to be up bright for work tomorrow morning.

He was sure to have listened to Mrs Hennessy. Ellen nursed her pride—if Harry wanted her, he would have to court her. If he came back, it probably meant he thought he could get things easy. Well, he could think again.

Ellen stood up. 'I might as well go to bed.'

~

Monday, Tuesday came and went without a sight of him. She would have to wait until next Sunday most likely. If he didn't call by then, he was just an ill-mannered pig.

Late Wednesday afternoon, Ellen sat at the table trying to get Billy to eat his tea.

Mam stood in front of the pantry cupboard. 'Will one of you go out and get a loaf of yesterday's bread?'

'I'll go. I need some air.' Ellen stood up. 'Alice, finish feeding Billy, will you?'

Alice took Ellen's seat, pulling faces to amuse the boy as she spooned the mash into him.

Ellen put on her hat and coat and went out into the street, pulling on her gloves as she started down Liverpool Street. Still lost in disappointed thoughts of Harry Woods, she almost collided with a man at the corner of Harrington Street.

She opened her mouth to tell him to watch where he was going and found she was looking up into Harry's face. He put out his hand to steady her.

'Ellen.' His eyes crinkled at the corners as he smiled.

'Harry.' For once, Ellen couldn't think of anything to say.

Passers-by muttered as they stepped around them.

Harry drew Ellen to the side of the footpath, his hand resting on her arm a few moments longer. 'I must call in soon and thank your mother for the sandwich.'

'She would like that.'

He looked at her as if to say, *And you?* No, she was letting her imagination run away. She braced herself and asked, 'Old Mrs Hennessy hasn't succeeded in scaring you off us?'

He frowned. 'I judge as I see and take no heed of nasty imaginings.'

She couldn't keep the bitterness from her voice. 'There's plenty in this town without a good word to say about us.'

'There was plenty said about my old man in Perth that wasn't true.' He clearly carried his own share of bitterness. He gazed into her eyes. 'As I said, I judge by what I see, not what others say.'

Her stomach somersaulted. She closed her eyes a moment at the relief. When she opened them, he was still gazing down at her with those lovely brown eyes.

'So you'll come for tea on Sunday?'

'That I will, Ellen.' He caught her fingers in his, squeezing them lightly.

Ellen watched Harry walk away up Harrington Street, holding on to the lingering memory of his touch. With some effort, she stopped herself from skipping all the way to the baker's and back.

14

Ellen pressed her cheek against the sheet hanging on the clothes-line. It was bone dry. A day of bright sunshine made all the difference.

She unpegged the sheet and pulled it from the line. Mary Ann took one end, and they folded it between them.

'So. *He* is coming again on Sunday?'

'That's what he said.' Ellen placed the folded sheet in the basket on the ground beside them. She wasn't giving anything away to her sharp-eyed sister.

Mary Ann unpegged a pillowslip and shook it out with a sharp crack to remove any creases. There was no unnecessary ironing done in the Thompson household. 'He's old, you know, nearly as old as Dad.'

'That is absolute rot, Mary Ann.' Ellen tugged another pillow-slip from the line. 'He's probably not much more than ten years older than you.' She looked down at the roughly folded mess in her hands. Mary Ann and her bloody prying! She shook the pillowslip out and started again.

Mary Ann twisted her mouth. 'I can't see the appeal myself.'

Ellen pulled a face at her sister. 'Well, he's a man.'

'Old Reg Hudson is a man.'

Ellen made a retching noise. 'You win. That's no good reason.'

'So why do you like him?' Mary Ann's tone was gentler.

Sighing, Ellen looked up and watched a gull soar overhead. 'He's not bad-looking. And he is always polite and such a story-teller—he's as good as Dad or the old fellow up the mountain. You can see they are related.'

'Do you think he's been married before?' Mary Ann gave voice to what had been nagging at Ellen but she had avoided facing. 'You do get the sense he's properly house-trained.'

'Dad's married and he's certainly not.' Ellen laughed. 'I think he might have been married once.' Yes, that would be it—he had come to Hobart Town to escape his memories, to put grief behind him.

'What do you want from him?'

'I don't know. It's too early to say.' If she said it aloud, it would never happen.

'Has he kissed you?'

'Hmm.' Ellen concentrated on unpegging the last few items from the line.

'You take care—we don't want a brother or sister for Billy until you have a ring on your finger.'

Before Ellen could snap back at her, Mary Ann added, 'I'd say he'd make a decent husband.'

Ellen supposed she should accept Mary Ann's stickybeaking and finger-wagging. She had been more than a sister, at times filling the role of mother. Ellen had not forgotten the time Mam had disappeared, locked up in the House of Correction at the Cascades for six months for stealing shoes—as if a shoemaker's wife would steal shoes! Mary Ann, at ten years old, had taken over the cooking and cleaning. She had cared for her younger brothers and sisters, rocking them, tucking them into bed, wiping their tears as they cried for their mother. Ellen had been four years old, Bessie two and George six. Will had said he was too old for hugs and kisses.

She smiled at Mary Ann. 'Seems that way.' Ellen hugged her dream tight—he would buy her a proper flash ring, and she would wave it under old Ma Hennessy's nose. 'And how's your sailor, Mary Ann?'

'Coming along nicely. At least when he's out on the ocean, I know he's not chasing after girls.'

'But what about those near-naked mermaids?'

'Too cold for mermaids out there. And they all reek by the time they get home—not even a fishy mermaid would go near them.'

They picked up the basket and carried it between them into the house.

~

On Sunday night, Harry was on the doorstep at half past five, a bottle of Mr Woods's spirit under his arm. He might see it as a gift for Ellen's father, but she knew, more than likely, it would be Mam who drank most of it.

After greeting Ellen's parents, he squatted down beside Billy who was playing with his blocks on the floor. He held out his hand. 'Good evening, young man.'

Billy pulled back slightly. Harry picked up one of Billy's blocks and placed it on top of his small tower. Billy grabbed another and placed it on top of Harry's. This time Harry carefully balanced his block off-centre. When Billy placed his block, the whole tower toppled over, Billy crowing with laughter. He started a new tower, Harry helping him, and knocked it down just as joyously.

Ellen came and picked Billy up. 'That's enough, my darling.' She kissed him on the tip of his nose and carried him to the table.

Billy went red in the face, bawling as he held out his arms for Harry. The boy settled as soon as Harry took him from Ellen.

'You've won a heart there,' Mary Ann said dryly.

'He's a fine lad,' Harry replied. He sat at the table, Billy on his knee.

'Do you want to help him eat?' Ellen asked.

'I'll give it a try.' He took the spoon from Ellen.

She passed him a tea towel to cover his clothes.

'You are good with children,' Mam said.

'Plenty of nieces and nephews. My sister Sarah had a child nearly every year and ...' he stopped himself, frowning.

'You're a natural, Harry,' Mary Ann said. 'Do you have any children of your own?'

'No.' His answer was firm. He kept his eyes on the boy on his lap.

Ellen was sure there was a story there—perhaps he had lost a child as well as his wife. One day he would tell her.

The meal over, they sat around the hearth telling stories and singing. Billy fell asleep in Harry's arms. Ellen gently eased him away and took him up to bed. When she came back, Harry and Bill were topping each other's tales. She wondered how much of it Harry made up. With her father she could rarely tell what was true and what was good storytelling. She wished Will was home—he was the best judge of character. He would know what to make of Harry Woods.

Ellen wanted to be cool and restrained, not let on what she was feeling but she couldn't hide it. She loved Harry's voice, especially when he sang. It was full and melodious, asking for duets. When she sang alongside him, she knew her face glowed. They could all read what she felt.

Harry stood. 'I'd better be off—work tomorrow. I've had a grand time tonight.'

'Come again next Sunday, Harry,' Mam said. 'We enjoy your visits.'

'Thank you. It has been like home, but I'm finishing at the mill on Friday.'

'You're going back to Perth?' Ellen gasped, blinking. She forced her eyes wide.

'No,' he grinned, 'I'm going back to the Springs. The weather's improving, and the old man needs my help. Climbers are starting to go up there again.'

Ellen opened her mouth to speak but couldn't say the words without the creak of her voice giving her away. Her barely formed dreams of marriage, of disappearing into the masses of the respectable where no one would look twice at Billy or dare to talk of bastards, crumbled. But Harry seemed content to be leaving. She had been nothing more than a bit of fun for winter. Ellen was certain had she offered more, he would have taken it but would still be on his way without a backward look.

'It's lovely there in summer,' Mam said.

Dad glanced across at Ellen. 'We'll have to come up and visit you.'

'I'm sure the old man would enjoy your company.'

Ellen rose from her seat and walked Harry to the front door. She followed him out, pulling the door shut behind them.

He turned to her, caught her hand and drew her close.

She closed her eyes but couldn't sink into his kisses, couldn't push the thought from her mind that he was happy to be leaving, that he wouldn't miss her at all.

He stopped, gazing into her face in the darkness. His grip on her tightened. 'Ellen,' he sighed. 'I'll miss you. More than you can imagine.'

It was all she wanted to hear. 'I *can* imagine.'

'I'll come to town when I can.'

If he made that effort, it would mean he truly cared.

15

Snow was constant on the mountain, some days extending as far as the Springs, other days merely dusting the pinnacle. Harry went about in hat and coat and gloves, the cold a persistent gnawing. Nothing warmed him through. The old couple were uncomplaining but spent most of the time wrapped in blankets hunched in front of the fire.

On days when the sky was a pristine blue and the snow in retreat, an occasional group of hardy men tramped up the track, more intent on reaching the top than lingering for the view. Once a group of picnickers arrived, visitors from interstate with a list of sights that must be seen before they went back home. They had brought a hamper with them with sandwiches, tarts and pies. Grannie pottered around, heating what she could and brewing tea. Harry led the men to the top. They stayed only long enough to smoke a pipe of tobacco while attempting to shelter from the wind beside the cairn. They returned to find the two women sitting side by side outside the door, glum-faced. When they finally left after eating their meal, their offering was paltry.

Grannie looked at the two pennies on her palm. 'No hope of getting drunk on this. I asked them in to bide by the fire, but they preferred to sit outside and moan that it was cold, the ground was damp and the wind icy.'

'People have changed,' the old man muttered. 'They used to appreciate what we do.'

Harry went into the barn and led the horse out to the shelter at one side, where a water trough and a feed rack were set up. Back in the barn, he set a log on the block and took up the axe. He stood legs apart and swung the axe. The log split cleanly down the centre. There was pleasure in the rhythm, the swing of the axe, the stretch of muscles, the scent of the wood. He picked up one of the split pieces, set it on the block and swung the axe again.

He knew what needed doing to make the place appealing to these interstate swells. The huts were in poor repair, and the cottage itself appeared to be collapsing into the bush. If visitors were to be encouraged to stay overnight, they needed somewhere clean and comfortable. Harry was as used as any man to making do, but he would think twice about staying here if there was a more inviting bed in town. And with that he smiled, thinking of Ellen Thompson. He brought his axe down into the chopping block and straightened up, stretching his back.

When Harry had left Perth, he had assumed he would leave his memories of Eliza behind. To his surprise, even after he arrived in Hobart Town, his first thought on waking had often been of her. Until he had kissed Ellen. Now he woke with his mind full of urgent dreams of Ellen. She had jostled Eliza into the past in a way time and distance had failed to do. Eliza had been neat and orderly, loyal and hardworking. Ellen, no doubt, was hardworking and loyal but she was bright, full of mischief, every part of her perfect, from her hair that often slipped free of its pins, the playful sparkle in her eyes, the shape of her body, to her ankles flashing out from beneath her hem as she moved, a skip in her step. When he was with her, he forgot everything but the here and now. The past no longer existed. In his saner moments, he reminded himself he was a few years older than Ellen but he had no sense that it mattered to her. She seemed to feel for him exactly what he did for her.

He worked his axe free and set another lump of wood on the block. He swung the axe smoothly down, splitting the log apart, segments bouncing across the ground. The need for money gnawed at him. Perhaps he could go back to the mill. If Davis saw him at the gate early, he was sure to give him work that day. He could work Monday to Thursday and spend the rest of the week on the mountain. But he would need to board again. Mrs

Hennessy was a businesswoman first and would want a full week's board even if he wasn't there half the time.

There was work closer to home, but the old man hated the log getters, stripping the lower slopes of the mountain, ripping up the pathways, muddying the water courses. They had camps on the mountainside, but Harry suspected their huts would offer fewer comforts than the cottage here. Besides, in the town there was the chance of seeing Ellen.

~

Harry walked out from the cottage at the sound of a sizable group coming up the track. He went back inside and put on his jacket and stood at the door, watching as the old man moved over to greet them. He swore under his breath—they had brought their own guide with them. By the look of him, someone they had picked up in town, claiming to know the mountain. A few pennies for a cup of tea would be the most they could hope for here.

The guide stood in front of the group, now milling at the top of the path. He swept off his hat with a flourish. 'Now I'll hand you over to our Old Man of the Mountain. What Mr Woods doesn't know about this place is not worth knowing.'

'George Thompson!' Grinning, Harry called out to him.

George strolled up and threw his arm around Harry's shoulder. 'Harry, mate, good to see you.'

'I thought you were their guide.'

'Met them at the fingerpost and I think I've convinced them they will get lost and die of exposure if they don't have you come with them. They're from South Australia and feeling the cold. I told them to have a tot of the old feller's best when they come back down. That should make them warm and generous.' He watched the group. 'How's business?'

'None too good. I should have stayed on in town another month. I might see if I can do a few days' work each week back at the mill until the weather picks up. I'm sure Davis would have me back. I was quite handy on the circular saw by the end.'

'Will you go back to Mrs Hennessy's?'

Harry shrugged. 'She'd want a full week's board and I can't afford that.'

'Look, I'm only home on and off, and Will won't be back until next year. Mam wouldn't mind if you bunked in with me. She wouldn't mind the extra coin either.'

'That would be grand, George.' He wouldn't need to be on his best behaviour the way he was at Mrs Hennessy's. And then there was Ellen.

'Anything for a mate.' He raised a sandy eyebrow and winked. 'But remember, it's me you'll be bunking with not my sister.'

Harry blinked, lost for words. Despite his imaginings, he was stunned George would be so unashamed.

George threw his head back and roared with laughter.

Harry changed the subject. 'Are you coming to the top with us?' He jerked his head towards the pinnacle.

'No, I'll wait here and have a cup of the old lady's *best* tea.' He ran his eye over the two younger women in the group. 'They don't want to get their dainty shoes muddy, so I'll have plenty to amuse me.'

Later, the climbers seen off towards the fingerpost where their carriage was now waiting and the evening meal served up and eaten, they all sat in front of the fire.

George jumped up and rifled in the sack he had brought with him. 'I nearly forgot.' He pulled out a flask of rum and passed it to Grannie. 'It's not whisky, but I thought you might like it all the same.'

The old woman's face broadened into a wide grin. 'I do like rum every bit as much. Will you take a wee dram with me, laddie?'

'That I will Grannie, but just a small one.'

They spent the evening telling stories, George's as far-fetched as the old man's.

'And do you know, Grannie, he jumped into the sea after her? Said she was the most beautiful creature he had ever seen. Last we heard, he was living with her on a Pacific island raising children, half man and half fish.'

Grannie frowned. 'And was she beautiful?'

George shrugged. 'Perhaps wherever he was from the women aren't much to look at, but as far as I could see, she was nothing more than a great ugly dugong.'

The old man wheezed with laughter. 'I knew a couple of fellers in the old days who were just as particular.'

Harry watched them. They were of a kind, his father and Bill and George Thompson. Would he have turned out more like them if his mother had stayed on here and they had sent for him and Sarah? Perhaps his life would have been less law-abiding and steady. He was certain it would have been far more interesting in all sorts of ways.

16

They strolled along Liverpool Street, arm in arm, as Ellen hummed the tune she had heard earlier that night at the dancing-room.

Harry had been staying with her parents from Sunday to Thursday for the last few weeks, in the front room, sharing with George when he was home. He was well-mannered, cheerful and had no more than a single drink most evenings. And each week, on Thursday night, he had taken Ellen, wearing her good dress with the bustle and overskirt, to the licenced dancing-room two blocks down Liverpool Street where there was no drinking and the men were generally well-behaved. Harry was a good dancer. She knew her happiness shone in her face as they spun about the room, his hand at her waist, his fingers linked through hers, or when he drew close and they sat to the side of the room, catching their breath. She waited all week for the walk home with him, the minutes spent in the dark of Watchhouse Lane before they went inside.

Ellen knew he liked her. She could tell by the way he looked at her, the light in his eyes when he smiled, the weight of his kisses. But he had said nothing of what he felt. It could simply be he was enjoying what was available—if he was still at Mrs Hennessy's and she had a daughter, Harry might be courting her instead of Ellen.

'I'll be staying at the Springs from next week,' Harry said.

Ellen stopped humming. 'Oh! No more dancing?' She couldn't hide her disappointment.

'I'm afraid not.' His grip on her tightened. 'If it was left to me, I'd be happy to keep on the way things are.'

They turned into the darkness of Watchhouse Lane, stopping beside the fence of the old watchhouse, now a private dwelling, across from the Thompsons' house. Ellen put her arms around

Harry and lay her head against his chest.

'Will you come down for Christmas? There is always room for one more at our table.'

'I'd love to, but the old man says it's a busy day—some even bring Christmas picnics up there.' He ran his hand across her hair, his fingers tracing her ear and down along her jawline.

Ellen buried her face against his chest. 'We'll have to come up and see you,' she murmured. His fingertips played against the nape of her neck. 'Not Christmas, but after New Year.' She couldn't concentrate. She reached up, brushed her lips against his, breathing his breath.

Harry pulled her tight against him and kissed her hard. Ellen pressed back against him, answering his kisses, clinging to him. She wanted Harry with an intensity she barely had the will to resist. All thought of courtship and rings on fingers fled.

She forced herself to break away. 'We can't have that get out of hand.' A few moments longer and he could have done what he wanted with her right there where they stood.

'S'pose not.' Harry's breathing was uneven. Although he loosened his grip, he still pressed against her.

Ellen made herself move away from him. 'We should go inside.'

'In a minute.'

He fumbled inside his jacket. 'Here, I have something for you, an early Christmas present.' He held it out. 'It's weeks away, but I don't know when I'll see you next.'

Ellen took the tiny paper-wrapped article from him and moved out into Liverpool Street, to the light of a street lamp.

She unwrapped the tissue. 'Oh, Harry,' she sighed, blinking fast against threatening tears. 'It's beautiful.' It was a brass bar with three flowers etched along it, each set with a cut-glass bead, each a different colour, glistening in the light from the gas lamp.

Harry had followed her and stood close beside her, not quite touching.

Ellen pinned the brooch beside the small spray of cloth rose-buds she wore near the neck of her bodice. She looked into Harry's face. She could barely breathe. She needed him to hold her, needed to feel his lips ...

She stepped back and grasped his hand. 'We should go inside.'

Harry resisted as she tried to pull him towards her parents' house. 'Should we?'

'Yes. Mam and Dad will be waiting up for us.' She stepped back to him and wound her arm through his. 'And besides, it's cold out here.'

'I could keep you warm.'

'I'm sure you could.' Ellen laughed lightly as she steered him across the lane. She needed to get some sort of promise from him before she let that happen.

~

George was on a trip to Adelaide so Harry had the room to himself. He had to be up early tomorrow but sleep wouldn't come. Staying with the Thompsons was like walking a tightrope. Harry needed to be sober for work, so he had to be careful what he drank until Thursday night. Even when he had taken Ellen out dancing, if George was home, he was expected to sit drinking afterwards until the small hours—it was as if George was trying to fit the whole week's drinking into one night. Often as not, Harry was woolly-headed as he made his way up to the Springs the following morning.

Then there was Ellen's constant presence and the feverish dreams that brought at night. She was lying in the room above him in nothing but her nightgown. He hadn't felt like this when he was courting Eliza. *Eliza.* He forced her from his mind. He wasn't going to be faithful to a memory.

There was the faintest gust of cool air as the door opened and shut silently. Ellen slid beneath the sheets, her scent washing over him. He went to say her name, but she hushed him, her hungry kisses stopping all thought.

~

Harry lay, his hands behind his head, staring at the ceiling. He closed his eyes, and again the world fell away as memory flooded through him, of heat and touch, the thrill of her hunger—as great as his—the breathless oblivion. It could be a dream but for Ellen's scent lingering on his skin. He wanted her here with him. He wanted her always. But he was moving back up the mountain with no idea when he would be down next, when he would see her again.

He heard someone come into the kitchen, the rattle of the stove door, the splash of water poured into a kettle or a pot.

He forced himself off the mattress. He hoped it was Ellen, but it would probably be her mother.

Beth turned from the stove as Harry walked in.

'Sleep well, lad?'

He wanted to laugh whenever she called him *lad*, but if it meant she saw him as close in age to Ellen, he was happy.

'Bit of a restless night,' he said. 'Couldn't sleep.' Best to stick close to the truth.

'I imagine you're keen to get back to the Springs.'

'I prefer being in town, but the old man needs me—there are climbers needing a guide most weekends now.'

'Have a drop of tea before you go.' She poured him a cup from the pot sitting on the hob and handed him a lump of bread and cheese. 'You've a climb ahead of you.'

~

Ellen stood at the bedroom window, her brush and hairpins laid along the inner windowsill, her brooch beside them. The sight of Harry, the set of his shoulders, the way his body moved as he walked, whistling, along the lane, took her breath away. She closed her eyes, remembered pleasures washing through her. It had taken all her willpower to force herself to leave him as the dull early morning light crept into the room. She had only just crawled into bed beside Billy when Mary Ann had groaned and hauled herself out of bed. Ellen had stretched as if she too were waking up. She would be home from work when Billy had his afternoon sleep and might have a snooze too—and dream of Harry.

The thought she might not see him for months had overcome all her sensible intentions. But she had regretted it in those first moments, lying in his arms, listening to the hammering of his heart, blinking back disappointed tears. Was that all it was even when you wanted someone so much, even when you loved him—yes, she did love him—brief moments of promise, over too soon, leaving you wanting more? Yet there had been comfort in lying close, her head on his chest. She had drifted to sleep in his arms. The sky was still dark outside when she had woken and moved away to go to her own bed. Harry had reached out and drawn her back to him, his almost gentle kisses persuading her to stay. His fingers sure upon her skin, he had forced away all sense of time and place, all knowledge of where she left off and he began, leaving only a breathless exultation.

Harry had disappeared now, turned the corner into Collins Street on his way to the Springs. Ellen picked up her hairbrush and tugged at the knots in her hair.

'So,' Mary Ann said quietly, sitting on the side of the bed where Jane and Bessie still slept. She pulled on her stockings. 'How's the tummy this morning?'

Ellen frowned, puzzled. 'The tummy?'

'I presume you had the gripes of some sort. Why else would you go out to the privy in the middle of the night?'

'Oh.' Ellen kept her back to Mary Ann and fought the slow smile spreading across her face. 'I'm fine now.'

'Ellen. You didn't!' She came over to the window and stood beside Ellen.

Ellen continued brushing, heat creeping up her neck.

'What about getting him to marry you?' she whispered.

Ellen glanced back at her sleeping sisters. 'He gave me this.' She picked up the brooch from the window sill, the glass sparkling in the light. 'I wanted to thank him.'

'You could have embroidered him a couple of handkerchiefs.'

'Embroidered handkerchiefs,' Ellen scoffed. 'What man we know uses embroidered handkerchiefs? Some don't even use handkerchiefs at all. Besides,' she sighed, 'no boy has ever bought me anything other than a glass of beer before.'

'He's no boy, and I wouldn't wonder if he didn't expect something in return.'

'Shhh,' Ellen hissed. 'Harry's not like that.'

'Isn't he?' Mary Ann lowered her voice. 'Seems he got exactly what he wanted.' She slipped her feet into her boots and knelt to tie them. 'We know next to nothing about him. He could have a wife in Western Australia.'

Ellen's eyes started to swim. 'Do you think so?'

'No. All I'm saying is you should be careful.' She stood up and came over to Ellen, put her arms around her. 'I don't want you hurt, Ellen. All we really know is that he's old Mr Woods's son.' She looked into Ellen's eyes. 'Now you've given him a taste, that will keep him keen. But nothing more until you have that ring on your finger.'

Ellen smiled at her and sniffed. 'You're right. You'll have to be my chaperone whenever he's around.'

'I'll have to be your guard and sleep across the doorway.'

Ellen laughed quietly. 'I promise I'll behave.' Yet she knew, after last night, she had little inclination to. Still, she wanted Harry Woods forever, and that wouldn't happen if she fell into bed with him every time she saw him.

17

The sun barely rose on Christmas Day. The mountain top was swathed in cloud that drifted, fog-like, around the Springs. Christmas was celebrated indoors. The old man had swapped two bottles of his own brew for a plump chicken on his last visit to town. Grannie roasted it with potatoes. She had made a pudding too. The *mountain dew* flowed, and between cackles of laughter, the old couple toasted everything from the top of the mountain to the ships that had brought them here. They sang the old songs, and the old man even got up and danced a brief jig.

Harry watched them as he sat nursing his mug. Each had no need of anyone but the other.

The days leading up to Christmas had been bright but chilly and the mountain clear of snow, but only a couple of small parties had arrived wanting a guide. He had expected the weather to be warmer—not the bright sunshine, heat and afternoon cooling breezes of a Perth Christmas, but something better than this seeping fog. The old man's assurances of scores of visitors trooping up on Christmas Day carrying picnic baskets had come to nothing. They might have once, but this Christmas there was not a single visitor.

Harry took a swallow from his mug and grimaced as it burnt its way down his throat. He wished he had accepted Ellen's invitation to have Christmas dinner with her family. If it wasn't for his duty here, he would be back in town, working a full week. He would have money enough to take Ellen out, buy her trinkets, set up a house with her where they could shut the door and lose themselves in each other.

The cloud cleared on Boxing Day but the afternoon brought snow squalls. They were hemmed in for two days. No visitors, no money.

He stood in the doorway staring at the snow.

'Never mind son,' the old man put a hand on his shoulder, 'it'll be clear by New Year's Day. They'll all come up then.'

~

The first of the climbers were on the doorstep before sunrise on New Year's Day. Harry sang as he led the party away from the Springs, 'Dabbling in the dew', the young men singing the man's part, the women the milkmaid's. Snow still lay in the crevices of the Ploughed Field, but the sky sparkled, not a cloud to be seen. That day he went to the top three times, the final journey returning to the Huon Road via the Silver Falls, Harry making the final climb back along the Fingerpost Track by moonlight.

A few days later, the sun rose hot and fierce. A single party arrived just after sunrise. Following their climb to the top, they had lingered over lunch at the Springs and were not long gone when thunder rumbled and the rain began. The storm continued all afternoon and into the night. Ear-splitting claps of thunder rolled on in waves, the sky cleaved by prolonged flashes of chain lightning. By nightfall, an eerie light shone almost as bright as day.

Harry watched from the doorway, awed. This was a place of stunning, unexpected beauty but, as he was learning, not one where anything could be relied on with certainty.

The weather was fine through most of January, and Harry made two trips most days. Grannie fussed around their visitors. The fruit was in full season so she offered ripe raspberries and blackcurrants with her scones and bread, the best bread in Hobart Town, many said. When the trippers brought meat and pies, she cooked them, had them ready for the party when they came back. Most of the parties Harry took to the top had women with them and went up at a slower pace. Yet there were young women, a modern confident type, who raced ahead, as sure and independent as any man.

Now and again a single climber, or a couple of men, stayed overnight, rising before dawn to make their way to the pinnacle to behold the breathtaking view of the sun breaking orange along the horizon, tinting the slatey river and the dark mounds of the hills, the rays touching down across the town, the streetlights eclipsed by the glory of the rising sun.

The locals treated Harry with the same respect as his father was shown. It was only the odd mainlander who saw him as nothing more than a porter. He had developed a method of dealing with them. He would lower the load that had been foisted on him, whatever it was, and walk over to the oldest of the group and strike up a conversation, weaving in his father's tales and knowledge. He would lead him off, and they would begin the next stage of the climb together, leaving one of the other lazy bastards to carry his own knapsack.

The only exceptions were the photographic expeditions. They were unfailingly courteous, careful of their equipment, reluctant to let unschooled hands touch it. Harry wondered what the cost would be to have Ellen sit for one. But an image wasn't enough, he wanted her beside him. She had said she would come and visit but hadn't said when. For that matter, he had said he would go down and see her. If he left it too long, she might think he had thrown her over and find someone else.

~

Mary Ann put her fork down. 'There were two of them,' she said, 'over at Bellerive. Tiger sharks.'

Alice and Jane gasped. 'Was anyone eaten?'

'No, luckily.'

Ellen shuddered but continued eating, her mind not on Mary Ann's story. It had been over two months, and she hadn't heard a word from Harry. Surely, he could have found time for one trip down the mountain.

She held Billy on her lap with one arm. He slammed his spoon into his own bowl, splattering gravy and potato everywhere.

'Billy.' She reprimanded him half-heartedly, glancing up from her plate as the door eased open.

Will slipped in. He looked a fright, his clothes grubby and torn.

Alice jumped out of her seat, but Will held a finger to his lips. The conversation around the table died as they watched him slide onto the bench beside Bessie.

'Keep talking,' he hissed. 'Act as if I'm not here. I might have been followed.'

'They caught them,' Mary Ann said. 'One was a female. They cut her open, and she was full of eggs.'

'Please, not while we're eating.' Bessie screwed up her nose.

'Do you want some tea?' Mam asked under the conversation.

'I'm famished, Mam.' Will's usually round face was thin, dark rings under his eyes.

'Wonder what fish eggs taste like,' Dad said. He drew his chair close to Will.

'Fish,' Mam said from over by the stove. 'Mrs Barrow, when I were working for her years back, she had some for one of her fancy parties. Tiny things they were, pinheads. They ate them on little bits of toast.'

'Did you try them?'

'We were warned not to touch them. They were expensive, not for servants. We all sneaked a taste when the cook weren't looking. They were fishy, nothing to be making a fuss over. Hen's eggs are much better.'

'More of a feed by the sound of it,' Dad said. He lowered his voice, 'What's the problem, son? Have you deserted?'

'Anyway,' Mary Ann said, 'if anyone wants a look, they have put the sharks on show at the George and the Dragon in Elizabeth Street.'

'Could we go?' Jane asked.

Mam set a plate of stew, a chunk of bread on the side, in front of Will.

'That's what they're saying.' He began shovelling the food in as if he hadn't eaten for weeks.

Dad frowned. 'What do you mean?'

Will swallowed his mouthful before he spoke. 'The *Emily Downing* is unseaworthy. We put in at Partridge Island because stores were running low and refused to put to sea again until she is made safe, so they had us on bread and water. We petitioned the Colonial Treasurer, but I doubt any good will come of it. Talk is we'll be charged with mutiny.'

Dad whistled between his teeth. 'That could get nasty.' He looked across the table. 'Here, Bessie, go over to the Rob Roy and get us a jug of beer.' He tipped the coins into Bessie's open hand.

Bessie clambered over the bench and grabbed a jug from the sideboard.

'Don't mention I'm here,' Will called after her.

She rolled her eyes. 'I'm not silly, Will.'

'I can't stay long, Dad. There are warrants out for us, and they are sure to come looking here.' He wiped up the gravy with his bread.

'We can hide you,' Ellen said.

'No, the traps would turn the place upside down. There are a couple of places I can stay they won't think of.'

~

Ellen brushed her hair and twisted it into a knot. As she pushed the pins in one side, the other unravelled. She wailed and flung her brush onto the bed.

Mary Ann picked the brush up. 'Do you want me to help?'

'Would you? Nothing is going right at the moment.' She had been lying awake half the night thinking of Will. And Harry too. Her worries about Harry should have paled to nothing beside Will's problems, but she couldn't help it. Why hadn't he found time to come and see her? And all her plans for a family trip to the

Springs had come to nothing. There was always some reason— Billy fretting with a summer cold, Mam's sprained ankle, Dad pretending he had work to do, George preferring to loaf at home or go to the pub when he wasn't working. She even tried to get a couple of friends to go with her, but they all came up with some excuse or other.

'Everything?' Mary Ann said, her voice sharp. 'You're not in the family way, are you?'

'No!' Ellen snapped. That, at least, was one small mercy.

'You're thinking of that blasted Harry Woods, aren't you? If he really wanted, he'd be down every week to see you.'

Ellen groaned. 'But summer is a busy time up there. He'd have too much to do.'

'There have been a few cold days.'

'He has to look after the old couple.' Her excuses sounded weak. She didn't believe them herself.

'Old Mr Woods finds time to ride to town at least once a week,' Mary Ann said, pushing the last of the pins into Ellen's hair.

Ellen's face fell. Harry had got what he wanted, and that was the end of it. Her eyes swam.

'Oh, Ellen,' Mary Ann pulled her to her roughly, 'he might be busy as you say. And the fact you haven't chased after him is a good thing. It'll give him the impression you're a bit shamed by what happened.' She almost cackled. 'He'll think you are modest and shy.'

Ellen glared at her, about to spit back a reply, when they both stopped.

A horse snorted in the lane below.

They peered out the window.

'It's Mr Woods.' Mary Ann arched an eyebrow. 'Perhaps he's bringing you a love letter.'

Ellen continued to stare. 'No. It's Harry.' She turned and bolted for the door.

'Slow down,' Mary Ann called after her. 'Don't look too keen.'

Ellen raced down the stairs but stopped at the bottom. Her heart was hammering. Harry's voice carried from the kitchen. She closed her eyes. She must stay calm, not rush in and throw herself at him. She could hear Mary Ann behind her.

She straightened her shoulders, brushed the front of her dress and walked into the kitchen.

All eyes turned on her.

'Harry.' She smiled at him—not too eagerly, she hoped. But it was hard to stop smiling now he was here, smiling back at her, the corners of his eyes crinkled with happiness.

'Ellen.'

No one else spoke, eyes moving from one to the other.

He stood at the far side of the table, turning his hat in his hands, and cleared his throat.

He's as nervous as I am, Ellen thought.

'Ellen, would you care to accompany me to the Circus tomorrow night?'

She opened her mouth and blinked.

He frowned slightly. 'Unless you have other plans.'

'No.' She beamed at him. 'I'd love to come.'

'Right.' He exhaled loudly, looking ten years lighter. 'I'll be by around seven tomorrow night.' He twirled his hat. 'I'd better be off, a few errands to run for the old man.'

Dad chuckled as the door shut behind Harry. 'That one's got it bad.' He drained his cup and stood. 'I'd better be going too.' He glanced over at Ellen. 'Alice should go as well, she can sit between you.' He took one look at Ellen's face and roared with laughter.

18

Harry walked, Ellen's arm through his, up to the Queen's Domain, the tract of bush and parkland running between the river and the town. A giant striped marquee had been erected in the quarry at the southern end. The evening light bathed the tent and those moving purposefully towards its opening in a golden glow. He had never seen so many people together in one place—hundreds and hundreds of men, women and children. Inside, dozens of gas lamps lit the tent almost to daylight. At one end a small orchestra played jaunty music, building the excitement of the crowd.

Ellen's eyes widened as they took their seats in the stalls. 'I thought we'd be in the pit.'

'It's a better view from here,' Harry said. 'And a bit more room.' They would have been in the pit had the price not dropped today from two to one shilling for a seat.

'Oh, Harry,' she grabbed his hand, squeezed it, and wriggled closer to him.

She was so pretty tonight in a blue dress, a lighter colour worked through the weave, the lace on her underbodice showed as she had left the top three buttons open because of the warmth of the evening. Her brooch sparkled near the neckline. The neat straw hat perched on her thick brown hair was trimmed and tied with blue ribbon. A tendril of hair had escaped and curled down her neck, resting against the hollow at the base of her throat. It was all he could do to stop himself from stroking the lock and winding it around his finger, from leaning over and kissing her.

He settled back beside Ellen and stared at the dozens of tall poles holding the vast tent aloft, strings of colourful pennants fluttering overhead. An older woman, in the seat beside Ellen, had greeted her and turned away but not before looking Harry up and down. Two young boys in front of them squirmed and elbowed each other, but luckily, they didn't block Harry and Ellen's view.

With a great fanfare, the ringmaster strode out into the middle of the ring. Dressed in a bright red jacket, his top hat raised, his whip in his hand, he stood in the spotlight and bowed. 'Ladies and gentlemen. Boys and girls. Come one, come all. Be amazed! Be astounded! Tonight, you will see sights undreamt of. Feats of skill and unimaginable daring. Sit back, forget your worries and be entertained by Burton's Great Australian Circus.'

The spotlight moved, and horses, coats shining, dyed ostrich plumes nodding on their heads, streamed into the ring as the music bounded along. Men and women in tights and satin blouses and tunics balanced bareback on the horses pacing around the ring. The crowd gasped as the performers leapt from horse to horse, one managing a double somersault. Clowns stumbled and shambled, their tumbling antics bringing gales of laughter from the audience. One strode along on six-foot stilts. Another, creeping up, teased his mate with a peacock feather. They were followed by a youth in red on two barebacked horses, leaping from horse to horse as they raced round and round the ring in imitation of a fox hunt, the energy and excitement heightened by the galloping music from the orchestra.

Ellen laughed and clapped and gasped with the rest. As she fluttered her fan in the heat, her perfume wafted over Harry. He was torn between watching the astounding antics in the ring and gazing at Ellen. At the interval, he pushed his way through the crowd and brought her back a glass of lemonade.

She gazed at him as she sipped, her eyes shining. 'This is the loveliest time I have ever had.'

He grinned. 'It is grand.' At that moment, he could remember no better time.

The clowns returned after interval, taunting each other with peacock feathers, balancing on slack wire, giving every impression they would fall, overbalancing by design and righting themselves when it appeared almost too late. Acrobats in tights performed gymnastic feats, climbing over each other with impossible agility to balance as a human pyramid. Dogs and monkeys walked and danced and acted more like humans than dumb beasts, mimicking the antics of the clowns. The whole company joined together in the finale. A mail coach and four was driven around the ring and bailed up by the ringmaster playing the highwayman Dick Turpin, to the rousing cheers of the audience, particularly those in the pits.

Ellen sat, blinking, as those beside them rose from their seats. She stood slowly and linked her arm through Harry's. 'That was wonderful.'

They moved with the tight crowd out into the night. In the crush, Ellen pressed close, Harry intensely aware of her bosom against his arm. They were swept along towards the town, but finally, as the crowd spread out, Harry thought he would suggest they stroll away towards the shadows of the trees in the Domain to watch the glitter of the light of the waxing moon on the river. He moved to whisper in Ellen's ear but she turned her head as her name was called.

Two young women of Ellen's age pushed their way towards them, elbowing each other and giggling. The taller, buxom and full of confidence, smiled at Ellen, but her attention was on Harry, assessing him with a keen calculation.

Judgement made, she said, 'You must be Harry Woods. Ellen has told us all about you.'

'Has she?'

A smile twitched at the corner of her mouth. 'What she hasn't told we can well imagine.'

Harry glanced at Ellen, who was glaring at the woman.

She smirked back. 'She's made us all jealous.'

'Let me introduce you,' Ellen said coldly. 'Harry this is Annie

Smith and Lily Walters. They live in Moodie's Row, further down Liverpool Street.'

Harry raised his hat. 'Lovely to meet you, ladies.'

'Likewise, Harry,' Annie said. 'You do have a lovely way with you, just like Ellen said.'

Harry was struck by how bold this young woman was—everything she said carried an undercurrent of suggestion.

'What has she been saying?' He glanced again at Ellen. She was staring straight ahead, her lips tight, her fury barely concealed.

'She's made you sound a real Prince Charming. Seeing her sitting there beside you in the stalls like any of the swells, fluttering her fan, you bringing her lemonade,' she gave a sly smile at Harry as she slid her arm through his free arm, 'seems she wasn't lying.'

Pushed along by the crowd, they moved towards Park Street, past the entrance to the railway station and into Liverpool Street.

'Now what about that circus? Have you ever seen anything like it?'

'I did see a circus in Perth ten years back, but it had nothing on this one.'

'And the bareback rider, the dark one—I wouldn't mind taking him home to meet mother, eh, Ellen?'

Ellen bent her head and spoke quietly to Lily.

Annie persisted. 'Ellen, how do you reckon we'd go in those short sparkling dresses the women were wearing?'

Ellen glared at her through narrowed eyes and continued her conversation with Lily.

'You'd all cause a stir,' Harry said, trying not to let his imagination wander too far along that path.

'Wouldn't we just?' She elbowed Harry in the ribs.

He felt the heat rising up his neck. He could tell Annie was fun, in all sorts of ways, but probably not the type who stood by you when life got rough.

He forced his attention back to Ellen. 'What was your favorite,

Ellen?'

The unsmiling glance she gave him seemed to say, *So you have finally remembered me, have you?* 'The fox hunt with that rider Annie is so taken with.'

They were now walking briskly along Liverpool Street. This was not the walk home Harry had imagined when he'd invited Ellen out.

'Where are you taking Ellen next, Harry?' Annie asked. 'The Theatre Royal is doing opera and stuff.'

'I don't know that I'd fancy that. I heard there's a steamer you can take day trips on.'

'The *Monarch*. It does trips to the races and to New Norfolk. You can go for the day, take a picnic, see the sights, have a laugh.'

'Sounds good.'

'We could get a party together.'

Ellen stared straight ahead, her eyes glistening in the lamplight. She seemed about to cry.

'Pretty busy at the moment,' Harry said.

As they drew level with Moodie's Row, Annie eased her arm away from Harry, her fingers trailing underneath his forearm. 'Been nice meeting you, Harry.'

'Oh yes,' Lily joined in.

Harry had barely noticed her.

''Night, Ellen.' Annie grinned. 'When you're done with this one,' she jerked her head towards Harry, 'I'll take him on.'

Ellen turned her back on Annie and marched away, Annie's laughter echoing in the empty street.

'Ellen,' Harry called after her.

She kept walking.

'Wait a moment.' He caught up with her at the corner of Watchhouse Lane and placed a hand on her shoulder. She shook him off and hurried towards her parents' house. 'They'll be waiting up for us.'

Ellen was right, the whole family was sitting around the table in the kitchen.

'How was it?' Bill asked.

'Oh, Dad, it was wonderful.' Ellen smiled but did not look towards Harry. 'There were acrobats and horses and monkeys riding dogs and dancing. A clown walking along a wire. You've never seen anything like it.'

Beth poured them both a cup of tea from the pot sitting on the hob.

'And, Mam, I was sitting beside Mrs Bryce. The look on her face! She gave a sickly smile when I sat down and didn't look my way again.'

'You should have poked your tongue out at the old besom,' Mary Ann said.

'It's a free country, lass,' Beth said, 'and you're every bit as good as her.'

'I'll drink to that even if it is with this tea.' Bill looked over at Harry. 'How would you feel about a drop of something stronger?'

'I need to be up at first light tomorrow, but next time I'm down, I'll bring some of the old man's brew.'

'I'll keep you to that, son.'

~

Harry lay on the bed, wide awake. The night was warm, the house rustling as if no one was sleeping, all tossing and turning in their beds. He had taken off his flannels and lay naked beneath the sheets. The evening had not gone to plan at all. He had known better than to hope Ellen could visit him here—he had expected George to be home—but he had hoped for some moments in the shadows beneath the trees in the Domain or, at least, in the lane before they came in.

That Annie. He wondered how Ellen came to have a friend like her. Or had it been a game, a test, to see how he behaved? If it was, he had failed.

He was drifting off, in the half land between wakefulness and sleep, when the door opened quietly and Ellen knelt beside the mattress. He held out his hand to her but she shook her head.

'So, are you planning to go off with Annie?' He could hear the hurt in her voice.

He eased himself onto his elbows. 'Why would I do that?'

'You seemed to be getting on with her.'

'I was being polite. What else could I do? She's your friend.'

'She's not my friend. She's just a neighbour.'

'Then we don't have to see her again.'

'Oh. Afraid you won't be able to control yourself next time?'

'Don't be ridiculous.'

'What's this, then?' Ellen slid her hand beneath the sheet. 'We start talking about Annie and look at the effect it has on you.'

Harry grabbed her around the waist and pulled her onto the mattress. 'That has nothing to do with Annie.' He slid his hands beneath her nightgown, running them across the silk of her skin. The weak moonlight lingering on the generous curves of her breasts as she raised her arms to take her nightgown off. She was beautiful, everything a woman should be, everything he could ever want.

~

Ellen woke in the grey dawn light. Harry was already up and dressing.

'Have to be on my way. The weather's fine—it'll be a busy day.'

She grabbed her nightgown from the floor and wriggled into it before getting up.

Harry pulled her to him, his jacket rough against the thin cotton of her nightgown.

She stretched up and kissed him, aware of the tension in him.

'Such a pity,' he murmured, 'but I do have to go.'

So she could not tempt him when his mind was made up. That was not necessarily a bad thing—it meant he was someone to be relied on. Ellen moved towards the door. 'Do you want a cup of tea first?'

'No, water will do, but some bread would be good.'

He sat at the kitchen table eating bread spread with jam as Ellen, her mother's shawl over her nightgown, cut a slice of bread from the loaf, smeared it with pickle and added a chunk of cheese. She wrapped it in a tea towel and set it on the table beside him. 'Think of me when you have your morning tea.'

'I think of you all the time, Ellen.'

She went to say, *Except when you are thinking of Annie Smith*, but thought better of it. She slid onto his lap.

He wrapped his free arm tight around her.

'When will you next be down?'

'Don't know, it's busy at the moment.'

'I'll do my best to talk them in to visiting one Sunday but they are a lazy mob.' It didn't matter that they wouldn't be alone, seeing him, knowing he was mad for her was half of it.

'A couple of months and the work will start drying up and I'll be back in town.'

A couple of months of stolen moments, and who knew what the future would hold? Ellen sighed and lay her head on his shoulder.

19

February 1879

Harry slowly chewed his bread and corned beef. The party he had taken to the pinnacle that morning had spread themselves around in front of the cottage eating the lunch Grannie had prepared for them. He took a mouthful of sweetened tea. It was a beautiful day. The view at the top had been exhilarating, the air brisk despite the warmth lower down the mountain. A daisytree at the edge of the clearing was in bloom, yellow flowers massed on its branches. The raucous call of wattlebirds filled the silences when the trippers stopped their chatter.

From his seat beside the door to the cottage, Harry could see down the path that led to the Fingerpost Track. A couple of men came into sight between the trees. He had promised to take the morning's party down to their carriage on the Huon Road, but his father could do that if this lot wanted a guide. He hoped they would give him time to finish his tea and have a smoke.

With an identical swagger, the two men strode up towards the cottage.

A woman appeared from behind them and a slow smile spread over Harry's face.

Ellen's smile was just as wide.

The second man had to be Ellen's brother Will. He was slightly taller than George and bearded, his face rounder, grey eyes to George's hazel. He had the same wiry strength and sense of danger about him.

Harry put his mug down and rose from his seat.

George grasped Harry's hand. 'Harry, mate, this is my brother, Will.' He turned to Will. 'Harry is old Mr Woods's son and sweet on our Ellen.'

Will looked Harry up and down before grasping his hand, a grip

111

almost strong enough to break bones.

'I'll see if Grannie Woods can give us some lunch,' Ellen said.

Harry went to follow her into the cottage.

'Woods,' Will Thompson called to him. He pulled a flask from the pocket of his jacket and took a swig. He offered it to Harry, 'Here, have a sailor's drink.'

Harry could hardly refuse though he had no desire to drink this early in the day. He took the flask and swallowed a mouthful. Rum. He hated the drink but forced himself not to grimace. As he passed it back, one of the men in the morning party beckoned to him.

'If you'll excuse me, I said I'd take them to the fingerpost.' He walked away, aware that every movement he made was watched and weighed.

~

Ellen came out of the cottage and sat on the bench beside the door. Harry was nowhere to be seen. She hoped she could manage a few moments with him without the others listening and watching.

Her brothers stood a couple of yards away, their backs to her.

'I want a talk with Woods without Ellen around,' Will said.

She went to open her mouth but stopped. They hadn't realised she was there.

Will pulled out his flask. He took a large swallow and passed it to George.

George drank, wiped the back of his hand across his mouth and handed the flask back to Will. 'Harry's fine. He hasn't put a foot wrong. Mam thinks he's a real gentleman.'

'All that shows is that he's a smooth one.'

'Whatever happens, he'll marry her.'

Will grunted, barely acknowledging George's statement. 'He's hiding something. He was wary when I shook his hand.'

'That might have been the way you nearly ripped his arm off,' George laughed. 'It was enough to make anyone wary.'

'We're not here all the time. If we were both off on a long voyage, there'd be no one to deal with any trouble.'

'Dad can still handle himself.'

'He's nearly sixty. He'd need help to make sure the bastard did the right thing.'

'S'pose.' George turned. 'Ellen, I didn't know you were there.'

'Clearly.' She folded her arms across her bosom, her mouth a thin, tight line.

Will sat on the bench beside her, unconcerned. 'What about lunch?'

'Grannie will give us some scones and raspberries. We should have brought lunch up with us.'

'It'll have to do.' Will shrugged. 'Now what's between you and *young* Woods?'

'That's none of your business.'

'A bit long in the tooth, isn't he?'

'He's not that old.' She waved her hand, dismissing the idea.

'Probably old enough to be your father.' He scowled.

'Rubbish,' Ellen said firmly. She frowned and stared out across the clearing. 'Look, I like him. He's polite. He doesn't treat me as if I'm here to love and leave. He's hardworking, doesn't drink too much, and he gets on well with Billy. What more can I ask for?'

Will leant back, crossing his arms. 'How far has it gone?'

She looked at him, her eyes wide and innocent. 'What do you mean?'

'Be careful, sis.' He watched the last of the party trailing the others down the track. 'Has he asked you to marry him?'

'Not yet—but I'm sure he will,' she said with a confidence she didn't quite feel. 'Married men walk away from their responsibilities too, so what difference does it make?' Ellen couldn't believe she had said that. It most certainly made a difference to the way people treated women, especially those with children.

'Not as often.' He stood up. 'I think I'll take a wander along the track. George!' he called to his brother, who was talking to old Mr Woods as he brushed down the horse over by the barn. 'Come for a walk.'

Will and George moved off together, jostling each other, just like when they were boys. Ellen's mouth twitched into a smile despite her annoyance.

~

Harry's pace slowed as he climbed the track. Voices carried from not far ahead.

'God, Will, couldn't it have waited until we'd eaten?'

The Thompsons. Harry stopped. Around him, the bush rustled and whispered. Nearby a currawong called, melodious. One hopped out onto the track, its head on the side, an intelligent beady yellow eye watching him. He hoped his meeting with Ellen's brothers didn't provide the bird with more entertainment.

He continued up the track until they came into sight.

'Thought we would walk back with you,' George said.

They fell in step, one at each side.

'Thought we'd have a little word.' There was a harsh edge to Will Thompson's voice.

Harry stopped and turned to Will. 'A word about what?' He had no intention of defending himself to anyone.

'What are your intentions regarding our sister?'

He sounded like some pompous old father. 'My intentions?'

'Don't play the innocent with me,' Will sneered. 'She's a pretty thing, and you seem to be sniffing around her a lot these days.'

Harry's eyes narrowed. 'Your father has no objections.'

'As long as you keep yourself to yourself.' Will glared at him. 'You put a step wrong and you'll have us to answer to.'

Harry stared back at him. With a jolt, he realised Will meant if he got Ellen in the family way. He stopped himself from smiling. The idea of having a child with Ellen pleased him.

'Whatever happens, I will take care of Ellen.'

Will grabbed him by the lapels of his jacket, pulled him close, menace in his voice. 'See that you do.'

Harry glared back, unblinking. He hadn't been in a scrap for years. Will Thompson was years younger and hard-muscled. Harry wouldn't stand a chance at all if George joined in. He understood now what people meant when they said to watch out for those Thompson boys.

He shook Will off and said with equal menace, 'I will.'

~

Ellen marched down the track. Her brothers seemed to have completely forgotten her, but she supposed her concerns were nothing compared to Will's. The police were out looking for him and his shipmates and they could end up doing months in prison. It was no wonder it seemed to be all Will could talk about.

'It was hopeless from the start. They didn't have enough stores and no plan to replace them. The vegetables ran out five months in, then the lime juice. Some of the men got scurvy.'

'It's all right for the owners,' George said, 'sitting at home in their flash houses, living off other men's work.'

'The mainstay blew away in a storm, and we doubted the state of the mainmast and the rigging.' Will gave a bitter laugh. 'And on top of all that, the whales were not about in the numbers you'd expect, so there was a chance we'd end the tour owing McGregor for tobacco and the clothing and bedding he supplies. With what he charges, you'd think he was putting us up at Webb's Hotel. He's claiming we are trying to get out of paying what we owe him. Of course, we damn well want to finish the tour. We want to come out of all those months at sea with something for ourselves. Whaling is dangerous enough without an unseaworthy vessel.'

'They make me sick. If McGregor was on board, or his sons, he'd take more bloody care.'

Ellen stumbled on a rock but managed to stay upright. She bent and rubbed her ankle.

'Ellen!' Will shouted. 'Slow. Down.'

She turned and watched as her brothers moved down the steep track towards her, more carefully than she had been going. She was lucky she hadn't turned an ankle, but she was so cranky with Will. He hadn't taken to Harry at all. She couldn't understand why—he was usually such a good judge of character.

Will walked along beside her. 'Has he told you anything of his life in Western Australia?'

'Yes, he has.' Not as much as she wanted but enough. And, anyway, who was Will to question her? He wasn't her father.

'Whatever he has told you, he's sure to have left plenty out. I know what men are like when they are chasing a girl.'

'And you think I don't?' Ellen snapped.

'Ah, Ellen.' He put an arm around her shoulder. 'I'm only worried for you. I don't want you caught up with another shiftless good-for-nothing.'

'Shit!' George, now ahead of them, stopped in the middle of the track.

Two policemen stood at the start of the track, along with two other men—labourers, by the look of them, roped in to help.

'Four of them to arrest one man,' Will said. 'I must be fearsome in a fight.'

'Don't overestimate yourself,' George laughed. 'Two of them are for me. If you want to head off into the bush, I'll hold them off for a couple of minutes.'

'I'll do my bit,' Ellen said. This was her fault. Will wouldn't be here but for her wanting him to meet Harry.

'No, you stay well out of this. These gutless mongrels are just as happy belting a woman as a man.'

'Thompson!' one of the coppers yelled up at them.

Will moved in front of George and stood, hands on his hips, feet wide apart. 'Which Thompson do you want? There are three of us here.'

'William Thompson,' the taller of the two yelled.

'Yes, *Cun*stable. How can I help you?'

'You watch yourself, Thompson,' the constable shouted, 'or you'll end up on a charge of obscene language as well.'

'Obscene language? Really? Calling a copper Constable is now considered obscene language?' He glanced at his brother. 'Did you hear that, George?'

George stood beside Will, breathing loudly through his nose, his fists balled.

'Do nothing, George,' Will hissed out the side of his mouth. 'Don't give them an excuse. They were going to catch up with me some time. And besides, you have to keep Ellen safe.'

Will raised his hands. 'I'm coming like a lamb, *Cun*stable.' He strolled the rest of the way, whistling as he went, Ellen and George following at a distance.

At the bottom, he presented his wrists for the manacles held ready by the second constable, a shorter man with the build of a blacksmith. Although Will showed no fight, they were rough with him, jerking his arms as they attached the manacles, pushing him in the back as he walked.

At least with so many witnesses the coppers couldn't claim he had resisted arrest. They were always looking for an excuse to give someone a belting. Ellen wished she were a man—with three of them, they could have made sure the coppers got better than they gave.

20

Late March 1879

Ellen buttoned her jacket and crossed her arms over her bosom against the chill wind. Scowling, she turned from Liverpool into Campbell Street and tramped along towards the gaol. When things were bad, they only ever got worse. And it was all her fault.

If she hadn't wanted Will to meet Harry, they wouldn't have caught him and six days later put him on trial with fifteen of his shipmates, charged with deserting their ship ten months into a twenty-month contract and with stealing two boats to get them to shore.

Ellen had sat through the two days of the trial, squashed in beside George at the front of the public benches packed with the families of the seamen. Nearly all of them were Hobart men, half of them younger than Will.

She had been hopeful to begin with. William Tarleton, the police magistrate, appeared almost fatherly with his high forehead and square grey beard, peering over his spectacles as he listened to the lawyers. But hope had faded when he began picking apart the letter the seamen had sent to the Colonial Treasurer with their worries about the state of the barque *Emily Downing*.

Most of the first day had been given over to the ship owner, old McGregor, standing in the witness box, smug and well-fed in a smart suit, his beard neatly combed. He was followed by his carefully chosen witnesses, spouting their lies to prove the ship was seaworthy and the men had no reason for complaint.

The second day was worse. Not only was time wasted arguing about Acts of Parliament and the meaning of words, but when Mr Clark, the seamen's lawyer, had asked that the men be permitted to give evidence, Tarleton had refused—it was against whatever stupid Act of Parliament applied in this case.

Everyone on the public benches had muttered and grumbled at that, so much that Tarleton had raised his voice and ordered them to be quiet.

Mr Clark had done his very best. He talked about the heavy weather, the lack of vegetables for five months, the lime juice running out, the scurvy, the way the mainstay had been blown away in a storm. He had finished by saying it was not desertion when men refused to put to sea in a vessel that was unseaworthy or if the provisions were scanty or bad.

But it all counted for nothing. Will and his mates had been sentenced to three months gaol with an extra month added for taking the boats.

The woman beside Ellen had begun to sob loudly.

Ellen was angry about what had happened to Will but it was so much worse for the wives of some of his shipmates. A number had young children to care for, to see they were clothed and fed and kept safe. Their men had been away ten months already with nothing to show for it. And now they wouldn't be able to work for another four. Even those with family to help would find it hard. Many were already living hand-to-mouth, relying on the Benevolent Society. There was no justice—those who did the dangerous backbreaking work ended up with nothing, while the ship owners lived in flash houses overlooking the Derwent and never knew a moment's want.

She marched across Bathurst Street, averting her face from the sight of the Police Court where Will had been tried.

And then there was her other problem.

It had started a week after the court case. A dull headache and feeling tired all the time but they were vague signs, easily explained away, especially as she also had a stuffy nose. Then she had missed her monthlies but she had told herself it was the worry over Will and the fact she wasn't well anyway. All the other signs had made their appearance one by one: the nausea, the sore breasts, the constant need to pee. And now she had missed another month. The only thing she hadn't done was throw up, so at least, no one else had noticed.

If she didn't think too much about the way the world worked, she was happy at the thought of another little darling like Billy. Harry's baby. But whether that was a good thing depended on Harry. He hadn't been down to see her since the circus, but—she told herself—there was so much work at the Springs in the warm weather, and there had been two big fires on Mount Wellington, not that they were near the Springs. Still, he wouldn't want to leave the old ones alone if there was any danger. But she knew, if she were a man and Harry her girl, she would have found a way.

She would have to tell him soon but she didn't want to go up to the Springs by herself—she needed someone to walk home with if he behaved like a mongrel. Once she told him, he might be off down the mountain and onto the next vessel leaving port before she had finished speaking, just like Billy's father.

But Harry wasn't John Collins. He might be so delighted with the news that he'd ask her to marry him. The longer she put off telling him, the longer she could nurse that dream.

She jerked her head. She wouldn't think about it anymore. She'd concentrate on being happy to see Will. She stopped outside the heavy prison gate and rang the bell.

~

Ellen clasped her hands tightly on the table in front of her and glared at the warder standing, arms crossed, against the wall of the poky room where prisoners were permitted to see their visitors for a mere fifteen minutes. Nothing they said to each other would be secret.

Will sat opposite her, his head and faced shaved. He looked boyish without his beard.

He grinned across at her. 'What's up, sis?'

'Nothing much.' Ellen forced a smile. 'Did you hear about the fire at McGregor's yard?'

He nodded. 'Pity there wasn't more damage done.'

'Good thing you're all in here, otherwise they might have blamed you.'

He grimaced. 'Gaol does have its uses.' He stared at Ellen. 'You're in the family way.'

The warder looked her up and down, clearly listening to every word they said.

'What makes you think that?' She glared at Will.

'I remember how you looked the last time. Have you told the bastard?'

'Not yet.' Her eyelashes fluttered. She wouldn't cry. 'I haven't seen him ...' Her voice trailed off.

'How far gone are you?'

She stared down at the table. She didn't want to be having this conversation where anyone else could hear. 'Two months,' she mouthed at him.

Will's face flushed. He stretched his fingers flat against the table between them. 'And he hasn't called in to see you in all that time?'

'I suppose he's been busy,' she said, her lips pressed tight, her chin puckered.

'But not so busy when he wants something.'

She should be fair—both times she had gone to him. But he hadn't said no, and besides, she didn't want to be fair. Tears pricking at the corners of her eyes, she looked at her brother's scowling face. 'I don't know what to do.'

Will reached over and grasped Ellen's hand.

The warder barked at him to sit back.

Will ignored the warder who now stood alongside the table. 'Don't do anything stupid like that McPhee woman.' He withdrew his hand.

The warder went back to stand against the wall.

Ellen gasped. 'I wouldn't.' The whole town was talking about it—a woman had bled to death following an abortion. The doctor who had performed it had been charged and was awaiting trial.

'I'd deal with it but I'm in here. Tell George to sort it out.'

'Leave it alone, Will,' Ellen groaned. 'Everything will be fine once I tell Harry.' She wished she believed that.

'It had better be.' He folded his arms. 'Whatever happens, we Thompsons stick together.'

She sniffed. 'We do.'

~

A glossy ginger cat strolled along Watchhouse Lane. Ellen watched it through the window as she brushed her hair, trying to think of nothing at all. She put the brush on the windowsill beside the pins laid in a row along it. Cats could have kittens and no one thought anything of it. She twisted her hair up and pushed the pins in. But if there were too many kittens, people drowned them without a second thought. She closed her eyes and shuddered. She couldn't bear to be a cat.

'So, Ellen,' Mary Ann said behind her. 'When are you going to let the cat out of the bag?'

'What do you mean?'

'You're getting tubby. They say it starts earlier when you have your second.'

Ellen moved back to the bed and sat heavily, her shoulders slumped.

'Have you told him?'

'I haven't seen him. He hasn't been down since the circus.'

'Ah, the circus.' Mary Ann raised a knowing eyebrow. 'Perhaps we should all visit the Springs on Sunday.' She sat beside Ellen and placed her arm around her shoulder.

Ellen turned to her sister. 'Could we?'

Mary Ann nodded. 'I don't see why not.'

'Please, don't tell anyone until I have a chance to speak to Harry. Especially not George.'

~

It was Ellen, her sisters and George who made the Sunday trip. It wasn't the brightest of days—grey clouds spread across the sky—but at least, there was no rain. They took a picnic basket with corned beef sandwiches, cake and a small bottle of rum for the old couple. To everyone but Ellen and Mary Ann, it was the last chance for a picnic before the weather closed in.

Ellen felt sick at the thought of facing Harry.

He was seated in front of the cottage beside old Mr Woods when they walked up from the track. He rose from his seat but waited where he was.

Grannie came out to meet them, a grin across her face. She looked from one to the other, the happiness fading a small measure. 'Ach. You haven't brought the wee laddie with you?'

'No, he's at home with Mam and Dad.'

'He's a sweet wee thing.' Grannie was wistful.

Ellen wondered if she had once had a boy of her own.

'Now would you lassies like a cup of tea?'

'That would be nice, Mrs Woods,' Mary Ann said. 'I'll give you a hand.'

'No, hen, you rest your feet after that long walk up the hill.' She grinned at George. 'And will you have a glass of beer? It's freshly brewed.'

'I can think of nothing better than a glass of your beer after a long walk, Grannie.' George sat himself beside Mr Woods.

Grannie brought out mug for the pair and disappeared back into the house to make the tea. Harry leant against the wall at the other side of the door, smoking his pipe. His eyes had not left Ellen since she had walked up the path.

She could tell he was pleased to see her—his face had lit up as she walked towards him. He was trying not to smile too obviously.

'Can I talk to you, Harry?'

He took the pipe out of his mouth. 'You can always talk to me,

Ellen.'

'Not here,' she said quietly. She could see the puzzlement in his eyes.

He placed his hand over the bowl of the pipe and dropped it into his pocket.

Ellen slid her arm through his as they strolled around the side of the cottage towards the track to the icehouse, aware of the others watching them.

Silence stretched out between them.

Ellen had to say something. 'You haven't been in town for a while.'

'Been busy, haven't had a chance to get away. It doesn't mean I haven't been thinking of you.' He pressed her hand. 'I think about you all the time.'

He did care. Perhaps this wouldn't be so hard.

They stopped on the track above the Springs and stared out towards Hobart Town and the hazy, rolling hills beyond, the river glistening grey in the dull morning light.

'Harry,' she said, staring at the dark brown waratah seedpods on the bush beside the track—the blooms were bright red and beautiful for a few brief months, then withered and gone. Doubt crept in again. This might be the last time she stood with him.

Ellen took a large breath and blurted it out. 'I'm going to have a baby.'

'A baby?' He turned, blinking. 'My baby?'

'Of course it's your baby.' She pulled away from him, anger rushing through her. What did he think she was? If he said another thing, she would call him every word she had heard her parents, her brothers, the drunks in the street use, and some more besides.

Harry lay his hand against the side of her face, his thumb brushing her cheek. 'Sorry.' He spoke slowly, as if he were stunned. 'I didn't mean that the way it sounded.' His eyes were shining. 'I'm going to be a father.' He gazed back to the horizon. 'I've never been a father.'

'You are happy?'

'Happy doesn't describe it.' He caught her by the waist and swung her around. He stopped suddenly. 'Must be careful.'

'I won't break.' Ellen laughed, happiness flooding through her. She loved him more than she had ever imagined possible.

'When?'

'In October.'

He pressed his lips against her hair.

'Harry.'

He looked down at her.

'What are you going to do about it?'

He blinked again, as if he didn't understand.

She would have to ask him outright.

Ellen chose her words carefully. 'You will have to take some responsibility—help support the baby.' It was the least he could do. But she wanted so much more from him.

'Oh, I will, but I can't leave the old ones here. They'll never agree to live in the town.' He held Ellen's hands in his. 'Will you come up here and live with me? I want you with me all the time.'

It wasn't the proposal Ellen wanted but it would do for now. Plenty didn't marry until after the first child was born.

'And Billy?'

'What about Billy?'

'Can I bring Billy to live with us?'

Harry looked puzzled. 'Why wouldn't you?'

'Many men make a woman choose—*I'll take you but not the brat.*' If he had said that, she would have walked away.

'But Ellen,' he grinned, 'haven't you realised I'm not like many men?'

'No, you're not.' She smiled into his face and stood on her toes to kiss him.

George strolled up the path towards them.

Ellen wound her arm around Harry's waist and smiled at her brother. 'I'm coming up here to live with Harry.'

'Are you, sis?' George said gently.

Ellen saw the question in his eyes. Mary Ann must have told him. Did no one in this family ever keep a secret?

'Yes. Billy will be coming too. It's lovely here in summer.'

'It is,' George said, his eyes on Harry. He turned back down the path. 'But summer is over.'

'It comes back every year,' Ellen called after him.

21

Ellen carefully lifted the loaf from the camp oven and carried it to the wire cooling rack on the table, the warm yeasty scent enough to stir the appetite of even a well-fed climber. By the time the party Harry had taken to the pinnacle returned, the bread would be ready to eat. Until Grannie had taught her, Ellen had thought of breadmaking as something only done by bakers with shops or by experienced cooks like Mrs Bryce's.

In the weeks she had been at the Springs, Ellen had learnt more about cooking, baking and brewing than her mother had ever taught her. Mam had no interest in cooking other than to make sure her family's bellies were filled. Her meals varied little and needed no great skill to prepare.

Ellen dusted one end of the table with flour and patted out the scone dough she had prepared while the bread was baking. She glanced across at Grannie, seated by the window crooning softly, Billy asleep in her arms.

'I'd better wake him once I'm finished here, otherwise he'll be wanting to play half the night.'

Grannie sighed and gazed down at the rounded, flushed cheeks, the perfect profile. 'He is comfortable here.' There was wistfulness in her gaze. 'I had a little boy once.'

The kettle hissed in the silence.

'What became of him?'

'He died. He was about the same age as little Billy.'

'Here? In Hobart?'

'Aye, at the Nursery.' Her sigh contained a world of longing. 'I called him George.'

Ellen clamped her mouth shut. The Nursery—the place where the children of convict women had been born and stayed on until they were old enough to be sent to the Orphan School, their mothers assigned to work elsewhere once the babies were weaned.

It explained why Grannie doted on Billy. He was toddling now, starting to talk properly, calling the old couple Grannie and Grandad—that seemed to please both of them greatly. Grannie sat with him on her lap, fed him, told him stories, took him by the hand and led him about the cottage and outside, watched as he played and, most importantly of all, kept him away from the fire and the boiling pot. Ellen wondered if it was the reason Grannie had such a soft spot for her brother George too. Perhaps, had he lived, Grannie's son would be the same age.

Ellen put the scones in the oven and heaped the coals over the lid. After cleaning the table, she went to the door. Grandad Woods was on the bench outside, puffing on his pipe. He was no longer capable of taking groups to the top. Some days, even the trip to the fingerpost and back exhausted him. Usually, he remained at the Springs on his seat by the door. Ellen understood now why Harry had visited so infrequently. Apart from the guiding, there was the work of keeping the tracks and the waterways clear. Although the weather had cooled, visitors still came—not in big groups like in summer but, most days, in ones and twos or small parties. The few days when snow had settled on the pinnacle had not deterred them.

Faint laughter carried down the track from the lower icehouse. The group were on their way back. Ellen turned back into the cottage and spooned tea into the kettle-sized teapot.

Grannie joined the old man on the bench beside the door. Billy, awake now, stayed close to her, warily watching the strangers. Ellen served them tea and warm scones. The old couple answered their questions and told their tales of old Hobart Town. The trippers did not stay long. Their tea drunk, they took themselves down to the fingerpost. It had surprised Ellen how polite these swells were to her—while they didn't treat her as an equal, they gave her more respect than she had ever had in town. She was young Mrs Woods, mother of a little boy. They knew nothing of the girl who had run along Liverpool Street at midnight throwing stones at doors, or at fourteen had brawled outside the Mountain Retreat Inn. Best of all, none of them saw her as a slut or Billy as a little bastard.

The noise of the group faded, leaving them to the chatter of nesting birds, the whisper of leaves nudged by the chilling breeze, the scutter of small creatures in the undergrowth. As the shadows lengthened, Grandad came in and took his seat by the fire, puffing on his pipe. With Billy calling the old man Grandad, Ellen had easily fallen into the habit.

She checked on the heavy iron pot that had been gently simmering all afternoon at the rear of the fire. She poured two mugs of the old man's *mountain dew*, as Grannie called it, from the flagon set on the sideboard.

She handed Grandad his mug.

'You're a grand lass, Ellen.'

She grinned back at him. 'It's grand living here.'

He savoured a mouthful of his brew and nodded. 'It is indeed.'

She took the second mug to Grannie who was sitting at the table feeding Billy his tea, a small serving of the stew the rest of them would eat later.

Ellen grabbed her shawl from the back of a chair and almost skipped out the door. She climbed the track that led to the ice-house. There was a spot on the track just above the Springs where, when the mountain was not enveloped in cloud, there was a view of Hobart Town in all her glory—a play of light and shadow, colour and shape. Even at this height the life of the town was clear—the narrow threads of the streets, the houses like tiny models, the vessels in the harbour, masts and yards still visible, and the steamer at the wharf, a whisp of smoke rising from its funnel.

Harry stood staring out, as he often did when the day was ending, the clouds pink-tinged by the slowly setting sun. Ellen slid her arm around his waist, rested her head against his shoulder. She closed her eyes, drinking in all that made the moment—Harry's presence beside her: the taut muscles of his flank, the strength of his arm holding her, the scent of wood resin and tobacco and the indefinable that was him alone, the curl of his hair against his neck, the sharp angle of his cheek, the curve of his lips, the memory of his touch in the dark warmth of their bed, the joy of waking beside him, the light in his eyes when he looked at her, the slow smile that told her everything she needed to know.

'There's a good view of Perth from Mount Eliza,' Harry said finally, 'though it's not so high, nor as breathtaking.'

She wanted to know so much more of his life there. 'You miss Perth?'

'I miss the warmth.'

She'd chance it. 'Anything else?'

He swung her around, lifting her off her feet. 'Nothing at all. I've everything I could ever want here.'

Ellen bent her head and kissed him on the tip of his nose.

'You keep me as warm as any Perth sunshine.' He lowered her to the ground. His face was serious, as if he were considering some weighty business. 'Ellen, I love you.'

No one had ever said that before.

'I love you, Harry.' She blinked back unshed tears. 'More than you can imagine.'

He kissed her, his lips firm and warm, promising more, promising her the world.

By the time they reached the cottage, Grannie was dishing up the meal—braised rabbit with vegetables grown in their garden. Grandad still sat at the fire, Billy on his knee, jigging him up and down as he sang a jaunty tune about a runaway horse.

Ellen thought her heart would break with joy.

22

Rain came at the beginning of May, short showers that did little other than wet the ground. In the middle of the month, a heavy storm blanketed Hobart Town with snow. From then on, snow was constant on the mountain, although it did not reach the Springs every day. June was colder.

The old couple sat indoors hunched over the fire, puffing on their pipes. Grandad had been into town this morning on his ancient white horse and brought back a neck of beef. Ellen had put it in the soup and left it to slowly simmer all afternoon. Eaten with Grannie's bread, it would be a tasty meal tonight with enough left for tomorrow.

Ellen helped Billy into his coat and led him by the hand outside. He pulled a wooden horse behind him, a stick with a head carved by Harry. Billy dragged it up and down the path at the front of the cottage. Ellen sat by the door watching him, her hand resting on her belly. She smiled softly. The fluttering movements of this child seemed more constant than with Billy. Perhaps this one would be a girl.

She pulled her shawl tighter.

It was nowhere near freezing, but it was colder than in town. Winter had not set in, yet life was already difficult. Visitors to the Springs were rare. She knew Harry worried about money—what might have kept the old couple didn't stretch far with five mouths to feed, even though Billy didn't eat much. Had they been living in the town, Ellen could help, perhaps go out charring for another month or two. Life would be so much easier, but the old couple would not move, and there was nothing she or Harry could do. They couldn't leave them here. Ellen doubted they would survive alone. She supposed she could stay here and Harry could go back to the sawmill, but he would be away days at a time. And he would need to pay board even if he were staying with her parents. She doubted she could live without him beside her.

Ellen looked towards the track—someone was coming. Her heart gave the little leap it always did at the thought of Harry.

She frowned. The man was the right height but he had only the beginnings of a beard, and the way he walked ...

'Will!' She jumped up and ran towards him. 'You're out.' She threw herself into his arms.

'That I am.' He caught her and lifted her off her feet. 'Nice rest it was too.'

She raised her eyebrows, disbelieving, as he set her back down.

'And I look like I'm in the family way.' He patted his belly.

'Rubbish.'

'No, they weighed me when I went in and when I left and I'm fatter now.'

'Was the food good?'

'So-so. It was the *hard* labour. They wouldn't know hard work if it bit them on the arse. Should try a whaling trip.'

Ellen put her arm around him. 'Come inside and have a cup of tea.'

'A mug of the old feller's brew would be better, but in a minute.' He inhaled deeply and gazed up at the sky. 'Enjoying the fresh air. On land or sea, I don't like the walls too close.'

Billy sidled up to him. 'How's my little lad?' He picked the boy up, swinging him in the air, Billy squealing, his face alight.

As he lowered the boy to the ground, he said, 'Billy, show me how well you can ride that wooden horsie.'

Billy toddled off to reclaim his horse from the path in front of the cottage.

Will followed him and sat on the bench by the door. 'Where's himself?'

'Heading towards Fern Tree looking for work.'

'Not much doing here this time of year, I suppose.'

Ellen shook her head.

'Are you happy, sis?'

Ellen sat beside him. 'I've never been happier.'

'Has he asked you to marry him?'

She turned her head, gazing across the clearing. 'No.' By the time she looked back, her face was under control. 'Once the baby is born, I'm sure he will. Summer is a nice time for a wedding.'

Will sat silent beside her.

'You don't like Harry, do you?'

He twisted his mouth. 'The man's hiding something.'

'Oh, Will,' she laughed, 'everyone in Hobart Town is hiding something.'

'Not all of us. Some of us are exactly what you see. Look, forget about it, I'm too suspicious for my own good.'

'What are your plans now?'

'I've signed on with another whaler. One of the crew died and a couple have deserted and disappeared, so they were happy to overlook my recent doings. I'll be leaving at the end of the week.'

Ellen slid her arm through his and held it tight. 'I'll miss you, Will.'

He squeezed her hand. 'You look after yourself, Ellen.'

'I will,' she dimpled at him, 'and you know Harry will take care of me.'

'I'm sure he will.'

Will didn't sound as if he truly meant what he said, but she wouldn't ruin the joy of having him here by arguing.

'You will stay for tea? It's a good thick soup.'

'I will.' He stood and stretched 'Time for a bit of a chat with the old ones. I've got a few tales Grannie will enjoy.'

23

The mountain was permanently capped with snow through winter. Even on days when the sky was clear in Hobart Town, clouds wreathed the pinnacle, shrouding the Springs in mist if not snow. But when the clouds cleared and the sun shone bright, it was as if they lived in another world.

Life had become almost hand to mouth, something Harry had not experienced before. He had never had so many people depending on him for the food they ate. He took what work he could, a half day here, a half day there, odd jobs at some of the farms along the Huon Road. Often as not, they paid him in kind. If he needed to go to town, he stayed overnight with Ellen's parents. He could then get a day's work at the mill—the foreman, Davis, putting him on if he saw him lined up with the rest at the gate. Harry wanted to move into the town but the old couple refused. When he raised the matter, both sat, their mouths set in grim lines, staring ahead, deaf to his reasonable arguments. If money were not a problem, there was work enough at the Springs—checking the watercourse was in good repair and clear of fallen branches and bark, chopping wood, building the wood pile in the barn where it stayed dry, digging out the winter vegetables in the garden patch, making sure the cottage was watertight. With every storm, something rattled or came loose. When the snow set in, he tried to keep a clear path from the track to the door.

Harry struggled up the Fingerpost Track using a staff, the way the old man did, to give him purchase on the slippery ground. It would be nightfall by the time he arrived home. His hat pulled down, scarf wound around the lower part of his face, thick gloves, and still he was freezing—he had never been so cold in all his life.

The sight of the cottage, the glimmer of lamplight through the curtained window, was always a relief. Harry pushed his way past the blanket hanging over the door to keep out drafts.

Ellen and the old man turned in their seats by the fire, hugging their blankets and shawls closer as the freezing air rushed in with him.

Harry took off his hat and dumped his sack on the table and went straight to the fire. Pulling off his scarf, shoving his gloves in his pockets, he stood on the hearth, his back to the fire, stamping his feet. The old man nodded at him, sucking on his empty pipe in silence. Grannie dozed beside him. Over in the bed, beyond reach of the lamplight, Billy was fast asleep under a mound of blankets.

Ellen eased herself out of her chair. She stretched up and kissed him, her mouth warm against his frozen lips as if she were breathing life into him. He buried his face against her neck and stifled a groan. Without Ellen, he could not keep going. He needed her beside him, needed the warmth of her body, her muffled laughter in the darkness, her constant touch as if checking he was not a dream, the unexpected kisses as she passed him about her daily tasks. No woman had ever wanted him with such passion, had ever made him feel he was the centre of her life. He could not live without her.

He lifted his head from Ellen's shoulder and gazed into her shining eyes. She kissed him again and helped him out of his coat, spreading it across her chair, draping the scarf and gloves on the seat.

She went to the table and emptied out the contents of the sack: sugar, flour, tea, a piece of bacon. 'I'll put the bacon in tomorrow's stew.' She smiled at Harry. 'Now sit down. You must be starving.'

He pulled out the chair at the end of the table nearest the fire. Ellen had barely placed the plate of stew—more vegetable than meat—in front of him, when he began eating. She sat on the bench at the other side of the table as he ate in silence. He was too tired to speak but he smiled across at her. Happiness shone in her face. She seemed untouched by their straitened existence, placing her faith in Harry to take care of her and Billy. There were moments when he feared her faith was misplaced.

He mopped up the gravy with a thick chunk of bread.

Ellen laughed as she cleared the plate away. 'You've cleaned this well. I won't need to wash it.'

'I was hungry.' He swallowed the last of his bread. 'And it was tasty.'

'It will be better tomorrow with the bacon.'

Harry counted out the coins from work over the past two days. He looked towards his father. 'It's not enough, Dad.'

The old man turned from the fire. 'We'll manage. We always have in the past.'

They may have in the past, but time had changed them. If he and Ellen were not here, the old couple would die of cold and starvation. 'I've asked around. You should be able to get a pension from the government—you have worked for years up here, keeping the watercourse and the paths clear and in good order, watching out for the climbers.'

The old man muttered under his breath.

'You need to write a letter to the Colonial Secretary.' Harry pressed his point. 'Bob Flanagan says he knows someone who could write the letter using the right words.'

'Don't like charity.' The old man was sullen. 'And I don't want busybodies poking their noses in my business.'

'They won't be. Everyone knows how things are.' He leant back against his chair, his arms crossed. 'I can't earn enough to support everyone through winter. I do my best, but it's not enough.'

Ellen went back to the fire and rearranged the clothing hanging on the chair. 'Harry. Come over here where it's warm.'

He sat and stretched his feet towards the fire. Ellen handed him a cup of black tea, sweetened with a little of the sugar he had bought. He rarely wanted to drink these days.

The old man stared at Harry's cup and shook his head. 'I'll think about it.' He got up and moved over to his bed in the corner nearest the hearth.

Grannie shook herself awake as he moved past her and followed him.

Ellen and Harry sat close together, their feet practically in the fire. 'Will you talk to him?' Harry whispered. 'Even if they gave him rations of some sort, it would help.'

'I'll do my best.'

If anyone could convince the old man, Ellen could.

Harry pulled her onto his knee and rested his hand on her belly, feeling the gentle movement of their child. Ellen pressed her cheek against his hair. They both stared into the glowing embers. Harry sighed heavily. 'Time for bed.'

~

Ellen lay in their bed at the corner along from the old couple's. It was too cold to sleep in the bedroom. An old screen, the paint on the panels chipped and faded, had been placed between the beds for privacy. Their coats were laid on top of the blankets for extra warmth. Billy slept deeply at the side of the bed closest to the wall. Ellen gazed on his perfect little face in the dim light from the fire. Despite everything, she was content, living with the two people she loved more fiercely than any other in the world.

The fire banked so that it would burn low through the night, Harry climbed into bed. Ellen slipped into his arms. She no longer felt the consuming hunger for him that had marked their first weeks together, but she needed him as she needed food and air. In that bed, cocooned from the world and its cares, they talked into the night. Ellen loved the sound of Harry's voice. He told her stories, tales of his childhood, tales of his adventures. In the darkness, she heard the changes in his voice, developed a sense of what was memory and what was embroidery intended to amuse her, aware of the pauses, the brief silences hinting at something held back. She wouldn't question him. She knew that one day he would feel he could tell her everything.

Early the next week, Ellen fussed around Grandad, getting him ready for his trip into Hobart Town. She brushed his coat and straightened the knotted kerchief around his neck.

'Don't make me look too flash—they'll think I don't need help.'

She laughed, as he wanted her to, but underneath she was afraid. This trip to town was a sign that winter had months to go, an admission that life had become a struggle. Perhaps more for Harry than anyone else. She would do anything she could to ease his burdens.

She stood at the door, watching as Grandad walked over to the barn where the old horse was stabled. The horse looked as old as the man himself; it almost seemed a cruelty to ride him. Yet they were a pair—old Mr Woods on his white horse had been a familiar sight in Hobart Town for all Ellen's life.

She paused before turning back into the cottage. Usually, she heard the conversation, the rumble of Grandad's voice, the snicker of the horse. This morning there was silence.

Grandad came out, his shoulders slumped. 'He's dead.' His eyes glistened in the morning light. 'We'll have to bury him.'

'We'll do that later, when Harry gets back.' She patted his hand. 'You need to be on your way—once you get to the road, someone will give you a lift into town.'

He seemed about to refuse, but he drew in a deep breath, tightened his jaw and took up his staff.

'Wait,' Ellen said. She reached up and kissed him on the cheek. 'Good luck.'

He winked at her. 'I can't fail with that on my cheek.'

Ellen watched as he plodded off down the track, a heavy weight in the pit of her stomach. When did well-fed officials in their smart suits ever do anything for ordinary folk?

Grandad was back mid-afternoon, a sack over his shoulder.

'Have you eaten anything?' Ellen asked as he handed it to her.

'Yes, I ran into your sister Bessie, and she invited me home. Your Mum gave me corned beef and tea.' He smiled at Ellen, his bushy eyebrows raised. 'I remember her when she was your age, pretty little thing just like you. A twinkle in her eye too. If your father hadn't been so quick, I might have been your dad,' he chuckled.

Ellen wondered if it were true. She would have to ask Mam.

She emptied the sack—three loaves of bread, some tea and sugar. 'No pension?'

He shook his head. 'Thinking about it. Meantime, they sent me to the Benevolent Society who gave me the rations.'

'Every little bit helps.' Ellen tried to sound cheerful.

24

October 1879

The mountain was still topped with snow but white blossoms were appearing on the snow gums, and in Hobart Town the days had begun to warm. Visitors were few, but Ellen did not mind, her thoughts turned inward to the coming of her child. She moved slowly, content with life—provided she didn't think too far ahead. She was cut off up here, no neighbours to send for should anything go wrong. She told herself over and over that nothing would.

She stood at the hearth, ladling porridge into a bowl. Grannie took it from her and set it in front of Billy, who was waiting, his elbows on the table, the spoon gripped in his dimpled fist. Harry and Grandad were already eating. Ellen began to fill Grannie's bowl.

'That's enough for me, hen,' Grannie said, 'put the rest in your own bowl.'

'You eat like a bird, Grannie.' She was afraid the old woman was going without to be sure Ellen had enough.

'I eat enough, and with a smoke and a wee dram in the evening, there's plenty to content me.'

Ellen brought her own bowl to the table and sat beside Harry. 'When you're next in town, will you ask Mam to come and stay?'

He shook his head slowly, his brow furrowed. 'I ask her nearly every time I see her, and her answer is always the same—she'll come when your time is nearer.'

Ellen exhaled heavily. 'I need her now. It could be soon.'

Harry leapt up from his seat. 'Soon!'

'Sit down.' She frowned, exasperated. 'Not right now—in a week or two. When the baby decides to come, there will be no time to send for her.'

'She thought it might be better if you went back home to have the baby.'

'This is my home,' Ellen snapped. 'Besides, I doubt I'd get as far as the fingerpost.'

'She said she will come in the middle of the month.'

'That might be too late—they say they come quicker each time.'

'I'll ask her again, beg her to come with me.'

'I know what she's like—she'll say that I have nothing to worry about, that I had no trouble last time. She had eight children without a problem.' Ellen drew a shuddering breath, fighting rising panic. 'Plenty do have problems, even those who have never had a problem before. Plenty die.' If she died, who would care for Billy?

Harry closed his eyes.

Ellen knew what she was doing to him but she needed him to feel her fear. More than that, she needed someone with her, someone who knew what she was going through, knew what to do to keep her and her baby safe. She needed Mam.

'Nothing will happen to you, Ellen.' Grannie placed her hand on Ellen's shoulder. 'I'll make sure of it, even if I have to sell my soul to Old Nick himself.'

Ellen gripped Grannie's hand and lowered her head, tears running down her cheeks.

Grannie bent forward and kissed the top of Ellen's head.

She might look as if the wind could blow her away, but Ellen knew she would fight as fiercely for Ellen and her baby as any mother.

~

The sun rose on a cloudless spring day. A pair of climbers from Melbourne arrived at the door not long after, asking for a guide. They were not in a hurry, lingering over the sights, asking Harry questions between long silences as they bathed in the beauty of the mountain and its broad vistas. They arrived back at the Springs near lunchtime to be greeted by a loud groan from the open door of the cottage.

The climbers turned to Harry, the alarm on their faces no doubt a mirror of his own.

He answered their unspoken question. 'My wife, she's having a baby.' His stomach lurched, a mixture of terror and excitement.

'Now?'

'Sounds like it.' Harry shrugged. What else could he say?

The door slammed shut behind him.

The climbers decided they could do without lunch and bolted down the track.

Billy sat on the bench outside, eyes wide with fear. Harry lifted him to his hip. The boy clung to him and buried his face against his neck. Harry had no idea what to do. Beth Thompson hadn't arrived. He wondered if she had ever intended to come.

The old man was sitting in the doorway of the hut beside the barn. He looked up at Harry, squinting into the sunlight.

'Don't worry, son, Ellen will be fine.'

'But we are so far away if we need help.' He felt ill, his stomach churning. He couldn't imagine a world without Ellen.

'She's a strong girl. And Jane knows what to do—she's helped deliver babies before.'

Harry nodded. There was nothing he could do, but somehow he needed to keep blind panic at bay.

He set the boy down beside the old man. 'Mind Billy. I've got work to do,' he said and walked off towards the barn. When he glanced back, Billy was sitting on the old man's lap, enthralled by another of the old man's fanciful tales of mermaids and bush-rangers.

He went into the barn and stripped off his jacket and shirt, down to his flannels. He set a log on the chopping block and picked up the axe. Adjusting his stance, he swung the axe. There was forgetfulness in the rhythm of the movement, the strokes of the axe as the logs split and rolled from the block. He lost sense of time and place as the split wood piled up.

'Daddy.'

Harry jumped. The axe bounced, the log flying sideways.

The lad stood barely three feet from him.

'Shit, Billy! What are you doing?' The wood could have hit him. If he had moved closer or faster, he could have ... Harry ran his fingers through his damp hair, drew a ragged breath and pushed the thought away.

'Hungry, Daddy,' the boy whimpered.

Harry squatted, his pulse still racing. 'Billy.' His voice was harsh. 'Never ever do that again. You don't come into the barn when I'm chopping wood.'

The boy's face crumpled. He started to sob.

Harry grabbed him, pulled him against his chest. He placed his lips against the boy's soft hair. 'I know, son. We're all frightened.'

He picked the lad up and marched down to the hut where the old man, head on his chest, snored in the sunshine.

'I asked you to look after him.'

The old man jerked awake. 'Sorry.' He blinked in the bright light.

'He came into the barn. I could have bloody killed him.'

He set the boy down and squatted in front of him. 'Billy, you stay with Grandad while I see if I can get us something to eat. Will you do that?'

The boy nodded, his thumb in his mouth, his eyes still shining with tears.

Harry stood up. 'Keep an eye on him this time,' he said gruffly and walked towards the silent cottage.

Grannie had left a tray covered with a tea towel on the bench outside the cottage. As he bent to pick it up, she opened the door.

'Don't look so worried, young Harry. All's well, going along just as it should.'

He wanted to see Ellen, but he had never heard of a man being in the room when a woman was giving birth. 'You'll come and get me if there are any problems?' He had to say it, although it felt like he was asking for trouble.

'Nothing will go wrong.' Grannie spoke as if her words were enough to make it so. He had to believe her.

25

Harry paced between the hut and the cottage. He needed to be doing something useful. He could go and check the watercourse, see that it was free of fallen branches and bark. But he couldn't leave the boy with the old man. Harry knew he would fall asleep again, and Billy might wander off, get bitten by a snake, fall down a gully. He pushed away the image of the boy's little body lying twisted at the bottom of a steep gully. If he took the lad with him, it would be the same—he couldn't watch him while he was working. Perhaps they could walk along the Watercourse Track, Harry taking note of anything that needed doing for tomorrow. A man should be able to take it easy on the day his first child is born.

They stopped often, Harry telling Billy the names of plants, showing him the early burst of bright red waratah blossoms, the flattened pink berries on the cheeseberry bush, the deep yellow bloom of the golden rosemary. He told the boy how to tell the differences between the trees and shrubs by their shape, their bark, their leaves and flowers. The lad was too young to take it in, but it seemed to amuse him all the same as he tried to repeat the names. They sat in silence on a log beside the track, watching birds flitting through the bushes or scrabbling in the leaf litter. A tiny native shrew stopped in the shadows beside them. Billy gaped, his eyes large with wonder, as it climbed over Harry's boot, its pointed nose sniffing his trouser leg, before scurrying back into the scrub.

The boy was quieter than usual, clearly still shaken by the noise of his mother's labour and by Harry's anger. Harry knew what it was like when your world tipped on its side. He didn't know if it was worse for a child of two with no understanding of the world or an eleven-year-old who not only knew but could imagine worse than was happening. He pulled his pipe from his pocket, teased out the tobacco and lit it.

Billy looked up at him. 'Billy too?'

Harry laughed, 'No, son. You're too young.' *Son.* He wasn't his son, yet Harry felt a care for this boy that he was certain was what a father felt for a child of his own flesh. Billy was a friendly lad, happy most of the time, and trusting. He snuggled against Harry, his thumb in his mouth.

Harry drew on the pipe, the slow breath in, the aromatic smoke spreading through him. Excitement swelled at the thought that he might, right at this moment, have a son of his own. Billy and this imagined boy would be brothers. Billy clearly was his mother's son—Harry saw no traces in his face that would point to who his father was. Harry's son and Billy would look alike and he wouldn't treat them any differently. He knew what it was to be pushed aside in someone's affections. The moment Tom Poland had come on the scene, he had been all his sister Sarah thought of—Harry had become an afterthought. He knew now it wasn't reason-able, but it was the way he had seen it then. Until Eliza. There had been other women before her, but none he had trusted enough, afraid that soon as he started caring they'd disappear. Eliza. She was so far in the past—it was as if she belonged to someone else's life. He looked down at Billy, asleep, his head resting on Harry's thigh. He gently brushed the silky brown hair from the boy's forehead.

The child murmured softly.

'Billy. Time to wake up,' Harry said. 'Time to go home and have some tea.'

The boy blinked and smiled at Harry. *Ah, he was a good lad.*

Harry carried him back to the Springs—it was too far a walk for a two-year-old. The door to the cottage was still shut but, as they walked past on their way to the hut where the old man sat, Harry stopped, frozen by the sound of Ellen's groan. He swallowed his panic and continued on down the path.

Harry lowered Billy to the ground beside the old man who was sitting just as Harry had left him. He must have dozed the whole afternoon away.

'Billy, you look after Grandad here. Make sure he doesn't get into mischief.'

The boy grinned up at him and giggled.

'I'll see what I can get for tea.'

Harry stood at the door of the cottage, his fist raised to knock, frozen by the sound of another groan. The memory of his mother's agonised groans and screams as she gave birth to his baby sister, Mary, were sharp in his memory. He had been seven, terrified his mother would die. Four years on, she had disappeared from his life along with little Mary and eight-year-old Jane. They had as good as died on the day that schooner had sailed away from Swan River.

Harry drew a shuddering breath and rapped on the door.

It took a moment for Grannie to answer. Behind her, the room was gloomy. He saw no glimpse of Ellen.

'How is she?'

'Doing well. It'll be a little while yet.'

'The lad's hungry and I've nothing to feed him.'

'And himself too, I'd say,' Grannie chuckled.

She shut the door. Harry waited on the bench, his elbows on his knees, and closed his eyes, each groan and whimper slicing into him. Beneath it all, Grannie's voice was a soothing drone.

He jerked around as she opened the door.

'Ellen says you can come in.'

Harry's heart hammered as he walked into the room, his eyes slow to adjust to the dim light from the fire. Ellen, dressed in nothing but her shift, leant on the table, her hands pressed flat against it, her head bent.

She raised her head slowly. 'Come here, Harry,' she gasped, 'rub my back while Grannie gets some supper ready.'

He stood behind Ellen, pressing his hands against her lower back. She straightened up and leant into him. He put his arm around her and held her tight, as if holding her was enough to keep her safe.

Over by the fire, Grannie had set the cast-iron rack in the fire and placed the frying pan over it. The smell of frying sausages filled the room, making his mouth water.

'Is there time for that?' he asked.

'Plenty of time—it will be a couple of hours more at least.' Grannie looked over towards him. 'You can take some bread, and I'll give you a pot of tea.'

Ellen moved away from him, a moan escaping as she braced herself against the table again, her face contorted.

How could so much pain not kill her? It tore at him. She was in agony, and there was nothing he could do. He had never felt so useless.

The pain seemed to last forever, but when it had passed, she smiled tiredly at Harry. 'Don't be afraid. It is going well. Put your arm around me and we can walk a bit.' When they reached the side farthest from the fire, she turned and took his face in her hands. 'My darling, I love you.' She brushed dry lips against his. 'You have no idea how I love children, and this one will be yours, and whenever I look at him or her, I will think of you.'

She gasped again, sweat beading her forehead, and clung to Harry.

As her grip on Harry finally eased, she said, 'Once Grannie has the food ready, you had better go because by the time this is finished, I'll be swearing like a whaler.'

Over by the fire, Grannie laughed. 'I'll teach you some good Scottish swears too.'

Harry thought of the effect Ellen's swearing had had on him when he'd first met her. She was unlike any other woman he had ever known.

He was ravenous by the time he left the cottage with the sausages and bread, carrying the pot of tea.

The meal eaten, the old man stretched out on one of the pallets in the hut, the blankets Grannie had brought down earlier in the day mounded on him. Within minutes, he was snoring loudly, although the sun had barely set.

Harry was too agitated to try to sleep. Ellen's cries now carried all the way to the hut. Billy whimpered. Harry picked him up and carried him as he paced, reciting the rhymes he had learnt over the last six months, some remembered from his own childhood.

The boy wrapped his arms around Harry's neck and lay his head on his shoulder, his eyes finally closing. Harry eased himself carefully into the battered armchair in the corner of the room. Billy curled against him. It seemed he had been sitting, staring into the dark for no more than a few minutes when Grannie pushed the door open.

'Come and see the babbie, Harry.' She grinned. 'A sweet wee mite.'

The old man struggled up from his pallet.

Harry passed Billy to him, not as gently as he could have, and the boy started grizzling.

Harry raced towards the cottage, stopping at the threshold. He took a deep breath. This was the most important moment of his life. A new, an unexpected beginning.

Ellen lay in their bed, the baby cradled in her arms. She looked tired, dark smudges under her eyes, but her smile lit her whole face.

He eased himself onto the side of the bed and pressed his lips to her forehead.

It was a moment beyond words. 'Oh, Ellen,' he sighed.

She held the tight-wrapped bundle out to him. 'Take her.'

Her. A girl. It was as if the boy he had imagined as Billy's brother had not existed even in his dreams. He had a daughter—a girl as beautiful as her mother. He would love her and protect her and show the world to her. He took the baby carefully. He had never held a child so small. He peered into her squashed red face.

So tiny, so helpless. This child was his.

'What shall we call her?' He gazed at Ellen through his tears.

'Jane.' Ellen smiled at Grannie, standing at the foot of the bed.

A fierce joy shone in her lined old face. 'Ellen, darling, wouldn't Elizabeth be better—your mother's name.'

'No.' Harry's voice was harsh. 'Not Elizabeth.'

Not his mother's name, not the name of the woman who had run away, the woman who had deserted him. He looked at Grannie—she had stayed by his father for nearly thirty years—and saw the hunger in her eyes. He stood up and walked slowly to the old woman and placed the baby in her arms. 'Jane it is—Janey.'

Grannie said the name, her Scots accent turning it to Jennie.

'Jennie,' he repeated, smiling at her.

The baby started squalling, a noise to raise the shingles from the roof. Grannie settled the baby back with Ellen. Seated on a stool beside the bed, Harry watched the tiny head with its hungry mouth nuzzling Ellen's breast. Ellen reached out with her free hand and wriggled her fingers into his. 'Are you happy?'

'More than I ever thought possible.' A happiness that dazed him.

The door slammed open. Billy bowled into the room scrambling onto the bed beside his mother. The old man followed him and stood beside his wife.

'Well done, Ellen. That one has a fine set of lungs.'

'That she has,' Ellen said. 'We're calling her Jane.'

He put his arm around Grannie's shoulder and gently squeezed. 'Now that's a grand name.'

Billy settled himself on the other side of Ellen, and Ellen curled her free arm around him.

Harry gazed at the three of them—his wife and his children—and all the cares of the harsh winter melted away. He could barely believe his good fortune.

26

December 1879

Harry paced outside the cottage, waiting. He was keen to be on the way. He wanted to be in Hobart Town well before nightfall, but Ellen had said she needed to feed Jennie first. The guilt he felt at leaving the old couple to spend Christmas by themselves was sure to fade once he got to town. He had tried to talk the old man and Grannie into coming with them down to the Thompsons', but they wouldn't budge, saying they would spend Christmas as they always had, together at the Springs. His father had insisted there would be visitors to guide on Christmas Day. It hadn't been that way last year, but the weather was better this time—Harry had taken two groups to the top today. But he wanted Ellen to have some time with little work to do, even if it was only a couple of days. And, if he were honest, he wanted the time away himself.

The old ones' disappointment was muted by the Christmas gift of a tin of tobacco, a small bottle of Scotch whisky and the prospect of the Thompsons visiting on New Year's Day. George, at least, would stay the night then. George brought a smile to Grannie's face, always had some unbelievable story for her. Grannie clearly had a liking for young men with a bit of *the divil* in them, as she put it. Perhaps that was what she had seen in Harry's father.

He stopped his pacing, sat on the bench and pulled out his pipe. He loosened the tobacco in the bowl and added to it from his tin. The pipe lit, he sucked on the stem, drawing the smoke in, emptying his mind of everything but the pleasure of the moment. When he opened his eyes again, a pair of green rosellas flew across the clearing and disappeared into the treetops. Their whistling and chattering carried on the still air.

Harry leant back against the wall of the house. Life was good.

December had been a pleasant month, only a couple of days of heavy rain, though snow still clung to the pinnacle. In the weeks since Jennie's birth, he had fallen into a routine. He worked on the garden beds between taking climbers to the top and, sometimes, the more adventurous home by way of Silver Falls and the Fern Bower. Less often he took small parties to Wellington Falls. In spring, he had dug the beds and planted seeds that were now sturdy plants. The raspberry and gooseberry canes, pruned back at the end of autumn, were fruiting. He had tidied the area directly in front of the cottage and patched the roof. He kept the pathways and tracks clear of fallen branches and bark as the need arose.

He loved the tranquillity of the mountain, but they could not live here forever. He wanted, needed, regular paying work in town. Then he and Ellen could get a small house with space for a garden. It would be easy if he could talk the old pair into leaving here. If ever they wanted it, there was a place for them at the Invalid Depot, the government asylum for the old and infirm poor of Hobart Town. The few times he had dared to speak of it, the old man's face had slammed shut before he said more than half a dozen words, putting an end to any discussion.

'I've done my time—not going inside again.'

Harry supposed they could go on like this for a couple of years. There would be more children, he had no doubt of that, more mouths to feed, yet each time he thought of Jennie his heart swelled—a child who would not exist but for him. Next time, perhaps, it would be a boy. His own son. A dream he had given up years ago. Every time he had that thought, he saw Billy smiling at him, trusting him, loving him. His own son would not change what he felt for Billy.

And Ellen. She did not need to say it. He knew she wanted him to marry her. He had thought the proper thing was to wait a few years, but the past was so far away. Before the next child arrived, he would put it right.

Whenever he caught Ellen's eye, no matter what she was doing, she smiled at him as if he were the centre of the world. She sang as she worked and was as good at making the visitors welcome as Grannie. She took the greater part, with Grannie keeping an eye on the little ones. When he looked at the old couple, he wondered if he and Ellen would be like them in thirty years' time. He knew with certainty that he would not stay—he would not die here, not on this mountain, not on this island. The cold got into your bones. There had been times last winter when he was sure he would never be warm again. He would never go back to Perth. South Australia perhaps? Adelaide was a warm, clean town. Would Ellen like it?

~

They arrived at the Thompsons' house in Watchhouse Lane in the late afternoon, having walked half the way before they were offered a ride on a cart heading into town. It seemed that most of those who usually travelled the road were already home making ready to celebrate Christmas.

As Ellen pushed the door open, the scent of warm shortbread wafted past them. Harry drank in the smell—it was Christmas. That and a burning heat that was decidedly lacking here in Hobart Town.

'Billy,' Alice squealed as soon as they were through the door. Alice had the same good-natured smile Ellen had—and a mind of her own, like all the Thompsons.

She swept Billy up and smothered him with kisses.

He squirmed away from her. 'No kisses.'

'Yes, kisses,' said Alice, chasing him around the table. When she caught him, she pulled him onto her knee and tickled him mercilessly, Billy squealing and giggling.

'Billy, do you want to come and see what the cat has given us for Christmas?'

She swiped two pieces of shortbread from the tray on the table and made a sprint for the door, Billy behind her. 'We'd better run for it before Gran comes after us with the wooden spoon.'

Smiling, Ellen handed the baby to Harry and pulled out a seat at the table.

'Cup of tea, my love?' her mother asked.

Jennie started squalling, and Harry tried jigging her up and down.

Bill stood and peered over Harry's shoulder. 'That's a fine pair of lungs there. Pity we don't know what she wants.'

Beth rolled her eyes. 'After eight children, you should have some idea.'

'That was years ago, forgotten it all.'

'She's telling us she's thirsty.' She smiled into the child's face. 'Aren't you, my wee darling?'

Ellen had unbuttoned the front of her dress. Harry laid the baby gently in Ellen's waiting arms. Harry had seen his sister feed her many children and thought nothing of it. But this, with Ellen and Jennie, made him weak with tenderness.

'Now, son,' Bill said, clamping a hand on his shoulder, 'I know you'd prefer something stronger than tea.'

Harry could hardly say that, right at this moment, tea was exactly what he wanted.

Bill filled two glasses with beer from a half-empty jug on the sideboard and said, 'Come outside and admire my tomatoes, the best crop I've ever had. We'll leave the women to talk of babies and who's in the family way and who's not.'

As Harry followed Bill through the door to the yard, he heard Ellen say, 'So who is in the family way?'

'Well,' said Mary Ann, 'you'd never believe it ...'

~

The evening meal eaten, the dishes done, the family settled themselves around the room.

'Dad, sing us one of your songs,' Alice said.

'I'd rather dance a jig—work off some of that fine stew your mother made. How about it, George, a proper hornpipe?'

George pulled out his tin whistle and blew a trill as the others pushed the table back and arranged the chairs along the wall. Bill stood in the centre of the space as George played the whistle. His feet hit the floor in rapid beats as he spun and leapt and twirled. Billy, snuggled up beside Alice, watched his feet, mesmerised.

'Come on, Beth.' Bill caught Beth by the hand and pulled her towards him. She was an energetic dancer, her skirts flying out as she skipped around him.

Alice put Billy down, the boy giggling as she twirled him.

Mary Ann took the baby from Ellen. 'Go on you two, get up.'

Jane and Bessie joined in and they all crowded together forming a squashed reel.

Three more dances and George said, 'This is thirsty work, time I had a drink.'

He went to the sideboard and poured a glass from the jug there. He looked over his shoulder. 'Dad? Harry?'

'Don't forget us,' Mary Ann called to him. 'And don't be stingy with it.'

Bill began to sing 'John Barleycorn', the family joining in, loud and enthusiastic.

Each sang a favourite song. When Harry's turn came, he began,
Believe me if all these endearing young charms,
Which I gaze on so fondly today ...
Ellen sat still, her eyes fixed on his face.
The heart that has truly loved never forgets,
But as truly loves on to the close ...
The silence stretched out when Harry finished. They were all watching him. It was one thing to say *I love you* in private, another to declare it in front of the whole family.

He glanced at Ellen. Her eyelashes glistened in the lamplight.

'Oh, Harry,' she whispered, winding her arms tight around his.

'That's a lovely song,' Beth said, a gentle smile on her lips. She began to sing softly,

Of all the money e'er I had,
I spent it in good company ...

George took up the tune on the whistle as the rest joined together. The children slept, Billy with his head resting on Alice's lap, Jennie in her grandmother's arms.

When the song ended, Ellen went and lifted the baby from Beth. Beth bent over the child and brushed her lips against Jennie's forehead.

Ellen carried Jennie, careful not to wake her. 'I'm putting Jennie to bed.' She bent close to Harry, her breath against his ear. 'We're in the room next door.'

Harry would have followed her straightaway, but knew how obvious that would be.

George sat himself in Ellen's seat, lounging, his legs stretched out in front of him. 'You didn't think to call the bairn, Elizabeth, after her gran?'

'No.' His voice was harsh. *Why would he name a child after a woman he had not seen for over thirty years?*

George lifted an eyebrow.

Harry realised George had meant his own mother.

'My mother was Elizabeth,' Harry scowled, 'but my grand-parents raised me.' His voice softened. 'Both gone now. Jane was my grandmother's name.'

George nodded, as if understanding. 'And it's Grannie Woods's name too.'

'Yes, that too.'

George took a long drink from his glass. 'Ever thought to try whaling, Harry? It's hard work but good money when the whales are about.'

'I'm no good at sea.' He grinned. 'My first trip from Fremantle, I pretty much spewed the whole way. Nothing's improved since.'

George frowned and said slowly, 'I thought you said you'd been a fisherman.'

Harry paused no more than a heartbeat. 'Tried my hand at it. I lasted two trips—spewed the whole time.'

Bill roared with laughter. 'Reminds me of one poor bastard on the way from England. We were divided into messes of eight men. One person was sent from each mess to the galley to collect the tucker in a dish called a *kid*. This bloke, 'the Boatman' we called him, was bringing the dinner down and was seasick. He vomited into the kid, right into the pea soup. I thumped him—there was no asking for a second serving.'

Harry laughed, but his mind was on Ellen lying in bed in the next room. He drained his glass and stretched. 'Time for bed.'

'Good idea,' George said. 'You need to be up bright and early— the whole family goes to church on Christmas Day.'

Harry's eyebrows shot up.

George let out a blast of laughter. He stood and slapped Harry on the back, 'Tell Ellen that and see what she says.' He headed out the back door.

Shaking his head, Harry walked along the passage to the front room.

27

Harry woke to daylight pouring through the opening in the curtain. He rolled onto his side.

Ellen, kneeling beside their mattress, gently lowered Jennie back into the basket. She smiled at him as she straightened up. He couldn't look away. She stood there in front of him, unclothed. He had never more than glimpsed her fully naked, only in the half-light of dawn or dusk. Life at the Springs gave them no privacy, no time to be completely alone, no time to come to know each other's body as much by gaze as touch. She was perfection, from the tangled hair around her shoulders, the curve of her breasts, the marks of motherhood across her belly to the strong line of her legs.

He glanced about the room. 'Where's Billy?'

'Upstairs, sleeping with his aunties.'

'I didn't notice he was missing last night.'

'And I wonder why that was.' She arched an eyebrow, a smile hinting on her lips.

Billy's squeals carried from the kitchen.

'Sounds like he's up already. I bet he's looking at his presents.' Ellen gazed into the basket. 'And this little one! Such a good baby, lying there playing with her toes.'

She walked over to the cabinet where a jug and bowl stood. Harry lay back, his hands behind his head, watching Ellen as she washed, her back to him. She pulled on her drawers and shift, picked up her stays from the chair and turned to face him.

'Aren't you getting up?'

'I will after you've dressed.'

'I'm not the main attraction at the Theatre Royal,' she said as she moved back towards him, tightening the laces at the back of her stays and tying the cord around her waist.

'I wouldn't say that.' He reached over and caught her hand, pulling her back onto the bedding with him. He kissed her hard. 'This is better than any show at the Theatre Royal.'

'Isn't it just?' She grinned at him, a dimple in her cheek.

She sprang up, pulling the sheets with her. 'Now it's my turn.' She gazed down at him, her eyebrows raised at the effect she was having on him. 'Harry, you must have been an absolute terror at twenty.'

'No.' He grabbed the sheets back. 'I didn't have you with me then.' At twenty, there had been no one. Even at thirty, it had been nothing like this. He swung his legs out, the sheets arranged modestly across his lap.

Ellen pulled on her petticoat and her dress, buttoning it as she walked towards the window. She stared through the opening in the curtains as she brushed her hair.

'Ellen,' Harry said slowly, 'how would you feel about moving back into town?'

Ellen put her brush down and turned, a smile lighting her face. 'When?'

'Not right away, but Dad and Grannie can't stay there much longer. It's too hard in winter. I don't know how we survived the last one, much less them.' He stopped. 'You do want to come back to town?'

'Oh yes.' She came and sat beside him. 'We could get a house of our own?'

'Yes. I'd be working a full week. It would be nothing grand, but a house with a small yard—I could grow vegetables, perhaps keep a few hens.'

'That would be wonderful.' Her eyes lit up. 'Perhaps we could get one of those sewing machines eventually. I could make curtains and sew shirts for you and clothes for the children.'

'We should be able to manage that. I'd find a house somewhere not far from your parents.'

She looked at him, thoughtful, a line between her brows. 'Do you miss your family?'

Harry stared straight ahead and said nothing.

'Your sister and her children?' she persisted.

He turned to her and brushed a curled finger down her cheek. 'You are my family.'

She drew his hand away from her cheek and kissed the palm.

He ran his fingers across her soft hair. There were moments every single day when Harry was still stunned by his good fortune.

Ellen stood up and went back to the chair. She sat, pulled on her stockings and slid her feet into her shoes.

'Don't say anything to anyone yet. It will take some time to convince the old man he would be better off in town.'

'I won't.' She lifted Jennie from the basket. 'They don't have to go to the Invalid Depot. They can live with us.' Happiness shone in face. 'I can't think of anything better than living in town, in our own house.'

~

Although, as children, the Thompsons had only received gifts on the rare occasions when there was money to spare, Ellen had said she wanted to give something to all her family this Christmas. With the number of climbers visiting the mountain, they could afford the spices and extra sugar she needed to make gingerbread. Adding to the festive atmosphere, her younger sisters had strung paper chains around the room. They had made toffee too, and Mary Ann had prepared a large plum pudding.

Billy was the centre of attention. He was given a pull-along cart made by Harry over the last few weeks and brought down a few days before Christmas. Billy dragged it from one end of the room to the other faster than the wheels could spin. He then decided it could be used to cart a couple of pieces of wood from the small stack beside the stove.

'There's a future for Billy,' Bill said. 'He could be a carter.'

George laughed. 'Perhaps he can work for Bob Flanagan.'

Harry nodded. 'Might be just the thing.'

George looked over at Ellen. 'You're looking like the cat that got the cream this morning, sis. Special Christmas present from Harry?'

Before she could answer, Harry said, 'I haven't had a chance.' He passed a small parcel wrapped in crumpled brown paper over to her.

Ellen unwrapped it, staring at an intricately carved backcomb, the small flowers along its edge picked out in bright paint.

'You made this?' She blinked quickly. 'Oh, Harry.' She leant over and pulled his head towards her, kissing him deeply.

'Give the man some air,' George groaned.

Harry blessed his dark colouring—without it, every set of eyes in the room would have seen the flush on his skin.

Ellen sprang up and rushed from the room.

Harry blinked, not sure what he had done. 'I should go after her.'

'Sit down, she's not upset.' George shook his head. 'You have a lot to learn about women, mate.'

A few minutes later, Ellen returned, her hair twisted up and held in place by the comb. She stood in the middle of the room and twirled.

'It's beautiful, my love,' Beth said.

'It is,' Bill agreed. 'Good Queen Vicky couldn't look grander.'

Beth rose from her seat. 'Now, you lads, take yourselves outside so we can get on with the dinner.'

It was the best meal of the year. Not roast beef but rabbits done with bacon and roasted potatoes, raspberries from the Springs as well as the plum pudding and custard and a large bottle of the Old Man of the Mountain's *mountain dew*.

The meal was noisy, all talking as they ate, laughing, joking and teasing good-humouredly. It was like the remembered Christmases

161

of Harry's childhood, with his parents and grandparents, his sisters and his aunt and uncles—before his childhood had been torn apart.

One day, like Bill Thompson, he would sit at the end of the table, his own boisterous children ranged along the sides, Ellen, his beautiful wife, at the other end. Uncles George and Will would be there, egging the children on to mischief. He would be head of his own family, no longer a guest at the side of someone else's table.

28

January 1880

Ellen sang as she kneaded the dough. She was now nearly as expert at breadmaking as Grannie. And Grandad could no longer tell which one of them had baked what he ate.

At midnight on New Year's Eve, she and Harry had stood on the track where they had a clear view of Hobart Town as it welcomed the New Year, the brilliant pinpricks of the Milky Way swirling in the dark sky above them. The harbour had been lit up with magnesium and coloured lights; sky rockets had been set off. They could hear the pealing bells and signal guns, muted by the distance. Down in Hobart Town it would be as noisy as the middle of any day. Harry had held her close and kissed her.

It had not occurred to Ellen until Christmas that they had never been truly alone—there was always someone in the room with them, always the need to be silent and discreet. They had never had the leisure to explore what more could be between them. But that day was coming closer. She hugged to herself the dream of a house in the town with a garden and children playing in it, her parents not far away. And Ellen loved the Springs and the old couple all the more because she knew the present would not last.

Outside, Billy chattered to Grandad, Grannie on the bench beside him. Ellen knew, because she had seen it so often, Jennie would be held against her, the ribbon on the old woman's bonnet gripped in the baby's chubby fist.

It had been a busy morning, a constant stream of visitors beginning at first light. Ellen smiled at the sound of Harry singing as he came up the track, Billy squealing, delighted. Whenever he came back from seeing a group of visitors off at the fingerpost, he would pick Billy up and swing him in the air. And each time Ellen loved him a little more, if that were possible. He could not treat a son of his own any better.

Had her hands not been coated in flour and dough, she would have gone out to greet him.

Harry came straight in to her and wrapped his arms around her waist from behind, nuzzling her neck as she placed the dough into the baking tin.

'You smell almost as good as that pie in the oven.'

'Almost?'

'I'm hungry.' He rested his chin on her shoulder. 'When I've eaten, ask me again.'

She twisted around to him, her flour-dusted hands held away and kissed him lightly.

'It's not ready yet. Do you want a slice of ...'

Feet pounded up the path.

'Ellen, Ellen,' George yelled as he burst into the cottage. 'Will's in hospital. They say he'll die.'

Silence slammed down, the birdcalls were soundless, the leaves moving without noise.

Ellen scrubbed her hands with her apron and slumped on the chair beside the table. It made no sense.

'But he's still at sea.'

'Back two days ago.' George's face was haggard, his eyes red-rimmed. 'He was out with that Patterson piece from Sackville Street. Went back to her place with a few others. He fell over in the corner of the room. She left him there, on the floor, left him there all night, didn't even try to get him to bed. Waited till this morning to go for a doctor. She said she thought he was drunk. The bitch!' He spat the word.

Time seemed to move slowly.

Billy was at her side, hugging her waist. She held him tight against her as he sucked on his thumb.

This couldn't be happening. Not Will.

The old couple stood in the doorway. Jennie, in Grannie's

arms, began to squirm and whimper.

Ellen held out her arms for the child.

'Where is he now?' She didn't want to think of this. It wasn't real.

She undid the front of her dress and settled Jennie at her breast. Ellen closed her eyes as the baby latched on, holding on to the peace that came with breastfeeding. She tried to hold Billy with her other arm. He buried his face against her side.

'At the hospital.' George pulled out the chair at the head of the table and sat, his head in his hands. 'If that slut had gone for the doctor last night, something could have been done. She's as good as killed him.'

'George!' Harry's voice was harsh. 'Ellen doesn't need this.'

George stood up, his chin jutting out. 'Her brother is dying.'

Ellen watched them. Were they going to fight? Nothing made any sense.

'I know,' Harry said, his palm laid on George's forearm, 'and I am so sorry.'

George shook him off, glaring as if Harry were to blame.

Ellen closed her eyes. 'I need to see him.' She fought down a sob as pain broke through her disbelief. 'I'll go back with you. Mam will need me.'

'I'll come with you,' Harry said.

Ellen looked towards Grannie, standing by the fire. 'Will you take care of Billy?'

'Of course I will, hen.'

'No.' George's voice cracked. 'He carries his uncle's name. He is the first man of the next generation of Thompsons.' He glared again at Harry. 'Billy's place is with us.'

No one argued. They sat, all eyes on Ellen, rocking gently as she fed Jennie. She kept her mind on Jennie. She couldn't think of Will yet. If she did, she wouldn't be able to do what must be done.

~

They trudged down the track in silence. Ellen carried Jennie close, wrapped tight in her shawl. Billy, piggyback on George, was silent too, taking his cue from his elders. Harry followed behind, the swag on his back with their blankets and clothing. They hadn't gone far along the Huon Road when a cart pulled up. It was half-laden, so there wasn't room for all of them. Harry was left to find his own way to town.

He dropped his swag by the side of the road and took out his pipe. Within minutes, a carriage from Hobart Town pulled up carrying a group of visitors. With only a moment's hesitation, Harry hurried up to them and offered his services as a guide. A smaller group arrived later in the afternoon, wanting only to collect waratah and to have a picnic at the Springs. By the time he returned to the fingerpost, the road was in shadow. Harry was in no hurry to get to town. He doubted Will Thompson would have any wish to see him, and Ellen was surrounded by her family should the worst happen. He moved back from the road and leant against a tall tree fern, pulled out his pipe and lit it. As he drew deeply, he emptied his mind of everything but the satisfaction of the smoke and the rustle of the surrounding bush.

He could hear the rattle of an empty cart coming from Fern Tree but stayed where he was. He dreaded what lay ahead, suspecting the Thompsons would be as enthusiastic in their grief as they were in the rest of their lives.

The carter drew on the reins, slowing the horses. He peered into the shadows. 'Want a lift, mate?'

Harry stepped out onto the road.

'If it isn't young Harry Woods.' Bob Flanagan pushed his hat back and scratched his forehead. 'Hop up, mate.'

Harry bit on his pipe, flung his swag in the back of the wagon and climbed up beside Bob.

'Thanks, Bob.'

Bob flicked the reins, and the horses trotted on. 'Late to be heading off to town.'

'Yes.' Harry stared ahead, his eyes on the road. 'The wife's brother is in hospital, thought to die.'

'Strewth,' Bob gasped. 'One of Bill Thompson's lads? Sorry to hear that.'

'Will, the whaler.' He took the pipe out of his mouth. It had gone out. He pressed the tobacco down with his thumb and dropped the pipe in his pocket.

Bob shook his head. 'It will be tough for his brother. They were like twins, always in scrapes of some sort when they were younger.'

They travelled on in silence. When they neared the edge of town, Bob said, 'I'm heading home now, along Molle Street. I'll drop you at the corner of Liverpool.'

'Thanks, Bob, but anywhere along Davey Street will do. I want a bit of time before I go in.'

'Fair enough. I don't envy you. If he goes, they'll take it hard. The Thompsons are a tight-knit lot.'

Harry wandered down Davey Street to the docks and stood watching as the light faded, the masts and yards of the sailing ships, the funnels of the steamers dark against the sky. The docks gave him a feeling of endless possibilities. He could get on a ship and go anywhere. At least as far as Melbourne or Adelaide to begin with. But he had no wish to go. The next few days would be difficult, but Ellen and the children tied him here. He'd only leave if they came with him.

He turned away and crossed the road. The low roar of conversation and laughter, the clink of pots, the aroma of cooking carried through the open door of a pub. He was hungry, it was hours since he had eaten, and he doubted he'd get a meal when he arrived at the Thompson's house. He would find a pub a few streets away and see what they offered.

The house was in darkness when Harry finally arrived well over an hour later. He pushed the front door open and walked along the passage to the kitchen. Bill Thompson sat alone in the moonlit room. He looked up as Harry came in and picked up his empty mug. 'Sorry, son, there's nothing left.' He pressed his hands on the table and pushed himself upright, swaying. 'Should go off to bed.'

Harry dropped his swag and went to him, held him tight. He felt the older man's tense effort at control.

'He was a good lad.' Bill's voice caught. 'They wouldn't let us bring him home. Tomorrow, they said.'

'It's too cruel,' Harry murmured.

Bill nodded. 'Life's a bastard.'

He peered at Harry, as if seeing him properly for the first time. 'You'll have to bunk in with George, and Will's mates.' He exhaled heavily. 'The inquest is at the Bird in Hand tomorrow afternoon.'

Harry went into the small room at the front of the house and spread his bedroll in the unoccupied space at one corner. He lay with his hands behind his head and stared into the darkness, wondering how he would manage to sleep with the rough snoring and the warm fug of exhaled beer, stale sweat and wind.

29

The men sat, grim faced, in the upper room of the Bird in Hand Hotel in Argyle Street, across the road from the Hobart Town General Hospital. Will Thompson's body was laid out for all to look upon while witnesses—two doctors at the hospital, Mary Patterson and her daughter as well as a shipmate of Will's—gave evidence. George, hunched in a seat at the front, muttered through the examinations. His father and another mate of Will's sat at either side of him, whispering now and again, keeping him in check. The jury seemed to take forever to come to their verdict of accidental death through falling and striking his head.

Before the coroner had even risen, George stood and shook off his father's hand. 'Knew there was no hope of justice here with that bastard in charge.' He jerked his head in the coroner's direction. 'He's the one who sent Will down last year.'

The coroner, judiciously perhaps, appeared not to hear.

Harry glanced around the room. Mary Patterson and her daughter had gone. It was clear George was spoiling for a fight, and it would be best if it was not with a woman.

The inquest over, the undertakers arranged Will's body in a coffin. The men walked in silence behind the hearse as it brought Will Thompson home.

The Thompson women and their neighbours had moved the bedding from the front room. The undertaker's men took charge, laying the coffin on a row of trestles, ensuring the family had time alone with Will.

The coffin lid removed, they each stepped forward and kissed Will. Beth, her eyes wet, each breath a ragged sob, lay her hand against the side of her son's blood-suffused face and began to keen softly. Her daughters surrounded her, helping her from the room.

George carried Billy to the coffin and held him up to kiss his uncle. The boy whimpered and tried to wriggle away. George forced the boy closer.

This was wrong—the child was far too young. Harry stepped forward. 'George, no.'

'What business of yours is it, Woods?' George snarled. 'You get no say in anything until you marry my sister.'

Bill raised his voice. 'Enough!'

He took Billy from George and passed him to Harry. 'He's best away from this,' he said quietly.

Harry nodded to Bill and carried Billy out into the lane.

He set him down and squatted, level with the boy. 'Are you right now, Billy?'

The boy, sniffing, smiled at Harry. He wound his arms around Harry's neck, sighing. 'Daddy.'

Harry kept Billy close through the evening as neighbours and friends passed through the house to pay their respects, many of the women bringing dishes of food. It meant, at least, that Billy did not go hungry, nor Harry himself for that matter. If he was expected to drink, he needed something in his stomach, but by keeping a filled glass close by, no one seemed to notice he wasn't drinking.

Billy went to bed with the younger Thompson girls, followed by Ellen with Jennie not long after. Other than greet her and hold her tight for a few brief moments this morning, he had done no more than watch her across the crowded room, surrounded by her sisters and friends—arms around each other, they leant together and wept, overwhelmed by the unreality of a loss so sudden and so cruel.

George kept vigil by his brother, some of Will's mates taking turns to sit with him. Harry saw no point offering. He had met Will once and knew he had no liking for him, an attitude George seemed now to have taken for his own. He took his place among the men gathered in the backyard, smoked with them and drank his warm beer slowly, answering the questions that came his way, and when most had left, he rolled himself in his blanket and slept on the passage floor with those who had no homes to go to.

~

The funeral procession set out for Queenborough Cemetery at half-past eight in the morning. Two mourning coaches followed the hearse pulled by horses with black plumes on their heads. No one could say William Thompson the younger was not seen off in style. The women wore black veils over their hats, the men black bands on their coat sleeves. As many as had followed the procession were waiting at the cemetery. Billy, all two and a half years of him, stood at the graveside between his grandfather and his uncle, as stoic as an old man. Ellen leant on Harry, her arm linked through his, her head down, the veil covering her face.

The graveside service was brief. As the coffin was lowered, Ellen tightened her grip on Harry, her body racked with sobs. He held her close, her face pressed against his shoulder as she wept. Harry looked up to see George staring at him with something that seemed akin to hate.

Shipmates, friends and neighbours then poured through the house and drink flowed as freely as the tears. The wake got into full swing—loud conversation, stories told, songs sung, laughter and grief dancing hand in hand.

Harry looked for Billy. He sat, comfortable, on his Aunt Mary Ann's lap. She seemed a sensible sort so Harry eased his vigilance.

Silence fell over the house as Bessie sang, her voice clear and pure.

> How cold the wind do blow, my love,
> And see the drops of rain.

Alice harmonised with her, her voice keening beneath the melody. Harry rose from his seat and moved towards the door.

> I never had but one true love,
> In cold clay, he was lain.

A plaintive sobbing, a sound to break the hardest heart.

He stopped and leant against the wall, mesmerised, as the two young women sang of love and aching loss.

The finest flower that ere was seen
Is withered to a stalk.

He walked from the house and up the rise in Liverpool Street and stared away across the rooftops to the horizon. His head was heavy; he hadn't eaten enough. This funeral was unlike any he had ever been to—it was almost riotous. He leant against a fence and pulled his pipe out of his pocket, loosened the tobacco, topped it up and lit it. The air was warm, the street quiet away from the Thompsons' house. If there had been a seat nearby, Harry would have lain on it and drifted into sleep. A longing for Eliza washed through him, her neat and careful ways, her mostly respectable family. He opened his eyes. Eliza was the past. He was betraying Ellen by thinking of Eliza.

'You know, Woods,' George's voice slurred behind him, 'Willie didn't trust you.'

Harry turned and stared into the red-rimmed eyes. 'Why was that?' He kept his voice even.

'He said you were hiding something.' He glared at Harry. 'And you drink like an old maid. Even Mam can put you to shame.'

Harry had no doubt about that. 'I've done my share today.'

'And another thing, *old man*. Why haven't you married our Ellen?'

'We'll get round to it, sooner rather than later.'

'See that you do.' He pushed his face into Harry's. 'Hurt any of mine and I'll hurt you.'

'I won't hurt her.' Harry stepped past him and walked back down the street to Watchhouse Lane.

George followed him. 'Now your dad, he's a good sort. Straightforward, no secrets.'

'I thought everyone in Hobart Town had secrets.'

He heard the intake of breath and turned to face George. George's eyes were narrowed, a nerve flickered beneath his eye, his shoulders tensed. Harry wondered why he hadn't punched him already. He squared up to George.

'George!' a voice called from the doorway of the house. 'What you up to out here?'

They were surrounded by seamen, shipmates of both George and Will's, full mugs were pushed into both Harry's and George's hands.

'A toast,' George said, raising his mug, staggering slightly as he tried to stand still. 'A toast to Willie Thompson, the best brother, the best mate, a man ever had.'

'Willie Thompson,' they chorused and downed their mugs.

Harry took a couple of mouthfuls.

George watched him. 'Swallow the lot, Woods, or I'll take it as a mark of disrespect towards my brother.'

Harry threw back his head and drained the mug. He drank on, meeting George Thompson drink for drink. His memory of the night became a blur of toasts and tears, of tall tales of fights on land and sea, of raucous songs and heartbreaking laments, George beside him, their arms across each other's shoulders like brothers.

30

There were moments when Ellen forgot, moments when the world seemed complete. She woke with Harry close beside her; she cared for the old couple; she played with her children; she served food and drink to those who came up the mountain; the sun shone and the birds sang. The pattern of her life had not changed and that made it so easy to forget. Will had been away from home for months, almost years, on end. It was not his absence but the knowledge that she would never see him again. She tried to imagine he was on a long voyage, a voyage that would last her lifetime, and that she would meet him at the end. It seemed like wishful thinking despite what she had been told on the few occasions she had gone to Sunday School. Most of those who went to church behaved the same as everyone else—they didn't act as if they believed anything they were told there, so why should she?

The minutes and hours of forgetting made her feel guilty, but worse were the moments of panic when she knew the reality that this would come to them all one day—Mam and Dad would die, Harry would die, even Billy and Jennie. She hoped she would not live to see any of her children die.

A group had just returned from the pinnacle, among them a tall bearded young man with reddish-brown hair. For the briefest of moments Ellen thought the impossible. Her eyes were drawn to him although he certainly wasn't Will, not with the way, like a puppy dog with his tongue hanging out, he was trailing after a pouty-lipped piece in a jaunty hat and a fashionable tight jacket and skirt trimmed with flounces. It was the girls who had chased after Will. She wondered how Puppy-Dog would stand up in a fight. Will would knock him out before he had his hands out of his pockets. Not a real man at all.

The men in the group, except for Puppy-Dog, were talking to Grandad, the women either sitting on chairs from the cottage, their skirts spread around them, or standing, teacups in hand. Grannie had brought out the pies they had left to be warmed as well as their cakes and sandwiches. She was now sitting to one side holding Jennie, Billy beside her playing with his wooden blocks. Ellen carried the teapot, filling cups. As she moved away from Miss Pouty-Lips, Ellen heard her say to Puppy-Dog what a pair of vinegar faces the two Mrs Woods were. Puppy-Dog's laugh was a donkey's bray. Ellen continued away from them as if she had not heard. Harry stood not far away, watching the pair, his eyes cold and hard. He had heard but did nothing. Ellen understood why, but she wished he would knock the girl over. Or better, Ellen could slap the stuck-up little puss across her simpering face, pull off her fancy hat and trample it on the ground. And knee Puppy-Dog in the balls for the fun of it. That would put an end to his braying. But they'd call it assault, and she'd end up in court. There was no money to pay fines, so she would spend at least a week in the House of Correction.

She almost laughed at the thought. What would Harry say to that? She sensed it was no struggle for him to be respectable. He seemed to lack the recklessness her brothers had, and that still simmered in her. Both her parents and the Woods must have had it—it was what had brought them here to Tasmania. But she liked that Harry was calm and reliable. He wasn't weak, though. His muscles were hard, and she was certain he could hold his own in a fight. He didn't swear much, which was strange, and it wasn't as if he was biting his tongue the way she was. But he didn't have brothers who had spent months at sea on whaling barques. She wondered if Harry could tell a barque from a schooner. And that brought her back to Will.

When the group finished their tea and disappeared down the track to the fingerpost, Harry went into the barn to chop wood.

Ellen walked off along the Ice House Track and stood staring out towards Hobart Town. She yelled to the wind every foul word Will had ever taught her and a few she made up herself. As long as she had those words, she still had something of him.

Grandad was sitting outside the door smoking his pipe when she arrived back at the cottage. He winked at her as she passed. She smiled back at him, the first time in two months. He understood.

~

April turned into May, the days were shortening fast, cloud and wind and snow a constant presence, not just at the pinnacle. In one of the increasingly infrequent bursts of bright sunshine, Harry stood on the track above the cottage, staring out towards the river with its flotilla of craft of all sizes, the forest of masts mere pencil lines at this distance.

This was not going to be easy. The sadness in Ellen's eyes was starting to fade. There were moments, recently, when he had heard her laugh with the children, when there seemed to be nothing but happiness in her voice. He watched as she walked up the path towards him. Today there was no spring in her step, no smile; the light in her eyes was dull.

He held out his arm to her, but she ignored it and stood beside him, a distance between them. He wondered if she would be better off in the town with her family, but he could not bring himself to suggest it. If he let her go, she might never come back.

'Ellen,' he said. This would make matters worse.

She moved close and lay her head against his shoulder. He closed his arms around her.

'It's George. He's gone.'

'Gone?' She frowned.

'I saw your father this morning. They don't know which ship he's taken, or where he's gone. He left a letter at the post office but said nothing about when, or if, he'd be back.'

Ellen began to weep, deep wrenching sobs.

Harry held her tight, lost for words of comfort.

He continued to stare at the horizon. 'There are places in Perth where you can stand and look across the river.'

She looked at him, her grey-blue eyes hopeful, trusting. 'Will you take me there?'

He would never go back to Perth.

He spoke slowly. 'Do you think you could leave your family?'

'As long as I have you and the children, I don't care where I am.' She clung to him tighter.

'But your parents, your sisters, you'd miss them?'

'I would get used to it.'

'One day,' he said, 'when we are tired of here, we'll go somewhere warm.'

She buried her face against him and wept quietly as Harry held her. It was best she let it out.

'Harry,' she said, her voice muffled. 'You won't ever leave me?'

'Ellen,' he groaned. 'I won't. Not ever.' He had put this off too long. 'Next summer, when I have money put by, I'll buy you a pretty ring and we'll get married.'

Her eyes glistened, not just with grief. 'Harry, I love you.'

He said it slowly, deliberately. 'I love you, Ellen.'

He had never loved like this. The depth, the completeness— Ellen was part of him.

~

The rest of the year was uneventful, following much the same course as the previous year. The winter held the mountain in a tight grip with rain, icy winds and frequent falls of snow. Only the most foolhardy attempted the hike up the mountain. Harry took work where he could find it, irregular days at the mill in Hobart Town, sleeping on the floor of the front room of the Thompsons' house. Not long after Will's death, they had moved from Watchhouse Lane to a house in Denison Lane off Macquarie Street. The yard gave a clear view of the mountain. When Harry stayed, he would walk out into the yard and look across at it, his thoughts on Ellen and the children. Twice a week, he carried the old couple's rations from the Benevolent Society up to them. The old man and Grannie kept to the cottage, in front of the fire, smoking their pipes and sharing a dram. They wanted nothing more than they had. Harry knew their time was running away. He could not, would not, wish them hurried to their end. He would do his best by them, but once they had gone, a new life would begin for him and his family.

31

December 1880

Christmas arrived. Ellen had no wish to go to her parents' house this year to sit at a table where too many faces were missing. At the Springs, she had little time to think of those she had lost as visitors arrived early with their picnic baskets. Grannie spent most of the day beside Grandad as he sat by the door, puffing on his pipe, telling those visitors who chose to sit, listening with rapt attention, tales of the mountain and of the early days. To hear him talk, he had lived here since Hobart Town's very beginnings.

Boxing Day brought furnace-like heat, fierce winds and no visitors at all. The curtains kept out the glaring light, but inside the cottage it was hot and airless. The walls and roof creaked in the high wind. Outside, trees threshed against the sky. The old couple lay on their bed, reluctant to move. The children flopped on the bed in the bedroom, fretting and whining. Ellen, wearing nothing but a camisole over her stays and her skirt drawn up to her knees, sat on a chair beside them, half-heartedly fanning herself and, when she remembered, the children. Harry went up to the icehouse to bring down some of the remaining ice, but by the time he got back to the cottage it had melted. Still, the water was cooler than what they had in the jug. Evening brought no lessening of the gale, but now the wind was tinged with ice. By morning the mountain was capped with snow and rain poured down over the town.

Harry had gone out to the barn early to chop firewood. He carried in an armful and stacked it against the wall along from the fireplace. He straightened up and looked around at them all. 'The lamp's broken, knocked to the ground in yesterday's wind.'

The old ones both gasped. Grandad turned and stared glumly into the fire.

Ellen stood in the doorway and shivered. The lamp was lying a

179

few feet from the door, broken apart, the glass shattered. 'I hope this isn't an omen for the year ahead.'

Grannie came and stood beside her. 'It is not the New Year yet.' She took Ellen's hand in hers and squeezed it. 'It's more likely the old making way for the new.'

Ellen glanced at her. She wasn't sure the old woman believed what she was saying, but Ellen needed to hear it.

She thought of all that had been lost this year. In a month's time, Will would be gone a year. She missed him. George too. She doubted she would ever see George again. Her heart ached but it was a dull, familiar aching, not the raging torment of near a year ago.

On New Year's Eve, she stood in the dark with Harry and again watched the distant flicker of fireworks over Hobart Town, which from the stroke of midnight would now be known simply as Hobart.

'Here's to a year far better than the last,' Harry said quietly.

'It will be for certain.' She caught his hand and laid it at her waist.

'Oh, Ellen,' he breathed, 'when?' She could hear the awe in his voice.

'Late July or August.' She wanted him to be as happy, as full of hope, as she was. 'It might be a boy this time.'

'It might, but it doesn't matter. I like girls too.' He took both of her hands in his and kissed her gently. 'I suppose we had better be married by then.'

Her heart skipped. He had not mentioned it for months, and she had been afraid to say anything in case his plan was for *one of these days*.

'When do you think?'

'Around Easter. We should have a party too—in town. We'll get the old man and Grannie down there somehow. I'm sure Bob Flanagan would bring them in his wagon.'

Easter was close enough for Ellen to start counting the days.

~

It had been a perfect summer's day, the sky bright and clear. Two large groups had come up the mountain, and they had both paid well. They were gone now, and Harry was outside with Billy. The bread was cooling on the wire tray on the table, the evening meal simmering in the pot, filling the room with a mouth-watering aroma. Ellen walked past the calendar Harry had bought early last month and pinned to the wall. The sixteenth of April was circled. They had decided it was best to wait until Easter was over and there were fewer visitors to the Springs. Each evening Ellen crossed off a day and counted those left. She glanced at the calendar as she passed by. After today, she would have only fifty-five days to wait until Harry married her.

She stepped outside and looked towards the treetops where currawongs called and whooped, her heart soaring with them. She glanced back at Harry. He winked at her and that wonderful butterfly feeling flared in her, no different from the first time she had met him. Harry went back to whittling the short whistle he was making for Billy. The boy was seated beside him, fascinated by the flash of the blade. Harry put his knife down on the bench and gave the whistle a blow. Clear notes tripped out. He passed the whistle to Billy, who blew, his cheeks puffed out and rosy, his chubby fingers waving, no attempt at fingering.

Grannie sat at the other side of the door, pipe in her mouth, Jennie snuggled close beside her. The pair were inseparable. The little girl toddled after Grannie, went everywhere with her, her small hand firmly in the old woman's gnarled hand. As Ellen turned to go back into the cottage, Harry caught her fingers and squeezed them. She bent and brushed her lips against his. She could not find words to express how much she loved him. She took Jennie from Grannie, and settled her onto her hip. The child snuggled against her, her head on Ellen's shoulder.

Ellen looked back across the clearing. A woman stood on the path from the track to the cottage, two bags on the ground beside her. She stared towards the cottage, her eyes fixed on Harry. Ellen glanced at Harry. The colour had drained from his face.

He stood slowly and walked towards the woman, away from Ellen.

32

Eliza stood, her eyes on Harry's face, as he walked down the path.

He stopped about a yard from her, wondering why she had come.

'Eliza.'

'Harry.' Speaking seemed to be an effort for her. She looked past him to the cottage.

Ellen stood in the doorway, holding Billy by the hand, Jennie on her hip. She was truly beautiful.

He didn't want to lose her, lose all he had here.

'Are they your children?'

He turned back to Eliza. 'Only Jennie. The baby.' The fact that he was a father made him happy. 'There's another due later in the year.'

He heard Eliza's sharp intake of breath, saw the stab of pain in her eyes.

'Mother's dead,' she said.

'I'm sorry to hear that.' It sounded weak—more something you would say if someone told you they had lost their cat. But it might explain why Eliza was here now.

He could see the tears welling in her eyes. Once he would have wrapped her in his arms and held her close. He couldn't do it. It was as if she were a stranger.

He supposed he would have to explain what had happened. And after that, she would go away.

'Seeing you're here, you had better come inside.'

He bent to pick up her bags. As he straightened up, he saw undisguised misery in her face. This was not the neat, bossy woman he had left behind. She seemed smaller. Her shoulders sagged, and although her clothes were tidy, there was a crumpled, uncared-for air about her.

He carried the bags to the cottage and placed them on the bench by the door, Eliza trailing behind him.

'Wait here a moment.'

Harry went into the bedroom and stood at the end of the bed, panic swelling in him.

Ellen was piling clothing onto one of the sheets she had stripped from the bed. Grannie sat on the chair against the wall, her arms around Jennie, weeping softly. Billy had crawled onto the bed and was watching his mother, worry written on his small face.

'You can't go, Ellen. It's too late in the day.'

She turned to him, her eyes narrowed. 'I know it's too late. It always was too late, wasn't it?'

He couldn't lose her. 'I want you to stay.'

'And how will that work? Will you sleep between the two of us?'

He closed his eyes. How could he make her understand? He loved her, not Eliza. His marriage to Eliza was dead. It had never occurred to him that she would travel nearly three thousand miles by herself.

'Trying to decide which one of us you'll fuck first tonight?'

He raised his voice. 'Ellen!' Ellen's fierceness, her passion, the fact that she swore occasionally had excited him. But this word ... No decent woman should use this sort of language.

He stepped towards her, stretched out his hand. 'There's no need—'

She slapped his hand away. 'You bastard!'

She wouldn't hear anything he said at present. Tomorrow, perhaps. He would find a way to work things out. He watched as she helped Billy into his coat.

She was leaving him.

'Ellen, I ...' Her look froze him.

'Go to buggery.'

The old man had come in and stood in the doorway. 'I'll walk you down.'

'We'll manage, Grandad,' Ellen said.

'I'm coming with you.' It was clear he would not be argued with.

Ellen kissed Grannie and took Jennie from her. She hoisted the child, well wrapped in a shawl, onto her hip, and slipped her free arm through the knotted loop at the top of her bundle of clothing.

She turned her head away as she moved past Harry.

A weight settled in his stomach. He wanted to say something that showed her that he loved only her, that this situation was not what he wanted but couldn't think how. And, no matter what he said, he knew, at this moment, she would refuse to understand.

The old man grasped his staff and took Billy's hand in his.

Harry followed them out.

Ellen marched past Eliza, standing quietly by the door, as if she didn't exist.

Harry stood in the doorway, staring after Ellen as she walked away from him and disappeared down the track.

~

They started down the Fingerpost Track in silence. Ellen wouldn't think of it now. She would wait until she was safe at her parents' house.

They were halfway down the track when Grandad said, 'I'm sorry, lass.'

'Did you know?' She braced herself for the answer. She didn't want to think that Grandad had kept silent and left her to make a fool of herself.

'I knew he had married years back, but I thought she must have died. He didn't speak of it, so I didn't either.'

'He should have told me.'

'He'd be afraid he'd lose you.' He stopped and leant heavily on his staff. 'He does love you, Ellen.'

'Doesn't do me any good when he has a wife.' She pressed her lips into a tight line and forced down a shuddering breath.

When they arrived at the end of the track, Ellen put her bundle down and hugged the old man, one armed. She looked up at him, his face blurred by her unshed tears. 'Can we come and visit you when they're not here? We are going to miss you and Grannie so much.'

'Of course you can, my lovely.' Grandad cleared his throat. 'And I'll have raspberries ready for you.'

He squatted shakily and shook Billy's hand. 'Now you take care of your mother, my boy, and your little sister.'

He pulled himself upright using his staff and looked along the deserted road. The warmth had gone from the day, and shadows stretched along the road.

'If a cart doesn't come along soon, walk back to the police office—I'm sure they will help.' He turned his head away and brushed his fingers across his eyelashes.

'A ride home with the traps—that would give Dad a laugh.'

Ellen reached up and kissed him on the cheek, squared her shoulders and tramped along the road, Billy beside her.

An ancient wagonette rattled past on its way towards Fern Tree. So late in the day, there would be few carts travelling towards Hobart. She hoped they wouldn't have to walk the whole way. Poor Billy would barely be able to put one foot in front of the other by the end.

A few minutes later, the waggonette drew alongside them. The woman riding in the back leant over and opened the door. 'Do you need a ride into Hobart, dear?'

'Yes, but aren't you going the other way?'

'Hop up,' the woman said, concern on her broad, kindly face. 'No decent person would leave a mother with two little ones walking along a lonely road at this time of the day. It'll be dark long before you get to town.'

Ellen was too grateful to argue they were going out of their way. She knew plenty in Hobart of the *better* sort who would have driven on past without a backward look.

'What's your name, lass?'

'Ellen Woods.' She said it without thinking.

'And I'm Mary Hansen. Now, Ellen, pass me that precious bundle you're carrying and sit up here beside me.'

Mr Hanson, seated at the front of the wagonette, nodded to Billy. 'What are you called, young man?'

The boy stared at him, wary. 'Billy.'

'Billy, would you like to ride up here with me?'

Billy nodded his head furiously. Mr Hansen climbed down and came around to Billy and lifted him onto the seat, tying him to the bench with a makeshift belt. Billy's eyes were shining, a grin on his face at what had suddenly become a great adventure.

As the wagonette bumped along, Mrs Hansen cooed to Jennie, rocking her to sleep in her arms. She smiled at Ellen. 'I have nineteen grandchildren, all angels like this little one once, some not so now.'

It didn't take much prompting and Ellen spilt out her story. She forced back her tears, refusing to let herself cry.

'Ah, lass,' the old woman said when she finished. 'You can be lucky and find one who will stick by you,' she nodded towards her husband, 'but in the end it is your own that matter most, your family who will stick by you and your precious children, not their useless fathers.'

It was her father's view of life.

The wagonette pulled up outside Ellen's parents' house just on dusk.

She lifted Billy down and said, 'Run inside, my darling, and ask Gran for something to eat.'

She took her bundle from the seat and slid her hand through

the loop.

Mrs Hansen carefully lowered Jennie into Ellen's arms.

'Thank you both. You have been so kind.'

'Ah, don't think of it,' Mr Hansen said. 'What's the point of life if you can't do a body in need a good turn?' He tipped his hat and shook the reins. 'You take care of yourself, missus.'

She watched them turn up the street, Mrs Hansen waving back at her.

Mam was standing at the gate. 'Let me take that.' She eased the bundle away from Ellen. 'What's happened, my love?'

Ellen closed her eyes, shaking her head. 'In a minute, Mam.'

In the kitchen, Billy was sitting at the table, devouring bread and cheese. Bessie, beside him, was spreading jam on another slice of bread. She looked up as Ellen walked in. 'We finished tea over an hour ago.'

Ellen shrugged. 'It doesn't matter as long as Billy doesn't go to bed hungry.'

Billy had placed the whistle on the table beside his plate. It was only that she knew it would upset the boy that she didn't toss it in the fire.

She could see them all, staring at her, wanting an explanation.

'He's bloody married. The wife turned up today.'

'The bastard!' Mam spat. 'The misbegotten piece of crap.'

Mary Ann was sitting on the other side of the table beside Jane, both sipping tea.

Ellen glared at her. 'Don't you dare say a word.'

'I haven't said a thing.'

'I know what you're thinking.'

Mary Ann raised her eyebrows and said nothing more.

Ellen knew exactly what she was thinking, smug cow with her sailor born and bred in Hobart, where everyone knew exactly who he was and every little thing he had ever done.

'If George was here, he'd fix him up,' Alice said.

'He would.' But if anyone was going to belt Harry Woods senseless, it should be her. It might feel good for five minutes but he would still be married with a neat little wife.

Jane put her cup on the table, came around and took the still sleeping Jennie from Ellen. 'I'll put her to bed.' She looked over at Billy. 'You coming, Billy boy?'

Billy grinned at her, grabbed his whistle, and jumped down from the chair. He ran to Ellen and planted a jammy kiss on her cheek.

Ellen rested her elbows on the table and held her head in her hands, rubbing her fingers against her forehead. She had the beginnings of a headache. The moment she had seen the woman, seen the look on Harry's face, she had known. His silences made sense. How could she have been so stupid? Will had been right, and she had ignored him.

'Can I cook you an egg and some bacon?' Mam asked. 'Or tea and toast?'

'Tea and toast, please.' Ellen nodded. 'Then I'll go to bed.'

Her father had sat quietly through it all. He stood up, and pushed his chair in.

Ellen looked up. His jaw was clenched, his normally laughing eyes, darkened and hard.

'Dad, don't do anything. I don't want anyone getting hurt, 'specially not you.'

'I've still a bit of fight left in me, lass.'

She didn't say what she was thinking: *But Harry is over twenty years younger than you and hard muscled. He spends his days labouring out of doors, not sitting inside making boots and shoes.*

'Please, Dad.'

He nodded slowly. As he passed behind Ellen, he squeezed her shoulder gently. 'Remember, lass, no matter what happens, we Thompsons stick together.'

Later, Ellen climbed into bed and eased herself between her two children. She turned her face into the pillow and cried herself to sleep.

33

Harry turned back into the cottage. Eliza seated now at the side of the table, stared straight ahead towards the far wall, her hands primly clasped in front of her. Granny was in her usual seat by the fire. Arms wrapped tight across her middle, she watched the flames, tears running freely down her cheeks. The only noise was the bubbling of the pot over the flames.

He felt hollow, as if all that was good in his life had been scraped out of him.

If it wasn't so late, he'd go out and chop some wood, work without needing to think. He went to the hearth and poured water from the kettle into the pot. A tea towel wrapped around his hand, he pushed the pot back from the flames. He didn't want Ellen's cooking boiling dry.

Both women sat in the shadowed room, silent, lost in their own miseries.

Harry lit the lamp on the table and walked outside. He hunched onto the bench by the door and took out his pipe. He'd wait until the old man came back.

The sun was setting and the clearing in darkness by the time his father plodded up from the track. Harry walked into the cottage ahead of him and went to the fire.

As he started dishing up the stew, Grannie groaned and got up from her chair. 'I'm going to bed.'

'But what about your tea?'

She scowled at Harry, her mouth turned down. 'Not hungry.'

'But, Grannie,' he said gently, 'Ellen made this. She wouldn't want you going without.'

Grannie ignored him. She glared at Eliza, her look poisonous, and climbed onto the bed. The old man watched her from his seat at the table, his eyes as sad as hers.

Harry placed a plate in front of Eliza.

She stared at it. 'Thank you.' She was unfailingly polite.

Harry seated himself at the opposite end of the table from his father and began to eat. Meals were usually a time of conversation and laughter, but tonight no one spoke, not even the old man. What could any of them say?

Eliza moved the pieces of meat across the plate with her fork and crumbled the slice of bread Harry had placed on the plate. She ate no more than one or two mouthfuls.

He wiped his bread through the gravy on his plate, looking up as he bit into the crust. Eliza was watching him. Her eyes flickered from the bread to his elbows on the table. Her mouth tightened.

The weight of her unspoken criticism sat on him, as it had for so many of their years together.

She stood. 'Where may I sleep?' Her eyes glistened in the lamp-light.

Where could she sleep? 'In there, I suppose.' He nodded at the door to the bedroom he had shared with Ellen. 'If you need the privy, it's around the back of cottage.'

She sniffed, colour rising up her cheeks as if he had embarrassed her. She picked up her bags and went in to the bedroom.

Harry took the plates over to the bench under the window and scraped the remains of Eliza's meal into the scrap bucket. Such a waste—it was a tasty meal, like all of Ellen's. At least Grannie had said outright that she didn't want anything to eat.

He heard Eliza quietly slip out of the cottage. She should be grateful—he had saved her the embarrassment of asking where the privy was. He had forgotten how coy she could be.

The old man, now in his usual place in front of the fire, puffed on his pipe as he stared thoughtfully at the glowing logs.

The dishes done and Eliza back in the bedroom, the door closed quietly behind her, Harry poured two half mugs of his father's brew and handed one to the old man.

'This is a fine mess.'

Harry grunted. As if he didn't know that.

'What are you going to do?'

'No bloody idea.' He wanted things to go on as they had. And that could only happen if he could convince Eliza to leave and Ellen to come back. He didn't want the life he had left behind in Perth.

The letter from his father three years ago had been a godsend, a chance for a new beginning, just the two of them. They had sat at the kitchen table as Eliza had read it to him.

'We could go for a couple of years and see how it is. It might be a good place to live.'

'No!' She had raised her voice. She hadn't even taken time to think about it. 'Our home is here. We can't leave.'

'Why not? It's not as if we have a tribe of children to make things difficult.'

She drew a shuddering breath.

He supposed that hurt her, but it was a fact. There was nothing stopping them.

'My parents need me.' Her voice quavered.

They didn't need Eliza in particular. 'Your sisters can look after them.'

'They're all busy with their own families.'

He crossed his arms and leant back against the chair. 'And if I say I'm going?'

She seemed to be near to tears. 'I will not leave them to go and live at the other side of the country with strangers.'

He breathed heavily through his nose. 'You are happy for me to leave, to go by myself?'

'You didn't expect me to go with you when you were working on the telegraph.'

'That was no place for a woman—it was a workmen's camp out

in the heat and dust. This is completely different.'

He stood up, rested both his hands on the edge of the table and opened his mouth to speak, but Eliza cut him off.

'Harry, I will not go.' She said each word deliberately.

He was back barely two months and she didn't care whether he stayed or left, probably would be glad to see the back of him. He might as well do exactly what he wanted.

He walked out into the backyard, slumped onto the chair by the door, crossed his arms and stared at the small garden he had planted three years earlier, plants of Eliza's choosing, planted where she wanted them. The old man had said he had a garden on his mountain. It would be a different life, out in the open again, not hemmed in by fences and buildings and everybody else's rules.

Eliza brought out a cup of tea, a peace offering, he supposed.

'Perhaps, in a year or two, once Mum ...' She swallowed and didn't finish.

'*My* father might be dead by then.'

She said nothing to that, but he knew what she was thinking— why did he care so much about a father who he hadn't seen for over thirty years, a father who hadn't bothered to come back for his son? If she said that, he would leave now.

He held his anger to himself, wondering if he had ever come first with her.

Three days later, she came into the bedroom as he was arranging his bed roll.

'You're leaving?' Her voice was sharp with surprise.

'There's a boat to Adelaide at noon.' He glanced up and saw the tears in her eyes, but he didn't care.

She stood there. She didn't plead with him, didn't ask him to stay, didn't say she would miss him.

He tied the straps around his swag and carried it past her. He stopped at the door and turned back, placing a brief, cold kiss on her forehead. He supposed he owed her that.

He walked out onto the verandah and took a deep breath.

Her father was sitting there, basking in the morning sun. He took the pipe from his mouth, coughing. 'Where are you off to?'

'Hobart Town.' He had slung his swag across his back. 'I'm off to see my father. Thought I'd try my hand as a mountain guide.'

'Never too late for something new,' her father had laughed.

'No,' Harry agreed. He had stepped off the verandah, whistling as he had opened the gate and strolled away towards the docks.

~

'Sorry.' Harry shook his head to clear it of memories. 'I didn't hear what you said.'

The old man took another puff of his pipe and said, 'You could take Ellen away from here, somewhere where nobody knows you. No one asks too many questions.'

It was one answer to this problem.

'But how would you two manage here by yourselves?'

'We managed well enough before you came.'

But that was the reason Harry was here—his father had said in that letter that they could no longer survive alone.

'Oh, Dad,' he groaned. 'I don't know.'

The old man stretched, then went outside.

He came back as Harry was banking the fire. 'Where are you sleeping tonight?'

'In one of the other huts, I suppose.' He pushed the fireguard into place.

'It'll be a bit cold. Bunk down on the floor by the hearth.' He tossed Harry a couple of the blankets Grannie had pushed to the end of the bed.

'That's a far better idea. I'll get a pillow from the bedroom.'

Harry eased the door open and walked in carefully.

Eliza lay stretched out near the edge of the bed, fully-clothed, a blanket over her. She made no sound or movement. He couldn't hear the regular breathing of sleep.

He grabbed a pillow and went back out. He lay on the floor near the hearth, the blankets wrapped around him, and buried his face in the pillow. It smelt of Ellen.

He should have gone after her.

He would go down first thing in the morning. But how could he explain? What could he say to her other than he loved her?

How was he going to fix this mess?

34

Harry woke to the morning chorus of birds. He reached for Ellen, but she wasn't beside him. He struggled up, groaning. What was he doing sleeping on the floor? It hit him like the kick of a maddened cow. He eased himself back down, his muscles aching, and folded his hands behind his head, staring into the darkness around the rafters.

It had never felt like it, but he supposed most people would say what he had done was wrong. Ellen had made it so easy. She was unlike any woman he had known—her eagerness, her playfulness, the fact she wanted him as much as he wanted her, that she made no secret of it. He thought of her, standing naked in the bedroom at Christmas a year ago. No normal man could be expected to resist that sort of temptation. She had made him feel there was life still to be lived.

And now? Did he owe Eliza any duty? If she had come with him at the beginning, he wouldn't have got involved with Ellen. His stomach fell at that thought. He was glad Eliza hadn't come.

His anger had been cold and hard. He had come back from Eucla after two years away, and there had been no space for him in Eliza's life. She had her parents to care for, her family to visit, the church and all its activities. There was never time for them to be alone, for him to share with her the things that had astounded him in his time away—the sunsets, the cliffs along the coast, the plants and the animals he had seen out there, the way seawater could be turned into drinking water. She hadn't asked a single question. She cooked and she cleaned for him. She shared his bed, but even that seemed to be nothing more than a part of her routine, something she permitted him, of little interest to her. Even after all that time away, there had been no welcome in her embrace. And afterwards, she had turned her back to him and fallen asleep. On the rare mornings he talked her into staying longer in bed, she rose from the bed afterwards, another duty done, and rushed off to put the kettle on and make breakfast rather than lingering five minutes more. Five minutes of murmured conversation or five minutes of comfortable silence—either would have been enough.

And then there were her rules—so many little rules, even where he was supposed to put his boots when he took them off. All Ellen demanded was that he love her and her children and not stray. Not that he had ever dreamt of that. But Ellen was not his wife—Eliza was. And Eliza was here.

He eased himself off the floor, every muscle, every sinew in his body screaming. He was getting too old to be sleeping rough.

The door to the bedroom was open. Harry peered in. The room was empty.

He walked outside once he was dressed and called Eliza's name. He was answered by the faint laughter of a kookaburra. He went back inside. Her bags were gone.

He thought of the misery in Eliza's face last night as she sat silent, crumbling a slice of bread. What she found here would have shocked her. She was a respectable woman. He supposed he should try to find her. While he didn't want her to stay, he should make sure she was safe. But he needed to see Ellen first.

Harry grabbed his hat and jacket and headed off down the track. There was no sign of Eliza when he arrived at the Huon Road. She would have been offered a ride by the first buggy or cart that came past.

He had gone about a mile along the road when a farmer heading into town pulled up beside him.

'Sure to be a scorcher today.' The farmer shook the reins and his horse trotted on.

'Looks like it.'

The sun was rising into a clear sky, the early morning coolness already burning off.

'You'll want to get your business done and be on your way home well before midday. I won't be spending a moment longer in town than I have to.'

'For certain,' Harry said. He wanted, as quickly as he could, to be back up the mountain with everything as it had been yesterday morning.

~

Ellen sat at the table watching Billy and Jennie as they ate their porridge.

'Mummy,' Billy said through a mouthful of porridge. 'Are we going home today?'

'Don't speak with your mouth half-full, my darling.' She closed her eyes, shaking her head slowly. 'I'm not sure when we are going back.' Or if they were going back at all.

Ellen placed her teacup on its saucer and rubbed her forehead. She was tired, her head ached. She felt as if her morning sickness had returned.

She opened her eyes as someone rapped at the front door. She gazed at her children. Poor little mites. How was she going to support them, see that they were fed and properly clothed?

Mam went out to answer the door. Her voice carried along the passage. 'What do you bloody want?'

It must be Harry.

'I'd like to speak to Ellen.'

Ellen loved his voice. But it didn't matter what she loved—he wasn't hers.

'Why would she want to speak to a lying turd like you?'

She walked up behind her mother and touched her lightly on the shoulder. 'Mam, I'll deal with this.'

Mam glared at Harry. 'You are lucky George isn't here, or you'd be picking teeth from your shit for weeks to come.' She squeezed Ellen's hand. 'Just call out if you need me.'

Harry looked haggard, his eyes puffy and bloodshot. So he hadn't slept well either. Good. Her stomach turned over. Or had he spent the night *welcoming* his wife back?

He stood staring at her, longing in his eyes. He opened his mouth to speak, but nothing came. Her last thought was probably unfair.

Ellen crossed her arms. 'Well?'

'Ellen, I'm sorry.' He swallowed. 'I never dreamt she'd follow me—she refused to come in the first place. I thought it was over.'

'Why didn't you tell me?'

'You would have had nothing to do with me if I'd said, *By the way, I have a wife back in Perth.*'

'No, I wouldn't.' She took a long breath, forcing back her tears. 'What happens now?'

He shrugged. 'She's cleared off. I'm certain she's going back to Perth.'

'I need to know she's definitely gone.'

'Then you'll come back?'

She twisted her mouth. 'I don't know.' She knew she wouldn't be able to help herself if the wife was gone, but she wasn't going to make it easy for him.

'Ellen, I love you.'

'But not enough to tell me the truth.'

'You know the truth now,' he said, a flash of anger in his face.

Was he really just like every other man? Say sorry once and expect to be forgiven straightaway no matter what he had done.

'Daddy!' Billy pushed past Ellen and threw himself against Harry.

Harry squatted and pulled Billy to him. He held him tight, his face pressed into the boy's shoulder.

Jennie had followed Billy to the door and stood, half-hidden, in the shelter of Ellen's skirts.

Harry held out an arm and she toddled across into his embrace.

Ellen couldn't stop the tears that ran down her cheeks. He did love the children, and for that alone she could forgive him nearly anything.

He stood slowly, Jennie still in his arms, Billy close beside him. As he passed Jennie to Ellen, he leant in and brushed his lips against hers. It would be so easy to give herself into his kiss, to relax into the safety of his arms, to believe that Harry was hers.

'Ellen.' His breath was ragged, his eyes as wet as hers. 'I promise you, I will work this out.'

And when he had, would that truly make him hers?

35

Harry walked down to Franklin Wharf, in no hurry. It was as if the longer he took to get there, the greater the likelihood that Eliza would be gone. If she had caught the steamer, that was the end of it. Life could go on as it had. Though she had not said it, he was sure Ellen would come back. Despite the hurt he had caused her, it was clear she still loved him. He deserved every word Beth Thompson had thrown at him.

A steamer lay alongside the Elizabeth Street pier. A group of lumpers were busy loading the last of the cargo onto the ship. Steerage passengers were milling under the open shelter on the pier, waiting to be let on board. Harry made his way through them and back again, looking from face to face. Eliza wasn't there. He approached a man of his own age, leaning against one of the posts of the shed, smoking.

'Excuse me, mate, where's this one heading?' Harry jerked his head towards the steamer.

The man took his pipe from his mouth and said, 'For Bluff.' He must have seen Harry's puzzlement. 'New Zealand.'

'Thanks.' He doubted that another steamer had left this morning. He walked back along the pier and over to the Tasmanian Steam Navigation offices.

There were only a couple of people waiting ahead of him, in a hurry to get out to the New Zealand steamer.

'How can I help you?' The clerk didn't look up. He stood at the other side of the counter, writing in a ledger as he spoke.

'When is the next steamer to Melbourne?'

'Tuesday. The *Southern Cross*.' He continued his writing. 'Do you wish to buy a ticket?'

'No.' Harry's voice echoed, louder than he intended, in the now empty office.

The clerk glanced up. He seemed tired, smudges under his eyes, his hair stuck up at the front where he had repeatedly run his fingers through it. It would be a lousy job for a healthy young man, Harry thought, cooped inside, dealing with disorganised, snotty people.

'Was there a woman in earlier asking about the steamer to Melbourne? So high.' He held his hand level with his chin. 'Blonde hair, blue eyes.'

The young man frowned slightly.

'My wife,' Harry added.

'Ah.' The clerk's face cleared. 'Yes, there was. An hour ago. She didn't buy a ticket, though.'

'Thank you.'

Outside, Harry stood at the edge of the verandah, looking up and down the street. He could go back to the Springs and let her work out what she wanted to do herself. But, he supposed, he should check she was safe. Where would she have gone? Perhaps somewhere she could sit and have a cup of tea?

He walked up Elizabeth Street, his hands shoved deep in his pockets. He glanced through the fence into Franklin Square, and there she was, sitting on one of the wrought iron seats. She was staring up at the statue set in the middle of the ornamental pond at the centre of the garden, her gloved hands folded in her lap, her feet neatly together, her bags on the ground either side of her.

She watched him come towards her, her face rigid with self-control.

He sat himself at the other end of the seat. 'I don't know what—'

'Don't explain.' She looked ahead, her eyes glistening. 'Nothing you say will make me understand.'

'If you had come with me ...'

She turned to him, her face flooding with colour. 'Don't you dare blame me for this. I didn't tell you to set up house with that woman. I didn't place her in your bed.'

'If you had been with me, it wouldn't have happened.'

She glared at him and stood. 'So it is my responsibility to keep you from yourself, to be your gaoler?'

He rose slowly and shoved his hands back in his pockets. 'You might as well be with all your damned rules and orders.' He spoke without thinking, all the petty irritations of the past pouring out. 'Wipe your feet; don't slurp your soup; haven't you had enough to drink; do you have to smoke that pipe; get out of bed we have to go to church. All your rules—even telling me what to plant and not plant in my garden. Our whole lives were run by your rules. And then, the one thing I want, you refuse.'

She closed her eyes, her anger seemed to drain away. Her voice was unsteady as she asked, 'Was our life together so very bad?'

He shrugged. 'Not when we were first married. But after I came back from Eucla, it was as if it didn't matter to you whether I was there or not. Your whole bloody family was more important than me.' He saw her wince at the word but didn't care. 'You wouldn't even go for a walk with me unless you had at least one of your nieces or nephews trailing after us. I thought coming here could be a new life, the two of us together. But you didn't want to be with me—when I said I'd go by myself, you didn't try to change my mind.'

'You didn't try to explain why you wanted to go.'

'You weren't listening to me—you were too busy telling me you wouldn't go.'

'I had my mother to care for,' she said quietly.

'Your sisters could have done that.'

Her chin quivered. 'Have you ever thought what it has been like for me?'

When he didn't answer, Eliza said, 'I tried to be a good wife—I took the best care of you I could. Yet you went off and left me, whistling as you walked out the gate. On top of caring for my dying mother, I have spent the last three years worrying what had become of you, worrying if you were still alive. I prayed for you morning and night. You never left my thoughts. All that time I longed for you.' She swallowed a sob. 'You clearly forgot I existed the moment you walked out the door. You set up house with a pretty young woman as if she was your wife.' Her voice rose, quavering. 'You even had a child with her.' She wrapped her arms around herself, her mouth tight as she fought to control her tears.

A couple of young women strolled into the square, arm in arm, took one look at Eliza and Harry and went out again.

Eliza walked towards the pond and stared down at the bright sky reflected in the water.

Harry hadn't given a thought to what she must have felt when he'd left. He had experienced no guilt at all, convinced she didn't need him or want him, would barely notice that he had gone. And when he had arrived here, it was as if he had stepped into a different world where he had no past. And what he had with Ellen—something so good could not be wrong.

He stared up at the statue. A seagull landed on its shoulder and did its business. Life went on no matter what mess people made of their lives.

Eliza pulled a neatly folded handkerchief from her reticule, wiped her eyes and blew her nose. She turned and faced him.

'What do you want, Harry?'

He had not totally lost the respectability his grandfather had drummed—occasionally beaten—into him. He couldn't bring himself to say, *I want you to go away so I can spend the rest of my life with the woman I love*. Instead, he asked, 'What will you do?'

She was fighting for control, still near to tears. 'I don't know.' She looked at him with the clear blue eyes that seventeen years ago made his heart skip a beat. He could remember what that was like, but those eyes stirred nothing in him now.

'I don't have enough money for my fare home and for a hotel room until the steamer leaves. May I stay at the Springs until then?'

He didn't want that but couldn't afford to pay for her hotel room either. 'S'pose so.'

They went back to the seat, and Harry picked up her bags. 'I need to get back to the Springs, but I have to collect Dad's rations at the Benevolent Society first.'

As he turned towards the street, Eliza took the smaller of the bags from him and slid her hand through his arm. He resisted shaking her away. He couldn't be that cruel.

Harry was aware of the puzzled looks of those who knew him and Ellen by sight as they walked out of the square. Give it a couple of days and the story would be over the whole town.

He left Eliza waiting in the street outside the Benevolent Society depot. He had no intention of introducing her to anyone.

The stores clerk looked up as he walked in. 'Ah, Mr Woods, we were wondering what had become of you. Old Mr and Mrs Woods came down themselves.'

Harry frowned. 'They've collected their rations already?'

'No.' The clerk shook his head. 'They've been admitted to the hospital. They were found collapsed in Anglesea Street at around nine o'clock this morning. The heat and distance, I suppose. I heard Mrs Woods is in a very bad way.'

'I left early ...' He could imagine his father and Grannie waking, seeing both of them gone and thinking he had gone back to Perth with Eliza. He cleared his throat. 'I had business here early.'

'I know what elderly parents are like. Sometimes they fix on an idea and it's hard to get them to shake it.' The clerk came out from behind the counter and opened the door for Harry.

'Thank you, I'd better go straight to the hospital.'

He needed to get back to the Springs as soon as he could—there was sure to be climbers wanting a guide today.

36

Harry was back at the Springs by the late morning. A group arrived not long after wanting to go to the pinnacle and return via Silver Falls as they had arranged for a carriage to collect them from Fern Tree. Fortunately, they were a talkative lot with a constant stream of questions, so there was little time for Harry to dwell on his problems.

He stopped off at the Fern Tree Inn for a drink, then took the longest way back along the Huon Road and up the Fingerpost Track. The clearing was in shadow by the time Harry made it back to the Springs. A lamp had been lit and placed in the window, as if he needed to be guided home. The smell of cooking drifted on the air.

Harry walked in, hung his hat on one of the hooks behind the door and looked around. The room had been swept and tidied, the old couple's bed made with a neatness Grannie had never aimed for. The lamplight glittered on the windowpanes. She had washed the damned window!

Eliza, Ellen's apron over her dress, was scrubbing the table. She glanced at Harry. 'I'll only be a few minutes more, then I'll serve dinner.'

He scowled. 'There was no need to do all this. It's not as if the place is dirty.'

But, of course, it wasn't up to Eliza's standards. Ellen worked from the moment she rose in the morning until she slid into his arms at night. Not only cleaning and cooking but looking after the children, the old man and Grannie and anyone else who wandered up the track. Was it any wonder she didn't have time to wash windows every day?

Eliza's eyelashes fluttered as if she were surprised he hadn't gone down on both knees and thanked her for all she had done.

'I had nothing else to do,' Eliza said evenly, 'and it doesn't hurt to give a place a good clean once in a while.'

He threw his jacket over the back of the chair by the fire and went to the sideboard. He poured himself a half mug of spirit and swallowed it in one long gulp. It burnt its way down his throat. He grimaced, fighting against a shudder. What was he doing? He hadn't even wanted a drink. He glanced back at Eliza.

She quickly looked away and got on with rinsing the soap off the table.

Harry fished out his pipe from his pocket and sat in the old man's chair. He got his pipe going, but there was no pleasure in it. Just as with the spirits, he was smoking to needle Eliza.

Once the table had dried, Eliza spread a tablecloth on it. She placed the lamp in the middle and set two places before calling Harry over. He sat in the old man's chair. Eliza seated herself at the other end.

She bowed her head and began to say grace. Harry didn't wait—he was hungry and he had left all that behind three years ago.

They ate in silence. The vegetable soup, along with Ellen's bread, made a filling meal. He had to admit Eliza was a decent cook. Every time he looked up, she was watching him, her mouth a prim line. Both elbows firmly on the table, he wiped the bowl clean with his crust.

Eliza sniffed and said, 'There's more in the pot if you want it.'

'I've eaten enough.' That sounded unnecessarily rude. He added, 'Thank you.'

She set her spoon down in her bowl. 'It's years since I've used a kitchen like this.' She nodded towards the open fireplace with its crane for the cooking pots and kettle, the large camp oven, the three-legged pots and cast-iron rack standing at one side of the hearth. 'Not since we left your grandparents' farm.'

What could he say to that? He supposed he should be civil. She had done nothing most people would consider wrong.

'The doctor said they could get the old man and Grannie—'

'Why do you call her that?' Eliza interrupted. 'She's not your grandmother. If anything, you should be calling her Mother.'

'Bloody hell, Eliza! She's not my mother.'

Eliza jerked back in her seat as if he had struck her. He supposed he had rarely sworn in front of her. But she was doing it again, telling him what to do, how to behave. 'Everyone calls her Grannie, even women her own age.'

Eliza said nothing. She watched him, her eyes wary.

Harry began again. 'The doctor said they could get the old man and Grannie a place in the Invalid Depot, but the old man won't hear mention of it.'

'Would they be separated?' She rested her hands on the edge of the table, the knuckles of her tightly knotted fingers white.

Harry paused. 'I don't know. I suppose they would keep the men and women separate at night.'

'I imagine they have been together every day for all their married life. It would be cruel to tear them apart.'

'I hadn't thought of it like that,' he said. 'I suppose this will give them a good rest. They won't be allowed home until they are properly well.'

Eliza stood and collected the empty bowls. 'Would you like a cup of tea?'

'No, thank you.' He didn't want to fall into any of the habits of their life together.

He stood and went again to the sideboard, this time pouring himself a small drink. He sat near the fire, now burning low. He drank slowly and smoked his pipe, staring at the glowing logs. Eliza clattered behind him as she did the dishes.

He heard her go outside, the trickle of water as she emptied the washing tub. She came back in and moved around, tidying.

The silence was uncomfortable. Harry wanted her gone. She probably knew that, and there was nothing to be gained by thinking about how that made her feel.

'I'm going to bed now, goodnight.'

Harry didn't answer.

She closed the door quietly behind her.

He drained what was left in his mug and stood, stretching. He would sleep in the old couple's bed tonight. By the time they were out of hospital, Eliza would have left and Ellen and the children would be back where they should be.

God, how he missed them.

~

The next few days were silent. Eliza spoke little; Harry said less.

No matter how many visitors came with their noise and chatter, Harry felt the echoing emptiness left by those he loved. He missed the old man spinning tales to eager visitors, Grannie's rattling laugh, the squeals of the children, Ellen's voice—singing, playing games with the children, running through nursery rhymes, laughing and joking with the old ones, politely passing the time of day with the visitors to the Springs. He missed her beside him, the smile meant only for him, the murmur of her voice in the darkness, her warm breath on his skin, the glorious forgetting in her arms. He missed her.

The weather was perfect over the weekend, and Harry was busy with climbers. Eliza took over what Ellen and Grannie had done without needing to be asked. She baked bread and made scones, poured tea and warmed any food the visitors had brought. She even made raspberry vinegar. Harry thought he would suggest Ellen make it too, when she came back. While Eliza treated the climbers with a quiet courtesy, she avoided conversation with them, retreating back into the cottage as soon as she had given them what they wanted. To those who knew enough to ask where Ellen was, Harry said she was visiting her parents. He said Eliza was family from Perth, knowing that was taken to mean she was his sister.

On Monday afternoon, Harry went down to the hospital. It wasn't a visiting day, but they let him in. The old man was sitting up, talking to an equally ancient man in the bed beside him about the old days. The nurse said he should be fit to come home in a few days. Harry's world would be back the way it should be by then—Eliza would be gone and Ellen home at the Springs.

He went into the female ward and stood by Grannie's bed. She lay with her eyes shut. He couldn't work out if she was truly asleep or pretending to avoid speaking to him.

The nurse, a stern, no-nonsense woman in a starched apron and veil, came over and stood beside him. 'There's no need for you to worry, Mr Woods. Your mother is doing well.'

He saw no point in correcting her. 'When do you think she will be ready to come home?'

'Doctor says if she keeps improving, she should be well enough by early next week.' She smiled at him. 'Young Mrs Woods's visit yesterday seemed to cheer her. It is lovely to see a daughter-in-law taking such care, sitting there holding the old lady's hand.'

'Yes.' Harry blinked hard. He knew his eyes were watery. 'They get on well together.'

It had been in the newspaper that his father and Grannie had collapsed in the street. Ellen would have come in because she knew he wouldn't be able to visit over the weekend. He wondered if, once he told Grannie that Ellen and the children were back at the Springs, she would make a miraculous recovery.

When he got back to the Springs, he went up and, taking his time, walked along the Watercourse Track, checking the channel was clear, before finally going into the cottage.

Eliza was setting the table for the evening meal.

As he hung his hat behind the door, he said, 'I called in at the steamer office, the *Southern Cross* is leaving at four o'clock tomorrow afternoon. I'll get you down there good and early.'

Eliza placed the cutlery on the table and stood rigid, her hands clasped together at her waist. 'I have decided to stay.'

He gaped at her. 'What do you mean?'

'My place is here with you.'

'You didn't think that three years ago.'

'That was very wrong of me. We are husband and wife and nothing you have done can alter that. You were right—there were others who could have cared for my mother. If I had come with you in the first place, none of this would have happened. But I can prevent it from continuing.'

She was staying to spite him.

He walked outside. What was he to do? He headed up the track above the Springs to the place where he stood most evenings, where Ellen would join him, and after a few minutes of companionable silence they would talk about the day. He should grab his swag and go down to Ellen and the children. They could catch a steamer tomorrow. It didn't matter where it was going. Would Ellen leave everything? Leave her family, leave Grannie with no one to care for her? It would be better to tell Eliza to go. Could he do that? Would she leave? And how would that look to everyone? It was one thing for a man to take up with a woman if his wife was absent, another altogether to turn a wife out onto the street so he could live with the woman he truly loved. His grandparents' respectability hadn't left him entirely.

He needed a drink.

Eliza rose from her seat at the table when he went back in. Her eyes were red and puffy, her cheeks wet.

Harry didn't care.

'I'll get you your dinner.'

'Forget it. I'm not hungry.'

He walked over to the sideboard, poured himself a full mug and proceeded to get miserably drunk.

37

March 1881

Ellen rubbed the shirt against the washing board, took a deep breath and rubbed again, more gently this time. The last thing she needed was to wear holes in shirts that were worth more than she could earn in a fortnight. She stopped and stretched, her hands in the arch of her back. She needed a job she could do through the winter. Mrs Bryce, for all Ellen had complained about her in the past, had been surprisingly kind. She had said she couldn't take Ellen back as a laundress—she had replaced Ellen when she left. Her eyes had travelled to Ellen's waist. She said that she had never employed anyone who was as good as Ellen in her care of delicate articles and asked if Ellen would be interested in doing her table napkins, lace-trimmed handkerchiefs and the odd item needing special care? Ellen had agreed willingly, though Mrs Bryce had not been overly generous in what she paid. Her parents had lent her the money to buy a couple of decent flat irons. She needed to be sure her work was perfect for Mrs Bryce. She had placed a small advertisement in the *Mercury* and two young men had answered it, and now she collected their shirts and under-garments once a week to wash and iron. But this would last only as long as the weather was fine and she could hang washing on the line in the backyard.

Harry had said he would come and get her once his wife had left. And she had believed him. She had wanted him to think, if only for a few minutes, that there was a chance she wouldn't go back, make him realise what he had done to her, but she would have packed her things as soon as he appeared on the doorstep. It had been over a month, and she hadn't set eyes on him. Grannie and Grandad were back home, and the wife was there with them.

Ellen stopped her scrubbing and went to the copper. She jabbed at the washing with the pot stick, moving it about.

So much for all his talk of loving her, not being able to live without her, never leaving her. He'd probably argue Ellen had left him. But what would have happened if she had refused to leave? Would the wife have walked away? She pressed her lips tight together. Harry wasn't hers to fight for.

She bent and pushed a couple of pieces of split wood into the firebox beneath the copper.

'Ellen.'

She straightened up.

Alice stood in the doorway of the washhouse, Jennie on her hip, Billy hiding in her skirts. She was the image of the little mother.

Please, Ellen wished, don't let her ever be as stupid as I have been.

'You have a visitor.'

Ellen pushed back a stray hair that had fallen across her face and went to the door. Alice and the children moved back towards the house.

Harry stood beside the door, turning his hat in his hands. He was wearing the red kerchief around his neck that she had made him the Christmas before last. He looked just like he did when he had called to invite her to the circus. Her heart contracted. He wouldn't be waiting at the door if he were free, he would have come straight to her.

Still, the breath caught in Ellen's throat. He was everything she wanted. He had the assured hardness of a man who worked out of doors, weather-beaten and strong. He had been good-humoured and didn't drink himself senseless and brawl. He had loved her, his desire, his passion equal to hers, yet he had been gentle and considerate when it was what she needed.

She wanted his arms around her.

Alice took the children back into the house. Billy stopped when he got to the top step and gazed at Harry.

Ellen could see his longing. His mouth moved. *Daddy.*

Harry hadn't once looked at the children. It was as if they didn't exist—not Jennie, who was his own flesh and blood, not Billy who he had made love him with all his little heart was capable of.

Alice gently drew Billy indoors.

Harry put his hat on the rickety chair by the door and walked towards Ellen, stood two feet from her.

She waited for him to speak.

'I'm sorry, Ellen. Eliza is staying.'

'That's hardly news.'

'I don't want you thinking ...' He gazed into the cloudless sky and groaned. 'I meant every word I said to you.'

'Meant it, not meant it.' Ellen shrugged. 'It makes no difference now.' Her chin quivered. She tightened her jaw, pressed her lips together and kept control.

'I would have married you.'

'But you had a wife. How did you forget that?'

'I didn't forget.' He looked straight at her, his dark eyes filled with the longing she understood so well. 'I thought we were finished. I never imagined she'd follow me.'

Even now Ellen wanted to run her finger along his eyebrows, down the line of his nose to touch his lips. To have those lips on her mouth, to slowly ...

Fat tears rolled down her cheeks.

Harry reached over, wiped them away with his thumb. Ellen caught his hand. She leant towards him, brushed her lips against his. He pulled her to him. Ellen wrapped her arms tight around him, her kisses hungry. She wanted him. She missed him, missed his touch, missed his fingers in her hair. This was what was meant to be. This was right.

She struggled against herself and pulled back from him.

'Harry, let's all run away together. We could go to Queensland. New Zealand.' Her breath was ragged. 'Somewhere far from here where no one knows us.'

Harry tightened his hold on her. 'I can't.'

Anger flared in her. She shoved him away. She had made a fool of herself. Again.

'Why not?'

'I can't leave my father and Grannie. If I go, Eliza won't stay. They'll die up there, alone.'

'So why did you come here?'

'I don't want there to be unpleasantness between us.'

'Unpleasantness! You piece of shit! No unpleasantness after humiliating me like this?' She crossed her arms, held herself tight. 'If you had married me, you would be a bigamist, but everyone would know you deceived me. This way they see me as nothing but a slut who moved in with a married man. If I'd known you were married ...' Her voice quavered. 'I would never ...' She shut her eyes tight, trying to force back the tears.

'I'm sorry.'

'Sorry isn't good enough. It does nothing. It doesn't stop people talking about me. It doesn't pay the bills, put food on the table.' She stopped, stifled a sob. 'It doesn't help Billy when he asks where his Daddy is.'

'I'm not his father.'

Her eyes narrowed. 'I know you're not, but for two years you acted like you were. You treated him like a son, answered when he called you Daddy—he sees you as his father, and he misses you.'

'I'm sorry but there's nothing—'

'I don't want apologies.' She scowled at him. 'The least you can do is help provide for Jennie and this one when he or she arrives.' She spread her open hands protectively across her stomach.

He blinked as if he didn't understand.

'Maintenance, Harry, money to help keep the children.'

'I can't afford it. You know what it's like—there's nothing to spare. I've got the old ones and a wife to support.'

'A wife to support,' Ellen scoffed. 'You have children to support too.'

'But you're here with your parents. It can't cost much at all.'

'There are eight of us living in this tiny house, and there'll be another in August when your next child is born. There's no room as it is. Why should my parents, my sisters, support your children?'

'At a pinch, I can help through summer, but not winter.'

'And until then we live on air?'

'How much do you want?'

'Three shillings a week.'

'I'll work something out.'

'Work something out? Where have I heard that before?'

Harry picked up his hat and walked away. Ellen watched him go. For over two years, she had been certain he loved her, that she was the most important thing in his life. And it had all been lies. She turned back to the washhouse, wishing he had never come.

~

'Ho, ho, listen to this.' Dad flattened his paper on the table, his finger moving beneath the line of print as he read the court report of a man robbed by two young women who invited him home after they had talked him into treating them to drinks at a pub.

'Pity they were caught.' Mam laughed. 'I bet the fool were forty and fat with a face covered by grog blossoms.'

'Some men have no sense at all.' Dad shook his head and went back to reading silently.

Ellen sat by the window, catching the last of the light, barely listening. She carefully darned the heel of an already well-darned stocking and wondered when she would be able to afford new stockings again.

'Ellen.' Mam broke into her miserable thoughts. 'I hear you had a visitor this afternoon.'

Ellen glared at Alice.

'I didn't say anything.'

'It were Mrs Ashwood next door,' Mam said.

'That old stickybeak!' Ellen threw down her sewing. 'Hiding behind the fence was she? Straining to hear every word?'

'She asked if you and Mr Woods had made up, said you were very friendly.'

'I should go in and tell the old busybody to mind her own business.'

'Sit down, lass, people are people. You'd have done the same in her shoes.'

'I wouldn't have told her mother.' She sat back down, picked up her darning, then threw it down again.

'What happened?'

'Harry bloody Woods wanted to *explain*.' She stared at the floor, trying to control her face. 'It makes no difference. He's with his wife. I'm here with his children.' She looked at her mother. 'I asked him for maintenance for Jennie.'

'And?'

'He says he can't afford it, maybe in summer.'

Her father looked up from his paper. 'You need to do something about that. A man has a duty to support his children. Use the courts to our favour for once.'

Ellen frowned, not understanding.

'Get an order for maintenance. Then he'll have to pay.'

Perhaps she should try. It would be the end if he were forced to pay what he wouldn't give willingly. She was a fool. Despite everything, part of her wanted him back, wanted things to be as they had been.

Jennie's squeals and Billy's laughter carried through the open door. Bessie was outside with them playing chasings, catching and tickling them. Ellen closed her eyes. No matter how sour things might become with Harry, she could not regret the relationship for what it had given her.

38

It was the sort of day Ellen had loved at the Springs—blue skies, light, high cloud, not too cold. There would be visitors, but not so many that it interfered with the housework. Grandad and Grannie Woods would be sitting outside, puffing on their pipes, telling far-fetched tales to all who wanted to listen. Ellen missed them. She had loved them—she still did. They were a lot like her parents—people whose lives had been hard, but at heart they were kind and not quick to judge. They had cared for Ellen and for her children, Grannie treating Jennie and Billy like they were her own grandchildren.

The thought of what she had lost, of Harry and his lies, of his wife who could let him go and reclaim him as she wished, made her cranky. She marched along Macquarie Street, giving way to no one, storming past the group of men lounging outside the Denison Hotel as she turned into the lane.

'Give us a smile, love,' one of the younger men called.

'Go to buggery,' she shouted back.

They all laughed as she slammed through the front gate of her parents' house. She kept her eyes on the house, avoided looking up. Wherever she looked in this blasted town, the mountain loomed. Even when it was covered by cloud, she knew it was there.

She opened the kitchen door. Mam was sitting on a chair at the door, watching Billy and Jennie playing in the backyard.

Ellen went over and stared out the door.

They were sitting at the bottom of the steps, Billy spinning the top she had bought him what seemed like a lifetime ago, before she had met Harry. Billy was almost an expert at getting it spinning now. Both were laughing, Jennie clapping when it tumbled onto its side.

Billy was such a good boy. He was three and a half and already protective of his little sister. He still asked for Harry, and it wrung Ellen's heart. The boy loved Harry. He took his wooden whistle with him everywhere. He didn't blow it but kept it like a charm, putting it under his pillow at night.

Mary Ann was over by the stove, making a pot of tea. She had called in, as she often did after work. She was starting to thicken around the waist—she was expecting a child about the same time as Ellen. Now called Mrs Budd, Mary Ann was living with Tom Budd near the end of Liverpool Street, not far from the wharves.

Ellen walked to the sideboard.

'Did you do it?' Mary Ann asked.

'Yes.' She frowned, pulling the pins from her hat and dumping it down on the sideboard. 'I'm going to court next week.' She felt so miserable. In two days, she would have married Harry—instead, she was suing him for maintenance.

'That'll show him,' Mary Ann said.

The legs of the chair scraped across the floor as Ellen pulled it out from the table. 'It's not about showing him. It's about him paying his share.' Her shoulders sagged as she sat down. 'I can't go on living here.'

'Ellen,' Mam said, looking away from the children, 'you can stay here as long as you need.'

'It's too crowded with all of us here and in August there will be another one.' She gently stroked her rounded stomach. 'And when George comes back ...' she trailed off. He had been gone a year and no word from him.

Mary Ann placed a cup of tea in front of Ellen. 'When George comes back, he'll see to your Harry.'

Ellen flushed. 'He's not my Harry.' She crossed her arms tightly across her bosom. He never had been hers, no matter what he said, no matter what she felt for him. He was his wife's, always had been. All the wife had to do was snap her fingers and he followed her like a trained dog.

'When will he hear?' Mary Ann pulled out the chair opposite Ellen.

'Tomorrow, I suppose, if he comes down to town. Otherwise, someone will have to go up to the Springs to tell him.'

'Ah, well, a man must pay for his pleasures.'

Ellen glared at Mary Ann—so smug with her man at home. She wanted to slap her.

~

Ellen was no stranger to the Police Court in Campbell Street. Her father, her mother, her brothers and Mary Ann had all made appearances there, over the years. She had been in the dock herself, aged eleven, with Mary Ann, charged with disturbing the peace in Liverpool Street after midnight, throwing stones at doors. Dad had been angry—he'd had to pay fines of ten shillings and sixpence for Ellen and one pound for Mary Ann. Next time, he said, it would be the House of Correction for them, that would teach them some sense. Even at that age, she had known he didn't mean it. Both he and Mam knew too well what life was like there to let their daughters be locked up if it could be avoided.

Two years ago, the court had moved from the rundown rooms attached to the police watchhouse to the red brick building with its elegant clocktower at the Brisbane Street end of the gaol. The courtroom, previously used for criminal sittings of the Supreme Court, was more impressive than the old Police Court. The walls were painted white with dark wood panelling halfway up. The magistrates' desk was on a platform, a wooden canopy over the desk and a coat of arms on the wall behind.

Ellen sat on the hard bench beside Mary Ann and Bessie. Jennie wriggled and chattered as Ellen jigged her on her knee. She glanced past Mary Ann and saw that Bessie was playing peekaboo. Perhaps it didn't matter if it kept Jennie entertained. As long as she didn't start crying, her noise was unlikely to be heard over the general hubbub of the rest of those who were packed on the public benches.

All those in the court stood, their noise dying away, as the two magistrates took their seats. One of them was the same mongrel who had sentenced poor Will two years ago. Ellen glanced around the court. Harry was nowhere to be seen. Would they order maintenance if he didn't show up? She didn't want to have to face this again.

The magistrates got straight to business. It was easy to understand why some came for a morning's entertainment rather than for business with the court. Ellen listened to the cases and tried not to think of her own. First up was a dishevelled older woman charged with being drunk and disorderly the night before. She looked to have spent an uncomfortable night in the watchhouse cells, her hangover a worse punishment than the five-shilling fine. Next was a man old enough to know better, charged with making a public disturbance by fighting in the street late at night. The old fool should have been at home with his family rather than making a nuisance of himself. The police magistrate, Tarleton, said as much. A cabman was fined two shillings and sixpence for driving his cab at faster than walking pace across the intersection of Liverpool and Elizabeth streets—not much of a crime at all. Case after case was heard. She wished they would all shut up and get on with it.

Then Ellen's name was called.

She stood, Jennie in her arms, and pushed her way past her sisters' knees to get out of the seat. The usher stopped her and told her to leave Jennie behind.

He held the gate open, and Ellen took her place in the witness box. When she turned, Harry was in the dock at the centre of the room.

She had done her best to look tidy and presentable. Her hair was neat beneath her hat, and her gloves were still good. With her coat on, no one could see the patches under the arms of her faded dress. At nearly six months pregnant, Ellen felt bloated and worn out. She clasped her hands above her belly and tried to stay calm.

And there he stood, the image of respectability, his hair and beard trimmed, his clothes neat. He was wearing a vest she hadn't seen before over a spotless shirt with a collar.

'Miss Thompson, what was the nature of your relationship with Henry Woods?' Police Magistrate Tarleton asked.

At least he was polite.

'I lived at the Springs with Henry Woods as his wife for around two years. He asked me to come there and live with him when I told him I was carrying his child.'

Tarleton looked over towards Harry. 'Is this the case, Woods?'

Harry did not answer immediately. Ellen thought for a moment he was going to deny he was Jennie's father.

'Woods, answer the question!' Tarleton snapped.

'Yes, that's about it.' He sounded petulant.

'Did you register the child's birth?'

'I did.'

'The case is clear—you have a duty to support your child.'

'I'm not a wealthy man, sir. I earn my living guiding people up Mount Wellington. I have to support both my elderly parents and my wife on the little I earn as a guide. I cannot afford to pay Miss Thompson anything.'

Ellen glared at him. Miss Thompson indeed!

'And where was your wife while you and Miss Thompson were living your mountain idyll?'

'She was in Perth. She joined me in February of this year.'

Tarleton peered over his spectacles. 'It would have been wise, Woods, although you two were separated, to have heeded your marriage vows. A man who wanders still has to take responsibility for his actions, even if that means supporting two households. Keep that in mind if you are ever separated from your wife again.'

Harry's face flushed, and he clenched his jaw. He kept his eyes on the magistrates.

Tarleton and the other magistrate spoke quietly together then Tarleton said, 'Henry Woods, I order that you pay four shillings a week for the support of the child, the first payment to be made today to the police clerk. In view of your circumstances, I am remitting the court costs in this instance.'

'Sir,' Ellen said, 'I am expecting another child by Henry Woods in August.'

'Come back to the court once the child is born, and we will deal with the matter then.'

Ellen stepped down from the witness box. Harry had already gone. She glimpsed his back as he headed towards the clerk's office.

Whatever he had felt for her had clearly disappeared. All that talk of love and never leaving her and how pleased he was to be a father, all worthless. But this wasn't the place to think of it.

Her sisters were waiting for her in the street.

'That wasn't so difficult,' Mary Ann said.

'No, it wasn't.' Ellen took Jennie from Bessie and twirled about, smiling. She was relieved. She would be getting a shilling more than she had hoped for.

'I can find a place of my own, somewhere not too far from Mam and Dad. Do you want to come and live with me, Bessie?'

Bessie's face lit up. 'I would. I could help with the children.'

Ellen would have just enough to get by. But her satisfaction faded when she thought of Billy. Had he been here, he would have been calling out to Harry, calling him *Daddy*. Of everything that had happened over the past two months what gnawed at her most was the way Harry had thrown Billy off as if he were nothing. Billy had spent more than half his short life thinking Harry was his father. And Harry had made the little boy love him. Now he acted as if Billy didn't exist. Jennie would never know her father and, perhaps, that would be easier. Ellen hoped, with time, Billy would forget too. Harry Woods was nothing but a useless mongrel.

~

Harry went and paid his four shillings to the police clerk in his cramped office. He had known it was over with Ellen when he saw her last, but this put the seal on it. She had her family to support her and the children while he had three people dependent on him. She knew how hard it was for him to make ends meet, yet she had persisted with this. He had no idea how he would find the money once winter set in.

He was relieved to see Ellen and her sisters were well away by the time he stepped out into the street. He started as a burly hand slapped him on the shoulder.

'Lucky for you George Thompson isn't in town,' Bob Flanagan laughed. 'It would have been more than four shillings to pay.'

Harry glowered at him.

'Don't look so shame-faced, Harry.' Bob grinned. 'You're not alone—you have your fun, you pay the price.' He chuckled and walked on.

That didn't make Harry feel any better. It was fine for Bob to laugh from the sidelines—he was not the sort who would ever find himself in this sort of predicament.

Eliza had offered to come with him to court. He supposed she saw it as her duty, but he wouldn't have asked it of her. It would have been salt to her wounds to hear Ellen talking of living with him as his wife so matter-of-factly.

The situation between Harry and Eliza had settled back into the pattern of a marriage. He couldn't say he loved her, but he was sorry for her. He would never have managed at the Springs without her—she was hardworking and courteous to the visitors. They had lived with long silences until the old man was back home. He was polite to Eliza from the beginning, chatted to her and told her his tales, asked her about her family and her life back in Perth. Harry could see her relief that someone was treating her as just another person, not an intruder. The stiffness faded from her face, and she smiled at the old man, occasionally laughing softly at his stories. Grannie barely spoke to her, any thanks was begrudging, and it was obvious in every action she wished Eliza gone. Harry glimpsed sadness beneath the calm surface. It was there in her eyes whenever she looked at him.

A few days after Harry had visited Ellen, the old couple had gone to bed early. The days were drawing in and the nights were cold. He had pushed the fireguard into place and turned to find Eliza standing beside the table watching him.

She stood stiffly, the way she had when she announced she wouldn't leave him.

She stared towards the fire behind him as she said quietly, 'I know how cold it must be out in that hut. I wouldn't want you to catch a chill or worse.' She paused, drew a deep breath and rushed on. 'If you wish, you can sleep in the bedroom with me. It would be much warmer. I would put a pillow between us, in the middle of the bed.' By the time she finished, her face was flaming red.

'Thank you, Eliza. That would be more comfortable.' He was aware of what the offer had cost her. She hadn't raised her eyes the whole time she was speaking.

When he came back from the privy, she was already in bed, her face to the wall, the pillow at the centre of the bed.

The next night he had woken, aware of her silent sobs shaking the bed. In all he had done, he had never thought to make her so unhappy. He had truly believed she didn't care what he did. He moved the pillow, only intending to hold her and comfort her. She hadn't pushed him away and with her in his arms it was natural to try to kiss away her tears. He hadn't meant to go further but Ellen wasn't coming back and Eliza was his wife and she hadn't objected. Afterwards, she had curled into a ball and wept again. He had felt such a bastard.

Scowling, Harry pulled his hat down and headed away from the court towards the Benevolent Society to collect the old couple's rations.

39

Harry slumped in his chair and stared at the banked fire, too tired to move. It had been a bitterly cold day, snow covering the mountaintop to well below the Springs. He exhaled loudly. He should get into bed. It would be warmer there but it took too much effort. He had been down the mountain today to collect the old couple's rations and had picked up a day's work at the mill. Jack Davis, the foreman, was a decent bloke. He had told Harry to call in whenever he was in the town and he'd see what he could find for him to do. Harry made sure he earned his pay. With a day's work a couple of times a week, the odd rabbit or wallaby he caught and the winter vegetables, they could get through the winter. Just. What was breaking him was the maintenance. Right from the start he had found it difficult. He had managed for the first five weeks but had caught a heavy cold—he could barely make it to town, much less work, so he had let the payments go. Ellen had ordered him to court and argued she couldn't survive without the money, and he had been forced to pay the twelve shillings he owed, clearing out nearly everything he had saved to tide them through winter. It was an impossible task—he was already behind three weeks again. He wondered if he could go back to court and explain exactly how things were. They might not let him off completely but, perhaps, they would reduce it.

He felt a hand on his shoulder. He placed his hand over Eliza's gloved hand and looked up at her. Her face was pinched, the tip of her nose red.

'You should be used to this, being English.'

'Harry.' She shook her head slowly. 'I was seven when I arrived. I can barely remember England. I am as used to the heat as you.' She dragged a chair over beside him, pushed her toes, clad in a pair of his socks, towards the hearth and pulled the blanket draped over her nightgown tighter around her.

'And winter has a long way to go. We'll be scraping a foot of snow from the door before it's over.'

He stretched his hand towards her and ran the back of his finger down the curve of her cheek. She turned her head and smiled weakly. In the glow from the fire, he could see the pain in her eyes, the unspeakable disappointment. She had not berated him since the day in Franklin Square. It would have been easier had she screamed and abused him for his faithlessness. Ellen would have taken after him with the old man's staff if their positions had been reversed. Instead, Eliza had silently wept in the dark, and he had slowly realised what his actions had done to her. It left him with the uncomfortable feeling that he didn't deserve her.

'I can't leave, Eliza, not now.' He nodded towards the bed in the corner where the old man snored loudly, Grannie asleep beside him.

'I know that.'

'If it's too hard for you,' he forced himself to say it, 'you could go back.'

She gave a slight shake of her head. '*Whither thou goest*, Harry.' She stood up. 'Come to bed. It will be warmer there.'

He knew Eliza was merely stating the obvious but he couldn't help himself. He answered as if she were Ellen. 'Is that an invitation?'

Eliza gave a slight gasp—he was certain it wasn't one of disgust. She lowered her eyelashes, blushing deeply.

He stood up, not so tired now, and pushed the fireguard in place. When he turned, Eliza was already in bed.

~

Harry arrived at the Police Court after Ellen and took a seat at the back of the public benches, well away from her. She had come alone, without her sisters or Jennie, and Harry realised he was

229

disappointed. Except for a glimpse in the court in April, he hadn't seen Jennie properly since February. She would have grown and would be walking well and talking. If he were honest, he missed Billy more. He had been so uneasy the day he had visited Ellen that he had ignored the children. It would not have helped to hold them tight, to have Billy crying for him, calling him *Daddy*. No matter what he felt for the boy, he was not his concern now.

He looked at the magistrates, Tarleton and Robertson and a third, Guerdon, with their smart jackets and starched collars. He wondered if any of them had a mistress. If he were a rich man, he could have a wife and a mistress. Set them both up in style. Be a proper father to his children. Of course, it would have to be kept a secret from Eliza. Would Ellen mind sharing him as long as he took care of her and the children?

Harry jolted out of his rather pleasant daydream as his name was called.

He stood in the dock and began by saying he would be happy to continue paying at the current rate if he had the money. 'Some weeks I don't have enough to pay it. I have to support my parents and my wife. The work guiding climbers on the mountain has stopped. No one comes up there in this weather. My parents are feeble, and my wife is caring for them, otherwise she would come down and get a job so we could make sure we had enough for the payments.'

Guerdon cleared his throat. 'It's a rum thing for a good woman to be working to pay for her husband's illegitimate children.'

Harry looked at the floor, hoping they would take Eliza's situation into their calculations. 'I can't work every day as I have to take rations from the Benevolent Society to my parents. We just get by.'

'Have you considered bringing them to the Invalid Depot?' Tarleton asked. 'They would be well cared for there.'

'I've considered it, but my father says he has lived the best part of his life on the mountain and will die and be buried there.'

'Sometimes the elderly won't do what is best for themselves,' Guerdon added.

'Very well,' Tarleton said, the other two nodding, 'we will vary the amount to half a crown. It will stay at this level for the months of July, August and September. It will revert back to four shillings a week from October.' He peered over his spectacles at Harry. 'Work should have picked up by then?'

'Yes, sir, things should be improving by October. Thank you, sir.'

'Do I get any say in this?' Ellen grasped the wooden barrier in front of the public benches and pulled herself upright. 'I can't manage on two shillings and sixpence a week.'

She looked tired. Her face was gaunt, but her dress strained across her bosom and belly. She must be very near her time. His tamped down feelings for Ellen flickered weakly to life. He wished he were rich enough to give her what she needed.

'You will have to make some provision for the child yourself,' Tarleton said evenly.

'Do you think I am not doing that already? And how much work can I do?' She seemed to be near to tears. 'Look at me, this baby is due in a couple of weeks.'

All three scowled at her.

'I didn't get this way by myself,' she snarled.

Tarleton looked down at the papers in front of him, then over at Harry. 'Woods, you do still owe arrears of maintenance. This is to be paid forthwith or, in default, fourteen days imprisonment.'

'Thank you, sir,' they both said at once, Ellen glaring over at Harry.

Harry left the courtroom and went to the clerk's office to see if he could defer payment until Friday. If he could work every day for the rest of the week, he could clear his arrears. And, fortunately, Tarleton had halved what he owed because the reduction was for the whole month of July, and July was nearly over.

~

Ellen sat at the kitchen table in the dark, her head in her hands. There was no money to buy candles or oil for the lamp, so Bessie and the children had gone off to bed as soon as the sun had set. She had taken the house when the court had first awarded her maintenance, but it had become a struggle to pay the rent. It wasn't as if it was anything flash. In Liverpool Street, on Moodie's Row, it was weatherboard, two rooms, no washhouse, no stove, only an open fireplace. It did have a front yard, but the back was shared with the other seventeen houses in the row. It was there that the single tap and the five privies that served them all were located. The house was barely furnished, and Ellen had no hope of making it more comfortable.

She shivered and hugged her shawl tighter.

She didn't know what she was going to do. She had no work. Once the damp weather had set in, she had nowhere to hang the washing so the laundry work had dried up. Mrs Bryce had been apologetic, but she'd said she had nothing else she could offer Ellen. Ellen doubted Harry would ever pay the maintenance regularly. He had paid the first five weeks, then stopped at the beginning of June. She had gone to court three weeks ago, and he had been forced to pay the twelve shillings owing but had paid nothing since. And now he had spun his hard-luck story to the court, they had halved what he owed her. Apart from the rent, she had the children to feed. They were both growing fast and needed new clothes. New clothes! All they would be getting was someone else's cast offs either from the pawnshop or the second-hand dealer. And Billy's shoes were worn out despite her father's mending. She gave a bitter laugh—all he would be getting was canvas shoes with only leather toes and him a shoemaker's grandson! Those sleek mongrels on the bench would never have known a moment's want, what it was to struggle to feed and clothe small children, put a roof over their heads and keep them warm and safe. She would have to see if she could get help from the Benevolent Society, but she was terrified that their answer would be to take her babies from her and give them to a stranger to care for.

And she was about to bring another baby into this mess, a poor wee mite who deserved better than Ellen could give him or her. All she could see ahead was darkness. Ellen crossed her arms on the table, laid her head down and wept.

40

Ellen woke to the sound of the door clicking shut. It was still dark outside, but she could hear Bessie in the kitchen, stoking the fire to life. As she eased herself out of bed, an ache began in her belly. She closed her eyes, spreading her fingers wide, holding on to herself as the pain swelled then slowly ebbed away. It was strong for a first pain. Perhaps they had started in her sleep. Her dreams had been troubled, but when weren't they?

She walked over slowly and opened the door. The kitchen was dark, the only light the glow of the fire.

'Bessie.'

Bessie looked up from the table, where she was spreading jam on two slices of bread in the gloom.

'It's started. Run and get Mam and tell her to bring someone to mind Billy and Jennie.'

Bessie blinked a couple of times. Sometimes it took Bessie a few moments to understand what needed to be done. She opened her eyes wide and almost sprang across the room, grabbing her hat and coat from behind the door.

'I'll be late for work,' she said as she swiped up the bread and jam.

'Tell her your sister's in labour.'

'Mrs Shaw will still dock me,' Bessie called as the door slammed behind her.

The kettle hanging over the fire hissed as it started to boil. Ellen took the teapot from the table and placed it on the hob. She poured water onto the leaves Bessie had already added.

She eased herself onto a chair at the table and, once the tea had drawn, poured herself a cup, stirring in a spoonful of sugar. Last week, Mr Witt from the Benevolent Society had arrived on her doorstep. A serious man, older than her father, he had walked in and looked around him, judging the place with a single glance. Billy and Jennie, who had been playing in the yard with a ball Bessie had found in the street, followed him in. They'd come straight to Ellen and stood beside her. She'd placed her hands on their shoulders, keeping them close.

Mr Witt had seated himself at the end of the table and taken out his notebook. He'd glanced at the children's bare muddy feet and Billy's patched pants, and asked how Ellen was managing, whether Mr Woods was paying his maintenance. Ellen had answered honestly. Mr Witt had a reputation for being able to immediately tell if a person was lying. He'd told Ellen to present herself at the next meeting of the Benevolent Society committee to request assistance. She had blurted out her greatest fear, that if she did that, they would take her babies from her. He had assured her no one would be taking her children. Children were better off with their mothers, provided those mothers weren't drunkards or living an immoral life.

So Ellen had gone to the Benevolent Society's depot in Bathurst Street where a group of clean, respectably-dressed and well-fed men questioned her thoroughly—what money she had, what she spent it on, who else she could turn to for help, was she drinking, was she *entertaining* men? She'd kept her answers polite though she wished she could have told them where to shove their prying questions, but pride was a luxury that would not feed her children. They had granted her rations. She was to come to the Benevolent Society depot to collect them twice a week. They would not be handed over to anyone else attending on her behalf. Ellen had left with sugar, tea, oatmeal, two loaves of bread and a jar of soup made in the depot's kitchen. Two days later one of the ladies from the Society had come to her door with a couple of nightgowns for the baby and clothing for the children. She had even brought a pair of barely worn shoes for Billy. And then Harry had paid all he owed at the end of last week, so Ellen could face the next few weeks without fear of being tipped out into the street.

She sipped her tea, savouring the heat and the sweetness, when another pain gripped her. She wished her mother would hurry. She was sure these pains were worse than her last time, but perhaps she had forgotten.

The children were still asleep when Mam arrived, Alice with her. Mam woke Billy and Jennie and made them porridge for breakfast while Alice was sent for the woman Mam had organised.

Alice took the two children off home once Mrs Miller finally appeared. She was not a trained midwife, but a woman who had helped at so many births there was little she didn't know. Stoutly built and of Mam's age, she was one who expected people to do exactly as she told them. She pulled a large white apron out of her bag, tied it around her waist and ordered Ellen onto her bed. She lifted Ellen's nightgown. 'Knees apart. You know what to do, Ellen. How often are these pains?'

'Quite close. I think this one is in a rush to get out,' Ellen gasped as another pain hit her.

'It will be a few hours more.' Mrs Miller straightened up and tugged the gown down to Ellen's knees. 'I'm dying for a cup of tea.'

Between cups of tea and trips to the privy, Mam and Mrs Miller seemed to have a fine time gossiping about old friends and neighbours, whose children were up to no good, whose had done well for themselves and who among the good and the great had secrets everyone but their spouses knew. There were a few snippets Ellen wanted to know more about, but she didn't have the energy to ask. She would ask Mam later—if she remembered.

They walked with Ellen, one at each side, helped her on the bed when she needed to lie down, tried to tempt her with cups of tea, and toast and jam. As the morning wore on, all she knew was the rolling waves of pain. She wanted it over. It was worse, it had to be worse than before. She couldn't remember. She groaned and swore and screamed. She was alone. There was no one to stand beside her and protect her and love her and her baby.

But Mam was beside her, Mam holding tight to her hand, brushing her hair from her face, crooning to her like she had when Ellen was a child.

It went on and on.

She heard her own scream and, rising above it, the bellow of a baby. Her sobs now were laughter. 'My baby.'

'It's a girl,' Mrs Miller announced as if she had done all the work herself.

'A wee lassie,' Mam laughed. 'And a bonny one too.'

Ellen held out her arms and Mam lowered the blood-slicked child, wrapped in a towel, onto her chest. Ellen's arms encircled the baby. 'My beautiful girl,' she laughed. Sorrow slid beneath the happiness. The child had a head of dark hair, Harry's hair, his colouring too. Oh, Ellen had loved him, perhaps beyond reason. Once.

Late in the afternoon, the family all trooped in—her parents, her sisters, her children. All the people she cared for most in the world were in the room, all except George. She wondered where he was now, as she often did, and hoped he was safe and happy.

Ellen lay against the pillows, the baby in the crook of her arm. Billy and Jennie tiptoed around the bed, their small faces serious.

Ellen gently brushed her hand over the mass of fine dark hair and held the tight-wrapped bundle so the children could see the baby's face. 'This is your baby sister.'

'Little baby,' Jennie said, wide-eyed.

'Both you and Billy were as little.' Ellen smiled at him. 'But look at you now. It won't be long and this one will be big enough for you to play with.'

'What's her name?' Billy asked.

'Elizabeth, like your Grandma and your Aunty Bessie.' It was not a name Harry would have wanted, but he no longer had a say.

'We'll call her Lizzie so we don't get all these Elizabeths mixed up.'

The children climbed carefully onto the bed for a closer look at their sister.

Ellen blinked back tears. Her three children, three fatherless mites.

'Don't cry, Mummy.' Billy crawled up the bed and put his arms around Ellen's neck. 'I'll look after you and the baby.'

The tears ran freely down Ellen's cheeks.

41

September 1881

Harry dumped the sack of rations on the table along with a few other bits and pieces he had bought: jam, bacon, cheese and tobacco. A climber had arrived last week wanting a guide to the top, the first in three months. Things would pick up from now.

He slapped a sheet of paper on the table beside the sack.

'Look at that,' he said to Eliza.

She picked up the sheet and read it. 'You know what this is?' She looked at Harry, a deep line between her brows.

He nodded. 'Yes. She wants more money—for the baby.'

Grannie turned from the fire, took the pipe from her mouth, 'Ellen had the bairn?'

'Last month.' It came out as a grunt.

Her old face broke into a broad grin. 'A boy or a girl?'

Eliza was watching him closely. He didn't dare show the mixed feelings he had. 'Don't know, didn't ask.'

Grannie scowled. 'So you won't know the bairn's name?'

'No,' he lied. It was a girl called Elizabeth. A poor little creature who would never know him.

Eliza must have read his thoughts. Her face hardened. 'Can you be certain it's yours?'

Harry blinked. He hadn't realised she nursed bitterness towards Ellen.

Grannie turned in her seat and stared, her eyes boring into Eliza.

Eliza sniffed. 'She's had children by other men.'

'Only one other child.'

'One child, then, but who knows how many men she has been with?'

If looks could kill, Eliza would have been dead a hundred times over. Grannie got up and stamped out of the room.

'There's no need ...' He knew Ellen had only ever had eyes for him. He had never doubted her feelings for him, not for a moment. Right to the end. He didn't doubt them now. She never hid what she felt.

Eliza spoke quickly. 'I'm pointing it out because if we have to beggar ourselves to pay for these children, you want to be certain they *are* your children.'

The old man rose slowly from his seat and, shaking his head, followed Grannie outside.

~

A murmur ran through the courtroom.

Ellen gasped as Harry repeated, 'I don't think the child is mine.'

'What! You bastard! You know she's yours. Everyone knows she's yours.'

The baby, wrapped in a shawl in Ellen's arms, woke and started squalling.

'Quiet!' Police Magistrate Tarleton bellowed. 'Control yourself Thompson or I will have you charged with contempt of court, obscene language and whatever else I think appropriate.'

'But, sir,' Ellen's voice was swollen with tears. 'Lizzie *is* Harry's child. I have never been unfaithful.' She rocked Lizzie, drawing as much comfort from the movement as the child.

'We don't have time for this now,' Tarleton snapped. 'Come back to court with witnesses on Friday, and we will examine the matter further.'

Ellen flounced out of the court ahead of Harry. Once in the street she turned and waited.

When Harry walked through the door, she pounced, pushing Lizzie towards him. 'Look at her, will you? She looks like you— same skin, same hair.'

He looked away. He wouldn't look at the baby, wouldn't meet Ellen's eyes. 'Could be anyone's.'

'So. You are going to perjure yourself to get out of paying?' She felt absolute contempt for him. 'You low gutter-crawling mongrel, you will be on oath.'

She walked away from him but swung back, her face contorted with anger. 'You are lucky George isn't here.'

She hated Harry Woods. She hated him so much.

~

Thompsons rarely faced court alone, and today the whole family had come, all except Mary Ann. She was at home mourning the loss of Rose, her tiny baby who had died within twenty-four hours of birth. Ellen had hugged Lizzie tight when she heard. Life was hard, but she knew her good fortune in having healthy children.

Her family all told the same story, all said that Ellen had been besotted with Harry, would never have looked at another man. Because it was true.

Harry had brought no witnesses. His wife hadn't come to stand by him.

As Dad stepped down from the witness box, Police Magistrate Tarleton stared to the back of the courtroom and called, 'Are you here to give evidence in this case, Mrs Woods?'

'That I am, sir.' Grannie hobbled forward, leaning heavily on her stick.

Ellen felt the ground fall away beneath her feet. Grannie was going to say whatever Harry had forced her to. She glanced across at Harry. He seemed surprised and a little wary.

As the usher led Grannie to the witness box, Tarleton said, 'Get Mrs Woods a chair.'

Once she was seated comfortably, he asked, 'Were you present with Ellen Thompson the whole time she lived at the Springs?'

'Aye, I was. A lovely lassie she is too, and such sweet bairns.' She smiled over towards Ellen.

'Your son says he doubts that the child born last month is his.'

'Ach, no,' Grannie said, 'his wife put him up to that.'

Tarleton raised an eyebrow. 'To your knowledge, Mrs Woods,

did Thompson show an interest in or act improperly with any of the male visitors to the Springs?'

'Never, sir. She loved young Harry, had eyes for no one else. She was always with me when there were visitors, serving the food, helping the ladies. If I'd had a daughter, I'd want her to be just like Ellen.'

When Tarleton had finished his questioning, Grannie shuffled away, out of the court.

Ellen blinked back tears, aware of the great effort it had taken for Grannie to get here.

Harry was examined next.

'Woods, when you were living with Miss Thompson, did you suspect her faithfulness?'

Harry paused.

Thinking how best to lie, Ellen thought. Or trying to remember what his wife had told him to say.

'No, but I might have been deceived.'

'Just like you deceived our Ellen,' Bessie called from the gallery.

Ellen tried not to smile. *That's my sister.*

Tarleton scowled into the public benches, tapping his fingers on the bench.

'Woods.' He paused, his eyes narrowed with concentration as he stared at Harry. 'Were there occasions when, with the benefit of hindsight, you now believe Miss Thompson went off with other men?'

'Not for certain, but she did have a child by another man.'

'When?'

'The boy is now four.'

The magistrate looked down at the papers on the bench in front of him. 'This is the boy, William John Thompson?'

'Yes.'

'That is irrelevant. The boy was born well before you arrived in Hobart.'

'But it says something of her character.'

'I wouldn't push too hard on character, Woods,' Robertson, the second magistrate, said. 'He who is without sin, as they say.'

'The family is not respectable.'

'We all know the Thompsons.' Tarleton breathed through his nose as if he was losing patience. 'I doubt you were unaware of that when you commenced your liaison with Ellen Thompson. Do you now dispute the paternity of your elder daughter?'

'No, sir.'

'Bring the child here.' Tarleton nodded towards Ellen.

Ellen walked to the bench and pulled the shawl clear of Lizzie's face.

'Come here, Woods.'

He looked from one to the other.

After a murmured exchange with Robertson, Tarleton said, 'Woods, I am satisfied this is your child. I order that you pay into the hands of Mr Collins, Clerk of the Police Office, the sum of four shillings weekly for the maintenance of this child. The first payment is to be made tomorrow. From the first of October, you are to pay eight shillings a week for the maintenance of both of your children.'

Ellen could have wept with relief.

Harry turned and strode from the courtroom.

The Thompsons were slower in getting out of their seats. Ellen, last to leave, noticed Grannie sitting on a chair outside the court, to one side of the door.

She grinned at Ellen. 'That young usher got me a chair, thought I looked a bit unsteady. Said I could sit here till I felt fit to leave.' She gave a soft cackle. 'And himself was in such a temper, he didn't even see me here.'

Ellen didn't want to think about Harry. She bent and kissed Grannie on the cheek. 'It's wonderful to see you again, Grannie.'

'Aye, it's grand to see you too. Me and the old feller, we miss you and the wee ones.' She looked longingly at the bundle in Ellen's arms.

'Here, hold her.' Ellen passed Lizzie to her.

Grannie gazed down at the child and pressed her dry lips to the child's forehead. 'May all the blessing of our Lord touch your life. May He send His angels to protect you on your way.' She looked up at Ellen, her eyes brimming. 'No matter what happens Ellen, you will always be in my heart.'

~

Harry paced back and forth from the cottage to the track, went off into the barn and furiously chopped wood, came out and paced again.

He moved in front of Grannie as she struggled up from the track, blocking her way. 'What did you think you were doing?'

The old woman jutted her jaw out. 'Telling the truth.' She shuffled past him, puffing, stopping every few yards and leaning on her stick.

He moved to grab her arm, but the ferocity of her look left him speechless.

When she got to the bench by the door, she fell onto it, gasping for breath.

The old man got up and went into the cottage. Within seconds, he was back with a mug, filled to the brim with his *mountain dew*, without doubt.

Grannie's hand shook as she took it. She smiled at the old man. 'I'd better be careful. It'd be a waste to spill any.'

Harry stood, hands on his hips, scowling at her.

'You know that bairn is yours,' she said. 'Did you want me to lie for you?'

'I didn't ask you to lie, did I?' he snarled. 'There was no reason for you to go down there at all.'

She turned to Eliza. 'You are a good church-going woman— you wouldn't want a man to lie on oath. If I'd not spoken up, he would have risked his immortal soul,' she added with a gleam of triumph.

Eliza, beside him, drew a sharp breath.

He could imagine how she felt being lectured about sin and souls by a woman with the sort of past he was sure Grannie had.

'I didn't lie,' Harry said, his teeth gritted. 'All I said was that I couldn't be sure.' Eliza might have suggested it, but he had seen the sense. How could he be absolutely certain?

The old man was puffing on his pipe, his eyes moving from Harry to Grannie and back, clearly enjoying the whole exchange.

Grannie turned to him. 'I saw the bairn, a beautiful wee thing. Ellen's called her Lizzie.' Her face shone with happiness.

Eliza walked away, into the cottage. Harry had no doubt that, although she didn't speak of it, this talk of his children hurt her. And no matter what she did for Grannie, the old woman wanted Eliza gone and Ellen back. She didn't seem to understand, or didn't care, that he now had to pay Ellen twice as much as he had been, money that could have been spent making life more comfortable for her and for his father.

Harry stalked off to the woodshed to lose himself in the swing of the axe and the clean scent of split wood, to forget the women of this damned island and the constant need for money.

~

Ten days later, Ellen stood in the office of the Registrar of Births, Deaths and Marriages, doing her best not to swear at the pale-haired young man behind the counter with his sad attempt at a moustache barely visible above his lip.

'No, Miss Thompson, the child has to be registered in your name.'

Ellen was sure he placed extra emphasis on the *Miss* as he carefully ruled a line in the spaces where the father's name and occupation should be written in the ledger.

'Everyone knows Harry Woods is Lizzie's father.' Her face

flushed. 'He has been ordered to pay maintenance for her. That is the court saying that my daughter Elizabeth is his child.'

'That's as may be,' his finger stroked the invisible moustache, 'but you will have to convince the father to come in and register the child if you want her to be known by his surname.'

Ellen glared at him. 'How likely is that, considering the way the bastard has behaved?'

The clerk sniffed and pushed the ledger towards her. Ellen nearly broke the nib when she made her mark. No matter what this pathetic halfwit said, her daughters would be known as Woods.

42

February 1882

Harry had worked hard through the spring and early summer clearing out, mending and painting the hut that stood beside the cottage and Eliza had made curtains and a bed cover. It was clean but basic overnight accommodation. Eliza had said, though, that most visitors would likely view it as nothing more than a painted shed. They needed to turn it into the sort of place where respectable ladies would be happy to stay overnight.

The days were now warm and long. The number of visitors had increased steadily and with them the amount of money they were earning. Many stopped at the Springs for refreshments—some brought food to be heated; others satisfied themselves with the tea, coffee and scones provided by Eliza. Just as many brought their own picnic baskets and needed nothing more than a cup of tea. And, worse, some brought their own guides from town.

The old couple did little except sit in the sunshine and talk to the visitors. Those who enjoyed their stories passed coins to them, which they gave to Harry to buy tobacco and the occasional flask of rum. The old man still shuffled out to his still, but Harry suspected, this winter might be a dry one as, with the amount he was paying Ellen, there was no money spare to stock up on the extras needed for the old man to distill his *mountain dew*.

Harry was certain those who came appreciated Eliza's courtesy and her care for their comfort. She was not as talkative with strangers as Grannie was once she got going or as Ellen had been. She never mentioned what he had done but he caught her, at times, watching him, sadness in her eyes.

She tried to go down to All Saints Church in Hobart at least one Sunday a month. She spoke of friendships she had made there with a couple of the women. Each time she invited Harry to go

247

with her, but he made his excuses, most often that in this fine weather there would be climbers needing a guide. He was not falling back into the habit of jumping to follow her every whim, no matter how sorry he was for the hurt he had caused her.

A couple of weeks ago, he had walked with her along the tracks to the Fern Tree Inn where a service was held each Sunday. The walk back had been pleasant, telling her stories of the mountain, pointing out plants she hadn't seen before. It had been, almost, as if he were courting her again. She had stopped, gazing at the shafts of light falling through the tall fern fronds, and smiled at him. She had reached up and brushed her lips against his. She hadn't done that when they were courting—she had never made the first approach. And it was this, the moments apart, that he had hoped for when he had suggested they come here.

He had heard her sing as she worked recently. But, he supposed, she was only truly happy when she forgot about Ellen and what he had done.

~

Ellen sat with Lizzie on her knee as the child made a mess of spooning mashed potato everywhere but into her mouth.

'She's got more in her hair than in her tummy,' Mam laughed.

'I fed her half before I let her have a go herself.' Ellen planted a kiss on Lizzie's potato-spattered cheek. 'You're a clever one, aren't you, my little darling?'

She looked across at her two other children, sitting quietly at the table, their plates empty. 'You two can go outside and play.'

They scrambled down from their seats and ran out into the yard at the front of the house. Mam followed them and stood in the doorway watching. Ellen could hear Jennie giggling. They would be building a tower of blocks in the back of Billy's little cart. He would yank the cart along the path to the gate and the blocks would tumble down to squeals of laughter. It seemed to be their favourite game at present. Ellen had left the toys behind at the

Springs, but one morning, a week after Harry had visited her in March last year, they had appeared on the Thompsons' doorstep. To Ellen, it was Harry saying he wanted nothing more to do with the children. He had placed the backcomb and the brooch he had given her, wrapped in a kerchief she had made him, in the back of the cart. She would never wear them again but she put them away to give to the girls when they were older—they deserved to know that there had been a time when Harry had cared about them all.

'Mrs Ashwood went to the Springs last Sunday,' Mam said.

'Did she?' Ellen carried Lizzie over to the tub of water on the bench under the window and wiped a damp flannel over her face.

'She said they've spruced the place up a bit, new curtains and painted chairs.'

Ellen said nothing.

'Some of those raspberries would be nice. There'd be a good crop by now.'

Ellen looked over her shoulder. 'They would, wouldn't they? I'd like to visit Grannie and Grandad Woods. Show them Lizzie. Grandad's never seen her.' She playfully pinched Lizzie's cheek. 'We'll show them what a beauty you are.'

She carried Lizzie outside and sat her on the ground near the door, putting a couple of the wooden blocks in front of her.

Lizzie picked them up and banged them together.

Ellen straightened up. 'We could go up on Friday. Are you working then?'

Her mother shook her head.

'We should start out early. He usually comes to town for rations on Friday morning. If we're lucky, she will have come with him. She does that most Fridays.'

Mam raised her eyebrows. 'You know their movements well.'

'People tell me. They think I'm interested. Still, it's good to be able to keep out of the mongrel's way.'

'We could take them some bread and cheese.'

'And a little bottle of rum.' Ellen grinned. 'They'd both enjoy that.'

~

Carts and buggies passed them by as they walked along the side of the Huon Road, but no one offered them a ride, possibly because there were so many of them. They took their time, Ellen carrying Lizzie, and Mam and Bessie taking it in turns with Jennie. Ellen had left Billy with Mary Ann, afraid that seeing the old ones would stir up his longing for Harry. For months after they had left the Springs, Billy had looked hopefully at any man who crossed their path. Of all the things Harry had done, his lack of concern for the boy made her hands itch to smash his nose flat against his face.

Ellen's heart danced as they climbed the track to the Springs. She loved it here—the clear air; the soaring trees; the tall ferns with their broad, lacy leaves; here and there clumps of scarlet waratah; the sound of honeyeaters, wattlebirds and currawongs; the shafts of golden light falling through the treetops. A honeyeater flew across their path, a flash of yellow and black, as they walked up the path towards the cottage. Stickybeak Mrs Ashwood had been right. Harry had put in a lot of work. The garden was neat, the raspberry canes staked and heavy with fruit. There were new curtains both in the cottage itself and the hut beside it. The whole place looked to be in much better repair than Ellen remembered it.

Grandad rested on the bench beside the door to the cottage, his eyes closed against the sun, basking like a cat. He opened them slowly and started up, grasping his stick. 'Jane, Janey. Come here,' he called into the cottage. 'It's Ellen and the little ones.'

Grannie came to the door. 'Oh,' she gasped and sat down heavily beside him, tears in her eyes.

Ellen was struck by their frailty. They were thinner, their skin almost transparent. She had seen Grannie just over four months ago, but Grandad she hadn't seen for a year. He had aged much more than she had expected.

'Let us see the babbie,' Grannie said, holding out her arms.

Lizzie was six months old, a healthy, cheerful child. She smiled into the old woman's face and reached out and hit her fingers against her nose.

Grannie cackled with laughter, 'Aren't you an imp, my little beauty.' She looked over Lizzie's head and saw Jennie standing beside Alice. 'Ah, Jennie, you don't remember me. You were a wee mite when I last saw you.' Alice brought her over, but she wouldn't sit beside Grannie, preferring to hide herself in Alice's skirts.

'You haven't brought the little lad with you?' Grandad asked.

'No,' Ellen sighed. 'He missed Harry so much when we left here. I was afraid a visit here would stir it all up again.'

'Such a lovely boy,' Grannie said, wistful. 'He'd be growing fast.'

'You'd hardly recognise him.'

'Will you make us a pot of tea, Ellen? I don't want to let this one go for a moment.' As Ellen walked into the cottage, Grannie called after her. 'Bring out some of the scones. They're made by herself, but they'll do.'

Ellen poured the tea, and Bessie passed around the scones and the raspberries Ellen had found in a bowl on the table.

'There's a waxworks show in Hobart at the moment,' Mam said. 'They say they're real lifelike, dressed in proper clothes, look fit to walk away. The Queen and those bushrangers, the Kellys, too.'

'Their father was here a while,' Grannie said, 'for stealing a pig, I heard. Then took himself off to Victoria after gold.'

'Plenty from here did that,' Mam added.

'And came away with little to show for it,' Grandad laughed. 'But shooting coppers, like those Kellys did,' he shook his head slowly, 'there's no surer way to get yourself hanged.'

'Handsome young men,' Mam sighed. 'Their poor mothers.'

Ellen thought of two other handsome young men missing from

their lives. She stood and handed Grandad the sack they had brought with them. 'May we buy some raspberries to take home?'

'Of course, my lovely.' He lifted the sack and peered into it. 'Bread, a pound of cheese and ... Ooh!' He fished out the flask of rum. 'This is a treat,' he beamed. But, unusual for him, he didn't sample it.

'We forgot to bring a basket,' Bessie groaned.

'Use this.' Grandad reached under the seat and pulled out a new-looking bucket. 'Bring it back next time you come up. It's a good excuse to get you here again.'

'We'll bring you a piece of corned beef when we come.'

'I do like a nice bit of corned beef,' Grandad said.

'Just the way you make it, Ellen.' Grannie smiled.

The young women went off to pick the raspberries, leaving Mam chatting with the old couple.

When the bucket was more than half full, Ellen came back. She shaded her eyes with her hand, staring into the sky at the clouds slowly building. 'We should be on our way.'

'I suppose you must.' Grannie's eyes glistened as she looked at Ellen. 'We do miss you and the little ones.'

Ellen shook her head. She couldn't change the way things were.

The sound of a man and a woman singing together carried up the track. They were too far off to hear the words clearly, or even the tune.

'What a pair of lovebirds!' Ellen laughed.

The tune became clearer. Her stomach turned over. 'The dark-eyed gypsy.' She had sung with him just the way his wife was now. Ellen had been sure he had sung the song for her alone, that she was the lady and he her dark-eyed Gypsy. And she would have given up everything for him—except her children. But it was nothing special, a song he sang with all his women.

'That's young Harry and his missus.' Grandad frowned. 'You'd better get out of the way. There's sure to be a row if he sees you.'

He looked about the clearing. 'Hide in the bush. Don't use the track.'

Ellen didn't think—she reacted to his words and hurried Jennie towards the scrub at the edge of the clearing, her mother and her sisters following, Bessie carrying Lizzie.

They made it to the bushes as Harry and his wife, arm in arm, walked up from the Fingerpost Track.

Harry stopped mid-note, let go of his wife and took after them. 'Hey! Hey! What are you doing?'

They stopped. If she had thought about it, Ellen would have stayed near the cottage—she had done nothing wrong.

He strode over. 'What have you got in that bucket?'

'Raspberries.'

'Wheedled them out of the old man for nothing, I suppose.'

He grabbed for the bucket Mam was carrying.

Ellen moved between her mother and Harry. 'Don't you touch them. They're paid for.'

'The bucket isn't.' His face was flushed, the muscles in his neck tight. 'Don't you think you've had enough from me without stealing my bucket?'

He lunged for the bucket again.

Ellen moved to block his way once more, but he pushed against her. Before she realised what was happening, he had pulled back his fist and driven it into her side.

The blow threw her off balance. She threw her hands out to prevent herself falling and caught onto Harry's coat sleeve.

With a jerk of his arm, he shook her off.

Ellen landed hard on the ground, the air forced from her lungs. Stunned, she felt no pain straightaway, only the sharp pressure of the stones on the earth beneath her.

'You bastard,' she gasped.

He stood there looking down at her as if he were shocked by what he had done.

For a moment, there was silence across the clearing. Everyone stared at Harry. Jennie hid behind Alice, whimpering, her eyes large with terror. Lizzie began to cry.

Ellen pulled herself up, holding her side. 'I'll send your bloody bucket back when I'm finished with it.' She marched away towards the track.

How could she have ever thought she was in love with a brute like that?

43

Harry stood, hands on his hips, and watched them go. How had he become involved with such a common, foul-mouthed woman?

The old couple were sitting by the door staring at him. Even from this distance, he felt the poison in Grannie's gaze.

Eliza was nowhere to be seen. He hoped she hadn't seen him punch the grasping bitch.

He walked towards the cottage, but before he was halfway, a party of men and women poured up from the track. They must have passed Ellen on the way but they were friendly, so Harry supposed nothing had been said as they passed.

Eliza came out of the cottage and busied herself providing the visitors with tea, scones, and raspberries. A couple of the men in the party said they knew the mountain well—they had no need of a guide. Harry watched them head off towards the Ice House Track then went into the barn.

'Harry.' Eliza's voice was soft behind him.

He turned to her.

'What happened?'

His thoughts tumbled into each other. *I've never hit a woman before—I don't do that sort of thing. She was taking what was mine. I'll never be free of her.* And the heart of it all, of everything that had gone wrong—*Ellen made me lose control.*

'Her mother had my bucket, and I tried to get it off her. Ellen pushed between us and, in the tussle, she was knocked to the ground.'

'That's what I thought.' Eliza nodded, no judgement in her clear eyes. 'Would you like me to bring you out a cup of tea?'

'Thank you, Eliza.' He leant his axe against the chopping block and went to her, folded her in his arms. He pressed his lips to the top of her head. 'It won't always be like this.'

'I know.' She reached up and kissed him. As she moved away, she said, 'Now, my dearest, I'll get you that cup of tea.'

Harry placed a log on the block and positioned himself. He brought the axe down with such force the piece spun across the shed, hitting the wall.

As the afternoon wore on, a heavy mist spread itself over the whole mountain, obscuring not only the pinnacle and the Organ Pipes, but even the farthest of the huts.

When they sat down to tea, the old man said, 'Did that big group come back?'

'No,' Harry answered. 'I suppose they returned by Fern Tree.'

'Many do that now. And they don't seem to need a guide.'

'I've noticed.' It was common knowledge that the old man was failing—they might believe there was no one here to help them.

Eliza lay her knife and fork on her plate. 'Perhaps we should advertise in the *Mercury*, remind people that a guide and refreshments can be had at the Springs.'

'Can we afford it?'

'It only need be a couple of times, and if more people come wanting a guide, the advertisements will have paid for themselves.' She leant forward, enthusiasm bright in her face. 'We should offer cocoa and biscuits as well as tea, coffee and scones. And I should start making raspberry vinegar again. That's always welcome on a hot day.'

He gazed at her. 'Eliza, without you ...' His voice choked. Without her calm presence, her hard work, her ability to see exactly what was needed and to make sure it was done, life would be lonely drudgery. They were working together, side by side, true partners finally. With Ellen, he had been aware of a growing burden of responsibility. He had realised recently, had Eliza not come, he would have ended up, well into his sixties, the father of twelve children, some mere infants. The thought horrified him. Life with Ellen had been a magnificent fevered dream. It could never have lasted.

He laid his hand on top of Eliza's. 'Without you, I would be lost.'

On the other side of the table, Grannie coughed behind her hand though it sounded more like a snort.

~

Harry woke from a deep sleep to a heavy hammering.

It was pitch dark outside. He opened the door, cautious.

The constable stationed at the Huon Road Police Office stood there with a lamp. 'Sorry to disturb you, Mr Woods. There's a party lost on the mountain.'

Harry pulled the door wide open. 'The group that went up earlier today? We wondered what had become of them.'

'Most made it back to town, but about six got separated. You haven't seen or heard them?'

'No, Constable, we haven't.'

The constable looked at him expectantly.

The old man snored in the background. Harry knew it was no use waking him—he could do nothing. And with no moonlight, wandering the mountain was dangerous. Harry had no intention of breaking a leg or worse for complete strangers who would not be in their current predicament if they had accepted his services as a guide in the first place.

'If they turn up here, we'll see they are fed and kept warm and I'll bring news of them to you.'

The policeman tipped his helmet and disappeared into the dark.

On Monday, in town for the old couple's rations, Harry heard the missing six had spent the night at the Ploughed Field, without food or shelter, though they had managed to light a fire. In the early morning, they had made their way to the Fern Tree Inn and been revived with hot coffee. If Harry had at least gone up the track past the icehouse he might have caught sight of the fire and could have guided them down. They would have had their reviving drinks at the Springs. His name would be in the *Mercury* today, his usefulness as a guide there for all to see. A better advertisement than anything he could pay for.

~

Twelve days later, Harry was again at the Police Court, listening as the whole tawdry mess of his life was put on display for the entertainment of the smirking population of Hobart. Eliza had found him a lawyer through her contacts at the church. A good one too, Alfred Dobson—he had been a member of the Tasmanian Parliament. He had said he would only charge Harry if he won the case for him.

Ellen had no shame at all, answering any question put to her, boasting almost.

'Yes,' she said, 'I lived with Harry Woods for two years at the Springs and had two children by him.'

'But Mr Woods was a married man,' Mr Dobson said. 'That was hardly a decent thing to do.'

Ellen glared at him. 'He never told me he had a wife. I wouldn't have had anything to do with him if I'd known.'

She gave the impression that butter wouldn't melt in her mouth standing there in a high-necked dress Harry was sure he hadn't seen before, her hair tidy beneath her hat. She didn't look as if she needed his money.

Police Magistrate Tarleton leant forward. 'Remind me, where was Woods's wife?'

'In Perth, I believe, your honour,' Dobson said. 'She had not come with Woods because she was caring for her elderly mother. The mother has since died.'

He continued his questioning. 'When Mr and Mrs Woods arrived at the Springs you began to swear at them—'

'I did nothing of the sort,' Ellen interrupted. 'I swore at Harry *after* he punched me. I have never said a word against his wife. I have only seen her from a distance, and I have never annoyed or taunted her.'

'You were tussling over the bucket, which was Mr Woods's property and you did not have his permission to use and, in the struggle, he accidentally struck you with a glancing blow, which did no real damage.'

'Glancing blow!' Ellen almost snorted. 'He punched me with his fist. I still have the bruise. Do you want to see it?' She made no move to rearrange her clothing.

Mr Dobson raised his eyebrows and looked along his nose. 'That will not be necessary.'

After Ellen had done her best to ruin any reputation Harry had left, her sister Bessie and her mother took their turns in the witness box. They did not lie outright but exaggerated in their attempts to portray him as a brute who set about dear sweet Ellen with his fists.

Then Harry was called.

'Tell us what happened, Mr Woods,' Mr Dobson said.

Harry knew he was on oath. All he could do was describe things as they seemed to him.

'I didn't intend to hit her. All I wanted was my bucket back. Her mother was holding it and Miss Thompson deliberately got in my way, so I tried to push her aside. I didn't raise my hand to her.'

He heard Ellen mutter from the gallery, 'No, you raised your fist.'

'I was trying to push past her to get the bucket, but she caught hold of me by the sleeves of my coat.' He had told himself this version so often he very nearly believed it. 'As I pushed her aside, she might have fallen.'

The magistrate didn't believe him. Harry was fined five shillings and costs. More money down the drain on account of Ellen Thompson. At least he didn't have the lawyer's fee to pay.

44

June 1882

Harry stamped the snow off his boots. Winter had come in with a vengeance. Snow covered the mountain. No climbers visited, so there was no money. And he owed Ellen two pounds for maintenance. It would be a lot more by the time the winter was over. He couldn't pay, and there was nothing anyone could do about it—he had no goods he could sell. Ellen would have to go without.

He pushed past the blanket hanging over the door. The room was chilly and in darkness, the fire nearly out. The old couple were in bed, cocooned in their threadbare blankets. He placed his sack with the rations on the table and went to the bed he shared with Eliza. She lay with her coat over the top of the blankets, her eyes shut, shivering. She had caught a cold at the beginning of May. The cough had lingered, leaving her breathless.

Harry bent and touched her forehead—her skin was burning. He squatted beside the bed and called her name.

Eliza whimpered and turned her head away.

He didn't know what he would do if he lost her.

He stood up, shivering. Before he did anything else, he should get the room warm. He went to the hearth and coaxed the fire back to life. As the room warmed, Eliza's shivering eased, but she muttered in her sleep, fretful. Harry hoped it was safe to leave her for an hour or so.

He rugged up and left the cottage, tramping around the traps he had set. Only one had a stringy rabbit caught in it. He took it home and gutted and cleaned it in the snow.

The chill was gone from the room, but Eliza was now hot and restless, groaning, throwing off her blankets. She didn't react when Harry called her name. Fear uncurled. He held himself taut, his fists clenched. He needed to act, to help her in some way. He would lose her if he didn't.

He grabbed a tea towel from the cupboard and went out and wet it in the snow. Folded, he placed it on her forehead. He hoped it was the right thing to do. He'd never had to do the little tasks that made up the daily care of another person. He had always been the one cared for.

He made soup with a few coarsely cut vegetables, some barley and the rabbit, and set it to simmer over the fire. The old couple were now out of bed, hunched close to each other at the hearth, sucking on their empty pipes. There was no tobacco, no grog of any sort to give them. Once the meal was finally served and eaten, they returned to their bed.

Eliza tossed and turned through the night, huddling close to Harry for warmth as she shivered, flinging the blankets off, sweating, groaning and threshing about. And all the time she coughed, harsh body-racking spasms. Her breathing between the bouts was laboured.

Most of the next day Harry spent at Eliza's side. He tried to get her to take a few sips of water. Her face was still flushed, her skin burning. She seemed not to recognise him or know where she was. He sat on a chair beside the bed, his head in his hands. With each deep, shaking breath he took, in time with Eliza's, he willed her to live, his throat aching with the effort. She mustn't die. She mustn't leave him.

He rose slowly from the chair, walked over to the hearth and stood, his back to the fire.

'This can't go on. We're not staying here any longer.'

The old man stared at him, truculent stubbornness on his face.

Harry shook his head slowly. 'Look around you—the cottage is falling down. We don't have enough money to keep four people through winter. Come into town. I'll have regular work, so we can get a small place with a bit of yard where you can sit, or garden if you want. Eliza will make it comfortable. You'll be warm and well-fed.'

The old man clenched his jaw. 'We're not leaving. We've lived on the mountain thirty years. We're not going anywhere.'

Beside him, Grannie nodded her head.

'I can't do it anymore, Dad.' Harry fought against the panic swirling through him. If they stayed any longer, Eliza would die, he was sure of it. 'Eliza and I are going to live in Hobart. We'll come up twice a week, bring the rations and see to whatever else needs doing.'

His arms crossed, the old man glared into the fire.

Harry went back to Eliza and stretched out on the bed beside her. She slept through the night, though Harry woke with her every movement. The darkness outside was fading when he realised her breathing was even between the bouts of coughing. He reached out and lay the back of his hand against her forehead. Her skin was dry and normal to his touch. He let out a ragged sob.

Eliza's eyelashes fluttered. With a moan, she turned on her side and gazed at Harry, recognition in her eyes.

'Eliza.' He made no effort to blink back his tears. 'I thought I had lost you.'

She wriggled her hand from beneath the blankets and laid it against the side of his face.

He grasped it and drew it to his lips. They lay together in a silence broken only by the snores from the other bed.

Eliza began to doze again.

Harry got up and stoked the banked embers, placing fresh wood on top of them. He set the kettle to boil and made a pot of tea. When Eliza woke again, he went over to her and straightened the bedding, helping her to sit up. He brought her a tepid cup of weak sweetened tea. Her hands shook as she tried to hold it, so he fed it to her sip by sip.

'We're going to live in Hobart as soon as I can arrange it.'

Eliza blinked. 'All of us?' she croaked and began coughing.

Harry sat, useless, until the bout had passed.

'No, just us. Dad and Grannie refuse to leave. I'll come up and check on them twice a week.' He stood and pulled the blankets up, tucking them around Eliza's shoulders. 'I'm going down to arrange somewhere to stay tomorrow or the day after, once I'm sure you're on the mend.'

Eliza drew her hand from under the blanket and held it out to Harry. He took it between his and chafed it, his fear for her stuck, like a lump, in his throat.

~

Harry sat in Mrs Hennessy's parlour, his hat on his knees. Her welcome had been polite but frosty, but she had invited him in.

'Mrs Hennessy, I'm not asking for myself, it's for my wife. She's been very ill. She's over the worst of it now, but I doubt she will survive the winter up there.'

He could see no sympathy in Mrs Hennessy, her face sterner than any of the magistrates he had appeared before over the last year or so.

'My guests are single men. I only have single beds in the rooms.'

'I'll sleep on the floor.' If she wanted, he would go down on his knees and beg. 'My wife is a good woman. She deserves better than what I have put her through.'

'I can't argue with that, Mr Woods.' She blinked slowly. 'I have heard Mrs Woods is a genteel lady from those who have been to the Springs recently.'

'She is.'

'It would still be board for two if I were to agree to it, as I'd be feeding both of you.'

'That's only reasonable.'

'And how do you propose to pay for your room? I believe you haven't been earning much lately.'

'I'll go back to the sawmill. And when Eliza is well again, she'll find work too. She's clever with the needle and an excellent cook.'

Mrs Hennessy pressed her lips together. 'Very well. But I am doing this for Mrs Woods's sake. If it was you alone, you'd not have put a foot in my house. Do you have the week in advance?'

'I have two shillings and sixpence but I will have the rest by Friday.'

'Make sure that you do.' She stood up. 'When will Mrs Woods arrive?'

'Tomorrow. I'll carry Eliza all the way if I can't pick up a ride on the Huon Road.'

Mrs Hennessy walked Harry to the front door. 'Now, don't be worrying yourself about picking up a ride. Bob will be waiting for you at the finger-post some time after eight o'clock tomorrow morning.'

45

Harry rose before first light, lit the fire and hung the large pot of soup, prepared the previous night, at the back of the fire. He had collected the rations yesterday, bread and oatmeal and tea—enough, he thought, until Sunday when he would be back. He had stacked a load of wood against the far wall so his father wouldn't need to go out in the snow.

After breakfast, he took his swag and Eliza's bag down to the fingerpost and hid them in the bushes. By the time he arrived back at the Springs, Grannie and his father were out of bed, sitting by the fire.

'I'll be back on Sunday, Dad.'

The old man grunted and stared at the flames.

Harry had no doubt his father believed he was deserting them, but his first duty was to Eliza. He had spent more of his life with her than he had with his father.

Harry shut the door firmly behind him and took Eliza's arm. They walked down the path past the huts, Eliza leaning heavily against him, still weak and unsteady on her feet. Silence and snow covered everything.

They had gone no more than a few yards when Eliza started coughing. Harry stopped and waited for the spasm to pass, rubbing her back as she bent over gasping for breath. He hoped the bitterly cold air wouldn't bring back her fever, though she was heavily rugged up with hat and coat, gloves and a shawl. Her nose, mouth and chin were wrapped about by Harry's scarf.

'It might be best if I carry you.' He swung her up into his arms, shocked at how light she was.

At the start of the track, Harry lowered her to the ground. 'This isn't going to work. I can't see where I'm walking.'

She gave a weak smile. 'If we go slowly, I'm sure I can manage.'

'Hold on to me.' He slid Eliza's arm around his waist. 'As you walk, stick your heel into the ground first. It will give you more grip.'

The descent was slow. They kept to the edge of the track, each step taken carefully, stopping often for Eliza to catch her breath. He saw the effort it cost her, her pallor, the film of perspiration on the little of her skin that was uncovered. This was a mistake. He should have waited a few more days, until Eliza was stronger, but it was too late to turn back.

On the final stretch, Eliza tumbled forward.

Harry grabbed for her, catching her as he slid to the ground, landing on his back.

He lay there, looking into the grey sky. Eliza lay on top of him, not moving.

Fear flooded through him. 'Are you hurt?'

'Not at all,' she gasped. 'What about you?'

He let out a long, slow breath. 'I can't feel a thing.' He wiggled his fingers and his toes. 'Too cold to feel anything.'

Eliza shifted off him as he struggled to sit up. 'Nothing broken except my pride.'

He pulled himself upright using his staff. 'And you are sure you're not hurt?'

'No.' Her eyes were sunken, her face almost as white as the snow covering everything.

She groaned as he helped her to her feet. 'I will be glad when we reach the bottom.'

'It's not far now.'

They plodded slowly on.

Bob Flanagan was waiting at the fingerpost. He jumped down from his wagon. 'Pleased to meet you at last, Mrs Woods.'

'Thank you, Mr Flanagan.' Eliza inclined her head. 'It is so very kind of you to take us into Hobart.'

'My pleasure. We couldn't have you walking all the way in this weather.' He helped her onto the driver's bench and laid a blanket across her legs while Harry loaded their bags into the back.

Once Harry was seated beside her, Bob on the other, they set off.

She grasped Harry's hand, tight.

Harry glanced at her. She sat stiff, her eyes shut, wincing with each jolt of the wagon.

Harry stared ahead, his mouth shut against a sob. *Don't let her die*, he prayed. *Please.*

As the road levelled out, Eliza eased her grip and relaxed against Harry, resting her head on his shoulder as she gazed at the snow covering the trees and mounded on the roadside. 'This is silly, but I am quite warm.' She laughed, breathless. 'I haven't been this warm for months.'

She jerked forward and started coughing.

Harry placed his hand on her back—fear sitting on him like a great weight.

'Won't be much longer, Mrs Woods, and we'll be in Hobart,' Bob said. 'I can't go too fast, not with all this snow. When we get there, Mrs Hennessy will have a big cup of cocoa ready for you.'

Mrs Hennessy was on the footpath as the wagon pulled up, smiling broadly. 'Welcome, Mrs Woods. 'Tis a pleasure finally to meet you.' She guided Eliza up the front steps, Harry behind, carrying their bags.

They had to stop three times on the staircase for Eliza to catch her breath.

Mrs Hennessy swung the door open to the room Harry had stayed in before. It almost touched the corner of a double bed. The bedspread and curtains looked to be freshly laundered and ironed. There was barely enough room for one person to stand between the bed and the chest of drawers. A tallboy stood at one end of the room, behind the door, and the washstand in the corner, a single chair squeezed between.

Pointing to the chair, Mrs Hennessy said, 'Now sit yourself there and I'll bring some hot water so you can have a wash. There's a clean nightgown under the pillow, just an old one of mine. I doubt you've had much chance to get washing dry up there this time of year.'

Eliza nodded. Her mouth held tight against a cough.

'And, if you give me your linen and himself there's shirts and unmentionables, I'll get your washing done.'

'There's no need Mrs Hennessy,' Eliza croaked.

'Ah, wisht now, you've been sick. You need to rest and not be worrying yourself about such things for a few days.'

Mrs Hennessy fussed about, bringing the washing water, and a hot water bottle wrapped in flannel that she placed in the bed, and finally a saucer with a spoon and a small jug with a beaded cover on it. She placed the saucer and jug on the chest of drawers and nodded towards them. 'I heard that terrible cough and thought this might help. It's a concoction of honey, lemon and vinegar. I swear it will break up the worst cough.' She smiled at Eliza. 'Take a sip whenever you need it. In a while, I'll be back to collect up your washing.'

As the door closed, Eliza burst into tears. 'It's like having a mother again.'

Harry drew her to her feet and wrapped her in his arms. 'It's been too hard for you, Eliza. I should have thought to do this last year.'

She sniffed, smiling at him through her tears.

He would do his best to make sure all would be well for her from now on.

Washed and in Mrs Hennessy's nightgown, Eliza lay back against the pillows, the blankets piled over her, her feet warm against the water bottle. The strain that had marked her face for months was absent.

Harry felt as if a great burden had been lifted from him.

He picked up the jug containing Mrs Hennessy's concoction. 'Do you want to try some?'

'I might as well.' Eliza tried to swallow her cough.

She sipped from the spoon and winced. 'That *will* cut through anything.'

He put the jug back on the chest.

'Harry.' She held out her hand to him.

He came back and sat on the edge of the bed.

Eliza leant forward and kissed him, her lips sticky with the syrup.

'You taste good enough to eat,' he said.

Eliza stared down at her hands on the bedspread. 'When I am a little better, we ...' Her voice faded as if she realised what she was about to say. Her blush was a deep red.

It was the boldest thing she had ever nearly said to him. Harry grasped her hand and kissed it. When he looked up, he could see what she felt for him shining in her eyes.

'Eliza, I love you.'

'I have loved you always, Harry, from the moment you walked into my father's shop.'

She straightened her shoulders and tried to be businesslike. 'As soon as I'm well, I'll start looking for work. Mrs Hennessy might have some idea and the ladies at the church too.' She was breathless by the time she finished.

'Oh Harry.' She coughed. 'We can go to church every Sunday.'

'We can, and take a walk in the Botanic Gardens on Sunday afternoons.'

'And the musical evenings at the church. It will be like being back in Perth.'

'Almost.' One day they would go back. He didn't want the life they had been living when he left, but he did miss the warmth.

Echoing his thoughts, Eliza said, 'I miss the Perth sunshine, but

I should have realised this a long time ago—as long as I'm with you, it doesn't matter where we live.'

He couldn't stop the tears that filled his eyes.

Eliza looked into his face. 'Harry, my dearest.' She squeezed his hand.

Harry took a deep, shuddering breath. Eliza had never left him. Every other person, from his parents on, had walked away from him and never cared enough to look back. She was the only one to have searched for him, to have come after him and found him. She was the only one who had ever truly loved him.

46

July 1882

Ellen stood in line outside the Benevolent Society depot, Lizzie in her arms. The child was swathed in a shawl to protect her from the damp. Billy and Jennie, wearing every item of clothing they owned, huddled close to Ellen's skirts, their faces pinched and drawn, their little noses red. Billy was still coughing from a cold he didn't seem able to shake off.

The air was freezing although the sun was out. Overnight snow lay in shadowy corners, elsewhere it had begun to thaw into a muddy mess.

When she was younger, Ellen had loved the falls of snow, racing about, throwing snowballs, skidding through the slush. Now all it meant was a deepening of the endless cold of winter, the miserable thought that they would never be warm again.

The doors of the depot opened, and the children all shuffled in, taking their seats on benches along the tables at the centre of the room.

Ellen pushed Billy slightly. 'Go on, go and get your share.' She watched from the door as, one hand tightly grasping Jennie's, he forced his way through the children still milling, looking for a space. She kept her eyes on them, sitting at the far side of the room. Billy was watching what the others did, stretching a hand out to stop Jennie hoeing straight into the soup and bread placed in front of her. The children all waited while grace was said, then they began as if they hadn't eaten for days. And for some, that might be true.

Many of the women waiting outside were like Ellen, unmarried with children to care for. But marriage was no safeguard—men disappeared or drank their pay. A number of the women looked like they could do with a decent feed as well. The Benevolent

Society provided meals for the children. They couldn't leave them to starve, but they reasoned they couldn't support adults who would then be encouraged to become dependent on them rather than try to support themselves.

One of the Society women came out to Ellen, her face stern and judgemental, and told Ellen to come inside to the desk near the door. Ellen sat with Lizzie on her knee. She drew back the shawl and brushed her hand across the child's soft dark hair.

'Is the child able to eat properly?' the woman asked.

'Yes, but she can't sit on a stool by herself.'

The woman pressed her lips together and walked away. Ellen wondered if she should stay where she was or go back outside. She was about to stand when the woman returned with a teacup filled with soup and a piece of bread. She set them on the desk in front of Ellen and handed her a spoon. 'This will fill her up.'

Ellen crumbled the bread into the soup and began to feed Lizzie, who swallowed the pap hungrily.

'Miss Thompson,' the woman began, but Ellen didn't give her time to finish.

'I'm sorry but I didn't have anything to feed them.'

'Don't worry about that—we do not want children going hungry.'

Ellen looked into the woman's sad grey eyes. Perhaps she was not stern, just resigned to the sorrows she had seen, possibly worse than Ellen knew.

'How are things with you?'

'It's too hard,' Ellen's voice almost broke. 'I don't know what we'd do without the help we get here. I haven't been able to find work, and Bessie only gets a few hours charring. That doesn't cover much more than the rent. And Billy's been sick, and I had to buy medicine for him.'

The woman reached across the desk and placed her hand on Ellen's. 'If your children are ill and need a doctor or medicine, in the future come here, and we will arrange for you to see someone at the hospital and get any medicine you need. You won't have to pay for it.' She patted Ellen's hand. 'Aren't you getting money from Mr Woods?'

Ellen forced her eyes wide. 'He's stopped paying. I've received nothing in over a month.'

'I can't give you anything at present, but I will send someone tomorrow and we'll see what we can do to tide you over. But you must go back to the court.' She frowned, her mouth pressed into an angry line. 'You didn't get into this situation on your own.'

Ellen blinked back her tears. It was the first time anyone other than family had shown any understanding of her position. 'Thank you. It will be better in summer. Both Bessie and I can work in the jam factory, and I will have enough to pay for someone to mind the children.'

The woman rose from behind the desk. 'That sounds an excellent idea. But don't let your head be turned again by a handsome face with an easy way with words.'

That would not be happening. Ellen was done with men.

~

Each day Harry's routine was the same. He came home from work, washed and changed into the shirt and trousers Eliza had laid out for him so he could come clean to the dinner table. Then he went down to find her.

As was now usual, she was in the kitchen with Mrs Hennessy, having a cup of tea before the rush of serving the evening meal.

Eliza was frowning. 'I must have been to every shop in Hobart that sells ladies' apparel as well as every baker and confectioner, but the answer is always the same—a shake of the head and *Sorry, we don't need anyone.*'

She placed her teacup on the saucer and rested her hands against the edge of the table, her fingers twisted tightly together. 'I could go out charring or, perhaps, see if I can get work at one of the factories.'

'Absolutely not!' It was louder than Harry intended.

Mrs Hennessy gasped, 'No, no!' at the same time.

Eliza's eyebrows shot up, looking from Harry standing in the doorway to Mrs Hennessy sitting opposite her, as if she was surprised to find them in agreement.

Mrs Hennessy's cup rattled as she put it on the saucer. 'Sit down and have a cup of tea, Mr Woods.' She stood up and bustled about getting Harry a cup. 'You do not want to be mixing with some of those girls who work at Peacock's and places like that. Oh no, not at all. What you need is work you can do at home.' Her brow wrinkled as she concentrated. 'That dress you're wearing, did you make it yourself?'

'Yes, I have always made nearly all of my clothing. I had a sewing machine back in Perth.'

Mrs Hennessy placed the cup of tea in front of Harry and sat down again. 'I have one, not that it is used much.' She drummed her fingers on the table. 'You could offer to do alterations. Many women here are not much good with the needle. Not everyone can afford new clothing, and some would certainly pay to have them fitted properly.'

'I could do that.'

'Of course you could, Eliza. It would be perfect for you.' Harry turned to Mrs Hennessy. 'Thank you, Mrs Hennessy. You are a wonder.' The thought of Eliza working with the likes of that friend of Ellen's, Annie Smith, horrified him.

Mrs Hennessy inclined her head and beamed at him. 'Thank you for the compliment, Mr Woods.' It was the first time she had smiled at him in the three weeks they had been boarding with her.

Mrs Hennessy made sure all of her wide circle of acquaintances knew she had an excellent seamstress living with her who, for a small fee, could alter or mend anything they needed. She let Eliza use the front parlour for the ladies who called for fittings.

In return, Eliza did all of Mrs Hennessy's mending and helped in the kitchen when she was needed. She seemed content with her life in a way she hadn't been at the Springs. Harry realised Eliza needed people around her, people who were like her. She leant on Mrs Hennessy as she would her own mother. He didn't know how much Eliza confided in the older woman, but Mrs Hennessy's attitude to him seemed to soften as the days passed. He supposed she would blame Ellen for what had happened. She had warned Harry about the Thompson family. He should have listened to her.

Harry and Eliza visited the Springs twice a week and tried to make the old couple comfortable. Occasionally, if there was money to spare, he bought them tobacco and a small flask of rum. He chopped wood, sealed the cracks that appeared every week—the cottage was falling apart bit by bit. Eliza tidied and cleaned, made a pot of stew that hopefully would last a few days, and took away any clothing or linen that needed washing. The old man and Grannie thanked them for what they did but said little else to them. Other than the necessities Harry and Eliza provided, they did not seem to need anything, or anyone, else. When they spoke, it was to each other and of times long past. Grannie sometimes sang lullabies softly to herself. It was as if they were sinking into their memories and like two dilapidated buildings were collapsing into each other. If one was taken away, the other was sure to fall.

47

Ellen, still wearing her nightgown, a shawl draped around her shoulders, poured tea into her cup and gazed out through the window. 'It looks to be a lovely day.' She came back to the table and added a couple of teaspoons of sugar. 'Let's take the children to the Domain. We could visit the Botanic Gardens too.'

Bessie, still chewing her mouthful of toast and jam, nodded. Lizzie, sitting on her lap, banged her porridge spoon on the table as if agreeing.

Billy stopped eating, his spoon mid-air. 'Can we, Mummy?'

'I don't see why not. But we'll have to rug up. The sun's out but it will still be chilly.'

Billy leant towards his sister. 'We are all going to the Domain, Jennie, down near the river.'

Jennie's answer was mumbled as she shovelled in as much of the congealed sugar from the top of the porridge as she could.

Bessie swallowed her toast and blinked slowly, as if her thoughts had been far away. 'Fresh air and sunshine would be a nice change.'

Ellen put her cup on the table and took Lizzie from Bessie. 'We had better wear our Sunday best in case we run into Mr Wonderful out there who will set us up so we don't need to work at all.'

Bessie opened her eyes wide. 'The one Mr Wonderful for both of us? He'd have to be very rich.' She clamped her mouth shut and stared at Ellen.

'No,' Ellen laughed, 'you can get your own. I don't believe in sharing men. Even rich ones who could give me bacon and eggs for breakfast and all those other bits and pieces Mrs Bryce has.'

Bessie let her breath out slowly. 'Imagine having that sort of breakfast every day. I bet you wouldn't feel hungry until teatime.'

'But it would mean having to get into bed with someone like

Mr Bryce.' Ellen screwed up her nose as if she had smelt something unpleasant.

Bessie made a retching noise.

Billy looked up from his bowl. 'What's wrong with Mr Bryce?' Bessie leant over and, in a stage whisper, said, 'He smells, Billy. He smells really bad.'

The children giggled, and Ellen joined in. It was as if she had not a worry in the world when they were happy.

Half of Hobart must have had the same idea. It seemed like a holiday rather than the Sunday respite between one drab week and the next. The air was brisk, but it was a fine, bright day—the top of the mountain was covered with snow, wispy cloud hanging about the Organ Pipes; the river sparkled; the light danced on the sails of the yachts on the river; the grass, the bushes, the trees were lush and green. The Domain looked better than it had last time Ellen was here. Old trees and shrubs had been removed, new trees planted alongside the pathways, and seats had been built here and there.

Jennie chased after Billy down the slope towards the Botanic Gardens, the ends of their scarves flapping over their shoulders, Bessie struggling to keep up. Ellen wondered what was wrong. Bessie moved more slowly than usual and seemed distracted. She was pale and her face thinner, but she didn't seem to have lost any weight. But how could Ellen tell? She was wearing nearly everything she owned to keep warm. Ellen hoped she wasn't ill. She relied on Bessie, couldn't manage without her.

Ellen followed them at a more leisurely pace, carrying Lizzie. The two children ran through a small flock of seagulls, squealing and laughing. She was aware of the disapproving looks from the more sober of the strollers, but most seemed not to care, there were plenty of children running about laughing and squealing.

They crossed the drive that ran past the gardens, Bessie holding on to the children's hands. As they passed through the impressive wrought-iron gates of the Botanic Gardens, she said, 'We all have to behave in here, there are lots of old people who will be very cross if we knock them over.'

'Yes, Jennie, we have to be careful,' Billy added, the serious older brother, 'they might break into bits.'

'Big bits?' Jennie asked.

'No, tiny weeny little bits,' Bessie said, 'so little no one will be able to put them together again.'

Jennie giggled. 'I be careful.'

They walked along the gravel paths past well-trimmed bushes, enjoying the sunshine on their faces. Plants were arranged in neat rows through the garden beds but few were in bloom, all waiting for spring.

'Let's go and look at the lily pond,' Ellen said. 'It might have some pretty flowers.'

The children behaved perfectly, walking hand in hand with Bessie.

An older couple strolled ahead of them, their arms linked, the man's head bent towards the woman, listening as she spoke.

Ellen slowed her step. There was something familiar about him. She stopped, a weight in her stomach.

She whispered to Bessie. 'See that couple ahead?'

The couple had reached the pond. The woman bent down, looking closely at the floating leaves.

'It's Harry and his wife.'

Ellen quietly called Billy and Jennie to her. 'These plants are boring, let's go out into the Domain and run a bit,' she whispered. 'But remember, we must be quiet until we are out of here.'

Once they were out of the gardens, Bessie said, 'The wife was smartly dressed. And that hat is almost new.'

Ellen's eyes narrowed. The wife's skirt and jacket were not truly fashionable, but they were not faded or obviously worn, and the jacket was nicely trimmed. Harry had looked neat; his jacket and trousers were pressed, his collar white—too respectable for colourful kerchiefs these days! There was grey in his beard and in his hair. He seemed so much older than the man she had fallen in love with. It was almost as if he was now a different man.

'I'd heard they were back in town,' Bessie said.

Ellen stopped and moved Lizzie to her other hip. 'And you didn't say?'

Bessie shrugged.

Surely, her occasional rant about Harry, and bloody men in general, couldn't have made Bessie afraid to speak in case it set her off. 'So they've left Grannie and Grandad to fend for themselves up there in the snow.' She shivered. The sun had slipped behind a cloud. They were an untarnished memory of life at the Springs, and there was nothing she could do to help them.

As they walked across the grass, she said. 'I've asked the police clerk to get him to pay what he owes me.' She pressed her lips together and fought back sudden tears. She knew he hated her— and the feeling was mutual. But why didn't he feel anything for his daughters?

48

Harry stood in the dock of the Police Court. Again. This was the sixth time in just over a year. He was tired of it. The magistrates today were two men he hadn't seen before, and neither showed the slightest understanding. The usual magistrate, William Tarleton, was far more sympathetic and knew the whole story, but he had had a stroke a few weeks ago. To these two, Harry was just another shirker.

'I don't have the money, sir,' he said in answer to questioning by Mr Barnard. 'I have to go up and down to the Springs at least twice a week to take rations to my father, so I can't work a full week. My wife hasn't been well, but she has begun taking in sewing. We bring in barely enough to meet our own needs much less what I have been ordered to pay in maintenance.'

'Woods, you must pay what you have been ordered by the Court,' the second magistrate, Mr Huybers, said.

'I believe I can meet the weekly amounts from now on, but I have no hope of paying the arrears at the moment.'

'If you paid each week as it fell due, you wouldn't be in this position.' Barnard scowled at him. 'We can't have men shirking their responsibility to their children, otherwise we would end up with hordes of the children of feckless men like you starving on the streets and going on to lives of crime.'

Harry breathed in through his nose, his mouth clamped shut. He was not bloody feckless, just poor, poorer than he had ever been.

'What goods do you own?' Huybers asked. 'They could be seized to pay the arrears.'

'Nothing but the clothes I stand up in.'

'There's nothing for it,' Barnard said, matter of fact. 'You will be imprisoned for two months. These court orders are not made lightly.' He looked down at the papers on the bench in front of him and said, without looking at Harry again, 'Two months in the House of Correction.'

Barely understanding what was happening, Harry was marched down the steps beneath the dock and along a whitewashed tunnel into the prison itself. And the humiliation began.

He was led into a room, where his details were taken and written in a ledger—his name and his age, the ship he had arrived on, his occupation, if he could read or write. He was measured—his build, the colour of his hair, his beard, his eyes noted. Stripped to the waist, any peculiarities, scars, tattoos, missing fingers were looked for—Harry had none. Ordered into the adjoining room, where seven battered baths stood in a row, he was told to sit on the chair inside the door. A warder then cropped his hair close and shaved his face. He sat stock still as the razor skimmed his throat. Even when this was over, his shaved head and face would mark him as having been in prison. He had not expected this. He couldn't believe it was happening to him.

He was told to strip and get into the nearest bathtub. Harry lowered himself into the water and soaped and rinsed off quickly. There was no pleasure in lingering in a bath of tepid water in a cold room. Shivering, he stepped out of the bath and dried himself on a rough towel. He put on the dark grey prison clothing and placed the leather cap on his naked head. His own clothing, roughly bundled and tagged, was thrown onto a shelf with other prisoners' clothing in the room where his details had been taken down.

Harry marched, a warder beside him, along a narrow path between two brick walls and through an iron gateway. His heart raced as the gate clanged shut behind him. He was locked in here with no way out.

They crossed the prison's entrance yard. To the left were two solid octagonal towers either side of the heavy gate that led out to

Campbell Street. Their shape brought back memories of the Roundhouse at Fremantle where his father had been held before his transportation here. He turned his head away. Opposite the gates stood a pleasant two-storey house with a verandah and balcony, creepers climbing the wall, a lush garden with cypress trees in front. He supposed it must be the governor's house, not what he could expect within the House of Correction. Two bells hung in a wooden frame in the entrance yard in front of the house.

The gate to the House of Correction was opened by an old man, a trusted prisoner by the look of him. Two two-storey buildings stretched on both sides of a long yard—the muster yard where the prisoners exercised, the warder said. Harry glanced at the sky. He could not imagine worse than seeing nothing but these walls and this patch of sky for the next two months. He swallowed his panic.

He was led to the building on the right, into the mess room, and directed to a seat along the side of one of the tables. There must have been near a hundred prisoners in the room, watched by two constables, trusted prisoners again, stationed one at each end of the room. They all stood, their heads bowed, as a tall, bald-headed prisoner recited grace.

Amen said, they sat and began to eat in silence. The meal of meat, potatoes, and bread was more and better food than Harry had eaten some days during winter at the Springs. No one seemed to take much notice of him, all intent on their own meals, though the beak-nosed old man beside him glanced his way several times.

Dinner over, the bald-headed prisoner said grace again. Once all their names had been called by the muster-master, the other prisoners lined up to receive a ration of tobacco before filing out into the exercise yard.

Harry was collected by the warder who had brought him in and shown to the dormitory where he would sleep. The mattress and bedding on all the beds were rolled to the end. The warder hung a tag at the head of the bed with Harry's name and particulars as well as his sentence, there for the information of anyone who could read. The afternoon was spent being shown the places he needed to know within the prison; the multitude of rules, regulations and routines were explained to him. The warder was civil and, Harry thought, surprisingly patient. Harry had never been in prison and understood little. He hoped he would remember it all. He had no wish to break any rule and have time added to his sentence.

Late in the afternoon, Harry was sent out into the exercise yard as all the prisoners were mustered in their work gangs, those who were in the workshops within the prison walls and those who worked at the quarry in the Domain and at the Botanic Gardens and the gardens of Government House. Harry joined the quarry gang. Tomorrow he would be out with them, breaking stone in a shed at the Domain. They answered as their names were called by the muster-master and were sent off to wash in the troughs near the lavatories hidden behind a creeper-covered screen at the end of the yard.

Following the evening meal of gruel and bread, eaten in silence, the prisoners collected their ration of tobacco and went out again into the yard. The full range of humanity were mingled together, talking in knots, pacing to and fro, many puffing on their pipes, the tobacco smoke a fleeting taste of heaven.

The old man from the dinner table shuffled up to Harry and introduced himself as Tom.

'What are you in for?' He took the pipe from his mouth and gave a wheezing cough.

'Didn't have the money to pay the maintenance the court ordered.'

'Sometimes it's easier to marry them,' Tom said, amusement in his inquisitive dark eyes.

Harry supposed he should answer. 'Couldn't. Married already.'

'You have your fun,' the old man gave a wheezing laugh, 'you pay one way or the other. At least she didn't give you a dose of the clap.'

Harry grunted.

'I'm doing two weeks for obscene language. The young copper told me to move on, and I told him where he could go. If he thinks that was swearing, he's got a lot to learn.' He coughed again. 'In the old days, the coppers and screws could swear as good as the best of us.'

Harry walked beside the old man, aware of the other prisoners around him, trying not catching anyone's eye, speaking only when spoken to, presenting his fear as menace.

The bells outside the governor's house rang, and the prisoners went to the dormitories. They spread out their bedding and sat on the beds, hands on their knees as the muster-master, accompanied by a couple of warders, called their names. The roll called, a whistle was blown and most got straight into bed. One prisoner sat in the middle of the room and read from a book for a lengthy time, tales of shipwrecks and adventures at sea. Harry drowsed as the story was read, but once the light was finally out, he couldn't sleep. He lay in his narrow bed beneath two thin blankets, staring into the dark.

He was here although he had done nothing criminal, nothing deliberate. It was only that he was poor and couldn't pay what the court had ordered. That bitch knew how difficult things were yet she had persisted and had him locked up. He had caught sight of her as he turned to descend the stairs. She had seemed as shocked as he was—he supposed it was the realisation she wouldn't be getting her money. If she was as decent as she had tried to pretend to the court, she wouldn't be in her current predicament. She had come to him willingly and it wasn't as if he was her first.

He twitched his shoulders against the mattress. He had been scratching! The place had bugs! His groan was lost in the chorus of snores. He would go back to Eliza lousy. He curled himself into a tight ball, shivering and scratching through the night, his sleep light and fitful.

The prisoners were roused by the bells before daylight and were out at their daily tasks as the sun slowly rose in the sky. The day passed in a haze of tiredness. Harry followed the rules, went where he was ordered, did as he was told, answered when he was spoken to. As soon as he climbed into his bed that night, he fell into a deep sleep and didn't hear the end of the tale of the shipwrecked man called Selkirk.

The following morning as he lined up in the muster yard, a warder pulled Harry aside.

'It's your lucky day, Woods. You've been bailed.'

Harry frowned. 'I'm free?'

'Once you change into your own gear and I let you out the gate.'

Almost light-headed with relief, he drew a deep breath and followed the warder towards the gate that led out of the House of Correction. He would make sure he never passed through it again.

Dressed like a normal person, his hat pulled well down to cover his naked head, Harry walked out into Campbell Street.

Eliza, waiting beside the gate, burst into tears when she saw him. She reached out and lay her gloved hand against the side of his face. 'What have they done to you, Harry?'

He wanted to hold her, to feel the solid reality of her body against his, to make what he had been through a dream. He stepped away from her. 'Don't come too close—I'm lousy.'

'Mrs Hennessy said to expect that.' Eliza smiled despite her tears. 'The copper is lit and the bathtub is waiting for you in the washhouse. And she has begged and borrowed clothes for you to wear until yours are properly clean.'

'She is a good woman,' he said.

'She is. And she is very angry about what has happened.' Eliza caught his hand in hers and squeezed it, her eyes still glistening. 'Oh

Harry, people have been kind. So many people dropped by and gave me money—one man even gave five shillings. You are needed out here, by your parents,' she sniffed back her tears, 'and by me.'

They walked along Campbell Street towards Bathurst Street. 'We must make these payments regularly.' Her face was rigid. 'It is making a criminal of you.'

A criminal like half the Thompsons. Eliza didn't say it. Harry doubted she even thought it. Who was he to talk? His own father had been twice transported—first to New South Wales, then from Swan River to Van Diemen's Land. And the traps had always been sniffing around when he was a kid. If the old man had stayed, Harry might have followed the same path.

'And once you've had your bath,' Eliza said with a forced brightness, 'we will have morning tea. Between us, Mrs Hennessy and I have made a Madeira cake.'

Once I've had my bath, Harry thought, *the first thing I'll do is hold you. And never let you go.*

49

'Hey, Thompson. I suppose you're pleased with yourself?'
Ellen turned and glared at Mary Cunningham standing, arms crossed, in the doorway of her house, along from Moodie's Row. Drunk again, in the middle of the day, and unpleasant with it.

'It's disgusting, a piece like you getting a decent man thrown into prison.'

'That was the court's doing, not mine.' Ellen kept walking.

Cunningham stepped onto the footpath and followed her. 'If you hadn't been hounding him, it wouldn't have.'

Ellen stopped and faced her. 'He owed that money to support his children. They can't live on air.'

'Are they even his?' Cunningham sneered. 'With a slut like you, they could be anybody's.'

Ellen didn't think. She threw herself at the older woman and slammed her fist into the side of her head.

Cunningham grabbed at Ellen's head, knocking her hat off, grasping fistfuls of hair.

A crowd gathered as they struggled, some cheering them on.

Ellen tried to prise Cunningham's fingers loose, sobbing with the stinging pain, but Cunningham held her grip. She was going to rip great tufts of hair from Ellen's scalp.

Ellen pushed at her, kicking at her legs, and dug her nails into her shoulders, but Cunningham twisted back from her.

'Mary,' a voice bellowed. 'Let her go. She'll call the coppers on you.'

Mary Cunningham stepped away from Ellen. Triumphant, she held up a handful of hair. 'See how you like it—being bald like a gaolbird.'

Cunningham's man, Ned Stevens, stood beside her. 'Now clear off, Thompson.'

'Clear off yourself.'

Ellen felt a hand rest lightly on her shoulder. Mrs Smith, from the house two along from hers in Moodie's Row, said, 'Come away, Ellen. They're not worth it.'

Mrs Smith squeezed Ellen's hand. 'Is your sister at home?'

Ellen nodded, afraid that if she spoke, she would burst into tears. She wouldn't give Cunningham the satisfaction.

Mrs Smith picked up Ellen's hat from the footpath and went with her to the house.

Bessie looked up as the door opened. She was sitting on the floor, playing pat-a-cake with Lizzie.

'Ellen's had a bit of a fright. She needs a strong cup of tea, Bessie, love.' Mrs Smith helped Ellen to a chair and left.

Ellen glanced down and realised her bag of shopping was still on her arm, had hung there through the entire fight. She placed the bag on the table and began to cry.

Bessie leant against one of the chairs as she hauled herself off the floor. She came over and put her arm around Ellen's shoulder. 'What's happened?'

'That cow Mary Cunningham,' she sobbed.

It wasn't just her stinging scalp and Cunningham's words, it was everything. She covered her face with her hands. She was tired of it. The struggle to care for her children—the help she got was barely enough to keep starvation at bay. The shabby house, the faded clothing not quite warm enough, lining the children up at the Benevolent Society depot for a meal of soup and bread when everything had run out and she and Bessie were living on tea and little else. Harry not caring about his children, paying maintenance only when he felt like it. That he had never meant anything he had said to her. It was winter. There wasn't enough work for anyone. The grey skies. The rain. The cold. Would it ever be any different?

Bessie gently brushed her hand over Ellen's tangled hair. Ellen whimpered with the pain.

'Let me look.' Bessie bent in close. 'There are a few spots here and there, but she hasn't ripped lumps out of your head. I'll get a cloth and clean it up.'

Bessie sponged Ellen's head gently. 'What happened?'

'I was on my way home, minding my own business, when that bitch came out and had a go at me because Harry went inside for not paying the maintenance. She said the children were probably not his. I couldn't stop myself. I thumped her. Then she started pulling my hair, said how would I like it being bald like a gaolbird.' She winced. 'Ow, that hurt.'

'Sorry, I'm being as gentle as I can.' She continued brushing.

Billy and Jennie had followed Mrs Smith in and stood quietly, close together, at the other side of the table.

'What's wrong, Mummy?' Billy asked. 'Were you fighting?' His eyes glittered with interest.

'I was,' she sniffed. 'That Mary Cunningham was rude to me and pulled my hair, so I boxed her ears.'

'You said we shouldn't fight.'

'Sometimes it can't be helped.' She sighed loudly. 'But fighting with your sisters is bad.'

Bessie stepped back. 'There, all tidy and pinned.'

'Thank you.' Ellen gazed across at the children. 'Now look at what I have here.' She took a paper bag from her shopping bag and laid it on the table, then held up a small newspaper-wrapped parcel. 'A beef neck. I'll make a big pot of soup that will do us a couple of days. But what about this?' She lifted a sugared bun from the paper bag. 'Today is Lizzie's birthday and we are having a treat. It's a bit stale, but it isn't squashed after that fight, and if we sprinkle some water on it and warm it, in a few minutes it will be as fresh as new.'

'Or almost,' Bessie laughed. 'I'll put the kettle on.'

'Now sit down. When the tea's made, I'll cut us all a piece.' She bent and picked up Lizzie, who had crawled over from where she had been sitting with Bessie and had pulled herself upright using Ellen's leg. 'Aren't you a clever one, my little darling?' She planted a kiss on Lizzie's cheek.

Ellen watched as Bessie placed the bun into the camp oven. 'Harry must have been shaved when he was inside.'

'He's got stubble on his face now.'

'You've seen him?'

'From the other side of Bathurst Street. He would have been on his way to the Benevolent Society depot.'

'I didn't want him to go to gaol. I get nothing if he does time instead of paying what he owes. Anyway, someone must have paid if he is out. I have half what he owes me, and there's no reason he can't keep up the payments. I hear he's working at the mill most days and his wife is doing clothing alterations. That would be a good job. If we had a sewing machine, we could do that home here and not have to worry about someone looking after the children.'

'But ladies would want to have fittings.' Bessie gazed around the room. 'Who would want to come here?'

Ellen was so used to it—she no longer saw the dirty, peeling wallpaper, the stained ceiling, the shabby furniture. Most days, in summer, she no longer even noticed the stench of the Hobart Rivulet at the other end of the Row. It was no different from most houses in places like Moodie's Row, where the poorest lived.

'I wasn't thinking of ladies, just people like us. Second-hand clothes always need something done to them.'

Bessie screwed up her face. 'Who could afford it in winter? And in summer you'd earn more working at Peacock's cutting fruit.'

'You're right.' Ellen rolled her eyes. 'But I can dream.' She had well and truly pushed away the last dream she had of owning a sewing machine—it went with a house with a garden and a man who cared about her and her children. It was the stuff of fairy tales.

50

Harry pushed open the door to the cottage and stood back, the floor was slick with water. He stepped in carefully and looked around. The old couple's bed, in the corner where the floor sloped away, stood in about three inches of water. The shingles had moved on the roof, leaving a gaping hole. Snow was mounded on the floor below. The hearth was a mess of cold ashes. His father and Grannie were still in bed. Everything that could be piled on the bed for warmth had been, even a couple of pieces of carpet.

Eliza followed Harry in. She stared at the roof. 'You go out and fix that. I'll clean up in here.'

Harry walked over to the bed. 'Dad, we're here now. We'll straighten this place up and get you something to eat.'

The old man nodded, his eyes still closed.

Eliza had put her basket on the table and was staring, her brow furrowed as if she wasn't sure where to start.

Harry went out to the barn and found what he needed to fix the roof. He carried the ladder over to the cottage and climbed up slowly, careful of the snow still on the roof. He did no more than push the shingles back together and nail a square of wood over them to keep them in place and make the roof watertight. The whole roof needed replacing. A job for spring. He paused for a moment, looking out across the clearing to the trees surrounding the Springs. The sun broke through the clouds, the whole scene shining a dazzling white. Harry shivered. No matter how beautiful, he preferred summer and its heat.

He returned to the barn and split logs for the fire. He carried an armful into the cottage. The floor was now dry, the hearth swept, a fire burning, bedding spread on chairs in front of it to warm. Eliza was sitting at the table, chopping vegetables to add to the soup she was preparing, the pot already simmering over the fire.

'I don't think they ate any of the stew I left on Sunday.' She stood and wiped her hands on her apron. 'It's so cold in here. We should get them out of bed and move it a bit closer to the hearth.'

She went over to the bed. 'Would you like a cup of tea, Mrs Woods?'

Grannie looked up and shook her head slowly.

'We'll help you out of bed. Then I'll bring you a cup of tea with a spot of brandy in it.'

'No,' Grannie croaked. She closed her eyes and turned her head away.

Harry came and stood beside Eliza. 'We'll get Dad out and fix the bed around Grannie.'

They helped the old man to the edge of the bed. As his feet touched the floor, his legs crumpled and he whimpered with pain. 'My leg!'

Harry held him upright. 'Let's get you into the chair by the fire.' Between them, Harry taking the weight of his father's body, Eliza his legs, they managed to get the old man into the chair. Once he was seated, Eliza draped a blanket over his shoulders.

Harry squatted beside his father and ran his hands carefully down his legs. The old man groaned, his face white and drawn.

'What happened, Dad?'

'Last night. Got up to use the piss pot,' he gasped. 'I fell.'

'I think it's broken. We have to get you to the hospital.'

'Not going anywhere,' the old man muttered.

There was no point arguing with him.

Eliza brought over a mug of tea, a tot of brandy splashed into it from the small bottle they had brought with them.

The old man wrapped his hands around the mug, warming his fingers as he drank.

Harry helped Eliza pull the carpet from the bed and straighten the blankets. Grannie, her eyes still shut, slowly followed Eliza's directions as she tried to make the old woman more comfortable.

The bed was dry beneath her. Eliza looked across at Harry, her brow furrowed. 'I doubt she has eaten or drunk much since we were last here.'

They dragged and pushed the bed closer to the fire, Grannie's weight making little difference at all.

Once the old man was back in bed, Harry went back to the barn and soon lost himself in the woodchopping. He finished up when his stomach grumbled, reminding him it was well past dinner time.

The old man lay against the lumpy pillows in his bed, Grannie quiet beside him. He turned to Eliza. 'It's warmer now, Bess.'

Harry's throat tightened. His father was away with the fairies.

Eliza glanced across at Harry before answering. 'I'm Eliza.'

'Is that what you call yourself now? You never should have gone, my lovely. I'd have looked after you. I've been straight for over thirty years.'

'Here,' Eliza said, 'have some soup.' She spooned the soup into the old man's mouth. He slurped at it hungrily. 'Do you want to feed yourself?'

He gripped the spoon, scooping it into the bowl Eliza held. His hand shook so much it splattered on the tea towel she had spread over the blankets. She took the spoon and continued to feed him. He began to doze once he had eaten his soup.

Eliza returned to the fire and dished up a bowl for Harry. She sat beside him as he ate.

'Who's Bess, Harry?'

Harry frowned and didn't answer.

'He called me Bess.'

'It's what he called my mother. You're nothing like her.' He didn't want to talk about his mother. 'If we keep the fire burning, they'll be warm enough tonight.'

'We can't leave them. One of us should stay.'

'I was thinking the same, but I'm supposed to be working

tomorrow.' He lowered his voice. 'They can't stay here by themselves any longer. I need to see what can be done about moving them down to the town, and let the mill know I won't be working. Can you manage here by yourself overnight?'

Eliza nodded. 'The house is warm and dry.' She reached up and rubbed her fingers against the short bristles of his beard. 'I'll be fine.'

He caught her fingers and kissed them. 'I'll be back as soon as it is light.'

~

Harry walked into the deep gloom of the room.

Eliza was asleep, her arms tight across her chest, her head against the side of the bed where Grannie lay. She jolted awake with the rush of cold air.

Harry went to the hearth and stamped his feet. 'There's near a foot of snow outside.'

Eliza shook herself properly awake. 'Sit down and take your boots off. I'll get you some breakfast.'

Harry hung his coat over the chair by the fire and eased off his boots while Eliza added wood to the fire. He wiggled his feet nearer the heat.

'When you are warm enough, would you go and sit with Grannie?' Eliza glanced at him over her shoulder as she tipped oatmeal into the pot hanging over the flames.

Harry got up and went to the bed. Grannie's eyes were closed, her chest rising and falling with each rattling breath. The old man slept quietly beside her. Harry had thought of sitting with the dying as women's work. With his grandfather, he had stood by the bedside and said his goodbyes, but it was Eliza and his grandmother who had sat through the long hours. Eliza had done the same for his grandmother and, he supposed, for her own mother. He now understood her reluctance to come with him, but still, a woman's place was with her husband.

Had she come with him when he first asked ... There was no point thinking of that. What he felt for Eliza now, what he was sure she felt for him, was better than anything that had gone before. He could talk of his life, all he had seen and done when working away from her, the desert, the night sky, the sunrises and sunsets, the sights on his climbs over the mountain, the people he met. And she listened now. She asked questions. She no longer hurried from his embraces as if scrubbing the floor or boiling the kettle was more important than he was.

Eliza came over and rested her hand on his shoulder. 'Your breakfast is ready. I'll sit here now.' She sat on the stool and slipped her hand beneath the blankets, taking Grannie's hand in hers.

He finished his porridge and leant back in the chair as he drank his tea. The cottage was silent except for the hiss of the kettle over the fire. He glanced over at Eliza. Her head was bowed, her eyes shut. She looked to be praying.

He put his tea down and went to the bed. He saw the stillness in the old woman's face and wished her Godspeed.

Eliza's eyelashes were damp. 'She's gone, Harry,' she whispered. On the other side of the bed, the old man shivered violently. Eliza went round and tucked the blankets tight under him.

'What do we do?' Harry asked. He had never had to deal with death—there had always been someone else to take charge.

'We can't leave her in the bed with your father.' She blinked slowly, her forehead puckered with concentration. 'We'll lay her on our old bed.'

Eliza pushed open the door to the bedroom; inside it was icy. Harry carried the old woman, as light as a child in his arms, and laid her gently on the bed.

'See if your father needs anything, then go down and tell the police. They will be able to arrange for the undertaker to come.' Eliza picked up the washbowl from the stand beside the window. 'I'll do what is needed here.'

~

Harry was back in the early afternoon. The old man was sleeping peacefully. Eliza sat in the other room beside Grannie, her head bowed.

Harry went over to the bed and gazed at the old woman. She was dressed in a clean nightgown, one of her frilled bonnets over her hair. Eliza had folded Grannie's arms across her chest and drawn the bedding up to her waist. In the peace of death, her face was smoothed out—she looked years younger than she was. She was not pretty by anyone's reckoning, probably never was. Harry had no doubt she had borne her share of sorrow. But she had stuck by his father—more than could be said for Harry's far prettier mother.

Eliza looked up at him.

'Inspector Quodling will be up as soon as he can get enough constables together.' He rested his hand on her shoulder—she was the steady point in this uncertain life. 'He said we should take the old man to hospital.'

'You know he won't go.'

'He's too sick to have any say.' Harry had made up his mind.

Inspector Quodling arrived with four constables early in the afternoon. They carried Grannie on a stretcher down to the finger-post where a hearse was waiting. He said as he left that he would bring the men up tomorrow afternoon and they would take the old man to the hospital. With a broken leg, it was the best place for him.

The afternoon was spent tidying the cottage. Eliza topped up yesterday's soup and tried to feed the old man. This time he called her Jane, and that troubled Harry less. They slept in chairs in front of the fire. Neither of them had any wish to sleep in the bedroom, and besides, it was too cold.

By the time Inspector Quodling and his men came for the old man, he no longer had any sense of his surroundings and went without argument.

Harry and Eliza pushed the bed back to the corner, stripped and folded the blankets, put the fire out and swept the hearth, leaving the room neat and tidy, everything in its place.

Eliza looked around her. 'There's work to be done, but not till spring.'

'And by then Dad might be well again.' Harry had to say it, although it was a faint hope. He bolted the door, wondering if it had ever been bolted before.

They buried Jane Woods the following Tuesday morning. A request had been placed in the *Mercury* for a subscription to help pay for the funeral to avoid Grannie being buried in a pauper's grave. Enough was collected for a plot that could take the old man too when his time came, but not enough to cover the cost of a headstone. Harry went back to the Springs the following Sunday by himself. He didn't go into the cottage but found a couple of lumps of wood in the barn that would do to make a cross. Over the next two weeks, he worked in Mrs Hennessy's shed at the bottom of her yard, fashioning a wooden cross. He carved a pattern of gum leaves along the edge and a waratah bloom near the bottom. He had asked Eliza to write both his father's and Grannie's names on a piece of paper. He carefully carved the letters of the old woman's name. If the old man rallied, they would all go to the cemetery and put it in place. There was space, too, for his father's name. Harry shivered—he would leave it for now. Harry had his father's name. It would be like carving his own gravestone.

Whatever happened, Harry was glad to have come to know his father again, to have filled one of the aching spaces left from his childhood.

51

Ellen pushed the door open and stepped into the darkened room. Bessie was seated at the table, her head lowered onto her arms.

'What is going on, Bessie?'

Bessie looked up at Ellen but said nothing. She lay her head back down.

Ellen marched over to the fireplace. 'Hell, Bessie, you've let the fire go out.'

She lit a candle, set it on the table, and rattled around at the hearth, trying to get the fire going. As if she didn't have enough to do. She had taken over Bessie's charring job. It was clear Bessie was ailing in some way. She was listless and seemed, more than ever, to be off in a world of her own. She had started missing work, so before her latest employer, Mrs Murray, could sack her, Ellen had talked the woman in to letting her take over the job. At least with Bessie home, she didn't have to worry about the children. She was sure Bessie was looking after them properly—she seemed happiest when she was with them.

The fire lit and the kettle set over the flames to boil, Ellen carried the candle to the bedroom door. The children were asleep, Lizzie snuggled between Billy and Jennie in Ellen's bed.

She pulled out the chair opposite Bessie. 'Did you give the children their tea?'

Bessie raised her head. She looked tired and dazed, deep rings under her eyes. She nodded. 'What was left of yesterday's soup. And bread.'

It was barely enough. But with the extra pay she had earnt this afternoon, doing the mountains of pots and pans and dishes after Mrs Murray's baking day, Ellen decided she would buy as big a piece of corned beef as she could afford, and they would have it with mashed potatoes and cabbage and bacon and they would eat until their bellies hurt.

'Any left for me?' Ellen asked.

Bessie groaned. 'I'm sorry. I didn't think.'

Ellen sighed loudly. Bread and dripping again—if there was any dripping left. What was wrong with the girl? Somehow, she would have to get Bessie to tell her.

Bessie started at the sound of shouting outside. 'What's that?'

'Some carry-on farther along Moodie's Row. The police arrived as I got home.'

Fear flashed across Bessie's face. She hugged herself tight and began rocking in her chair. 'They'll hang me,' she sobbed.

A chill crept down Ellen's back. 'What's wrong, Bessie?' Her voice was shrill. 'Tell me what's wrong.'

'I had a baby.'

'What?' It made no sense

Bessie repeated herself. 'I had a baby.'

'When? Where?' She wanted to shake Bessie. Where was this baby? Was she making it up? Ellen took a deep breath. Berating Bessie made her retreat into silence.

Ellen moved to the other side of the table and sat beside her sister. She put her arm around Bessie's shoulder and said more gently, 'When did this happen, Bessie?'

'Last week. When you were at Mam and Dad's.'

Once a week Ellen took the children to their grandparents. The weekly meal they had there was one of the things that had got them through winter. Her parents had little to spare themselves.

Ellen remembered coming home to find Bessie in bed, sleeping deeply. She could see Bessie had cleaned and scrubbed the floor and that had cheered her, thinking that finally Bessie was over whatever was wrong with her. She hadn't thought more about it—she had been too angry at what Dad had read from the newspaper. It had said there that Grandad was in hospital and Grannie had died at the Springs, neglected in the cold of the mountain. Bloody Harry Woods!

'You had the baby here? Alone?'

The candle flame flickered, light glistening on Bessie's wet cheeks.

'Yes.' She wept quietly. 'It hurt so much. I'd think the pain had stopped but it would start again. When it was over, I fainted.' Her eyes glazed. She was no longer seeing Ellen. 'When I woke there was a mess of blood and stuff on the floor and the baby was beside it. He was cold and still.' She looked at Ellen now. 'A little boy. He was so tiny. I wrapped him in my shawl, but he didn't get warm.'

Ellen pressed her lips tight, forcing back her own sobs. She thought of Billy, the first time she had held him—red, bellowing, kicking, full of life. That poor wee mite.

'Oh my poor girl.' She pulled Bessie's head against her bosom and stroked her hair. 'Why didn't you tell me?'

Bessie drew a ragged breath. 'I was scared you would turn me out into the street. You are always angry about men and how hard it is. And this was another mouth to feed and I wouldn't be able to work and we'd have no money.'

'Bessie. Bessie. Babies don't cost anything to feed. We would have managed. It's not being able to work that makes things so difficult.' She paused then asked the question that had worried her from the beginning. 'Where is the baby now?'

Bessie shivered. 'I knew he was dead so I buried him.'

Ellen loosened her embrace and eased herself back from Bessie. 'Where did you bury him?'

'In the garden next door, wrapped up in my shawl.'

Ellen rubbed her hand across her face. 'We will have to tell the police. Someone, some time, will find that poor little baby.' She pulled Bessie closer. 'It's better we tell them rather than someone else finds him and the police start looking for his mother.'

'But they'll hang me,' Bessie wailed.

'No. They won't. You didn't kill the baby. The problem is the baby isn't buried in a proper place.'

The police had already left Moodie's Row and were a couple of houses down Liverpool Street when Ellen went out.

'Constable! Constable!'

The two policemen turned and waited for Ellen to catch up to them. The light from the street lamp glittered on the belt buckles and buttons of their uniforms. With their helmets, they towered over her, tall and menacing.

She swallowed. 'You need to come and talk to my sister. There's something she needs to tell you.'

'What exactly does she need to tell us?' the taller of the two asked. He wasn't old, but his face was hard and stern.

Ellen didn't want to explain in the street where there were always other ears. 'You need to hear it from her.' She lowered her voice. 'It's about a baby.'

They exchanged a quick glance, but neither said anything. They followed Ellen back to the house.

The candle on the table guttered out as the police came through the door.

The shorter, middle-aged constable placed his lantern on the table and stood, his arms crossed.

Bessie looked ill, sitting there, staring into the bright light of the lantern.

Ellen stood beside her, her hand resting on Bessie's shoulder.

The taller constable pulled out a chair and sat facing Bessie across the table. 'What do you have to tell us, Miss ...' He looked up at Ellen.

'Thompson. My sister's name is Elizabeth Thompson.'

'...Miss Thompson?'

Bessie continued to stare into the light.

'We can't wait all night,' he said, taking no trouble to hide his impatience. He scowled at Ellen. 'You will have to tell us.'

Ellen opened her mouth and forced the words out. 'Bessie has just told me she had a baby last week.' She told herself she wasn't betraying Bessie, she was trying to save her. She hoped, by telling them rather than waiting for them to find the baby, any punishment would be less. She sucked her breath in and rushed on. 'And she said he died straightaway so she buried him.'

That caught his attention. His scowl deepened. 'Do you know where this baby is buried?'

'Bessie said it was in the yard next door.'

'You will need to be more specific.'

Ellen squatted beside Bessie. 'Can you tell us exactly where in the yard the baby is?'

Bessie slowly shook her head and said nothing.

'Right.' The constable picked up the lantern. 'Both of you wait here.'

Ellen and Bessie sat in the dark together, Bessie's head resting on Ellen's shoulder. No louder than a whisper, Bessie began to sing, 'How cold the wind do blow, my love ...'

A slow tear slid down Ellen's cheek.

The police seemed to be gone forever, but Ellen supposed it was only half an hour.

The middle-aged constable came back, lantern in hand. 'We will have to take your sister with us, Miss.'

'To the watchhouse?' Ellen started up from her seat. They were going to arrest Bessie. She should have kept quiet. Perhaps the baby would never have been found.

'No, to the hospital. She will need to be examined by a doctor.'

'Bessie's not well. She can't walk that far.'

'Don't worry, we'll take her by cab. I expect she will be there a few days. Tomorrow is a visiting day, you can call in and see her.'

'Now stand up, Miss Thompson.' He was fatherly in the way he spoke to Bessie. 'We are taking you to the hospital.'

Bessie stood slowly and walked with him to the door.

'Wait.' Ellen grabbed her own shawl from the back of the chair and wrapped it around Bessie. 'You'll feel better once you are in hospital. They'll look after you.' She kissed her on the cheek. 'I'll come tomorrow and see you.'

Bessie didn't react.

The constable placed his hand over Bessie's wrist and led her into the street.

Ellen sat in the darkness, her elbows on the table, her head in her hands.

'Mummy, what's wrong?'

She opened her eyes. 'Oh, Billy, my darling.' She pulled him onto her lap, holding him tight. He wriggled loose and slid back to the floor.

'I'm too big for that.'

'You will never be too big for that as long as I'm around.' She smiled. These children of hers, they were the best part of her life, no matter what happened.

'What were all the voices?'

'Aunty Bessie isn't well, so she's been taken to hospital where they'll make her better.' She kissed him. 'Now you go back to bed. I won't be long.'

She sat pinching the bridge of her nose. Why was life so hard? She had to go to work tomorrow morning and now had no one to mind the children. She would take them to Mam and Dad's early. Hopefully, Mam or one of her sisters wouldn't be working. She couldn't take them to Mary Ann—she was about to have another baby any day. And she needed to visit Bessie. She hoped Mrs Murray wouldn't want her to work late. She didn't want to miss visiting Bessie. Ellen groaned. What had she become? Here she was worrying about work and practical things when all she should be thinking of was Bessie and her lost boy.

52

An inquest was held a week on. Ellen sat with Bessie and her father in the upper room of the Bird in Hand Hotel. Bessie had been home from hospital a couple of days. She didn't look as pale and tired but she still seemed to be in a daze.

The taller, hard-faced policeman, Constable Delaney, gave evidence about finding the baby. He was followed by a doctor from the hospital who had examined the baby and Bessie. When the doctor said the baby could have died of exposure in as little as ten minutes if Bessie had been unconscious, Ellen was hopeful the jury would say that the baby died of natural causes.

Ellen had to give evidence about what she knew of Bessie's pregnancy and the birth, which was exactly nothing. And then Bessie was called. She explained it just as she had to Ellen and ended by saying she had hidden her pregnancy and the baby's body because she was afraid Ellen would turn her out of the house.

Ellen closed her eyes. She would never have done that.

The jury was quick in making its decision. Barely daring to breathe, Ellen held tight to Bessie's hand as the foreman stood and announced the verdict—death by natural causes. There was loud muttering in the reporters' box. Ellen wondered what those mongrels would write in their newspapers tomorrow.

Dad and Ellen walked home, one each side of Bessie. No one they knew would have dared comment. In the afternoon, Mam brought the children back home and sat with them while Ellen went out and bought hot saveloys and bread for tea.

She looked across the table at Billy and Jennie, sitting side by side, mouths full, eyes shining, chins glistening with grease. The enjoyment glowing in their faces made the extravagance worthwhile—they all needed something to cheer them and the best way, when you had very little, was a full belly.

After Mam left, they all went to bed. Ellen put the children together in her bed and climbed in beside Bessie. She held Bessie close as she sobbed, her heart breaking.

'My poor darling,' Ellen murmured. She couldn't shake the feeling that none of this would have happened if she had taken the time to speak to Bessie when she first noticed she was ailing. She had been so caught up in the endless struggle to feed and clothe her children, her anger at Harry and the way the world worked against her that she had not seen what was happening in her own house.

When Bessie's tears had subsided, Ellen asked gently, 'Do you want to tell me who the father was?'

Bessie sniffed. 'His name was Jack. He said he was a shipmate of Will's and was at his funeral. And he sounded like Mam.'

That narrowed things down—a Scottish whaler called Jack!

'How did you meet him?'

'I was on my way home from work when he called out to me. He introduced himself and knew I was Will's sister. He was polite, asked after Mam and Dad. He said he was about to have dinner and asked me to come along. It was a lovely meal, Ellen, roast beef and potatoes and gravy. Pudding too. He sent out for wine and gave me some, and I must have drunk too much. I felt giddy so he walked me home.'

'Where was I?'

'You were at Mam and Dad's with the children. And ...' her voice trailed off.

Ellen let out her breath slowly. It was nowhere near as bad as she had imagined.

'Ellen, I don't understand why you all do it. There's nothing nice about it. It hurt, and it went on and on. I won't do it again.'

Ellen smiled into the dark despite herself. 'You might meet someone you really like, and if he likes you too, it will be better than that. But in the future, when you're out with any bloke, don't drink too much and don't let him get his hands up your skirts the first or even the third time you go out with him. Once they've got what they want, most of them disappear into thin air.'

'I know,' Bessie sighed. 'Jack said he'd come and see me again, but he never did.'

Ellen hoped the inquest was the end of Bessie's problems, but the following Friday a copper came to the door asking for Bessie. He told her she was to come to the Police Court the next morning. There Bessie was charged with concealment of birth and remanded to appear again the following Wednesday.

She was led down the steps beneath the dock into the prison before Ellen had realised what was happening. There had been no time even for Bessie to glance Ellen's way.

On Wednesday, she was committed to stand trial when the Supreme Court of Tasmania next sat to hear criminal cases. Bessie stood quietly in the dock, her shoulders hunched. She was wearing a brown prison dress and a white cap on her head. Her arms held tight across her bosom, she stared around the room as if she had no idea where she was.

Ellen peered at her. She had no scratches or bruises that Ellen could see. Women could be cruel to those they thought had killed babies. She didn't know how Bessie would survive in prison without her sisters to look out for her. She pressed her lips tight to stop a sob. Ellen had known all along that something was wrong but hadn't taken the care to ask Bessie what it was. If she had, Bessie wouldn't be in this situation.

53

September 1882

Ellen poked her head around the door of the hospital ward. There was no nurse at the desk in the middle of the room, nor anywhere in sight. Lizzie on her hip, she shepherded her two older children over to Grandad's bed.

He was sitting up in a bed at one side of the fireplace, puffing on his pipe. As soon as he caught sight of her, his thin pale face crinkled into a broad smile.

'We wanted to come and see you, Grandad.' She set Lizzie on the bed beside him.

He beamed at the child. 'What a bonny little lass!'

'That she is. She's a year old now.'

'She has the look of Harry to be sure.'

'She does.' There was no point in talking about Harry's attempt to disown Lizzie. She would never forgive him that.

Grandad turned to Billy. 'And how are you, Billy me boy?'

Billy stared at the old man, recognition slowly breaking across his face.

'Grandad,' he said and pulled the wooden whistle from his pocket. He offered it to his grandfather, who took his pipe out and started to play a sprightly tune on the whistle. He broke off, wheezing and coughing, and held the whistle out for the boy to take back.

When he had his breath back, he relit his pipe, placing his matches on the small table between his bed and the next. 'How old are you now, son?'

'Five, Grandad. I'm going to school next year.'

'Probably not until the year after.'

Billy kept his eyes on Grandad as if Ellen hadn't spoken.

She didn't understand why Billy was so keen. Children didn't need to go to school until they were seven, but Ellen thought she might stretch the truth slightly and say he was already seven at the end of next year.

'You'll be learning to read and write. Never needed it much in my day, but the world is changing.'

He looked down at Jennie standing beside Ellen. 'And you, young miss, aren't you a pretty one, like your mum?' Jennie smiled shyly at him and moved farther into the safety of her mother's skirts.

'How are you going, Grandad?' Ellen asked.

'Getting better.' He took a puff on his pipe. 'They strapped my leg and reckon it will be a few weeks before it's mended, then it'll be as good as new. I'll be taking trips to the pinnacle again.'

'Leaping from stone to stone across the Ploughed Field?' Ellen asked.

'And blowing on my cornet while I do it. I did that once, blew it the whole way to the top and down again. I was fit in my time.'

'Are they feeding you well?'

'The food's fine, but not a patch on your cooking. What you couldn't do with a rabbit!' He stared through the door opposite his bed to the verandah. 'But they don't let me have a drink in here.'

'I have something for you.' Ellen turned away and slipped her hand into her jacket pulling out the small flask she had wedged into the top of her stays. When she had arrived at the hospital, she had declared to the gateman, with wide-eyed innocence, that she had nothing for the patient. Any food or drink was to be handed in at the gate, and she knew there was no chance the rum would ever get to Grandad if she did that. The gateman had told her to check with the nurse before she took the children into the ward, but Ellen was having none of that.

She slipped the flask underneath the bedclothes.

'I'll have to ration that.' He winked at her. 'And keep it well out of sight.'

Visitors wandered into the ward to see other patients. A nurse came to the door and scowled at Ellen's children who were all now sitting on the bed. She looked ready to come over and order them out, but someone called to her and she moved away.

Ellen grasped Grandad's hand. 'I was so sad when I heard about Grannie.'

A single tear trickled down Grandad's lined cheek. 'She was the best mate a man could wish for.' He took in a deep breath and started a wheezing cough. When finally he could breathe easily, he said, 'I'll be joining her soon enough.'

'Oh, don't say that.' He was family, her daughters' grandfather. Hadn't she lost enough of her family already?

'I've had a good life, seen the world, made merry. I'll be glad to join my Janey.' He winked at Ellen. 'She'll have a wee dram ready for me when I get there, wherever it is, upstairs or downstairs.'

Ellen blinked back her tears. 'That she will.' She bent and kissed Grandad on the cheek. 'I suppose we shouldn't stay too long—you never know who might arrive.'

'No, we don't want any rows.' He chuckled to himself. 'I didn't mind watching them, though, 'specially when it was two women.'

Ellen laughed softly. 'You must have been a devil in your time.'

He nodded. 'I was indeed.'

She rested her hand on his and kissed his cheek. 'We'll be back as soon as we can.' Although it made her sad to see him like this, it was the sadness of ordinary life and a respite from her worries about Bessie.

As she walked along the corridor, she noticed a woman coming towards her, staring intently at her and the children. She seemed most interested in Lizzie. Ellen had never seen her this close. She was blonde with washed-out blue eyes, well into her thirties by the look of her, thin and neat, a kindly face until she realised Ellen was watching her. Ellen smiled at her as she passed by. She wanted to say, *No hard feelings, you're welcome to him.* If she could only find a decent man who would take her *and* her children, she wouldn't give Harry Woods another thought.

~

Despite the illness and death, life was finally moving calmly. Harry didn't want to admit it to himself, but there was relief that these last few years were coming to an end. If things went on as they were, he would be putting money by despite having to hand over eight shillings each week at the police office.

There was a routine now that the old man was in hospital. Harry was working a full week, Eliza doing a bit of sewing and visiting the old man on Tuesdays and Thursdays, the weekdays visitors were allowed at the hospital. Harry went with her on Sundays. They had the sociability of meals with Mrs Hennessy and her boarders in the evening, singalongs in the parlour afterwards if they wanted. Then they could retire to the privacy of their room.

Harry lay back against the pillows, the lamp turned low, watching Eliza sitting on the chair at the end of the bed, brushing out her hair, firm strokes along the full length. The image of another woman, sitting on the side of a bed, brushing her hair with a more languorous movement slithered into his mind. He shoved the thought away.

'I passed Miss Thompson and her children the other day. She was leaving as I arrived to see your father.'

Harry held his breath. Eliza had rarely spoken of Ellen.

'I am sorry, it was wrong of me to suggest that child was not yours, Harry. She is the image of you.' She paused, sat straighter in her chair, and said, 'I know life is very difficult for her, raising those children alone, and wondered if, perhaps, we—'

Harry sat bolt upright. It would be easy to pass Lizzie off as Eliza's child. And to have one of his children with him ... He felt again Jennie's arms warm around his neck, Billy's chubby hand in his. And Lizzie, the child he had barely seen, the child he had never held. The pain of their absence washed through him. He could not let Eliza finish, could not let the idea take hold.

'No!'

Eliza sat still, her brush in her hand, watching him.

'Ellen would never give a child up. There would be hell to pay if anyone was to suggest it to her. She loves her children more than anything on earth.'

Eliza nodded her head slightly and continued her brushing.

He forced the thought away, forced himself to think of something else. 'Bob says we could get a lease on the land at the Springs at a very small cost.' He lay back against the pillows. 'It would stop people believing they had the right to barge into the cottage any time they wanted.'

'Yes.' Eliza turned to him. 'And we could offer refreshments for picnic parties so they needn't bring heavy baskets with them. We would have to get a proper stove.'

'And,' Harry said, warming to the plans, 'we could build a large cabin for visitors to stay in, a place suitable for ladies.'

'We wouldn't need to stay there through winter. We could come down at the end of May and work here, put some money by, have a rest and then go up again in October.'

'It would work, wouldn't it?' He felt a thrill of excitement. Eliza seemed as enthusiastic as he was. 'Could you write the letter to the Hobart Council?'

'I'm not sure I'd know the right things to say, but I'll ask around, see who would best help us.'

In the end, the letter was written by Mr Dobson, the lawyer who had defended Harry in court last summer. Harry was granted a five-year lease at one shilling a year provided he kept the water course clear and made sure it was in good repair. The day following the Council decision, the old man died. It was as if he had now passed care of the mountain on to Harry.

~

Henry Woods, the Old Man of the Mountain, was buried in the

same grave as his faithful wife, Jane. And now Harry had nothing that tied him to this place. There were his daughters but he doubted, even if he lived to his father's age, that he would ever be part of their lives. He wondered how much longer he would stay.

He stood beside Eliza as Reverend Curwen from All Saints Church said the prayers at the graveside. Eliza's head was bowed. Harry thought it more likely that she was thinking of her own mother than the old man they were burying. It didn't matter. She had done more than her duty by the old couple even though Grannie, in particular, had not appreciated her efforts. There had been none of the easy friendship they had with Ellen. Eliza had said when she visited him in hospital, his father had said very little to her, giving brief answers to her questions about his health. Sometimes she could get him talking of the old days. More often she read to him—the story of the marooned man. Harry had wanted to know the end of the story he had heard in the gaol, so Eliza had bought a used book that told the story in greater detail, calling the man a different name. She read it to Harry of an evening.

He gazed at the mourners. There was a fair turn-out. Some had come for his father but a number of the women, whom Eliza counted as her friends, were here for her. He expected to see Ellen somewhere at the back, but she wasn't there. She had the right to mourn the old couple, but he knew the mere sight of her would make him angry.

The next day Eliza wrote to the *Mercury* to publicly pass on both Harry's thanks and hers, to everyone for their assistance, both financial and personal, especially in helping to pay for the funerals. The world was, as Eliza said, full of good kind people.

54

Despite being in the same building as the Police Court at the Brisbane Street end of the Campbell Street Gaol, the Criminal Court was formal and frightening. The judge, Justice Dobson, in his red robe and large white wig, sat at the front behind the raised wooden bench. He was the brother of the man who had defended Harry when he had punched Ellen. She hoped he wasn't going to be horrible to Bessie.

There were lawyers everywhere, wearing dark gowns and small white wigs. This was the court that sentenced people to hang. Dad had said the worst that could happen was that Bessie would do time, that if they had wanted to hang her, they would have charged her with murder. It didn't make Ellen feel any better.

Bessie stood in the dock looking bewildered.

When the clerk asked her how she pleaded, she mumbled, 'Guilty.'

Justice Dobson leant forward and spoke directly to Bessie. 'Are you admitting that you buried the child in order to conceal ...' he paused, '...to hide the fact that you had given birth.'

Bessie frowned, blinking slowly. 'Isn't that what you are meant to do if someone dies? Bury them?'

The judge sat back in his chair and said to the clerk, 'Enter the plea as not guilty. We will defer this case until later in the session.'

A warder escorted Bessie down the stairs beneath the dock. She hadn't looked Ellen's way once.

Ellen clambered out of her seat and went to the usher. 'Excuse me, where are they taking my sister?'

'Back to the gaol. She will be brought back this afternoon when her case is heard.'

'Can I go and sit with her? She'll be frightened.'

'I'm afraid not, Miss.' His eyes flickered over Ellen, making immediate judgements. 'Are you giving evidence in this case?'

'Yes, I am.'

'You shouldn't be sitting here in court if that is so, Miss. Your sister's case won't be heard until well after luncheon. I suggest you go home and be back here by two o'clock. Come and see me then. I will take you to the room where the witnesses wait.'

Ellen knew arguing would get her nowhere. It was clear this polite, mild-mannered man knew every rule inside out and would never change his mind.

She came back at two o'clock and was taken to a waiting room with a grimy window. She wished she hadn't eaten any lunch even though it was only bread and jam and a cup of tea. Ellen waited for so long that her queasiness went away, but then she started worrying that they had forgotten her, and Bessie had been tried without a friendly face in the court. Bessie would believe they all had abandoned her.

The light was fading by the time the usher came for her. Bessie was already in the dock when Ellen was brought into the court-room. The gaslights had been turned on. In the yellowish light, Bessie looked very ill, the rings under her eyes darker.

Ellen was led to the witness box, placed on oath and questioned.

'Bessie ...' She stopped and began again. 'Elizabeth Thompson is my sister. She lives with me in Moodie's Row.'

The lawyer prosecuting, Mr Adams, asked, 'Were you aware that your sister had given birth?'

'Not at all. I didn't even know she was expecting.'

'How is that possible? The pregnancy came almost to full term.'

She glared at him. 'It's winter. It's cold. We don't always have enough money for wood. Everybody looks stout because we wear all we own some days.' Her voice caught. 'And it's still not enough to keep warm.' He had no idea how so many of them were forced to live.

Without acknowledging her answer, he moved on. 'When did you discover that your sister had given birth?'

Ellen glanced over at Bessie, sitting in the dock with her head bowed. She wished they hadn't ordered her to come here and give evidence.

'When I said the police were outside, she told me that she had given birth and buried the baby. She was very upset. I don't think she understood what she was doing.' Tears pricked at Ellen's eyes. She took a long, shuddering breath through her nose. 'If I had known she was expecting, none of this would have happened. I would have been with her and that little boy would be alive.'

Ellen was allowed to step down after that. She went and sat on the public benches.

John Delaney, the scowling constable who had been there that night, took Ellen's place in the witness box. 'We searched the yard at the front of a house in Moodie's Row and dug up the body of a newborn infant. I attempted to question the mother, Elizabeth Thompson, but she said nothing. We then took her and the body of the infant to the Hobart General Hospital. When questioned again at the hospital, she stated that the infant never lived.'

Constable Delaney was followed by Dr Graham from the hospital. He, at least, had a kinder face than Delaney.

'I am a qualified medical practitioner. I remember the dead body of a male child and the mother, Elizabeth Thompson, being brought to the hospital. The woman was in a very weak state and had been confined eight or ten days previously. In conjunction with Dr. Giblin, I made a post-mortem examination of the body. We found that the child had breathed and consequently were of the opinion that it was born alive. Had it been properly cared for, it should have lived as the mother was capable of giving it nourishment. It was a healthy-looking child, and there were no external marks of violence on the body. A short period of exposure to the cold, during the presumed unconsciousness of the mother, would be fatal.'

When Dr Graham finished and left the witness box, Bessie was asked if there was anything she wanted to say in her defence.

She looked up at the judge, her shoulders sagging, misery plain in her face. 'No.'

Justice Dobson briefly summed up everything that had been said. He ended by saying to the jury it was clear that the prisoner showed limited understanding of what had happened, perhaps even of these proceedings. He was saying, more politely, what the newspapers had said after the inquest—that Bessie was *dull-witted*. Who wouldn't seem that way after everything she had been through? Although it made her angry, Ellen hoped it meant Bessie would be spared further punishment.

This time too, the jury seemed to take no more than a few minutes before they returned.

Bessie was told to stand when the foreman of the jury rose from his seat. She hung her head, her knuckles white as she gripped the edge of the dock.

The clerk asked, 'How do you find the prisoner: guilty or not guilty?'

'Guilty.'

Ellen wished she could go to Bessie and hold her in her arms, tell her everything would be all right. But that would be a lie.

The foreman continued to stand. 'May I make a comment, Your Honour?'

'You may.'

'We, the entire jury, would strongly recommend that Your Honour exercise mercy in your sentencing, taking into account the inexperience of the prisoner.'

'Thank you, you may now sit.' Justice Dobson turned his attention toward Bessie. 'Elizabeth Thompson, having taken into consideration what you have already suffered and the recommendation of the jury, I sentence you to imprisonment for one calendar month.'

Ellen's sob echoed through the room as Bessie, her shoulders hunched, disappeared down the stairs again.

More than ever, Ellen felt to blame. She had been too wrapped up in her worries and her bitterness towards Harry to notice what was happening. She had treated Bessie as someone to lean on, forgetting that Bessie was a young woman just like she was. For the last year and a half, everything Bessie had done was for Ellen and her children, nothing for herself alone. Ellen had no idea what Bessie's hopes and dreams were, if she wanted a husband and children of her own, if she wished she could go out dancing, if she had the money, was it hats or fancy shoes she would buy first. When she was released, Ellen would make sure Bessie had the chance to enjoy life the way a young woman of only twenty-one should.

55

December 1882

Ellen walked across lower Macquarie Street in the late afternoon sunshine.

Despite everything, today it was good to be alive. In a couple of months, it would be two years since Harry's wife had arrived and the worst two years of her life had begun, three when she counted Will's death. There had been so many deaths—not only Will, but Grannie and Grandad Woods, and Mary Ann and Bessie's babies. George had disappeared, and she had discovered that the man she loved was a heartless liar.

But they had survived. Bessie was home, although she was quiet and sad. She was working at Peacock's, and most of the women there were kind to her. Ellen had been forced to give that snotty cow from Ragged Lane a blooded nose. She wouldn't be talking of sluts and murderers in Ellen's hearing again, nor would any of the other women at the factory.

Ellen stopped at Mary Ann's front door, watching a group of boys playing football in the middle of the street. The boys ranged in age from around five to ten or so, the little boys rougher in their play than some of the older ones. Billy was there amongst them. He had the ball and booted it high over the heads of the others, who turned and raced along the street after it, Billy with them. Ellen was happy to see him playing without a care.

She pushed open the door, calling out as she went in.

Mary Ann turned from the stove where she was stirring a pot. She sniffed. 'Strawberry jam today?'

'Yes, you can smell it out in the street.'

Mary Ann looked past her towards the door. 'Bessie not with you?'

'She's working late.'

Mary Ann frowned. 'I don't like her walking along Liverpool Street alone after dark. She can stay here any night she wants.'

'Annie is working late so they'll walk home together.'

'Ah, that's good. I pity any drunk who tried anything with Annie she didn't want.' She pushed the pot to the back of the stove. 'How is Bessie? Has she spoken at all about her time inside?'

'Not much.' Ellen sat down at the end of the table. 'She wasn't with the other women because she was in the gaol, not the House of Correction. Something to do with being tried at the Supreme Court.'

'I suppose that was for the best,' Mary Ann frowned, 'but she would have been lonely.'

'I couldn't imagine being by myself.' Ellen had rarely spent longer than an hour by herself that she could remember. There was always someone around and at night always someone warm beside her—her sisters, her children, Harry. She was sure her heart would break without those she loved near her. She jerked her head to get rid of the thought.

'Bessie is quieter than she was, but when she's with the children, she seems happy.' She glanced over at her daughters. 'And how have my angels been today?'

Jennie was standing by the cradle at the other side of the room, gently rocking Mary Ann's baby, Thomas Henry, born six weeks after Bessie's. Lizzie, sitting on the floor beside her, was holding a rag doll with a painted face, babbling away to it.

'They're good kids and play well together.'

'I'm grateful you can mind them.'

'It's no problem at all. And the coin comes in handy.'

Ellen yawned. 'I had better get them home and cook tea.'

Mary Ann took a small paper-wrapped parcel from the meat safe hanging in the corner of the kitchen, covered with damp hessian. She placed the parcel on the table in front of Ellen. 'Here are the sausages you wanted. I sent Billy out and he talked the butcher a ha'penny down. I'll have to use him to do my shopping. He's a fine little lad.'

'He is.' Ellen smiled, as she always did when someone complimented her children. 'Would you like some raspberries? The first of the season should be ready. Annie wants me to go to the Springs with her on Sunday to buy some. Mam said she would mind the children.'

'Is that a good idea?'

Ellen screwed up her face. 'He's paying maintenance regularly, so I've no complaint with him. I'll hang back and let Annie do the talking. I loved it up there. I'll walk up the Fingerpost Track and wait there while Annie gets the raspberries.'

'That sounds reasonable. You'd be well out of his way.' She nodded. 'Yes, I'll have a few.'

Ellen stood and pushed the chair in. 'Come on, girls.'

Mary Ann, now sitting in the chair by the window, unbuttoned the bodice of her dress and settled the baby to her breast. She looked content, her sorrow over the loss of little Rose last year faded, but Ellen knew the tiny infant would never be forgotten. How could you forget any of your children?

'We'll be back tomorrow, just after half-past six.'

'I'll be awake. This young man here is an early riser.' Mary Ann bent her head, her gaze on the child.

Ellen smiled. Motherhood had mellowed her older sister.

As she walked out into the street, Billy ran up. 'Are we going home now?'

'Yes, and I'll cook those sausages you got me and mash some potatoes. How does that sound?

'Scrummy, Mum.'

Mum! He was already growing up. He took Jennie's hand, and they skipped along in front of Ellen as she carried Lizzie, sitting comfortably on her hip, her head resting on Ellen's shoulder. Ellen sighed, realising she was happy. Bessie was getting better. Ellen had heard her laughing as she played with the children. Ellen would be working at Peacock's jam factory until the end of March and, if she was lucky, she would be kept on longer. The money was reasonable, and she was paying Mary Ann to mind the children. It was a relief knowing they were with someone who cared about them. And Harry was paying the maintenance. She had begun, week by week, to replace the children's clothing that was worn or too small. She might even manage some more furniture—a dresser perhaps, or a sofa. When winter came, life would be hard again, but she would be prepared. They would get through the next few years. And when they were old enough, she would see the children went to school. She could find a morning job then—laundry or charring if she had to. The future was not as bleak as she had thought as little as two months ago.

~

Harry walked down the path from the cottage past the barn and the huts. He was pleased with the progress he had made in the six weeks they had been back at the Springs. The garden behind the barn was in order. He had planted potatoes, cabbages, carrots and leeks. The berry canes were staked—there was a good crop of raspberries coming on, some already ripe. The roof was watertight but it needed to be replaced. He had lined the walls of both the cottage and two of the huts with timber boards, and painted them. The bedding on all the beds had been replaced, and Eliza had made curtains and bedspreads. It wasn't luxurious but it was clean and comfortable, a place there was no need to be ashamed of. That had eaten into what he had saved down in the town, but climbers were coming up regularly. Each week money was left over after he had paid the maintenance. In April, once the visitors started to drop off, he would build a large cabin from scratch. What wasn't done before winter set in, he would finish in the spring.

Two groups of climbers had arrived within minutes of each other this morning. Harry had taken those who wanted to the pinnacle, but a number of the women had been happy to stay at the Springs and enjoy the peace and quiet. The whole crowd was now sitting outside the cottage, eating sandwiches and the pies Eliza had made. She had said that if they got any busier, she would need a girl to help her. Finally, everything seemed to be going right.

Women's voices carried up the track.

He had to be mistaken.

Ellen, her young sister Alice and the friend who had flirted with him after the circus, loudmouthed and forward Annie, came into sight.

He walked towards them and stood blocking the path. 'Clear off, you're not wanted here.'

'Annie wants to buy some raspberries. I'll stay here while she and Alice pick them,' Ellen said. 'You have nothing to worry about.'

It was a reasonable request. But Harry didn't trust her.

'Anyway,' Annie butted in. 'We can go where we want. You don't own the mountain.' She stood there with her hands on her hips, as if she were spoiling for a fight.

'I may not own the mountain, but I lease the land here at the Springs so I get to say who comes here. And I don't want the likes of you up here, disturbing the peace of decent people.'

'Decent people?' Annie scoffed. 'You're not counting yourself as one of them, are you? There was nothing decent in the way you treated Ellen, tricking her into thinking you were going to marry her, then making out those children had nothing to do with you. She should do you for breach of promise.'

'Breach of promise!' He was breathing through his nose, his fists clenched. 'From what I remember, she didn't need any encouragement.'

He had said too much.

Ellen glared at him, eyes narrowed, and said each word clearly, 'You are such a low bastard, Harry Woods.'

The conversation over by the cottage had stopped, each person sat, teacup in hand, watching them. A couple of the men stood up.

'You mind your language,' Harry snarled. 'My wife is over there.'

'Oh, one of those, is she?' Ellen sneered. 'Wouldn't say *shit* for a shilling but do it all the same.'

She was no better than her friend Annie. He went to move forward but couldn't, his arms held tight by a couple of the climbers.

'Not worth it, mate,' one said.

'We'll see them in court.' The other eased his grip. 'Someone has gone for the police.'

A sturdy middle-aged matron marched over to the women. 'You foul-mouthed creatures are not fit for decent company. On your way! We will be reporting you to the police.'

Annie looked the woman up and down. 'You can just go and fuck yourself, you old bag.' She pulled on Ellen's arm. 'Come on Ellen, let's go to the Fern Tree Inn. It's safer there. I hear this one's missus pisses in the tea.'

'Arseholes.' The word carried up from the track. It was young Alice, not more than thirteen. Where had she learnt that sort of language? Stupid question. The mother swore like a whaler.

Harry turned and looked back towards the cottage. Eliza was nowhere to be seen.

He walked past those sitting, silent, outside. Eliza was standing in the shadows in the far corner, her arms wrapped around herself, sobbing.

She lifted her head. 'I can't go on, Harry.' Her cheeks were wet with her tears. 'I can't.'

He put his arms around her and held her tight. 'They'll be charged, Eliza, and banned from coming here.'

Eliza took a deep, shuddering breath and moved away from him. She stood at the hearth, her head bowed.

Harry didn't know what to do, how to comfort her, how to set things right.

She raised her head, blew her nose and dabbed her handkerchief at her eyes. Her head erect, her back straight, Eliza walked into the sunshine.

Outside, conversation had started again. One of the women was carrying the teapot. A second sat Eliza down and brought her a cup of tea. Another asked her how she managed to get her scones so light.

Harry knew that, in the end, he was the cause of Eliza's pain. Ellen may be a foul-mouthed slut but if he had been faithful, none of this would have happened.

56

M am set a cup of tea on the table. 'If you can't pay the fine, I'm sure we can scrape it together between us.'

Ellen stood at the kitchen door, staring into the yard, trying not to listen. The plum tree in the corner was loaded with fruit. 'We could make jam from the fruit on that tree.'

'The sugar would be expensive,' Mam said.

Ellen came back and sat opposite her mother. 'Or stew them and have them with custard.'

Mam sipped at her tea. 'Do you need money for the fine?'

'I wish I hadn't gone up there with Annie,' Ellen groaned. 'I wanted to see the place again and remember them. I never got to say goodbye to Grannie. And there would have been a row had I gone to Grandad's funeral. Visiting the grave and having a drink to their memory just didn't seem enough.' Ellen flicked her fingers with annoyance. 'I'm not paying the fine.' She looked over at her mother. 'How much were you fined last time you were up for obscene language?'

'Twenty shillings and sixpence.'

'What? But Harry was only fined five shillings for punching me.'

Mam shrugged. 'I've lost count of the number of times I've been fined for it. You won't get that. It'll be five shillings.'

'Five shillings?' Ellen got up and paced the room. 'The same as him. I say two words to him and they consider that every bit as bad as punching a woman and knocking her to the ground.'

'Which two words?'

'*Bastard* and *shit*. I wasn't even trying.' She sat down again. 'I am not paying. I'll do the time instead. I won't give him the satisfaction of saying I'm spending his maintenance on court fines.'

Paying the fine seemed like throwing money away. 'You'll look after the children for me? Bessie has to go to work.'

Her mother nodded. 'Of course, my love. Between us all, we'll work something out.'

Ellen rubbed her fingers between her eyebrows. 'Because it's over Christmas, I'll only lose half a week's work. They won't hold the job for me, but the boss said they would be putting on more women after Christmas. I'm a hard worker—I'm sure they'll take me back.'

'Can you talk your way out of this?'

Ellen shook her head. 'There were too many witnesses.'

'If there's no need to make a good impression, don't wear your best clothes to court. They'll go in the cupboard with everyone else's when you get to the House of Correction. You don't know what will ride home on them when you get out.'

Ellen shuddered. 'Do you think we'll have roast beef and plum pudding for Christmas dinner?'

'Plum pudding at least. They do roast potatoes on Sundays—I'd say you'll have them as well.'

'Something to look forward to,' Ellen said glumly.

They pleaded not guilty, although there was no hope of getting off. Harry wasn't in court. Ellen supposed he wasn't needed with all the other people willing to give evidence. And it wasn't him taking her to court, but Inspector Quodling charging them with the crime of breaching the *Police Act* by using obscene language in a public place, a far more serious offence than merely thumping a woman!

Mam had been right, Ellen was fined five shillings and, as she said she couldn't pay, she was sentenced to seven days in the Female House of Correction. As it wasn't her first time, Annie was fined ten shillings, but she paid up. Luckily, the case against Alice was dismissed because of her age, but she was lectured about mending her ways. Alice listened with bored resignation, jingling the coins in her hand that Dad had given her to pay any fine.

Before Ellen turned to descend the twisting stairs beneath the dock, she passed her hat to Alice. She wasn't having that squashed in any prison store cupboard. The clothing she wore was a disgrace, the petticoat fit to be torn up and used as cleaning rags. She had left off her stays, her dress was the oldest she had, only worn when she had dirty work to do. Good thing she hadn't tried to argue that the witnesses were mistaken in what they heard—dressed as she was everyone would believe the worst of her.

She was taken along a tunnel beneath the court and up some stairs, along a narrow pathway, through an iron gate and out into the entrance yard of the prison. The two yards that made up the Female House of Correction were to the left when they faced the great iron gate to Campbell Street. The warder accompanying Ellen rang a bell beside the heavy door set in the wall. It was opened by a stern female warder who took Ellen through and locked the door behind her. She explained the routine of the prison as they walked. The first yard held the mess rooms where the women ate their meals. The second, entered through a doorway under the verandah of the prison building, was the yard where, under cover at one side, a laundry was set up with washing troughs, mangles, and lines across the yard. The bottom of the yard was closed off with a tall fence of iron railings, a gate at the centre. A sentry box stood on the path outside against the high stone prison wall.

Ellen went with the warder into the receiving room, set between two of the laundry sheds. Here her details were taken and she stripped off her own clothes and bathed. Her hair wasn't cut. Mam had said they didn't do that anymore. Ellen roughly dried it and put on a plain shift and a pair of ugly stays that seemed intended to flatten any curves. She sat and combed out her hair and pinned it up. The drab brown prison gown was nearly as ugly as the stays. Ellen tied the white apron she was given over it and pinned the white prison cap to her damp hair.

The warder took her to the dormitory on the ground floor of the prison building, one of several rooms with eight beds, each carrying a tag on the bedhead with the name and description of the prisoner. Ellen looked at hers. There wasn't much written there other than her name, her height of five-foot four, two words she assumed were obscene language and her sentence of seven days. She was taken back out into the laundry yard, where she was put to work. The women prisoners did the laundry for the General Hospital, Government House and some of the hotels. It amused Ellen to think of stuck-up women lying between sheets that had passed through the hands of the sort they liked to pretend didn't exist—thieves, drunks, beggars, prostitutes and the foul-mouthed like her.

Prison life wasn't so bad. Three female warders and a matron kept their eyes on forty-odd prisoners and were no problem as long as you did what they said. There were no fights that Ellen saw— there were no men about to argue over and no one had anything worth stealing. The women were no different from many of those who lived in the streets Ellen knew well, where life was difficult at the best of times. There was one woman, Martha, with a little girl the same age as Lizzie. She was in for theft, but who could blame her for thieving? Her man had run off, and she couldn't find work because she had no one to care for her daughter—not even now she was in prison. Like others before her, Martha had been permitted to bring her small child with her. When they had time to exercise after meals and the women walked or sat and chatted, Ellen got to cuddle Martha's daughter and think of her own children. That made her weepy, but she fought it. She was only in for a week.

The greatest annoyance, apart from being without her children, was that she had to go to church twice, once on Sunday and once on Christmas Day. The women filed into the prison chapel with its high roof and sat in pews at the front, screened from view of the men on the tiered seats behind them. The curtain certainly wasn't to stop the women ogling the men. Most were sure, like Ellen, that they were finished with men, more trouble than they were worth. The minister's sermon droned on and on. The old girl beside Ellen snored through most of it. She was in for assaulting a copper whilst drunk and incapable but surely, if she was incapable, she couldn't have assaulted anyone. Then there were the hymns sung by those who knew the words, to the music of a wheezing harmonium. Ellen wondered if this church service was a taste of the hell that the minister seemed so keen to send them to as punishment for their sins. But when it was over, there was dinner. And the food wasn't bad at all, three meals each day and meat every dinner time—not a great deal, but meat all the same. She understood why Will said he had got fat inside. And she got the special Christmas dinner, with a small serving of plum pudding and custard. It was better than wasting five shillings for the pleasure of calling Harry Woods a bastard.

57

Exactly a week after she had appeared in court, Ellen walked along Liverpool Street, the breeze in her hair. She pushed the door to her house open, but there was silence inside. They would all be up at Mam and Dad's.

She went over to the hearth. The fire was out but the kettle hanging from the crane was still warm. She couldn't be bothered lighting the fire and waiting for the water to heat. She dragged the wash tub from the corner of the room, set it in front of the fireplace and went out to the tap in the shared backyard to bring in a bucket of water. The yard was unusually empty, only old Mrs Webster doing her washing at the far end of the Row. She waved to Ellen, and Ellen waved back.

The first two buckets Ellen poured into the tub and the third she left to stand. She lifted the heavy kettle down and poured a little warm water into the tub. Most of the rest went into the bucket, leaving enough for a tepid cup of tea later. Ellen locked the doors and closed the curtains in the kitchen and the bedroom at the back. She stripped off her clothing and dumped it in a pile on the hearth. Kneeling in the unpleasantly cool water, she thoroughly soaped every inch of skin from her toes to her scalp, shivering as she scooped water from the bucket into a jug and poured it over her head. Once she had dried herself off and combed the knots out of her hair, she went into the bedroom and laid out her clothes. They were nothing special but were much softer than the clothes she had worn in prison. She put on her new dress—a pretty greenish-blue with a row of lovely glass buttons down the front of the bodice that caught the light the way Mrs Bryce's rings had. She had bought it with her first pay from Peacock's. It was second-hand and a decent quality but going cheap because there was a stain at one side of the bodice and both seams were split and frayed. It was too wide but she had spent every spare moment over two weeks taking it in and mending it. It was now a good fit with the stain out of sight.

Dressed, Ellen made herself a cup of weak, barely-warm tea, dragged a chair out into the front yard, beside the door, and sat in the sun drinking the tea while her hair dried.

The front yard was a mess of weeds, except for the path and a cleared patch in front of the house. She'd had plans for a vegetable garden but nothing had come of it, especially with the way this last year had been. Maybe next year—she was sure Billy would help.

Gaol hadn't been difficult. Just a group of women together, the usual drunks, swearers, thieves and those who had nothing to sell but themselves to make ends meet. No one you didn't meet every day on the street. She understood why some tried to get themselves inside in winter—the food was better and there was more of it than she, Bessie and the children had been surviving on.

She got up, rinsed her cup and did her hair. She dumped the clothes she had worn to court in the tub—she would clean it up later. All she wanted to go and see her children. She felt a thrill of excitement at the thought of the three of them, wondering how much they had grown in a week. Would Lizzie have learnt a new word?

She stepped out into the street, a spring in her step, resisting the urge to skip all the way.

Even before she opened the door, Ellen heard the sounds of home—adults talking all at once, laughing, children squealing. Her mouth watered at the aroma of roasting meat even though she'd had a bowl of porridge for breakfast.

Mam's face broke into a wide grin. 'You're home, my love.' She came over and threw her arms around Ellen. 'How was it?'

'Pretty much as you said. Plenty to eat but nothing but tea to drink.'

Mam moved back to the oven and pulled out the roasting pan,

spooning the drippings over a sizeable lump of meat.

'What's this for?' Ellen asked.

'A late Christmas dinner to share with you.'

Ellen pressed her lips together and forced her eyes wide, fighting back tears. 'And I haven't brought anything.'

'Yourself is enough.' Mam hugged her again.

The sound of children squealing carried from the yard, and a burst of male laughter, more than just Dad and Tom Budd. Ellen's heart leapt. George was back!

She rushed to the door. Her happiness fading a little at the sight of the young man who was spinning Billy around by the arms, the child whooping. It wasn't George.

He glanced at Ellen as she came down the steps. 'We better stop now, Billy, or you might get sick.' His voice had a lovely Yankee twang, like a shipmate Will had once brought home for tea.

He slowly brought Billy to the ground and, smiling, inclined his head at Ellen. 'I'd take off my hat, but I'm not wearing one at the moment.'

'Mum!' Billy squealed and threw himself at Ellen. She staggered backwards. 'You're back.'

'I am, my darling.' She squatted down and hugged him. Over his shoulder, she saw Jennie and Lizzie standing close. She opened her arms and they ran to her. She held them tight, her eyes squeezed shut, drinking in the scent of them. Her children.

She held on too long, and they started to wriggle, so she let them go and stood.

The young man was still watching her.

'I thought you were George.' She wished he was George, but he was not like him at all. He was taller and of a slenderer build, his hair much darker, and his deep-set eyes were a beautiful clear blue. A seaman, tattoos showing beneath his rolled-up shirt sleeves—a woman's head on one forearm, *KR* on the other.

'Sorry to disappoint you, ma'am,' he said.

'Ma'am!' Ellen laughed. 'I've never been called that before. You had better call me Ellen or I'll start getting ideas about myself.'

'Jim Doran.' He held out his hand to her. 'And I did see George a few months back. He said to call in here if I was ever in Hobart Town.'

She took his hand, her fingers tingling at his touch. 'Where is he now?'

'England. I met him in Liverpool.'

'Our George has been seeing the world,' Dad said from his seat in the shade of the plum tree.

Mary Ann and Tom sat beside him. Bessie was holding little Thomas, rocking him in her arms. Alice and Jane now had Ellen's three playing ring-a-rosie. They fell on the ground, giggling. It was a happy family scene, but Ellen saw those who were missing.

'It's a pity he couldn't find his way home for Christmas,' she said and turned back into the house.

She heard Jim ask, his voice carrying through the open door, 'Is Ellen's husband a seaman too?'

'The *husband* is a sore point,' Dad said. 'When Lizzie, the baby, was on the way, Ellen discovered the fine upstanding man was already married.'

'That's a low trick to pull.'

Ellen stood close to the door, her arms crossed.

'It is,' Tom said.

Ellen knew Mary Ann would be nodding her agreement.

'She's just done a week inside for telling him what she thought of him,' Dad added.

'Not much of a man if he runs off to the police when a woman cusses him out.'

Dad laughed. 'I'd spend my life hiding at the police office, if I was as particular.'

Ellen didn't know whether to laugh or to cry—there were no secrets in this family.

'Don't stand there eavesdropping,' Mam said. 'Set the table and we'll get this lot fed.'

Ellen was sure they hadn't had such a raucous, happy meal since both Will and George were home. Jim entertained them with his tales of foreign places—not just England and America, but India and other exotic places Ellen had never heard of. He described the cities he had visited, their streets teeming with people, the strange cargoes carried by the ships he had sailed on. On his last trip from Calcutta to Adelaide, they had brought out camels, nasty, snarling, spitting beasts.

Billy listened, his mouth open. 'Have you ever ridden one?'

'No,' Jim said, 'but I've been on an elephant.' He leant over towards the boy. 'They dress the elephants with bells and coloured cloths and put tents on their backs for ladies to ride in.' He winked at Billy. 'How do you think your ma would like to ride in one of those?'

Billy's eyes lit up, clearly taken with the idea. 'That would be grand.'

Ellen struggled to hide her smile. What was the wretch doing? Flirting with her through the boy?

After the dishes were done, they sat in the yard enjoying the late afternoon sunshine. Ellen smoothed her skirt as she took the chair beside Jim. 'I imagine your family is missing you the way we miss George.'

'I do write now and then.'

'George has been gone nearly three years and not a word from him until you arrived. Have you been back home at all?'

Jim nodded. 'I did a run to New York five months ago.'

'Where are you off to next? Timbuctoo?'

'Not likely,' he laughed, 'that's in the middle of the desert.'

'Shows how much I know.'

'I'll have to teach you some geography.'

Ellen laughed for no reason other than she was happy to be with her family on this lovely day and sitting beside an attractive man. She looked at those beautiful blue eyes watching her and thought, *What harm is there in a little flirting?*

58

On Sunday, just after lunch, Jim appeared on Ellen's doorstep, offering to take her small family to the Domain.

'I hear there's a band playing.'

'The children would love it,' Ellen said.

Bessie came too, carrying Lizzie.

'Allow me,' Jim said and took the little girl from her.

So, he could be a gentleman.

Lizzie peered up at him, concentration on her face as she decided whether she would allow this stranger to carry her. The decision made, she grabbed for his hat before settling against him.

'It suits you, Lizzie,' he said as he adjusted it so she could see.

Another point to his credit, Ellen thought—he remembered the children's names.

Jennie walked hand in hand with Bessie. Billy strolled along beside Jim, chatting away, asking about ships and the sea, whales and fish and strange countries far away.

'My uncles were seamen.'

'I've met your Uncle George.'

'Uncle Will, he chased whales, but he's out at Queenborough now.'

Jim glanced at Ellen. He seemed to have sensed this was not another town.

'The cemetery,' Ellen said quietly.

'How did you become a seaman?' Billy asked.

He looked down at the boy. 'I wanted to go to sea but my father had other ideas, so I stowed away. They set me to work when they discovered me as the ship was too far out at sea to send me back.'

'Were you very old?'

'Eighteen or so.'

'That's an old man.'

'It is indeed, Billy. And I'm older now.'

Lizzie pulled Jim's hat off and sent it flying.

Ellen chased after it and brought it back. 'I'm sorry about that. I'll carry it for you.'

'You could wear it for me.'

'You'd have to wear mine.'

'A sailor does like a pretty hat.'

'Yes, we all know that.'

Bessie smiled gently at Ellen, an eyebrow arched. Ellen raised her eyebrows back at her. It seemed like forever since she had flirted with a man. There was no harm in it.

Jim was good with the children—perhaps he had nieces and nephews at home. Ellen supposed seamen missed family life at times, not wanting to spend their whole time on girls and grog. Or children of his own. A girl in every port! She must be careful.

They wandered through the Botanic Gardens, watched a game of cricket from the rise above the enclosed cricket ground in the Domain for a while, then sat on the grass, listening to a brass band practising and watching the light dance on the water and the sails of the yachts on the river.

Billy jumped up and yelled, 'Look, Jim!' and turned three perfect cartwheels down the slope.

Jim laughed. 'I can do that too.' He managed one turn before crumpling in a heap. He pulled himself upright and grabbed Billy's hands, whirling him round as the boy squealed with delight.

He brought Billy carefully to the ground, and the boy flung himself out on the grass, arms and legs spread wide, a great grin on his face, the world still spinning about him.

Bessie sat with Lizzie on her lap, Jennie nestled between her and Ellen. Jim came over and squatted in front of Jennie and said, 'Would you like a turn too?'

Jennie nodded, eager. Jim spun her gently, the child gurgling with laughter.

Ellen thought, *If this isn't a show merely to impress me, I could want this man forever.*

~

It was a surprisingly quiet Sunday, dry despite overnight rain and the light cloud cover—a good day for mountain climbing. But by lunchtime there had been not a single visitor to the Springs.

Harry drained his teacup and set it on the saucer. 'Why don't we take the afternoon off? I doubt we will get any visitors now. We could go down to the Botanic Gardens and perhaps have an early tea in the Melbourne Café.'

'That's a wonderful idea.' Eliza's eyes lit up. 'I'd be interested to see the sort of refreshments the Melbourne Café offers.' Eliza turned to Kate, the girl she had employed to help her over summer. 'You'll come with us, Kate?'

It wasn't a question. Harry knew Eliza wouldn't dream of leaving a fourteen-year-old girl here on her own.

'Ooh yes, please,' Kate nodded. 'I've never been to a café.'

It was a pleasant day for a stroll, not hot, but the gentle breeze and the sunshine bursting through the clouds reminded them that it was summer. The Domain was like a painting with the grand mansion that was Government House overlooking the Botanic Gardens, the river glittering behind it. Harry turned and gazed back at the mountain, majestic, the Organ Pipes picked out in the sunlight. Hobart was a beautiful place. If only it wasn't so cold in winter.

They meandered towards the gates to the Botanic Gardens. Harry gazed over at a young family enjoying the bursts of sunshine. The women sat comfortably, young children on their laps, looking on as the father played with his son, turning cart-wheels and swinging the boy around him. He thought of those moments when he had returned to the Springs, swinging Billy high in the air, his happy squeals.

The boy now lay on the ground, and the father was swinging his daughter about, his wife smiling at him.

With a jolt, Harry realised that the *wife* was Ellen. The child the young man was swinging was *his* daughter Jennie. It was like a knife beneath his ribs. He hadn't realised but lying deep was a real hope that one day he would be part of their lives, that they would know he was their father. But they wouldn't notice his absence. Maybe, already, his children were calling this man *Daddy*.

The man had set Jennie down and lay on the grass beside Ellen, resting on one elbow, his long legs stretched out. Ellen was laughing at whatever he had said to her. He was tall, clean-shaven except for a moustache, his hair dark, a slender build—the hard-muscled, wiry type. Harry should have known that one day Ellen would find someone to replace him, another man who would have everything he had once had with her. Memories washed through him. He did not want her back, but this ... This was another twist of the knife.

He had stopped walking. He jerked his head, shaking unwanted thoughts away. Eliza and Kate were well ahead of him, walking arm in arm, looking like mother and daughter. He and Eliza would have had children Kate's age if life had been kinder. Perhaps that was why Eliza had enjoyed the company of her nieces and nephews so much. Harry had not understood.

He hurried down the slope after them and slid his arm through Eliza's free arm. They walked on together to the Gardens.

~

They finished the day with tea and scones in a small refreshment room in Elizabeth Street that had just opened to serve its evening customers. The children were so well-behaved—Ellen was proud of them. And no one stared at them as if they were somewhere they shouldn't be.

Jim walked them to their door afterwards and handed Lizzie to Bessie, who took the children indoors.

'Thank you, Jim,' Ellen said politely. 'It's been a lovely day.'

'I've enjoyed it.' He bent down and kissed her on the cheek. She turned her head, brought her lips to his and kissed him properly. His arms went around her waist, and for a few moments she was completely lost. Close by, someone whistled.

'Well.' She smiled at him, not sure what else to say.

He grinned back at her. 'Well indeed!'

'You're not married, are you?'

His eyebrows shot up in surprise. 'No, definitely not.' His face cleared. She supposed he remembered why she might want to know.

'So, who is *KR*?'

He frowned, puzzled.

'On your arm. The girl you left behind?'

'No.' There was a twist to his smile. 'The girl who couldn't be bothered waiting.'

Perhaps she shouldn't have asked, but now she knew.

'Do you think you'll visit Hobart again?' She warned herself not to raise her hopes.

'Oh, I'll be back. There are plenty of regular runs between Hobart and Adelaide.'

He kissed her again, for nowhere near long enough. 'I'll be back in a couple of months and I'll take you out dancing.'

Ellen went with him to the gate and watched him walk towards Liverpool Street, whistling. He turned and waved back at her. She smiled to herself, her knees still deliciously weak. When he came back ... She corrected herself. *If* he came back, she would take the advice she had given Bessie and make certain he was what he seemed to be before things went any further.

59

March 1883

H ey, Ellen,' Annie Smith poked her head around the door, 'are
you doing anything later today?'

'We are going to Mam and Dad's.'

'Cup of tea, Annie?' Bessie got up from her seat and went to the
stove. She picked up the teapot sitting on the hob.

'Thanks, Bessie, that would be nice.' Annie pulled out the chair
beside Ellen. 'Are you interested in some work? Lily and I are
supposed to be working at Mrs Watkins's later today—she's having
a big party because her son's back from England—but Lily's got
the gripes. Do you want to come instead? It's only kitchen work—
scrubbing pots, washing dishes and whatever the old bat of a cook
wants done.'

Ellen sipped her tea. 'Where is it?'

'One of those flash houses out at New Town.'

Bessie placed the cup and saucer in front of Annie and sat down
again.

Outside, Jennie and Lizzie laughed and squealed, their feet
thudding along the path in the front yard as they bounced their
ball.

'What time does it finish? I don't fancy walking home in the
dark all that way.'

'Every time I've worked for her, she's had a cart bring us home
and drop everyone off in Elizabeth Street.'

'It would be useful. Peacock's is closed on Monday because of
this holiday for the wedding anniversary of the Prince of Wales.
Nice for the nobs to have a day to lie in bed, but the rest of us go
short without the work.' She looked across at Bessie. 'Will you be
right, minding them all?'

'Of course I will.' Bessie rolled her eyes. 'I'll take them to Mam and Dad's as usual and we'll be back here in bed by the time it's dark.'

Bessie seemed to be her old self again, but there were moments when Ellen caught her unawares, sitting gazing at nothing, a heart-breaking sadness on her face.

'We have to be there by five o'clock,' Annie said, 'so we should leave before four—we don't want to rush. Don't wear anything flash, it'll just get wet and dirty. And we have to bring our own aprons. She doesn't care much what we look like as none of the guests will see us.'

~

Mrs Watkins's place was an older house, sprawling back from the road, single-storeyed with a verandah on three sides. A row of tall windows glittered in the afternoon sunshine. Several young men and a couple of women in eye-catching hats sat on the verandah, chatting and laughing. Two men leant against a trellised verandah post, drinks in their hands, watching Ellen and Annie as they walked along the path leading to the back of the house. Ellen recognised the pair—William Cook and Thomas Armstrong. Two nuisances who had liked hanging around the illegal dancing rooms that George had preferred where grog was available.

Ellen knew better than to stare back at them.

'Did you see that pair?' Annie said as they neared the house. 'Looking us over like we are on display in a shop window? They'll tell you anything to get what they certainly won't be getting from the pretty misses inside. And once they've had what they wanted, they treat you as if you have just done the whole town.'

'Isn't that most men?' Ellen said.

'S'pose.' Annie gazed at the garden with its neatly trimmed bushes and colourful beds of dahlias and late roses. 'I wouldn't mind living in this sort of place. I'd even contemplate a fat old fool of sixty if it meant having servants and plenty to eat all year round.'

Ellen frowned. Could she put up with someone she had no real liking for in exchange for never having to worry where their next meal was coming from?' 'I doubt I'll ever get that sort of offer.' She furrowed her brow. 'I don't know that I could.'

Annie shrugged. 'You like that lovey-dovey stuff too much, Ellen. It might be fun to start with, but look what happens most of the time—a couple of babies and he doesn't give a damn about you anymore. He's drinking his pay, comes home drunk and cranky and belts you, then he clears out and you're left with half a dozen kids lined up at the Benevolent Society.'

'Not everyone is like that. My dad's not. Neither is Tom Budd.'

'No, but it's not easy to work out who's decent and who's not, 'specially when he's turned your head and you think the sun shines out his arse.'

Ellen laughed. 'Don't I know that?'

'Speaking of turned heads, have you heard anything of that sailor I heard took you and the kids to the Domain?'

'No. And my head wasn't turned. He was polite, good with the children, and being a seaman, he sailed away.' It had only been a couple of months, but Ellen wasn't holding any hopes he would be back. What she needed to concentrate on was getting through the coming winter.

The kitchen extended away from the back of the house, a neat vegetable garden beside it and, beyond, several outhouses, possibly storerooms, and the laundry. They went through to the kitchen and presented themselves to the cook, and were taken straight to the scullery, where a mountain of baking tins and moulds, bowls and crockery awaited them.

Ellen tied on her apron and whispered out the side of her mouth, 'And we are being paid one and six to do all this?

'Yes,' Annie answered. 'If the cook is happy with us, she'll throw in some leftovers to take home.'

'Not much considering this is just the start.' Ellen waved her hand towards the piles beside each sink.

'Better than a poke in the eye with a forky stick.'

'Much better,' Ellen laughed.

As the evening wore on, in the brief breaks in the clatter of pans and the cook giving orders, they could hear faint snatches of music and laughter and what Ellen supposed was polite conversation, broken by the odd braying laugh that wouldn't be out of place in a waterfront pub.

It wasn't hard work but it was continuous. Ellen was amazed by the sheer number of pots and pans used. The cook wandered in and sorted through the baking tins and dishes, holding them up to the brighter light in the kitchen.

'There's food still on this one.' She banged it down on the bench beside Ellen.

Ellen was surprised—and relieved—it was only one out of the dozens she had washed.

With the effort they were putting in, she thought they should be paid twice the amount. There were three of them. Annie and Ellen doing the washing and scrubbing and Mary, a thin quiet girl, drying and stacking the dishes away.

The smell of the cooking was mouth-watering, beef and fish and roast vegetables—but all that was offered to those brought in to work, halfway through the night, was thinly sliced bread with a scraping of dripping.

The maids were carrying in trays with empty bowls that had held trifle and puddings, plates with dainty cakes barely nibbled. Ellen hoped Annie was right and she would get some cake to take home to Bessie and the children.

Mary dropped her damp tea towel into the washing basket by the door. 'I've run out of clean towels.'

'There should be dry ones out in the laundry,' Annie said.

Mary went to the door and stood peering out. She shivered. 'It's dark out there.'

'I'll get them, Miss Mouse,' Ellen laughed. 'I could do with some fresh air.' She picked up the basket and hoisted it onto her hip. 'I'll take these out too.'

The new moon slipped behind a bank of heavy cloud, the only light now coming from the kitchen windows. Ellen understood why Mary didn't want to come out.

The aroma of tobacco smoke drifted on the air.

As she neared the laundry, she saw them leaning against the wall, the tips of their cigarettes glowing in the dark.

'Ellen. You've decided to join us.'

Her mouth went dry. It was that bastard Thomas Armstrong. She had danced with him once or twice years ago, a decent dancer but hands everywhere. George had thumped him. Why, out of all the girls he had annoyed over the years, had he remembered her name?

'No. I have work to do.'

'I'm sure you'd rather have a bit of fun with us.' Armstrong dropped his cigarette and ground it onto the path.

'All Hobart knows how you like to have fun.' Cook laughed. 'We read it in the newspapers.'

Armstrong placed his hand on Ellen's shoulder.

'Piss off.' She shook him off and marched past them into the laundry. Her eyes adjusting to the darkness, she emptied the basket into the trough. A pile of clean tea towels sat on the bench beneath the window.

Her shoulders tensed. They had followed her.

She turned.

Armstrong grinned. 'Ellen, don't be a spoilsport.'

Behind him, Cook blocked the doorway.

60

The house was in darkness. Ellen quietly closed the front door and latched it.

She couldn't control her shivering. Her hair was flattened against her head. Water dripped down her face and neck onto her sodden clothing. They had been driven home in an open cart. It was spitting when they left, but the sky had opened, drenching them as they got to Burnett Street. Annie, like the rest of them, had lifted her jacket over her head to keep as dry as she could. Ellen had sat and let the water run over her. She didn't care. The others had chatted around her, Annie and one of the men flirting simply for the fun of it. Ellen had done the same years ago. Mary had been laughing along with them. What if Mary had gone out? Would they have done the same to her? She was Alice's age! Ellen had clamped her mouth shut. If she began to weep, she would never stop.

She stirred the banked fire to life and put a couple of small logs on, dragged the tub in front of the hearth and picked up the bucket.

On her way through the bedroom, she paused. Bessie slept with Lizzie beside her; Billy and Jennie were snuggled together in Ellen's bed. She longed to crawl in with them, wrap her arms around them, and forget.

With the rain pelting down, no one was outside to ask what she was doing carrying buckets of water at this hour.

She topped up the kettle and half filled the tub, then went and checked that both the front and the back doors were locked. As long as she had things to do, she didn't have to think.

She stood, waiting for the kettle to boil, her arms tight across her middle.

She hauled the kettle over to the tub once it began to hiss, pouring the boiling water into both the tub and the bucket. She tossed in the scrubbing brush and the carbolic soap. The soap was supposed to be good at removing vermin from the head. She hoped it would rid her of all trace of human vermin.

She stripped off her sodden clothing, dumped it on the hearth beside the empty kettle and stepped carefully into the tub. She dropped down, the tepid water slopping over the tub onto the floor. The fire was burning low, the night air cold on her skin. She shivered.

Ellen soaped her hair and every inch of skin with the carbolic, rubbing it in with the brush, scrubbing away until her skin stung. She tossed the brush out and picked up the jug. Her mouth closed against a yelp of pain, she poured a jug of still-hot water from the bucket over her head and shoulders, tears finally leaking out as the water ran over her.

Her arms wrapped around her knees, she lowered her head, racked by silent sobs. This was not her fault. She had done nothing but her work. Who were these two who thought they could have what they wanted even though Ellen's refusal was plain? What right had they? Cook was no better than Armstrong. He had pushed her down, held her there. His whole weight on her arms.

She sat in the tub, rigid with anger.

Your turn, mate.

Nah, don't want to catch anything. I'm getting married in a few months.

A snarl. *I'd better not have caught anything from you.*

She had found her voice as she struggled up from the floor. *I'm more likely to have caught something from you. Pig!*

He had punched her in the stomach.

She had wanted to say, *Is that the Armstrong version of a goodbye kiss?* but was too much of a coward. All she'd wanted was to get away from them. To be somewhere safe.

She lurched up from the tub, water flooding out across the floor.

They were nothing. Less than nothing. Worthless.

She poured jugfuls of water over her hair, not caring about the mess pooling on the floor.

All for a single shilling. The cook had noticed she was missing and refused to pay her the full amount. Ellen had argued, said she had the gripes, she wasn't gone for that long, but the cook was the one holding the purse, and the work was done. The shilling in her hand, she had said, 'So, next time, you want me to shit on the floor where I'm standing.' There wouldn't be a next time, even if the old bag offered her twenty times the amount.

Her hair wrapped in a towel, she tiptoed into the bedroom and got her nightgown, checking the back door was locked. Shivering so hard her teeth chattered, she went back to the other room, opened the front door and threw buckets of dirty bathwater out into the rain.

Finally, the front door locked, the fire out, her soiled clothes in the empty tub, Ellen eased herself into the bed beside Jennie. The child turned and curled in towards her. Ellen's shivering eased. She stretched her arm across Jennie, resting her hand on Billy. How was she to keep them safe when she couldn't manage it for herself?

~

Mary Ann was sitting by the window, patching the knee on a stained pair of work trousers, little Tom asleep in his basket beside her. Billy lay on his stomach in front of her, a stub of a pencil in one hand, scribbling away on a piece of crumpled brown paper. His sisters, lying opposite him, were intent on the movement of his hand and the patterns appearing on the paper.

Mary Ann slid the needle into her sewing and carefully stepped past the children. 'You look like you could do with a strong cup of tea.'

Ellen nodded. 'I could.' She sat down and rested her elbows on the table, rubbing her hands over her face.

Billy was now sitting in Mary Ann's chair by the window, his sisters cross-legged in front of him. He held his piece of paper out as if he were reading and began, 'Once upon a time, far back, there was a broonie, full *towsie* and *poukit*.' It was one of Mam's old stories, and Billy told it with something of her lilt. Her children truly were the best thing in Ellen's life.

Mary Ann placed the cups on the table and pushed the sugar bowl towards Ellen. 'You look awful.'

'Thank you.' Scowling, Ellen stirred the sugar into her tea.

'I mean it. You don't look well.'

'I'm fine, just headachy.'

'Bessie said you haven't been well since you came home from that extra job on Saturday.'

Ellen stared at her sister, her lips tight, her chin puckered. 'Been gossiping, have you?'

'No,' Mary Ann said evenly. 'We're your sisters. We worry about you the way you do about us. She said you spent Sunday in bed.'

'Well, she's lying. I got up and did my washing.' That made it sound worse—washing on a day pouring with rain. Ellen blinked rapidly and looked into her cup, afraid the shine of her eyes would betray her. It would be easy to spill it out, to have Mary Ann come and put her arms around her, to weep with her. But what good would it do? She had to get a grip on herself and keep going.

'I think I had whatever it was that stopped Lily Walters from working.'

Mary Ann raised an eyebrow. She looked as if she didn't believe Ellen. 'If you aren't feeling better in a couple of days, you should take yourself to the hospital.'

'I will.' There was nothing wrong with her that a hospital could cure. She picked up her tea and sipped it. 'A good night's sleep would help.' She fell asleep straightaway at night but woke within an hour or two, so much tumbling through her mind. Why her? Could she have stopped it? If there had been only one of them? And then there were the flashes of memory, the weight of Armstrong on her, his hand over her mouth, the coldness of the flagstones on her back, the laughter, his beery breath, the stink of him. But worst of all, her own powerlessness, the fear that froze her, like nothing she had known. And the rest. She would not think of it. She would not go over every detail as if it was something she wanted to remember. This was not her fault. She would not take the blame for it. She had done nothing wrong.

Over by the window, Billy finished his story. 'And the broonie put on the green coatie and was seen no more. Many think he went off to an easier life with the fairies.'

She couldn't fall apart, her children needed her.

Mary Ann was staring, her brow deeply fuurrowed.

Ellen dropped her shoulders as she sighed. 'We had better be getting home.'

Mary Ann came around the table and hugged her tight.

'Don't worry about me, Mary Ann, I'll be all right.' She had no choice.

61

Harry stood on the track above the Springs, drawing on his pipe, staring out across Hobart to the horizon. Each evening it was the same—the gentle noise of the bush at the end of the day, the slanting light of the late sun behind him, the worries and petty annoyances of the day melting away with each breath.

It had been a good summer except for that incident at the beginning of December. And there had been no problems with Ellen since. Eliza had placed a notice in the *Mercury* letting people know they now provided both accommodation and refreshments and Harry was available as a guide. It made a difference—they had been busy, the occasional small group staying overnight. Debts were paid and maintenance forwarded, and they were putting money by. But autumn was turning towards winter and it was time to move down the mountain. He took his pipe out of his mouth. There was nothing to be gained freezing up here with no work.

He heard Eliza's footsteps as she climbed the track towards him.

The pipe had gone out. He dropped it into his jacket pocket.

Eliza slid her arm through his, rested her head against his shoulder.

'I've been thinking about winter.'

'It'll be on us in no time,' she said. 'Kate has just left with her father. She has been such a help. I gave her a written reference but said, if she wished, I would be glad to take her on again at the end of October. Have you spoken to Mrs Hennessy and to the mill?'

'We could as easily spend winter in Perth.'

'Really?' She looked up at him.

'It would be warmer. Almost like a holiday.'

'Oh yes.' She glowed with a sudden happiness. 'It would be wonderful to see everyone again.'

351

He knew she missed them—her father, her sisters and brothers, all her nieces and nephews—there would have been changes in the time they had been away.

'These past few years have been hard. And, there's nothing to keep us here.'

'But ...' She stopped herself.

He knew she wanted to say *But what about your daughters?*

His daughters—would he recognise them in the street? Would he recognize Billy? Did they even know he existed?

'This place is the old man's dream not mine.' He frowned. 'I don't want to die here.'

'Don't talk of that.' She grasped his hand and squeezed it.

'I'm not planning on it happening for years.' He laughed. 'But I am getting older. I barely had a grey hair when I arrived and look at me now.' He turned and took both her hands in his. 'So. What will it be—winter here? Or in Perth?'

He wasn't sure what he was truly asking. To go back for winter or for good? It didn't matter. They could make up their minds when they were back in Perth.

'Oh, Harry.' Her voice choked. 'You know my answer already.'

~

Harry stood on the deck of the *Southern Cross* as it pulled away from the dock, his eyes fixed on the mountain, snow extending down its slopes as far as the Springs. He had barely been able to look away from it when he arrived. He remembered how he had felt then—for the first time in his life he was free to do whatever he wanted, no past, nothing expected of him. And Ellen had only added to that feeling of freedom—young, beautiful, eyes for no one but him. Who wouldn't have done what he did? She had made him feel half his age. It had been a magnificent madness. And his guilt—it was not for what he had done, but for the hurt he had caused Eliza.

This part of his life was over. He wouldn't speak of it again.

Neither would Eliza. But he would never forget.

His girls, Jennie and Lizzie, would have no memory of him, and there was nothing he could do about it. In them, he would leave something of himself behind. The thought gave him no comfort. He felt the hollow space in his life where his children should have fitted, Billy too, a child of his heart if not his flesh. Time might wear away the sharp edges but it would never close it. The ache would always be there.

He thought again of Ellen, the first time he had seen her, the light in her eyes, the mischief in her smile. Bessie had sung a lament at Will's wake—what had it said of lost love?

> *The finest flower that e'er was seen,*
> *Is withered to a stalk.*

The sun broke through the clouds, shining across the Organ Pipes as it had at the beginning.

And now it was finished. Harry let his breath out slowly, the rancours of the past slipping away. He wished Ellen a better future.

The steamer's horn blared.

Harry caught Eliza's hand. She smiled up at him, happier than he had seen her in years.

'Let's walk to the front and see what lies ahead.'

~

Ellen kicked the door shut behind her and stared about the room. There were toys on the floor, clothing hanging over the back of the chairs, the remains of lunch congealed on the dishes still on the table.

Bessie was crawling on the floor with Lizzie on her back, Jennie beside them trying to hold her little sister upright.

'This place is a mess! What have you been doing all day?'

Bessie stared at her. Lizzie slid off her back and started to whimper. Jennie moved close to Bessie, as if for protection.

Billy ran in from the street, the door slamming behind him, his hair messy, dirt on his face.

Ellen rounded on him. 'Where have you been?'

'Playing football with Fred Rowe and some other boys.'

She barked out her questions. 'And what else? You're not spending the day running round the streets? Making a nuisance of yourself? Stealing?'

'No, Mum.' He backed away from her towards the safety of Bessie who now stood, Lizzie on her hip, the child's face turned in towards her aunt's neck, Jennie hiding in her skirts. 'We played football and we dug up a bit of Fred's yard. His dad said we could dig a garden.'

They stood looking at Ellen as if she were an ogre of some sort.

And she was an ogre—shouting and snarling at them when they had done nothing wrong.

Ellen flung herself onto a chair, her arms tight across her chest. She hated this. Hated the way she was. Always angry, turning on those she loved. She wanted it to end, to wipe away the memory of it, to go back to the way she had been when as dire as her worry about feeding the children had been, it was more bearable.

They were still standing silent, watching her.

'I'm sorry. I just ...' Her voice trailed off. What could she say?

'You've heard, then?' Bessie said.

'Heard what?' Her voice was rougher than she intended.

'That they've gone.'

Ellen rolled her eyes. 'Spit it out, Bessie, who's gone?'

'Harry Woods and his wife. Left on the *Southern Cross* the day before yesterday.'

Ellen shoulders dropped. It all crashed down on her. 'There goes the maintenance through winter. Good thing I'm still at Peacocks.'

But that wasn't going to last. It would be like last year but far, far worse.

She stood and went into the bedroom, crawled onto the bed and curled into a ball. And wept. Not the silent weeping of loss when Harry's wife appeared and her dreams had died, but deep gut-wrenching sobs. What had she done to deserve this? She wasn't to blame, yet she was the only one being punished.

62

Ellen woke, the daylight almost gone. The door to the bedroom had been shut. Her children were on the bed with her, curled up close, fast asleep. All she wanted was the best for them, but life plotted against her.

In the other room, she could hear someone talking quietly to Bessie. The aroma of cooking drifted under the door. There was comfort in it, the sounds and smells of home.

She eased herself off the bed, trying not to wake the children, and went out into the kitchen.

Mam came straight to her and held her tight. 'What's wrong, my love?'

'Do you really want to know?' She stepped back, stood alone, her arms crossed, her chin raised.

'Of course I do.'

'I'm pregnant.' A tear ran down her cheek. She brushed it roughly away.

Bessie turned from the stove.

She would say it, say the ugly words exactly as they were.

'Last March. I was working at Mrs Watkins's. William Cook held me down while Thomas Armstrong raped me.'

Mam's face contorted as she began, 'The misbegotten son of a *cankert* whore ...'

Ellen had never seen her mother as angry, never heard her abuse so foully inventive. When her anger had subsided to tears, she held Ellen tight and said, 'Wait until I get my hands on this piece of shite and his mate.'

'No,' Ellen said. 'You are to do nothing. And you are not to tell Dad his name. I don't want anyone getting themselves into trouble trying to sort things out for me.' She looked over to Bessie. 'And that goes for you too. You are to say nothing to anyone.'

'I know a couple of old lassies who would be more than happy to hold the bastard down while I made slow work of his tackle with your father's awl and pincers.'

'Oh, Mam.' Ellen didn't know whether to laugh or cry.

They sat back at the table, Mam still gripping Ellen's hand.

'I saw in the cupboard that you've bought yourself a great bottle of gin.'

'Horrible stuff.' Ellen shuddered. 'I drank one glass and threw it back up.'

'It doesn't work anyway.' She squeezed Ellen's hand.

'Mam, I'm scared. I'm so angry and full of hate. How can I love this child?'

'Ah, my darling girl.' She drew Ellen's head onto her bosom. 'You will.' She brushed her hand over Ellen's hair. 'Do you see that Collins lad when you look at Billy or Harry Woods in your girls' faces?'

'Billy is Billy—nothing but a Thompson—but I do glimpse Harry in the girls.' She sat up, and wiped her fingers over her lashes. 'I loved him, and I am sure he did love me, the weak, lying bastard. But this one, I feel nothing but anger and hate.'

'Love will come. Babies bring it with them.'

'And I worry how we'll manage.'

Bessie, who had been standing quietly by the stove, came over. 'I'll help. Once the baby's weaned, I can look after it. I'll take such good care, and you'll be free to work as much as you want.'

'Thank you, Bessie.' It would be like most families, one out at work, one at home with the children, taking extra jobs where she could. The only problem was Ellen would never earn as much as a man.

'You should go to the police, get the bastard done for the rape. Then you can charge him for maintenance. The worthless piece of shit should pay one way or another.'

'Who would believe me—a whore with three little bastards and another on the way?'

Mam's eyes flashed. 'Don't you dare talk about yourself and your little ones that way. You are a better woman, a better mother than any of the nobs I have worked for over the years.'

'The police won't believe me. When are the likes of Armstrong and Cook ever punished for what they do to us?'

'I'll come with you.'

Perhaps she should do it. There was a slim chance the police might take it seriously.

'Promise me, Mam, you won't let loose if they laugh at me.'

Mam sniffed as if offended. 'I can behave when I've a mind to.'

The bedroom door creaked behind Ellen.

'Billy, my wee darling.' Mam held her arms wide.

'Gran!' Ellen could hear the delight in the boy's voice. He ran past her and threw himself into his grandmother's arms.

Ellen felt a stab of sadness. She was the one he had always come to first. Her anger was ruining the trust her children had in her.

'And how's my laddie?'

'Grand. Are you staying for tea?'

'No, my sweet. I have to go home and make your granda's tea but I'll be back tomorrow.' She planted a loud kiss on the boy's cheek and stood up. 'We'll get through this together, Ellen, and we'll help you as we can. Now. I should take that gin home with me. I don't want you being silly with it.'

Ellen couldn't help smiling, but she knew her mother well. 'You can have it tomorrow. If I give it to you tonight, there's a chance you'll have a head on you in the morning and won't be able to keep from telling the coppers what you think of them.'

Ellen went with her mother to the police office in Bathurst Street the next morning. The building, backing onto the Campbell Street House of Correction and containing the city watchhouse, had seen far better days. Water stains spread from one corner of the ceiling of the charge room; the paint on the ceiling and the walls was cracked and peeling; ink spatters marked the wall beside the desk where a young constable sat. The room looked no better than most found on Moodie's Row.

There was fear in the constable's eyes as Ellen explained what she was there to report, but that might have had as much to do with the way Mam was glaring at him. His relief was plain when an older constable walked over. A man in his thirties with a thick black moustache, Ellen knew him by sight.

He didn't introduce himself. 'What's your complaint?'

She drew a deep breath and spoke quickly. 'On the tenth of March, while I was at Mrs Watkins's house in New Town, Thomas Armstrong raped me while his mate William Cook held me down.'

The copper stood, his arms crossed, not a scrap of sympathy in his face. 'How can you be so sure of the date?'

'It was the Saturday of the celebrations for the Prince of Wales's wedding anniversary.'

'And what were you doing at Mrs Watkins's house?' He looked her up and down. 'She's hardly someone who would mix with the likes of you.'

Ellen pressed her mouth shut and breathed in through her nose. 'I was working in the kitchen there. She was having a party, and they needed extra people to wash dishes and pots and pans. I went out to the laundry for clean tea towels when the b—' She stopped herself. 'When Armstrong and Cook grabbed me.'

'Any witnesses?'

'What do you think? How often are there witnesses who aren't mates of the b—' she stopped herself again, 'the rapist? You men wouldn't get away with it all the time if there were witnesses.'

'What do you mean, *you men*?' he snarled. 'Are you accusing *me* of raping you?'

'No, I am not.' She knew she had not a hope of having this taken seriously. 'I have no idea what your dirty little secrets are.'

His eyes narrowed as the colour rose up his face. 'Why have you left it this long? If you were truly concerned about whatever it was happened to you, you would have come here straightaway.'

He stared at Ellen, his nostrils narrowed as if someone had slammed a ten-day-dead dog on the desk in front of him. 'Really, *Miss* Thompson, what's one more among hundreds?'

She hissed her breath in. 'You b—'

'Constable Hunt.' The middle-aged constable who had taken Bessie to the hospital came into the room. 'I'll deal with this now.'

Hunt glanced at the constable, a look almost of contempt, and stepped away from the desk.

'If you'll come with me, Miss Thompson.'

Ellen expected he would take her into an office where he would write down what she had to say, but instead he led her out into the paved entrance yard. Behind her, the young constable said something Ellen couldn't quite hear. Hunt's harsh laughter in reply followed her as she walked down the steps.

Someone had taken the trouble to plant a flower garden against the walls of the building, though, with it being late autumn, only the fuchsias and pelargoniums showed any colour.

The constable walked over to a bench against the street wall. 'Take a seat, Miss Thompson.' He nodded to Mam. 'You too, Mrs Thompson.'

'I'll stay standing, thank you.' Mam glared at him.

He sat himself at the other end of the bench and turned towards Ellen. When he spoke, his voice was soft, no hint of judgement. 'You would know rape is very difficult to prove. It is rare there are witnesses who are not involved in some way.'

Ellen pressed her lips tight. He was saying the same as bloody Hunt, only more politely.

'If we managed to get it to court, the men you accuse would have expensive lawyers who would turn every word you say inside out.'

'In other words, I haven't a hope?'

He shook his head. 'It's not right. It shouldn't be this way. I've seen cases of young girls, barely eleven or twelve, where we have the right man and the evidence and, even then, juries won't convict.'

Ellen stared at the paving, her arms wrapped tight across her bosom.

'You should try to put it behind you.'

Ellen looked up at him, her eyelashes damp. 'But I can't. I'm pregnant.'

His eyes were a sad grey. 'I'm afraid paternity is never accepted on the word of the mother alone.'

'Ellen!' Mam's voice was shrill. 'We're wasting our time here.'

The constable kept his attention on Ellen. 'Miss Thompson, I can take your statement if that's what you want, but you have a hard and almost impossible road ahead.'

'There's no point.' Ellen stood up. 'Thank you, Constable.'

She walked away, her back straight, Mam close behind her.

Out in the street, she said, 'So they're not all complete bastards.'

'He's about the only one. He's not one to charge you with obscene language the moment you drop a *bloody* or a *bastard*.'

As they walked up Bathurst Street, Ellen said, 'Well, that's that then.' She was still angry, but at least, her anger wasn't at herself. She straightened her shoulders. 'Let's go home and have a cup of tea. Or gin if you want. And when you and your old lassies do Armstrong and Cook over with Dad's awl and pincers, you can have a go at Hunt too.'

63

August 1883

Ellen trudged up Macquarie Street. Coming home this way added as much as ten minutes to her walk. She was tired, her legs ached, and a pain nagged its way from her buttock down the back of her right leg. She had never felt this bad with the other children, but with them she had worked at home and there had been time to sit and have a cup of tea, not the relentless business of working at the jam factory six days a week.

This extra walk was to avoid Mary Cunningham. Once it had become clear Ellen was pregnant, Cunningham took every chance she could to jeer at her.

'Who's the father this time, Thompson?'

'Can't blame poor bloody Harry Woods for your latest little bastard.'

'Whore!'

If Ellen didn't react, most people didn't take much notice, thinking it was old Cunningham drunk again and shouting at the sky. And as much as Ellen wanted to smash her in the face, she had to ignore her. She didn't want to get into a fight—she knew she'd come off second best.

She turned into Molle Street, plodding doggedly down the dip in the street, bracing herself for the climb up towards Liverpool Street. Most of the time Ellen was glad she had let the police know what Armstrong had done to her. She was certain she wasn't his first and wouldn't be his last. Perhaps the police would overlook the fact that he came from a *good* family the next time a woman was brave enough to tell them. Other times she wished she hadn't gone to them. She was afraid that bloody constable, Hunt, would spread it about that she'd been raped. She could imagine the joke he'd make of it, someone like her thinking she could point to the

362

father of her child. The bastard! It was something she didn't want people knowing—one day some vicious cow would tell her baby that he or she was born of rape, a child Ellen had never wanted. It wasn't the child's fault.

Mr Witt stood outside her house, rapping smartly on the door. Come to check on her to see she wasn't selling the rations—or her body, for that matter.

Ellen opened the gate and walked slowly towards him.

'Miss Thompson.' He raised his hat to her—he was always polite. 'I've been trying to catch you. You haven't been at home each time I've called.'

Ellen unlocked the door and held it open, but Mr Witt gestured for Ellen to go in ahead of him.

'I'm still working at Peacock's.'

It was dim inside. She lit the candle in the middle of the table. 'Bessie hasn't been able to find any work since the end of the fruit season so she minds the children.'

She went to the hearth. The fire had been carefully banked. She stirred it with the poker and placed a piece of split wood on top of the embers. She straightened up slowly, her knuckles at the arch of her back.

'Can I make you a cup of tea?' She swung the kettle over the centre of the fire.

'Thank you, no. I won't stay long.' Mr Witt pulled a chair out from the table and sat, his hat on a chair beside him. 'I wanted to check all was well with you.'

'We are getting by.'

'And I see you are expecting again.' He pulled out a notebook and pencil from his satchel.

'Yes.' What else could she say.

'And the father?'

The father. It made Ellen angry when she thought of it. *He* could do what he wanted, do something that was actually against the law, and nothing happened to him. She was the one who faced the consequences. She forced the thought of it away. She managed to do that most of the time but her anger still spilt out. Not often onto Bessie and the children now, but she snapped at other members of the family when things went wrong. And her words could be vicious to those outside her family who tried to belittle her in any way.

She twisted her mouth, stared past Mr Witt and unclenched her hands. 'On the tenth of March, when I was working over at Mrs Watkins's place at New Town, Thomas Armstrong raped me while William Cook held me down.'

Mr Witt blinked and sat up straighter, surprise on his normally unreadable face. 'Did you report this to the police?'

'I did. But they say it's too hard to prove. Constable Hunt laughed at me.'

He frowned deeply, his steely grey eyebrows a straight line as he scribbled furiously in his notebook. 'Thomas Armstrong.' He looked at Ellen. 'And William Cook?'

'Yes.'

At least someone was taking it seriously enough to write down their names. But Mr Witt always wrote everything he was told in his notebook.

He exhaled loudly. 'I am sorry, Miss Thompson, the police are right. It is a very difficult charge to prove, especially when you are accusing men from good families like the Armstrongs and Cooks.'

Good families! Money and education didn't make them good. There was so much Ellen wanted to say, but she kept her mouth tight shut and breathed through her nose.

Mr Witt slipped his notebook into his satchel. 'Do you have what you will need for the baby?'

'Yes. I gave the clothes I had for Lizzie to my sister, Mary Ann, but I'll get them back. Her baby will turn one next month.'

Mr Witt stood up. 'I'll call by closer to the birth and see how you are going.' He put on his hat. 'And if Bessie continues to have difficulty finding work once your baby is born, she can come into the depot some mornings and split kindling for rations. We have a few women do that. It will leave her free to look for work in the afternoon.'

He nodded his head to Ellen and walked to the door.

Ellen shut the door and blew out the candle. She still could see as it wasn't fully dark. Mr Witt and the other members of the Benevolent Society were busybodies but kind in their own way. Not fools either, they knew when people were spinning stories. There were many in Hobart, women like Ellen without men or those whose men were either sick or good for nothing, old people, children, who would not survive without the help they got from the Benevolent Society.

The kettle was boiling now. She made a weak pot of tea and went back to the table, resting her feet on the chair opposite. She drank her tea and waited in the quiet for Bessie and the children to come home. She could hear a couple screaming at each other farther down Moodie's Row, the sounds of a baby crying, raucous laughter, loud conversation. They all lived so close together here. Sometimes it made her feel safe, knowing neighbours were nearby. Other times it was frightening—a flimsy door, a pane of glass, all that kept the screams and the shouting out.

It would be good to live somewhere quieter, and cleaner, where the neighbours didn't know as much about her. She had worried Armstrong would track her down, think he owned her after what had happened. But he hadn't. He was the sort whose main interest was in the number of women he had, thought it made him more of a man. Still, the worry lingered.

There was noise outside. She lit the candle again, holding her hand up to shelter the flame as the door swung open. Billy and Jennie raced in ahead of Bessie.

Billy placed a tea towel wrapped package in front of Ellen.

'Gran said to give you this. She said she bet you wouldn't have bothered to make yourself any tea. It's a corned beef and pickle sandwich. We had corned beef and—'

'And, and, cabbage and potatoes,' Jennie joined in. She rubbed her tummy. 'Full.'

'You'll sleep well, my darlings.' Ellen knelt, gripping the table to keep her balance and held out her arms. 'Not too rough,' she said as Billy and Jennie threw themselves into her embrace.

Bessie lowered Lizzie from her hip to the floor, and the little girl toddled over to join them.

Ellen sighed. Her children were everything. As long as they were fed and happy, she could survive.

As she struggled upright, she noticed dark spatters down Billy's shirt.

'What's this?' She picked up the candle and drew him closer. There were grazes on his face, a purple bruise around his left eye.

She gaped at him. 'You have been fighting!'

'Yes, Mum,' he said proudly. 'You should see the other boy. I think I broke his nose. There was blood *all* over his shirt.'

'But why, Billy?' Her voice creaked. 'Haven't I told you not to fight?'

'I had to, Mum. He called you a rude name.'

Ellen wailed and slumped onto the chair. A boy needed to be able to stand up for himself, to learn how to defend those he loved, but Billy had only just turned six.

'Come here.' She opened her arms to him and hugged him until he started squirming. She let him go, but not before planting a loud kiss on his right cheek.

She hugged her girls and kissed them in turn.

'Now, all of you, off and use the pot, wash your faces, rinse your mouths and get into bed.'

'I'll clean that shirt tomorrow,' Bessie called over her shoulder as she followed the children into the bedroom. 'Dad took a look at him and said there was no damage done.'

Ellen rested her elbows on the table and rubbed her fingers over her brow. This was the wrong way about—she should be fighting for Billy.

Once the children were in bed, she sat and ate her sandwich, the meat still slightly warm. Opposite her, Bessie sipped a cup of tea.

'Bessie, I think we should move somewhere else. A place that's a bit bigger, away from the stink of the Rivulet in summer. Somewhere without damp walls and peeling wallpaper.'

'How could we afford that?'

'If it was somewhere cleaner than this, with a yard that was sunny for half the day, I could take in washing over summer when I can't work. Maybe you could go back to Peacock's.'

Bessie nodded. 'I wouldn't mind being back with those women. Most are pretty good.'

'Mary Ann is planning to work at Peacock's over summer, so you'd have her for company. We should be able to manage even if we had to pay two shillings more in rent. And if it isn't working out, if the place has more than two rooms, we could get someone in to help with the rent.'

'It would be good to leave.' Bessie gazed into the dark corners. 'A lot of sad things have happened here.'

'Yes.' There had been happy times, like Lizzie's birth, but even that had been tinged with sadness.

It was as if the house was waiting for Ellen—five minutes from where they were but it seemed a world away. A narrow terrace, one of three, at the steep end of Molle Street—one large room upstairs and two below. The kitchen ceiling was heavily smoke-stained. The fireplace had a small oven set into it beside a grate for the open fire. There was a washhouse out the back and a yard that caught the morning sun. Five houses shared two privies in the common area of the yard but each house had its own washhouse and tap. The upstairs room looked out towards the mountain. Ellen no longer minded. Harry and his wife were gone and she liked to remember the best of times there with Grannie and Grandad. And although Harry had proved to be a lying mongrel, he was not the worst man in the world.

She was certain this would be a good place to begin again—a solid building, warmer in winter and cooler in summer, with stout doors and more sunlight. And here she would learn to love her new child.

64

November 1883

Ellen struggled to the side of the bed and hauled herself upright. She felt the weight between her hips as she stood. The baby must have settled overnight. There were twinges as she walked across the room, nagging little pains, not the regular cramps of early labour. She had had them before her labour with Billy. It was hard to say when it would begin properly, but she didn't want to spend the day at the factory feeling the way she did.

'Bessie.' She shook her sister gently. 'Bessie, could you go down to Peacock's and let them know I won't be in. I think the baby will probably come today.'

Bessie lurched up still half-asleep, forcing her eyes open.

Ellen put her hand on her shoulder. 'There's no need to rush. It hasn't started properly.'

She went down to the kitchen, still in her nightgown, and raked out the ashes and kindled a fire.

Bessie was dressed by the time Ellen came in from the wash-house with the filled kettle and hung it on the hook over the grate.

'I won't wait for the tea,' Bessie said. 'I'll ask if I can take over your job.'

'Are you sure?'

'Yes. It can be such a laugh at times, when you are doing work you don't need to think much about.' She went to the cupboard and brought the bread to the table, cutting herself a slice.

Perhaps it would be good for her. Ellen wanted the old Bessie back. She wanted the old Ellen back too. But, first, she had to get through what was ahead of her.

'See if they'll give you what they owe me for the week so far.'

Bessie swallowed her mouthful of bread and jam. 'Will you be all right by yourself?'

'I'll send Billy for Mam if things start properly.'

Ellen slowly went about what she knew needed to be done—dressing, getting the children up, feeding them. She would have preferred to lie on the bed and curl into a ball but thought grimly that if she tried that, some part of her would ache. She had the dull fear that had been present with every birth, fear she would not survive, fear that her children would be left motherless with no one to love them the way she did. In the past that had been set against the excitement that came with the thought of a new baby, each one different, each one delightful, holding something of the good that was in both her and their fathers. This time she had nothing of that joy, even when she had felt those first fluttering movements. All she had was dread. When she looked down into this baby's face, would she see its father looking back—a constant reminder of what he had done to her?

Bessie was back an hour later. 'They won't take me on, and I can't get your pay until payday.'

Ellen placed a bowl of porridge in front of her. 'You must be hungry after that, on one slice of bread.'

'I had a cup of tea at Mary Ann's after I went to the factory.' Bessie began to eat, speaking between mouthfuls. 'They are going to advertise next week—I'll go along then.'

Billy scraped his spoon across the bottom of his bowl. He looked up, his brow puckered with concentration. 'What's wrong, Mum?'

He really did notice everything that was going on.

Ellen placed the saucepan in the washing dish and came over to the table, planting a kiss on the top of his head. 'Nothing, my darling. I won't be able to work for a while because this baby will be here by tomorrow.' She forced a wide smile, hoping it put him at ease. 'Aunty Bessie is going to work at the jam factory instead of me. You go off and play with Fred now.' She kissed him again. 'Make sure you come home at lunch time. I might need you to run messages.'

'I will.' He nodded furiously.

He looked serious and responsible at that moment. All of six years old, he saw himself as the man of the house—when he wasn't out with his friends, racing around the streets, playing football. He needed a father who could show him how to be a man, to keep him on the right side of the law. But even with a father, things could go wrong. George had made his first appearance in court aged eleven, his head the only thing that showed over the dock. That had ended with him spending seven days in the House of Correction for stealing six eggs. She didn't want that happening to Billy. If George were here, he would teach Billy to be tough, how to look after himself but, she knew too well, Billy might learn from him other things that could get him into trouble.

Ellen's pains began in the middle of the night. She eased herself out of bed and went downstairs. Between the well-spaced pains, she built the fire and set the kettle to boil. She paced the room, sat when she was tired, wrapped about with her fears. Just before dawn, she called up the stairs to Bessie.

Billy followed Bessie down.

Ellen lowered her head and grasped the back of a chair, groaning as a pain hit her. When it finally eased, she looked up to see Billy standing opposite, terror in his eyes.

'Come here, my darling.' She held him close and kissed the top of his head. 'Don't worry, everything will be all right.'

Billy sniffed back his tears, looking as if he didn't believe her.

'Get yourself dressed and go and tell Gran the baby's coming.'

He ran towards the stairs, his feet thumping on the floor.

'Quietly, Billy. I don't want your sisters awake yet.'

Mam arrived with Mrs Miller, the midwife, just after breakfast, then Bessie took the children down to Mary Ann's. Ellen climbed the stairs, back to her bed, and rested between the pains.

Mrs Miller was as bossy and competent as ever but complaining that she had to tramp up and down the stairs for cups of tea and the privy.

As the afternoon wore on, it seemed to Ellen this child was as unwilling to face the world as Ellen was to welcome him or her into it. Towards evening, finally, time contracted to unstoppable waves of pain and pressure, an ever-present fear rolling beneath them.

The sun had set when Ellen heard the first yell of her newest child.

'A bonny wee boy.' Mam smiled down at the child as she carried him, tightly wrapped to Ellen.

Mam's smile was not so bright when she looked into Ellen's face. She could not possibly know what Ellen was thinking.

Ellen lay against the pillows, relieved. It was over, but there was none of the swelling joy that had come with the other children, only sadness, not for herself, but for this child—a poor wee scrap of a boy who never should have been. She watched him, latched on to her breast. He looked like a little old man. How would she ever learn to love him?

Later, when Bessie brought the children back, they crowded around the bed, keen to see their little brother.

Jennie was unimpressed. 'What does he do?'

'Eat and sleep for the moment, but soon enough you'll be playing peekaboo and pat-a-cake with him.'

Lizzie piped in. 'I play peekyboo.'

'I can play football with him,' Billy said. 'And take him to school.'

'You can, my darling. But not for a while yet.'

Ellen smiled at her children, blinking fast. Perhaps they would teach her how to love this child.

Bessie's gaze had not left the baby since she entered the room, her hunger to hold him plain.

Ellen beckoned her over.

Bessie cradled him in her arms. 'What's his name?'

'George.'

'A lovely name.' She gazed at the infant, her face suffused with the love Ellen couldn't summon. 'He is beautiful,' she breathed.

Poor Bessie.

Three days later, Ellen sat in the early morning light, feeding *wee Georgie,* as his grandmother called him. When the rest of the family had visited, Alice had said he had his grandfather's nose, Mam adding she was sure he would have his grandfather's laughing hazel eyes.

George's cheeks had rounded out, and his dark wispy hair was angel's down—no longer a little old man. He did have his grandfather's nose, and there was something of Billy in his face.

Ellen smiled at her boy, her beautiful boy, tears trickling down her cheeks.

65

March 1884

Ellen sang as she scrubbed the front step. Farther along the passage, George lay on a blanket, his chubby feet kicking the air as Jennie played peekaboo through her hands. Beside them, Lizzie, her dress pulled up to her neck, fed her doll. Billy was at school and Bessie at work. The washing Ellen was paid to do was flapping on the line in the backyard. The sky was a clear blue, the breeze blowing warm.

Occasionally, someone walked past, keeping well clear. The sensible knew not to get in the way of a busy woman with a bucket of water.

Footsteps sounded on the footpath, work boots by the heavy tread. They came to a halt beside Ellen.

Ellen stopped her scrubbing and dropped the brush into the bucket. She sat back on her heels and gazed up into a pair of blue eyes.

Jim Doran lifted his hat and said, 'Good morning, Ellen.'

'Good morning, Jim.' She got up off her knees and dried her hands on her apron. 'It's a long time since we've seen you.'

He grinned at her. 'You're a hard woman to track down.'

She stepped away from the door. 'Go into the kitchen. I'll be along in a minute. I'm nearly finished here. And don't put your feet on the wet step.' She watched him walk along the passage, his kitbag slung over his shoulder, pausing to look at George lying on his blanket. The girls clambered up from the floor and followed him.

Ellen wiped the step dry, threw the dirty water out into the gutter, and left the bucket in the doorway of the front room. She could hear Jim talking to the girls.

'How do you know our names?' Jennie asked.

'I've met you before.'

'No.'

Ellen could imagine Lizzie shaking her head, stubborn certainty on her face.

'Was that when Mummy came home from gaol?' Jennie asked. No doubt about it, Jennie was a Thompson—treating what others thought shameful as matter-of-fact. 'I thought you were Uncle George. Everyone talks about Uncle George.'

'I've met your Uncle George.'

'George our baby,' Lizzie said.

The front door shut, Ellen called down the passage. 'I won't be long.'

George was fussing and crying so loud it was almost a roar.

After changing his wet nappy, Ellen carried George into the kitchen and deposited him on Jim's lap. 'I have to wash my hands.'

When she came back, Jim was sitting upright, holding George awkwardly, the baby red-faced and bellowing.

'He won't break unless you drop him.' She scooped George up. 'And I thought you were good with children.'

He smiled at her.

He did have a nice smile.

'I'm fine as long as they can talk.'

'I need to feed George. Could you manage to make us a cup of tea?' She turned away and unbuttoned the front of her bodice, settling the baby to her breast.

'I'll try. But, first, I've brought a couple of things.'

He picked up his bag from beside his seat and pulled out a paper bag, a newspaper wrapped parcel and five bananas.

The girls left off playing with their dolls and came over to the table, watching, eyes large, as Jim took a pound cake out of the paper bag and unwrapped a big bunch of grapes.

'This is a treat, isn't it, girls? What do you say to Jim?'

'Thank you, Jim,' they said together.

Ellen raised her eyebrows. 'You *bought* all this for us?'

'I did.'

'Just wondering—seamen on the docks, crates slip, what's inside accidentally falls out.'

'I paid for them all.' There was a sparkle in his eyes. 'Though I may not have gone to a fruiterer.'

Ellen laughed. He was not much different from her brothers.

He went over to the dresser, Ellen telling him where to find the cups and plates, the tea tin. She sensed he was on his best behaviour and wondered why.

'Girls, if you sit up at the table, Jim might cut you a nice piece of cake.' They didn't have cake often. She would leave giving them lunch until they were hungry.

Jim finally sat down and looked across at her. To his credit, he kept his eyes on her face.

He sat sipping his tea. Although he was neat and freshly shaven, he looked slightly worse for wear. His eyes were bloodshot, dark smudges beneath them, grazes on his knuckles. She was sure if she kissed him, he would taste of the grog he had drunk the night before. Why was she thinking that? She had no intention of kissing Jim Doran or any other man.

'You are hard to track down, Ellen.' He smiled across at her. His blue eyes were truly the nicest Ellen had seen.

'I called last November when I was in town, and no one down at Moodie's Row had any idea where you had moved to. I went to your parents' house, but no one was home there either. I haven't managed to run into any of your family each time I've been in Hobart. It was sheer luck I saw Bessie last night on her way home from work.'

That might explain why he hadn't been surprised by George.

'Funny, she didn't mention it.' She would kill Bessie if she had told Jim everything. 'So, what have you been doing?'

'I'm on the *Strathmore*, mostly along the coast—Hobart,

Garden Island, Mersey, Launceston.'

He asked politely about her family, no comment at all on the presence of a new baby.

'And Billy, where's he today?

'Billy is at school—learning to read and write.'

'That's good. He's a fine lad.'

'He is indeed.' She supposed she should ask, after the gift of cake and fruit. 'Would you like to stay for lunch? It's only bread and cheese.'

'I could take you all out for lunch.' She saw the spark of hope in his eyes.

'Thank you, Jim, but I doubt that would work. What if George wants to be fed? Babies are hungry creatures.'

'I didn't think of that.'

He did stay for lunch.

The girls' appetites had not been spoilt by the cake. While they ate, they told Jim stories about their Gran and Grandad and their aunts, not all of them completely true, and the time Billy got a black eye and had given the other boy a blooded nose.

Jim seemed reluctant to leave. He offered to do a few odd jobs, so Ellen got him to fix the latch on the front window and the loose hinge on the kitchen door.

George was asleep in his basket, the girls playing quietly in the backyard when Ellen walked Jim to the door.

'It's been lovely seeing you, Jim.' She meant it. It was a reminder life had been fun once, perhaps it could be again. One day.

'Tell Billy I'm sorry I missed him.' He raised his eyebrows, and grinned at her. 'May I call in when I'm next in Hobart?'

She could see he expected her to say yes—he was just like her brothers. 'Of course, we'd love to see you.'

He reached over and pecked her on the cheek.

Ellen stood where she was and resisted placing her hand against the side of his face.

He tipped his hat and walked away.

She wondered why he had come. What possible interest could he have in someone like her, with four small children, when there were so many young unencumbered women. She hadn't asked him if he had seen her brother George, perhaps he had called as a favour to him.

He looked back up the street when he reached the corner, a grin on his face, and waved.

Ellen waved back. She remembered last time he had turned and waved as he left her and the vague silly dreams she'd had then. Life had certainly knocked them out of her.

66

June 1884

Ellen sat by the kitchen fire, George asleep in her arms. She should put him in the basket he slept in down here, but she didn't want to disturb him, and besides, he was almost too big for it. He was sleeping peacefully, his dark eyelashes resting on plump cheeks. The image of the perfect baby. She resisted planting a kiss on his pink cheek.

Bessie, not long home from her day charring, was playing hop-scotch outside with the girls, giggling along with them, no doubt pretending to be as wobbly on one leg as Lizzie. Billy hadn't come home from school yet. He often didn't arrive home until just on dark, which wasn't too late as night came on early this time of year. His excuse was always that he was playing football with his mates. It worried her, not only the thought he might get into mischief, but of what could happen to him. He could hold his own in a fight with someone his own age, but what if he was up against a bigger boy?

She turned at the cold gust as the front door opened.

Billy burst into the kitchen, his face bright from the wind, his hair standing almost on end. There was mud on his knees and one side of his pants.

'Mum, you've got a visitor.'

Mr Witt walked in behind him.

Barely pausing for breath, Billy said, 'I'm hungry. Can I have something to eat?'

'First, go out to the washhouse and clean yourself up—and wash your face and hands properly. Then you can cut yourself one slice of bread, and not too thick.' He'd hack off half the loaf if he wasn't watched.

'And jam?'

'Yes, and jam.' She smiled as he ran out into the yard.

Mr Witt had walked over to the window and was staring into the yard. He turned back to the room.

'That smells tasty.' He nodded towards the pot suspended over the flames.

'Soup for tea,' Ellen answered. She sensed he approved of the way she was managing.

He pulled out a chair at the other side of the table. 'Your sister must be a great help.'

'She is. I couldn't manage without her.'

'I hear she has been attending the Sunday services at All Saints Church.'

Ellen, hiding her surprise, nodded. So that was where she was off to some Sunday mornings. Ellen had assumed she was visiting their parents. She wondered why Bessie had kept it a secret.

'Bessie is out charring three days a week, and I go out two mornings. It covers the rent but not much more.'

Mr Witt was scribbling in his notebook.

'We are grateful for the rations we get for the children.'

Billy was back, busy cutting his bread and slathering it with jam. He didn't bother with a plate. He headed towards the back door, his mouth already full.

'Billy!' Ellen called him back. 'Put the bread and jam back in the cupboard.'

With a huff and a slouch, he did as he was told and then went out the back to create mayhem among his sisters.

'He's a good little lad,' Mr Witt said.

Ellen laughed. 'Most of the time.'

George stirred and started coughing. Ellen held him upright against her shoulder, rubbing his back. She felt so useless. All she could do was to wait the long minutes until the coughing passed.

Mr Witt frowned. 'That is a nasty cough. Has he been unwell long?'

Ellen grimaced and let out a long sigh. 'I don't know that he's ill. We all had heavy colds last month—coughing, sneezing, runny noses. Everyone else is over it, but George's cough won't shift.'

Mr Witt came around the table and touched the back of his hand to the baby's forehead. 'He's quite warm.'

'I've got him rugged up. And we are sitting by the fire.'

'Does he sweat at night? How is his appetite?'

'It's just the cough that's the problem.' If she were honest, his appetite wasn't as good. He was nowhere near as interested in solid food as he had been before they had caught that cold.

The coughing had stopped, and George now sat in Ellen's lap gazing up at Mr Witt.

Ellen could see sadness in the old man's eyes. She knew what he was thinking—she would not allow herself to contemplate it. She rubbed her nose against the boy's neck, blurting against it. The child squirmed and giggled. Really, there was nothing wrong with him.

'You should take him to the hospital.' Mr Witt held up his hand as Ellen opened her mouth to object. 'There's no harm in going— it will set your mind at rest. Go tomorrow and, on your way, call in at the depot and I'll have a letter ready for you to give to the doctor.'

There was no point arguing. 'I suppose it won't hurt.'

Ellen did as she was told and, the following day, took George, wrapped in a shawl, a woollen bonnet on his head, to the hospital.

The doctor read the letter and asked her to undress George. Seeing him lying there on the doctor's bench, she knew he was thinner than he should be. The doctor poked and prodded him, tapping his chest with his fingers. George wriggled and began to cry, his cries turning to coughing. The doctor listened to his chest with a fancy ear horn. He sat back at his desk watching and, Ellen supposed, listening as she dressed George and tried to calm his coughing. He had the same worried look Mr Witt had.

She knew what he was going to say.

'I'm sorry, Miss Thompson, your little boy has consumption.'

'He can't have it—he's not coughing blood.' She had clung to the idea. 'People with consumption cough blood.'

'Small children often don't. They swallow what comes up.'

Ellen raised her head, clenched her jaw. 'Why does he have this?'

'For a long time, we haven't been sure of the cause. It has been thought it could be inherited from a person's parents or grandparents or perhaps the result of bad air and poor living conditions or changes in the temperature.'

'But no one in our family has consumption, not my children, my parents, my sisters or brothers.'

'What about your baby's father or his family?'

Ellen jerked her head. Was Armstrong to blame? 'We have nothing to do with any of them.'

'Hmmm.' He tapped his fingers on the desk. 'Unlikely to be the source. Doctors are coming to the view it might be caused by infection, passed from one person to the other through the air.'

George started to cry. 'Can you cure him?' She jigged the child on her lap.

The doctor shook his head slowly. 'There is very little I can do. It's clear you care for him well ...'

What did that mean? That he wasn't dirty and smelly? It was clear she hadn't cared for George anywhere near well enough.

'... all you can do now is to take your little boy home, keep him warm, feed him well and make sure he gets plenty of fresh air. But I want you and the rest of your family back here on Thursday. I need to examine you all.'

Nausea washed through her. 'My other children aren't sick.'

'It's best to be safe. In the early stages, the disease may not be obvious. If we catch it early enough, we can slow its progress.' He walked Ellen to the door and held it open for her.

George was still fussing, so she stayed in the waiting room and fed him. She had her coat on, and although she had the front of her dress unbuttoned, she wasn't on display. She glared at the fat old cow on the other side of the room with her narrowed nostrils and her mouth pursed like a cat's bum. Her baby needed to be fed, as much for comfort as anything else, and if anyone said a word, she would tell them what they could do with themselves.

They trooped back to the hospital on Thursday, all inspected by the doctor, who declared none of them showed signs of the disease. Ellen could have wept with relief except he said she should keep watch on her other children. He said he couldn't explain how George had it and no one else.

Later, Ellen remembered old Mrs Galloway, one of Mary Ann's neighbours. She had taken care of George for three weeks while Ellen had worked at the jam factory back in late February. They were short of women because more than expected had left the factory early to go to New Norfolk for the hop picking. Mary Ann's sister-in-law had minded the girls but couldn't manage another baby—she had her own child and Mary Ann's Tom as well. Mrs Galloway was a sprightly old woman with bright eyes and pink cheeks, the picture of the perfect grandmother except she was thin. She had loved George, bouncing him on her knee and kissing him the way a grandmother would. She had lived close enough to the factory for Ellen to come and feed George during the dinner break. She had a cough, but she smoked a pipe, like so many old people. Mary Ann had mentioned that she had died recently of phthisis, the fancy name for consumption. The doctor was wrong about the idea of it travelling through the air; Ellen would have it too if that were true.

Life was as it always had been—completely unfair.

67

August 1884

George faded, week by week, losing his lovely roundness. His laughter lessened. He was listless, no longer interested in games of peekaboo and funny faces. He coughed and coughed—sometimes leaving flecks of blood on his lips—and broke into sweats at night. But his eyes, so heart-breakingly beautiful and trusting, still gazed up into Ellen's.

He was curled against Ellen as she held him on her lap. She had tried to feed him watery porridge for breakfast, but he didn't want it. He had the spoon in his hand, waving it half-heartedly about. Three months ago, he would have been banging it on the table and laughing.

In the backyard, she could hear the bounce of a ball and the girls squabbling. Bessie was out there trying to keep order.

Billy slammed through the back door and threw himself down, arms crossed, on the chair opposite her. 'Can I go out in the street?'

'No, Billy. It's Sunday morning—no one will be out. Go and play with your sisters.'

'Don't want to play girls' games.' He slouched in the chair, pouting. Ellen closed her eyes. She could see trouble coming. Billy would be seven later this month. He needed a stronger hand than hers to guide him.

Bessie came in and swung the kettle over the fire. She glanced back at Ellen. 'Cup of tea?'

'Thank you.' She looked down. George had fallen asleep despite the noise.

'Can I go and see Fred Rowe?'

'Fred's father is off the grog and has a bad dose of religion. If you turn up there now, they'll haul you off to church with them.'

Billy's eyes lit up. 'That sounds like fun.'

384

'It isn't. There's an old man stands at the front and goes on about nothing very interesting, and then everyone sings boring songs. And you have to sit up straight and be quiet.'

'It's not that bad. The songs are nice, and sometimes they have tea and cakes afterwards.' Bessie sat still, as if she had admitted to something she shouldn't have.

Ellen wouldn't ask. Bessie would tell her about her churchgoing when she was ready. 'They'd have to be good cakes to convince me to sit through that.'

'Please, Mum,' Billy whined.

'Very well, but don't say I didn't warn you. Wash your face and hands and comb your hair first.'

'We will see if he is as keen next week.' Ellen smiled across at Bessie, who was staring at nothing, her thoughts miles away.

Billy ran in from the back, and down the passage, yelling, ''bye.' The door slammed behind him.

A couple of minutes later, he was back again.

'Mum! Mum!' He pounded back into the kitchen. 'We've got a visitor.'

Jim Doran stood in the doorway, his hat in his hand. 'Good morning, ladies.'

'Jim! It is lovely to see you.' And it was. He was a reminder of sunnier days.

He didn't have his bag with him, but he was carrying an oddly shaped red kite with a long tail wound around it.

He pulled out a chair and sat, placing the kite on the table.

Billy was beside him. Ellen could see his fingers itching to pick it up.

'This is a special kite, Billy. I got it from mate called Tommy Ah Chong, and he had it all the way from China. You won't see anything else like it flying down on the Domain.'

'Are you here for long?' Ellen asked.

'I've signed off. Decided to spend a few weeks on dry land.'

George gave a little cough in his sleep. She carefully lifted him, making him more comfortable.

Billy placed his hands on the table, the fingers of his left resting beside the kite.

'I wondered if you wanted to come to the Domain and fly the kite. We could have something to eat while we are down there.'

He seemed as eager as Billy.

'I'm sorry, Jim. It's a lovely idea, but George isn't well, and I can't take him out in the cold.'

She could see the disappointment in his eyes. They were lovely eyes, so blue in the light from the window.

'Mum,' Billy wailed. 'Please.'

'I can mind George,' Bessie said. 'You go and get some fresh air.'

'I can't. He will want to be fed when he wakes.' She looked back to Jim. 'If you could take Billy, that would be wonderful.'

'I'm sure the girls would enjoy a run with the kite too.' He smiled at Bessie. 'You'll come along, Bessie?'

Ellen could see the pleasure shining in Bessie's face. She was rarely asked directly—it was assumed Bessie would go along with everyone else. Despite her best intentions, Ellen still took Bessie for granted. Her sister deserved better than that.

They came back late in the afternoon. Ellen was seated by the fire, George still in her arms. There were days when he did nothing but sleep. But the sleep was easily disturbed, so she sat still and quiet.

Jim looked across at George, a line between his brows. Bessie must have told him.

The children were talking all at once about the kite and their lunch and the cake they had eaten.

'I doubt they will want any tea after all they ate.' Bessie smiled. She was happy in a way Ellen hadn't seen for a long time. 'It was a wonderful afternoon. Thank you, Jim.'

'It was my pleasure, ma'am.'

Ellen shut her eyes. It was these moments that hurt the most—when life was going on around them, people happy, and she knew her little boy would never have any of it.

She felt a hand on her shoulder.

Jim stood beside her. 'I've got to go now.' His voice, so different from those who surrounded her, was a comfort. 'I'll be here for a few weeks. I'll call in again, if I may.'

'We love seeing you, Jim. All of us.' She placed her hand over his and squeezed it. And there it was, that same spark as when he had first shaken her hand. How could she possibly feel that at a time like this?

He withdrew his hand and put his hat on. 'And don't forget, the jam tart on the table is for you. The kids have promised not to wheedle a bite of it.'

'Thank you—' She had to stop herself. She had nearly called him *my darling*, as she did those she truly cared for. It was his kindness. She didn't understand why he was doing it but it lessened the gloom.

~

George was a frail elfin creature, slowly slipping away from her. Ellen had set up a cot for him in the kitchen, where he could lie while she cooked and cleaned. She tried not to think that he should now be under her feet, crawling along the floor or skidding on his backside. He lay in his cot, his eyes following her. When she went out to the washhouse, she sang so he could hear she was not far away.

Life went on. She had to go to work, but she knew he was safe. Bessie cared for him just as she did. Whenever she walked in from work, Bessie had him in her arms, rocking him, crooning to him, soothing him.

Ellen gave George all the love and care she could, but she knew she wasn't giving her other children what they needed. They were washed and fed, hugged and kissed, but her mind was always on

George. They knew he was sick and watched what happened to him, silent, not truly understanding. Often enough now, the girls squabbled, slapping each other and pulling hair. Billy would have spent the whole day away from home if she let him. The only way to control them was by shouting and threatening, and she hated it. Was this what happened as children grew up? Or was she a bad mother?

Jim appeared most Sundays and took Bessie and the children out. When it was cold and wet, he spent the afternoon in the kitchen with them, talking. Ellen loved the sound of his voice as he spoke of his family and the place he had come from. Brooklyn. It seemed like Hobart with people from everywhere, but he said the weather here was milder, not as hot in summer nor as cold in winter. It struck her she had no sense that he was hiding anything about his past, that there were secrets he would tell her one day. He was what she saw sitting across the table from her. She wondered why he hadn't signed on to another ship but didn't ask. Perhaps he had a girl down Wapping, where he had a room. If that was the case, she didn't want to know.

The house was quiet as she came in from work on Saturday afternoon.

Mam was sitting out in the yard, George lying in her arms.

She smiled at Ellen as she opened the door. 'It's lovely and warm in this corner, out of the wind. Drag up a chair, my love.'

It would be pleasant to sit in the sun and close her eyes. 'I've a pile of mending to do. Billy's pants need patching nearly every week. This time he's got a three-cornered tear on the seat. I have no idea what he gets up to when he's out of my sight.'

'You can easily do that here in the sun.'

'Where is everyone?'

'I sent them off to our place. Alice has a new kitten. And Billy can have a kick of the ball with the boys along the lane. That boy hates being cooped inside.'

'He does but I can't have him running wild.'

Mam laughed. 'Aye, but that one thinks he's nearly a man.'

Ellen rolled her eyes and went in to get her sewing.

'And how are *you*, Ellen?' her mother asked when she settled onto the chair beside her.

'I don't know.' She closed her eyes and shook her head slowly. 'Life is too hard.'

'You know his time is near,' Mam said gently.

'Yes.' Her voice was barely louder than a whisper. She squeezed her eyes tight against the tears.

Mam reached her free hand out and rubbed it along Ellen's forearm.

'You have done everything you can. All that can be done now is to love him while he is with us and mourn him after.'

Tears trickled down her cheeks. 'How did you manage when you lost the baby before Alice?'

'Our other little Alice.' She rocked George as he coughed, so weak that he barely stirred the air. 'It were sudden. She had a fever and convulsions. She went too quickly. We didn't have time to do anything. Just five weeks old.' She lifted George up, resting his head on her shoulder. His breathing seemed easier. 'It were as if my heart had been shredded with a knife. But you have to go on for the others. And, as you know well, I find a wee drop always eases life's pains.'

'Oh Mam.' Ellen smiled through her tears.

'And then, eighteen months later, there was our Alice Eva, and this world would be a much sadder place without her.' Mam stared up at the scudding clouds overhead, her eyes glistening in the sunlight.

'And where do they go, these little ones?'

'It would be good to think there is a better place than this where the little ones are never hungry.' Mam gently rubbed her hand against George's back. 'Wherever they go, they are away from the sorrows and pains of this life.'

Ellen hoped there was a place where children who had known nothing but suffering were warm and well-loved.

68

October 1884

Ellen woke in the grey light of early morning, George in the crook of her arm, his breathing shallow. He seemed not to have the energy to cough. He turned his head away when she tried to feed him. His nappy was dry. Her shawl over her shoulders, she carried him downstairs to the kitchen. She stoked the fire and sat by the hearth, rocking George, stroking his downy hair, softly singing the lullabies he had once gurgled and clapped to.

She did not see the moment he left her, but she felt the great rip in her heart. Ellen bent and kissed his forehead, her beautiful boy. She carried him to the door, pulled it open and said, 'Fly away my darling, my little angel.'

Sunrise touched the clouds overhead. A dusky robin took flight from the fence at the back of the yard, its plaintive call carrying on the cool morning air.

Ellen went back to the fire and sat cradling George, her cheeks wet with tears.

The sun slowly rose, filling the room with light.

Bessie came into the kitchen and went straight to Ellen. She knelt in front of her and kissed George's cool cheek.

She looked up at Ellen. 'He's with my little boy now.'

'Did you name him?' All babies had a name.

Bessie nodded. 'I call him Peter. George will be with Peter, and they'll play together. In heaven.'

George was gone where there was no pain, where he could breathe and laugh and learn to run and play. She must believe it. And perhaps Will was there too, watching over his nephews. She must believe it.

Billy and the girls came down the stairs not long after. Telling them was not as difficult as she thought.

'He was very sick,' Jennie said.

Lizzie said nothing. She shuffled close to Jennie who put her arm around her. They clung to each other.

'And George is in heaven now,' Billy said. 'It's where all babies go.'

Ellen stared at him.

'They tell us about it at school.' He proceeded to explain the joys of heaven to his sisters, a place that had everything a child growing up in shoddy housing with thin clothing and not quite enough to eat would enjoy, nothing like the eternity of boredom described by the minister in the gaol.

The following day, early, George was buried with his Uncle Will at Queenborough Cemetery. The minister from All Saints said prayers by the graveside. Ellen had left her girls with Mary Ann who, at eight months pregnant, was in no state to walk all the way to Queenborough and back. There were no mourning coaches or mountains of flowers, no money to pay for them. It was simple, just family—Mam and Dad, Alice, Jane and Bessie. Billy stood beside Ellen, Jim Doran behind her. She was glad of Jim's kindness. His presence had been a bright steady point these last months. Ellen's eyes were dry as the tiny coffin was lowered into the ground but every muscle, every fibre screamed her sorrow.

There was no wake. They went off to their jobs, but Mam said that on Sunday they would get together and raise a glass to *wee Georgie's* memory. Ellen thought she would buy a bottle of beer, and tonight, after the children were in bed, she and Bessie would share it and sing to the memory of their lost boys. She could hear Bessie's beautiful voice.

How cold the wind do blow, my love,
And see the drops of rain.

~

There was no time for mourning, for special clothes, for staying inside like rich people did. Ellen straightened her shoulders and walked down to the Registrar's Office and told them her boy was dead, that he had died of consumption. The young man behind the desk had been polite. She thought he might be the same fellow who had refused to register Lizzie as a Woods, but she couldn't remember.

Jim called in later in the day, to see how she was.

'Back to work tomorrow early.' She shrugged. 'What else can I do?'

'I've signed on with the *Charles and Arthur.*'

'Oh.' He could have no idea how much she would miss him. 'When did you do that?'

'Yesterday afternoon. I've run out of money, and I can earn more than what I've been getting here on the docks.'

'When do you leave?'

'Next Monday but I will be back.'

She wanted to say *When? Next month? Next year?* But she had no claim on him, no right to ask these questions.

'But you will come to Mam and Dad's on Sunday?'

'I wouldn't miss it for the world.' He smiled. 'May I call in and walk you all up there?'

'Yes, I'd like that.' She smiled back at him, wishing he would hold her. She wanted to be held tight by someone stronger than herself.

On Sunday, the children were keen to leave, the girls to see Alice's kitten, Billy to play with the boys who lived along from his grandparents. Ellen sat alone with her thoughts and waited for Jim.

Everything else that had happened in these past few years paled beside George's illness and death. She knew the pain would fade— life could not be lived if it didn't—but George would always be there in her heart. She would never forget him.

Jim knocked at the door and walked in. He no longer waited for the door to be answered. 'Where is everyone?'

'They've already gone to Mam and Dad's.'

'Even Billy?'

'Yes, even Billy.' Ellen smiled. 'Your charms have faded—there are two boys living in the lane along from Mam and Dad.'

He grinned at her. 'I'm heartbroken, but I suppose two boys are more fun than an old man.'

'You're not so old. And Billy will miss you when you're gone.'

'And you? Will you miss me?'

She had to look away from those blue eyes. 'I will.' She took a deep breath. 'I don't know how I would have got through these last months without you here.'

'Ellen, I wish I could stay, but I need the money.'

'The real money's whaling, but for that you could be away for anything up to two years.' She couldn't bear not seeing him for two years.

She stepped towards him, told herself it was the hug a sister would give a brother about to sail away. But as soon as his arms were around her, she knew what she had been missing—the strength of someone else, protecting her, making her feel she wasn't the only one holding up her world.

She stretched up and kissed him. It was meant to be no more than a peck, but her lips touched his and there was no pretending he was her brother. A tiny corner of her mind told her this was reckless—she could be left alone with another child. But all that existed was this moment and the ache of longing and loneliness it answered.

There was no thought left but the newness of him. Little things she already knew were revelations: the mint on his breath, the smell of his cologne, the tickle of his moustache, the hardness of his muscles, the darkness of his hair, the shape of his ears, the light in his eyes. The familiar and the unexpected. Murmured laughter and breathless silences. Oblivion and awareness soaring together. Glorious exaltation slowly settling to ordinary joy.

She lay across him, listening to the hammering of his heart, her fingers tracing patterns on his skin. The faint pealing of the bells from All Saints Church brought her back to the present, to the weight of her sorrow, the realisation that no more than a few days after his death she had forgotten her little boy. She shut her mouth on a sob as her tears dripped onto Jim's chest.

'Ellen,' he slid down the bed, 'I'm sorry. I shouldn't have ...'

She gazed into his eyes. 'Jim, don't say that. You've done nothing I didn't want.' She laid her hand against his face. 'It's too soon to let him leave my mind but I wanted you ...'

He kissed her again. It would be so easy to slip back into that forgetfulness. Ellen eased herself away. 'We should get dressed. They'll be waiting for us.'

She reached over and picked up her shift from the floor beside the bed, pulling it over her head before she got out. As she dressed, she watched Jim from beneath her lashes. He moved about the room collecting his discarded clothing, no shame in his nakedness. It was for the best that he was leaving. She could love him if she let herself but was it truly what she wanted? She needed time to mourn George and to love her other children before she could decide.

The afternoon was spent with those who meant most to Ellen—Mam and Dad, not perfect, but they loved their children without judgement. Mary Ann, steady and sensible, almost as big as a hot air balloon, Tom Budd at her side. Their little Tom, two-years-old and playing with Lizzie and Jennie. Billy, running in now and then to help himself to food, happy out with the other boys. Jane and Alice, both pretty young women, full of laughter, twenty and fifteen. And Bessie. She had been by Ellen's side since her world with Harry Woods had fallen apart. She had loved George as she never had the chance to love her own son.

Jane and Alice were teasing her as she talked about a young man she knew from the church.

'Hens?' Alice squealed.

'Yes, hens. He has all sorts. He has this breed he said goes back to the Romans. They have an extra toe.'

Bessie had clearly had a lengthy discussion about chooks with him. Or, at least, had been an admiring audience.

Alice frowned, puzzled. 'What are Romans?'

'People that lived years ago,' Jane said. 'Older than Mam and Dad.' She frowned. 'How old is your young man, Bessie?'

'He's not my young man.' Bessie's face flushed. 'He's my age.'

That blush gave Bessie away. Ellen hoped that this young man brought some fun into Bessie's life but, more importantly, she hoped that he was kind. The church seemed to be a good place for Bessie. As long as she didn't turn Temperance and start telling Mam not to drink, all would be well.

And Jim. He was sitting between Dad and Tom, an easy banter going on between them. No one who called in would think he wasn't one of the family. Ellen had no sense that he was anything other than what she saw. But he was leaving tomorrow, and despite what he said, who knew if he would return.

She thought of lost moments—days at the end of summer, the aroma of baking bread drifting from the cottage, Grannie and Grandad sitting outside smoking their pipes, Billy squealing as Harry tossed him in the air, Jennie comfortable on Ellen's hip. She had been happy, and she had loved Harry beyond reason. But he had turned out to be a lying bastard. Still, he had given her Jennie and Lizzie, and that alone made it all worthwhile. And then there was her George, her beautiful boy. His chubby cheeks, his wispy brown hair, his gurgling laugh, his babbling chatter, his beautiful hazel eyes. His trust in her. His love for her. He had broken her heart.

But she could go on. She had those she loved around her. And George would never be gone from her as long as she could see echoes of him in the faces of her children, as long as his name was remembered.

Epilogue

Late February 1885

Ellen eased the tray of scones out of the oven and carried it over to the cooling rack on the table. The scones had risen perfectly, golden brown on the crown. It was a pity there was little time for baking with the long hours at the jam factory. She should make some of Grannie's bread—it was the best bread she had ever tasted. Maybe in winter, if she wasn't kept on at Peacock's. Life was either feast or famine—more hours than she wanted or not near enough.

She walked to the window. Jennie and Lizzie were on the chair outside, sitting squeezed together swinging their legs as they whispered to each other, both watching Billy. He was farther down the yard digging, not quite with the force needed to turn the patch over. He had come home with the idea of having a garden like Fred Rowe's father. When Billy was out, Ellen thought she would go over it herself. They could plant potatoes and cabbages. Maybe carrots too.

Whenever all the children were together, she could almost see George with them. Not as the pale boy he was for so many months, but round-cheeked and happy, toddling on wobbly legs, as he would be now.

She went back to the table and turned a scone over, tapping the bottom. Perfectly cooked. She slid them from the tray onto the rack to cool properly. She would take them to Mam and Dad's house when they went later. These Saturday evenings with all the family, friends and neighbours often dropping in, had got her through so far, that and the forced routine of work. She couldn't afford to give in, even though there were days when she wanted to crawl back into bed and weep. Today wasn't one of them.

Ellen returned to the window, resting her hands on the bench beneath. The sun was shining, the birds were singing, the children were happy, she had money in her purse. What more could she want? Well, there was no point thinking about that. Four months and not a word. She wasn't sure, though, whether the *Charles and Arthur* had called into Hobart at all in that time. She didn't regret what had happened, but she was glad she hadn't been left with a memento.

She couldn't spend the afternoon staring out the window. She picked up the enamel jug to go out to the washhouse for water.

She gasped, the jug slipping from her fingers and clattering onto the floor.

'Shit, Jim. You frightened me.' She held her hand to her chest, her heart hammering, not only from fright.

He dropped his kitbag on the floor and strode over. 'Sorry.' His grin lit his whole face. He lifted Ellen off the floor and swung her around.

Laughing, she slid into his kiss. He was back. She was glad he was back. He tasted nice—mints. His cheeks were smooth—he'd had a shave. He smelt of soap and cologne—he had been to the baths. And was that a new shirt? Was he trying to impress her? Did she want to be impressed?

'So you're back.' She couldn't help smiling.

'I am.' He was still smiling, sheer happiness bubbling in him.

Billy stood at the door, hands on his hips—the image of an angry father.

'Billy.' Jim went over and grasped his hand as if he were a man and not a boy of seven and a half. 'I have something for you.'

Billy's scowl melted away.

Jim looked over at the two girls standing side by side in the doorway. 'Jennie, Lizzie, you come over too.'

He grabbed his bag and went to dump it on the table.

'Not there! Not in the middle of my baking! Use the chair.'

Jim put his bag on the chair and winked at Billy. He rummaged in it and pulled out a small cloth bag and handed it to the boy.

Billy loosened the drawstring and gasped. 'Marbles!' He lay a couple in the palm of his hand, smooth greenish glass twisted through with thin threads of colour. He gazed at Ellen, his mouth open. 'Look, Mum.'

'They're wonderful, Billy.' Jim certainly knew his way to the boy's heart. All Billy had was a handful of chipped marbles, muddy colours, discarded or lost and picked up in the street, one by one.

Billy threw himself at Jim, hugged him tight. 'Will you play with me? If I ask to go and play in the street, Mum will just say no.'

'I will, in a while.'

The girls stood at the table, waiting patiently as Jim pulled out his gifts for them.

Ellen noticed then that his bag was stuffed with clothing. He must have come straight from the baths and hadn't yet organised lodgings.

'Mummy, oooh.' Jennie held a tube to her eye. 'It makes pretty colours.' She adjusted it against her eye. 'It changes when you move it.' She held it away, shook it and squinted into the tube again.

Lizzie waved a painted stick with ribbons unfurling from one end, laughing as the rainbow colours fluttered around her head.

Bessie walked in, a bag over her arm.

'Jim.' Her face lit up. 'It's lovely to see you again.' She went over and pecked him on the cheek.

'A delight to see you too, Bessie.' He returned the kiss.

How had she missed this? Ellen hadn't realised there was affection between them. But more, she hadn't noticed that Bessie was no longer the timid girl, easily pushed around. There was a quiet strength that hadn't been there before.

'Now this is for you.' Jim handed Bessie a length of cloth.

She shook it out, a swirl of colours, spangles glinting in the light.

'Scarf or shawl, I'm not sure. It's from India via the exotic port of Adelaide. And now,' he turned to Ellen, 'what do I have to give you?'

She almost expected him, conjurer-like, to produce a bunch of flowers from his sleeve.

'Hold out your arm.' He clipped a bracelet on her wrist, a series of hinged panels, the edges bevelled and carved in a lacy pattern.

Ellen ran her fingers over the enamelled disks at the centre of each panel. Their bright colours glowing in the light. She had never seen anything like it.

'From India via the exotic port of Adelaide?' She smiled at Jim. She wanted to kiss him again. But not here, not with everyone watching.

'It is indeed.'

'It's beautiful. Thank you.' She hoped her eyes told him what she felt.

'Would you like a cup of tea while I tidy up here?' She laid a tea towel on the table and arranged the scones on it. 'We are going to Mam and Dad's when I'm finished.'

'Oh.' His smiled faded. 'I was hoping to take you out dancing.'

Ellen blinked. 'I don't know ...'

'I've wanted to for a long time.'

Bessie, her scarf still wound around her neck, placed the contents of her bag in the pantry cupboard—potatoes, onions and carrots—and shut the door. 'You go, Ellen. I'll look after the children. We'll walk back home with Mary Ann and Tom. There's nothing for you to worry about.'

Why was she thinking she shouldn't go? Bessie and the children were safe and happy. There was no reason she shouldn't.

'I'd love to go dancing, but I need to change.'

She was as nervous as she had been as a girl getting ready to go with Mary Ann and one of her brothers to a dancing room. She went up and quickly washed, using the water still left in the jug, and put on the green-blue dress with glass buttons, her old bustle pad tied underneath. She had barely worn the dress in the last two years. She had thought about pawning it, but something had stopped her. Hope that a time would come when she had reason to dress up and be happy? She brushed and pinned her hair, checked it in the hand mirror. She would do. There were a few drops in the scent bottle. She had hardly worn that either. She stopped herself from running down the stairs. She wasn't a girl of sixteen, she was an old woman of twenty-six. But she didn't feel old today.

Bessie had tidied the children by the time she came down. The girls were standing quietly, watching as Billy and Jim played marbles on the floor.

As Ellen walked in, Billy collected up his marbles and shoved the bag in his pocket. He led the way along the passage, no doubt eager to show them to the boys in Denison Lane.

They went together along Molle Street and across Liverpool Street—Ellen had no wish to walk past old memories at present.

The children chattered away, Billy once again hogging Jim's attention.

At the corner of Collins Street, Ellen said, 'We are going this way.' She squatted and held out her arms, hugging Lizzie and Jennie together.

'Are you too big for hugs and kisses?' she asked Billy.

'I'm not a little kid.'

She resisted saying, *Oh, yes, you are*. Instead, she planted a kiss on his forehead.

'Now, all of you, be good for Aunty Bessie.'

'And you two have fun,' Bessie said.

Billy stood in front of Jim. 'And be sure to bring Mum home in the same state as she left here.'

'Billy!' Ellen gasped. 'What are you saying?'

'It's what Fred Rowe's dad says when a boy takes his sister out.'

She opened and shut her mouth, didn't know where to begin.

Jim took off his hat and said, 'You have my word, sir.'

She could see how pleased Billy was with himself. She would deal with it later. Tonight was not for worrying.

They walked down Collins Street, Ellen's arm through Jim's. 'I'm sorry, he had no idea what he was saying.'

Jim laughed in reply.

'Where are we going?'

'I thought dinner at the Melbourne Café and then the dancing room in Liverpool Street.'

'You know your way around for a stranger.'

He squeezed her hand. 'Not such a stranger.'

'Not a stranger at all.' She already knew his character better, perhaps, than any of the fathers of her children. But there was more to know, and it could be fun finding out.

'Are you here for long?'

'I've decided to have a few weeks' break, take some jobs on the dock.'

'And where are you staying?' She had noticed he had left his kitbag behind.

He grinned, a light in his eyes. 'Thought I might stay with you.'

'On the sofa?'

His eyebrows shot up. 'Not quite what I had in mind.'

It was her turn to grin and raise her eyebrows at him. 'We shall see.'

Ellen glanced along the street. It was empty, not even a buggy heading down the hill. 'Let's skip to the next corner.'

'Why not?' He grabbed her hand.

Halfway along the block, Jim caught Ellen around the waist, and they danced. The street was no longer empty but Ellen didn't care. The world spun about her: the great mountain watching over them; the river shining in the slanting afternoon light; the buildings old and new; the past and the present; the people she knew, those she didn't, those she loved most of all. Her skirt flying out, her feet skimming the ground, she smiled into laughing blue eyes. A moment of pure happiness. A moment promising more.

Historical Note

Nine months later, on 19 November 1885, Alice Eva Doran was born, Ellen and Jim's first child. They married on 11 January 1891 at the church of St John the Baptist, Hobart, three weeks before the birth of their third child. Ellen's sister Alice Eva was one of the witnesses, the other, John Jackson, the husband of Ellen's sister Jane. Ellen and Jim had seven children together, all of whom lived into middle age. Ellen died at Queenstown on the west coast of Tasmania on 6 February 1910. Jim Doran did not remarry after Ellen's death. He died at Moonah on 27 February 1940. They are now buried together at Cornelian Bay Cemetery, Hobart. From the foot of their grave, kunanyi/Mount Wellington can be seen in the distance.

Sarah Ellen Thompson and Henry Woods the younger are my great-great-grandparents. I am one of the numerous descendants of their daughter Elizabeth Woods, the child Harry claimed he was 'not liable' for in 1881. The court did not believe him, and genetic genealogy has most definitely proven him wrong.

First and foremost, *Cold Blows the Wind* is a work of fiction. It is, however, firmly based on the lives of my great-great-grandparents and their families as found in public records and the glimpses of their personalities offered by newspaper reports of their activities. There are many gaps in information when dealing with the lives of ordinary people. I have filled these gaps with plausible imaginings. Where people have disappeared from the records, I have imagined how their lives might have continued. Where the records are ambiguous, I have made choices that allow this story to work well as fiction. I do not know when Ellen went to live at the Springs; the date I have chosen may be later than she actually did. I do not know the circumstances of the rape, but I do know the date it happened, the names of Ellen's attackers and the fact that it was reported to the police who took no action. The greatest liberty I have taken is to have Ellen meet Jim Doran in December 1882. Documents recording Jim's first arrival have conflicting and ambiguous dates. I have chosen a date that allows a note of hope through the next sections of the novel, which are particularly dark.

Ellen's story struck me from the moment I uncovered it through my genealogical research. I have a letter written by my grandmother in 1964 listing Ellen's children and mentioning 'another son, he died quite young'. I have found that children who died as infants are usually not remembered by their young siblings and certainly not by nieces and nephews born years later. Elizabeth Woods was only three when her brother George died. His memory, initially, would have been kept alive by Ellen, passed on to Elizabeth and then to my grandmother. When later I discovered the circumstances of his conception, I realised just what an extraordinary woman Ellen Thompson was. Over a period of five years, Ellen experienced all those things women fear most: betrayal, abandonment, poverty, rape, unwanted pregnancy, death of a child, death of other loved ones. She was a woman whose life revolved around family. She appears in the records registering the births and deaths of her sisters' children, in court for the assault of a woman she thought was initiating an affair with one of her brothers-in-law, and her house was the place of birth for one of her sister Alice's children, her son Billy later registering this child's death. Her sister Jane's first child was called Ellen and Mary Ann's fourth child Sarah. Ellen's is a story of love—a mother's love for her children, a woman's love for her family and, those most troublesome loves of all, for the men in her life. Most of all, Ellen's story is one of the resilience of the human spirit.

Harry and Eliza Woods did not return to Hobart. In the year after their arrival back in Western Australia, Eliza ran the newly established Burnett Coffee Rooms, a Temperance hotel, at the corner of Barrack and Hay Streets, Perth. She was frequently described as the 'indefatigable manager' of the place. Harry and Eliza then moved to 474 Murray Street, Perth, where they ran a small fruiterer's and confectionary shop. Harry died on 24 August 1908 and Eliza on 19 January 1922. They are buried together at Karrakatta Cemetery, Perth.

Nineteenth-century Tasmania, like so many other places at the time, viewed poverty mainly as an individual moral failing and believed that charity weakened individuals' resolve to help themselves. The Hobart Benevolent Society, a Protestant organisation, established in 1832 but operating continuously since 1859, did try to ease the situation of those in need; however, the Society, in its annual reports to Parliament, frequently expressed the view that if people were encouraged to put money by for times of sickness and for their old age, cases of pauperism would become rare. It was never explained how this was to be achieved when wages were low, work was insecure and sickness or death of the breadwinner could quickly throw a family into dire poverty.

In Tasmania, initially, outdoor relief to those in need was managed by the Charitable Grants Department. This government body, established in 1873, was administered by the Hobart Police Magistrate, William Tarleton, a far-sighted and compassionate man. He believed in granting aid even when parents were, in the view of the mores of the time, 'undeserving' because, without aid, children would starve (*Charitable Institutions. Report of the Royal Commission. 1871* p.62). Most of the assistance given went to elderly people in poverty and to destitute children. In 1871 the basic level of assistance for children under twelve years was two shillings and sixpence per child. Children over twelve were considered old enough to work and mothers were expected to support themselves.

In 1880, the government passed responsibility for the administration of outdoor relief to the Hobart Benevolent Society, who continued to provide support for the elderly and for children, not for able-bodied adults. Applicants were closely questioned to ensure they were genuine, and rations were given rather than money to prevent it being used to buy alcohol. Those seen to be lazy, alcoholic or immoral—in other words, the 'undeserving poor'—were not assisted. The assistance Ellen received, after the first three months provided by the Benevolent Society, was funded by the government.

First-time mothers who were not married received assistance from the Benevolent Society at their lying-in home. The Society also attempted to find work for the mothers once the child was born. Those women who made a habit of having children by men they were not married to only received the government assistance the Benevolent Society administered. The biggest problem for women who were on their own with children, married or unmarried, was finding someone to care for their children while they worked. This was compounded by the lower level of wages paid to women.

The attitudes of those at the lower level of society towards women who had illegitimate children seems not to have been as censorious as those of the more 'respectable'. Many unmarried women kept their children and ended up marrying someone who was not their older children's father. Children from previous liaisons would then be known by the name of their mother's husband. While they were young, Ellen's daughters, Elizabeth (Lizzie) and Jane (Jennie), were known as Doran, possibly for convenience. When they both married, they gave their surname as Woods and recorded Henry Woods as their father. William John (Billy) Thompson was known as William John Doran for most of his life.

Ellen prosecuted Harry under the *Tasmanian Deserted Wives and Children's Maintenance Act 1873*. This covered illegitimate children as well as those born to married couples. The Act was predicated on the understanding that a father had an obligation to support his children. In the case of children born to unmarried parents, for a woman to be able to sue under this Act, the parents must have been cohabiting for twelve months and paternity was not accepted on the word of the mother alone. Even had a rape been proven, it is unlikely that Ellen would have been able to successfully sue Thomas Armstrong for maintenance. I do not know if confirmation of her pregnancy was the reason Ellen reported the rape to the police, but I have used it as a possible motivation. There are many reasons today why a woman does not report a rape immediately—if ever, and this was even more the case in judgemental and censorious societies of the past.

By the middle of the nineteenth century, Australian working-class men were known for their use of colourful language, and though women of all classes were expected not to swear, many did. All the colourful words and phrases I have used, with the exception of one (*piss off*) were in use in the nineteenth century, most carrying more sting than they do today. The most colourful of obscenities used in the scene at the Springs in December 1882 is an example of a phrase in use far earlier than the dictionary suggests. It is found in a Hobart Lower Court record of 1851, yet the *Oxford English Dictionary* tells us it was coined around 1895 in the United States. It was clearly in far more widespread use earlier. With this in mind, I have used words and phrases and Australian idiom that, according to the dictionary, were coined a little later than the period covered by my novel. It is conceivable that they were in use several decades before they made it into print. That said, some modern-sounding words and turns of phrase are sometimes far older than the *Big Book of Everybody Knows* would suggest. For example, *What's up?* first appeared in print in 1838 and its contraction, *Wassup?* in 1903. *To look out for* somebody, as in to show care or concern for a person or to act in their interests, has been around since 1752. Even *scrummy* found its way into print as a form of non-standard London English in 1844.

All poetry and folk songs used in the novel come from nineteenth century sources; in some cases, folk songs have been adapted slightly, as they often were in the past.

The older generation, in particular, of those who lived in Hobart and throughout Australia, came from everywhere within the British Isles. I have tried to hint at this in the speech patterns and word use of people like Beth and Bill Thompson and Henry and Jane Woods. As happens today when people of different backgrounds live together, they take on some of the other's words and speech patterns, and children also draw on their parents' heritage in the way they speak. Some of the older generation had mixed heritages themselves, so their speech patterns would not have been pure examples of the areas they came from—William Thompson, from Stoke on Trent, had a Scottish father and an English mother, and Jane (McCurrie) Woods, from Glasgow, was born in Antrim of Irish Catholic parents. The richness of the vernacular of the British Isles has contributed greatly to the development of a uniquely Australian idiom.

I hope I have given a sense that the people who move within the pages of this novel were once living people, in so many ways like us today—people who wanted shelter, warmth and enough to eat, who hoped for love and security, freedom from illness and, most of all, a better future for their children. It is the daily heroism of ordinary lives, their survival over generations, that has given most of us, up until now, a life far better than that experienced by any generation before us.

Melbourne
April 2022.

Acknowledgements

Writing historical fiction is not a solitary occupation. We would not be able to create past worlds without the work of others, those who research and write the books we consult, those who manage websites and curate historical collections, those who read our work when it is not fully formed and those closest to us who put up with our obsessions. So, with this in mind, I would like to thank all those who have helped me on the road to publication.

Thank you to friends and colleagues who have read and commented on *Cold Blows the Wind* at the various stages in its development: Francis Kirby, Janine Smith, Gabrielle Higgins, Heather Lyndsey and historical novelists Brook Allen, author of the Antonius trilogy, and Jean M. Roberts, author of *The Heron* and *The Frowning Madonna*. Especial thanks is due to Vivienne Brereton, author of the wonderful Tudor series *The House of the Red Duke*. Vivienne not only read the novel, several times, but has been a patient sounding board and has offered unique insights into the behaviour of my characters. From the moment she met Ellen on paper, she has become one of her greatest champions— Vivienne, you are now an honorary family member. Thanks also goes to Sarah Kirby for her patience and meticulous proofreading.

Special mention should be made of two Australian institutions without which the research for this novel would have been incredibly difficult: the National Library of Australia and the Tasmanian Archives. Both have an extensive program of digitis-ation which makes records and images available to the public online for no charge. The NLA's newspaper digitisation, via its *Trove* interface, is an invaluable resource for all Australian researchers. The Tasmanian Archives has an extensive collection of digitised records and images easily available online. I have made numerous visits to the Archives in person and am grateful for all the help given by the knowledgeable staff that led me to make discoveries I never would have found alone. I consider the Tasmanian Archives online catalogue the easiest to navigate of all state archives in Australia (and I would bet anywhere in the world).

I am indebted to the wonderful Tasmanian community of researchers and historians and their willingness to share their knowledge both through their many publications and also by personally answering my questions. These include Irene Schaffer OAM, an expert on so many facets of Tasmanian history, who I first made contact with about fifteen years ago when I was beginning my search to identify Henry Woods, father and son; Joyce Purtscher with her extensive knowledge of social welfare in Tasmania and the operations of the Hobart Benevolent Society; and Maria Grist with her love of kunanyi/Mount Wellington and her encyclopedic knowledge of its history. Maria has published works on so many facets of its history and has been generous in answering my myriad questions. I am particularly indebted to Brian Rieusset, an historian specialising in convict and penal history, for his patience and generosity in answering my detailed and convoluted questions regarding the operation of the Campbell Street Gaol in the nineteenth century. People who have helped me in other areas include Gayle Faulkner on women's clothing, Laurence Hewson on pipe smoking, and Bernie Kirby on how to pack and fire a blunderbuss (one day I am sure I will have practical, not just literary, use for this information). Thank you all. Any misrepresentation of what you have told me is entirely my misunderstanding.

Immeasurable thanks go to Jenny Quinlan of Historical Editorial, who provided a range of detailed editorial help as well as designing the book's beautiful cover. Jenny's insights and advice were critical in adding depth to the story; she also nudged me where I would have preferred not to go but this resulted in a more honest retelling of Ellen's story.

Last, but by no means least, I would like to thank my family. I would not have reached this point without you and your tolerance of my strange interests, my neglect of domestic responsibilities (but, hey, we survived) and my lengthy obsession with 'these dead people'.

About the Author

Catherine Meyrick is an Australian writer of romantic historical fiction. She lives in Melbourne, Australia but grew up in Ballarat, a large regional city steeped in history. Until recently she worked as a customer service librarian at her local library. She has a Master of Arts in history and is also an obsessive genealogist.

You can find out more about Catherine, her books and the background to her stories at catherinemeyrick.com

Also by Catherine Meyrick

Forsaking All Other

Love is no game for women; the price is far too high.

England 1585.

Bess Stoughton, waiting woman to the well-connected Lady Allingbourne, has discovered that her father is arranging for her to marry an elderly neighbour. Normally obedient Bess rebels and wrests from her father a year's grace to find a husband more to her liking.

Edmund Wyard, a taciturn and scarred veteran of England's campaign in Ireland, is attempting to ignore the pressure from his family to find a suitable wife as he prepares to join the Earl of Leicester's army in the Netherlands.

Although Bess and Edmund are drawn to each other, they are aware that they can have nothing more than friendship. Bess knows that Edmund's wealth and family connections place him beyond her reach. And Edmund, with his well-honed sense of duty, has never considered that he could follow his own wishes.

With England on the brink of war and fear of Catholic plots extending even into Lady Allingbourne's household, time is running out for both of them.

The Bridled Tongue

Death and life are in the power of the tongue.

England 1586

Alyce Bradley has few choices when her father decides it is time she marry as many refuse to see her as other than the girl she once was—unruly, outspoken and close to her grandmother, a woman suspected of witchcraft.

Thomas Granville, an ambitious privateer, inspires fierce loyalty in those close to him and hatred in those he has crossed. Beyond a large dowry, he is seeking a virtuous and dutiful wife. Neither he nor Alyce expect more from marriage than mutual courtesy and respect.

As the King of Spain launches his great armada and England braces for invasion, Alyce must confront closer dangers from both her own and Thomas's past, threats that could not only destroy her hopes of love and happiness but her life. And Thomas is powerless to help.

Made in United States
Orlando, FL
20 August 2022